To Ann B.

A Frontier Adventure

Rod L. Hodg

Best Wishes
August 2009

By
Roderick L. Hodgson

PUBLISH AMERICA

PublishAmerica
Baltimore

ISBN: 1-60836-436-4
PUBLISHED BY PUBLISHAMERICA, LLLP
www.publishamerica.com
Baltimore

Printed in the United States of America

Contents

PART III: Ten Years Later—1837

To my grandchildren

Zoe, Joy and Thea Zeeman.

Also by the Same Author:

Historic Hudson—Part II
ISBN: 1-895821-03-7

Historical Industries & Services of Hudson, Quebec 1841-2004 (co-authored
with Margaret A. Peyton, Martin R. Hofton & Daniel Vigneault)
ISBN: 1-41205453-2

Historic Buildings of Hudson and Area 1792-1913
ISBN: 1-895821-13-4

T.B. Macaulay & Mount Victoria Farm
ISBN: 1-895821-15-0

(The above books are available through the Hudson Historical Society,
P.O. Box 802, Hudson, Québec, J0P 1H0.)

Defenders of the Flag
ISBN: 1-4120-3946-0
(Available directly from the author at rhodgson@videotron.ca)

Les Auberges d'Hudson—The Inns of Hudson
ISBN: 1-4120-9166-7
(Available directly from the author at rhodgson@videotron.ca)

100 Years of Worship—The History of Wyman
Memorial United Church: 1907-2007
(Available directly from Wyman Memorial United Church, 513 Main
Rd., Hudson, Québec, J0P 1H0)

Dreams to Remember
The Hudson Yacht Club Inc. 1909-2009
(Available June 2009 directly from the
Hudson Yacht Club Inc., 10 Yacht Club Rd.,
Hudson, Québec, J0P 1H0)

Author's Note

This is a work of historical fiction. Many of the events actually occurred and many of the participants mentioned were actually there. The main characters have had their names changed from those who actually settled in Cavagnal (Hudson, Québec) in the early part of the 1800's. Their actions and conversations have been largely fictionalized though many of the events that are mentioned are based on historical fact. Other characters are imaginary and only resemble real persons out of sheer coincidence.

I have also tried to use the broken English that maybe the early 19th century working class French Canadians might have used after they had learned some English. I hope that it would be similar to what is spoken today. I have tried to make it as realistic as possible.

R. L. H.
January 2009

Acknowledgments

Special thanks go out to my niece Katherine Whalen and Drew Gough of Ottawa, Ontario who were very kind to do the final editing of this immense project. I could not have completed it without them.

A second and very important "Nia'wen" (thank-you) goes to Mr. Ronnie Gabriel and his daughter Angela Gabriel, both of Kanesatake, Mohawk Territory, Québec for their Mohawk translations and words they provided for this book.

A finally I wish to thank the late Margaret A. Peyton who initially edited this immense project so many years ago and encouraged me to continue.

PART I

Chapter 1
Westmorland

The winter of 1823/24 had been a tough one for the residents of Dufton and for the first time in many years there was still snow in the valley below Dufton Pike at Easter. George Henderson looked down from the western side of the Fell, admiring his home village that slept before him. 'How long before we are settled in our new land,' he wondered. The ship is to leave Maryport in a fortnight and we must be there on time. I must get that big stag before noon if we are to have meat for the voyage. Then off he went tracking the huge stag that had eluded him for the past three days.

Down in Dufton, Mary Henderson was stirring in her warm bed not knowing that her beloved husband had left two hours before for the long climb up the snow covered Pike. Outside a dog barked as the first rays of dawn began to creep into the snow covered valley. George had put a few extra logs on the fire before he had left so their house would be warm and cozy when his family got up.

Lying in bed, Mary smiled to herself and thought of how wonderful it would be to sail across the great ocean, carve out a new life for their family, and be among friends from Westmorland and Cumberland. England was changing and with the threat of Bonaparte now gone and peace in North America, life was going to be hard for those who remained in England. So many troops and sailors had returned home and there were so few jobs for them. 'We have to go,' she thought, 'even if it means leaving our families here in Dufton.'

It would not matter to George too much as he was alone now in England. His two brothers were far away in North America and Australia. Supposedly Joseph, his elder brother, was in a prison near Sydney and hopes of him ever being released were slim even if he were still alive. John Henderson, George's younger brother, was serving with the army at a large Canadian garrison town called Kingston.

Mary Henderson had never left Westmorland except for the occasional trip to Penrith and once down to Lancaster when she was a child. This upcoming voyage was something to look forward to but she was also worried for her children. Rumours had spread around the Counties of many ships being wrecked off some sandy island east of Nova Scotia. "Sable Island," she recalled. Others had been wrecked heading up the St. Lawrence River, especially at this time of the year when ferocious gales swept down from the heartland of Canada. At least that is what the papers said these past few months.

Taking seven children across the North Atlantic in a small sailing ship was not going to be an easy task. And winter was not over yet. Friends had told Mary of the terrors of the North Atlantic in winter. Three thousand miles of open ocean, then a slow journey of another one thousand miles up the gateway to Canada—the mighty St. Lawrence River.

"At least I will see where grandfather fought with Wolfe in 1759," she thought. What a battle that had been. Her grandfather had often talked about his life in the army as a member of the 47th Regiment of Foot, better known to those who served in it as "Wolfe's Own." He had been proud to serve under General Wolfe at Québec in his own regiment and at a great victory.

Too bad Christopher Black was not here. He would have wanted to come and finally get his wish to settle in Canada. He had died in 1819 from heart failure.

"Mother," whispered John Henderson from just outside her room, "where is father? I hope he did not go out hunting this morning."

"He has," Mary replied in her soft voice, "he has."

"But I was supposed to go with him today," John whispered.

However, his mother only smiled and then slowly got up from her warm bed.

John Henderson was a strapping boy for his age, almost six feet tall and already twelve stone and he would only turn seventeen in August. Hopefully by then the whole family would be on their new land in Canada. He was the eldest boy of the seven Henderson children. George relied on him a greater part of the time for work around their small farm due to his size.

John had done well in school and like his parents had learned to read and write, something that was not too common among the farmers of England in 1824. George had also used his ability to read and write to become an elder in the local Church of England often acting as a lay reader on Sundays and special holiday services.

The Hendersons were a popular family in Dufton and their leaving was going to be hard to accept. George had heard that a distant cousin of his, Thomas Grantham, from up north was also planning to move to Canada. George's grandmother had been a Grantham from Castle Carrock and she was Thomas' great-aunt.

Already other families from the area were planning to move to Canada, to a small community just west of Montréal. Very few were from Westmorland so the gossip in the Appleby market went. Most of those planning the long voyage were from over in Cumberland, near Penrith. Penrith was just a few miles west of Dufton, across the Eden River.

Mary Henderson had asked her husband about this place "just west of Montréal" and George had promised to find out more, as it seemed to be a nice safe place with fellow Englishmen, few Frenchmen, and lots of good land for the taking. Especially for decorated army veterans on pension like himself.

George slowly raised his rifle and eased back the hammer as he took careful aim on the magnificent stag. He estimated its weight to be about eighteen stone. That would provide almost enough meat they would need for their two-month journey across the Atlantic. Of course they planned to take some sheep and a cow with them but they wanted to begin a new herd in Canada. George was hoping that someone would have a bull so he would be able to breed his prime Ayrshire cow.

The big gun let off a great boom and for a few seconds George could not see if the stag was down or not as the smoke from his old rifle obscured his vision, just as it had so many times in battle.

"Yes," he said as the smoke cleared and the big deer lay dead some one hundred yards below him. The big rifle had done its work once again.

"Now the hard job," George mumbled to himself.

"I should have brought John along as he'd wished. Maybe he'll be smart enough to get up early and follow my track. No one else is up this way today. At least it is down hill all the way. Maybe John heard the shot and is now on his way up the winding trail."

George was noted for his prowess with a rifle, having won every shooting match in the region, even some over in Cumberland at Penrith. He'd only lost once. A mysterious stranger had arrived in Dufton, wearing a green jacket, similar to the old tattered one George had in the hall closet. He seemed familiar but George could not place him. It had been many years since he'd served in Spain with the 95th Rifles under Wellesley. This stranger must have been there as he spoke of many of the now famous battles.

The 95th Rifles had been formed earlier in the war with Napoleon and had been issued with a new type of gun. The rifle that was very accurate, unlike the old "Brown Bess" that the rest of the infantry used. The Baker rifle had special grooves inside the barrel called rifling to make the bullet spin. The old "Bess" had a smooth bore and was not very accurate. A soldier was lucky to hit the enemy at seventy-five yards and never at anything over one hundred yards. However, the Baker was deadly accurate up to two hundred yards and an excellent rifleman could hit a target at four hundred and fifty yards. George thought of that stranger as he walked over to the huge stag that lay before him.

Isaac Kirkbride, a yeoman from over in Keswick, had been the stranger and had once served with George as a skirmisher at the greatest of all battles nine years before, Waterloo. Isaac had changed a great deal, putting on at least three stone of weight and he'd lost an eye. Luckily for Isaac it was not the one he aimed his rifle with. They both had been at Badajoz in Spain and had survived the hell there.

"That old soldier could really shoot and drink," George thought to himself. He'd lost his eye it in a drunken brawl in Calais after Waterloo, not in battle. They had not seen each other till that day on Dufton's square at the annual May Day Shoot in 1821.

After losing the shoot to Isaac three years before, the two men had renewed their friendship. Keswick was not that far away and from time to time they visited each other's farms to celebrate the victories of the famed 95th. They were the chosen few who had excellent shots and who proved themselves time and again. The perfect skirmishers. Deadly shots. But at Waterloo the French had outnumbered the riflemen three to one and many had fallen in that isolated sand pit in front of the British lines. Many good men like Henry Bathurst of Carlisle, Sergeant Thomas Hogarth of Kirkoswald, Captain John Grainger of Aspatria on the west coast and others. Too many fine men that day were lost to stupid senior officers who prided themselves with the "glory" and "sport" of it all.

"Thank God for Blücher," George said out loud, surprising himself as he gutted the deer. The foul smell did not bother him at all. If you could survive the stench at Waterloo, the stench of a dead deer's guts was nothing but perfume.

George and Isaac had a grand view from Wellington's left flank of the final few minutes of the battle. What was left of Kincaid's Rifle Brigade was now taking shots at the Old Guard as they marched up the slope to their doom.

When it was all over that day in June 1815, over fifty thousand men were dead or dying on both sides of the valley. But Regimental Sergeant Major George Henderson and his pal, Isaac Kirkbride were alive. Three fourths of the Rifle Brigade were dead or dying, many who had fought with them from Portugal to Spain and up into France. Long time friends, gone forever. As George carved up the big deer, he made a pact with himself that Isaac Kirkbride would accompany him and his family to Canada. Isaac was a lonely man and maybe he would find someone to settle down with.

"Hope it is not my daughter though," he said out loud.

"What did you say father? Were you talking to me?" The suddenness of hearing John's voice made George curse as he jumped up quite startled.

"Don't you ever do that again," George bellowed at his son who quickly backed down the hill a few steps. "The last thing I need to do before our voyage is to slice my finger off." John apologized to his father and they set about loading the meat and hide onto the sledge John had hauled up with him.

"I heard just one shot and knowing you, I decided to bring this. Maybe we can ride it part way down the Fell. It would be fun and probably our last time too," John said.

George agreed and thought, "This boy of mine is as smart as well as strong. He is going to really like it in Canada. This family of ours has a bright future ahead of it."

George was glad his son had struggled up the Fell with the heavy sledge. He was forty-eight years old now and despite still being in great physical condition, the years at war had taken their toll on the huge body. At six-foot five, George Henderson stood inches over most men in Dufton and besides being an excellent shot, he was no person to tangle with in a fist fight.

Mary Henderson was happy too, as she was pregnant with their eighth child. The pregnancy had been an easy one as all of hers had been since the birth of their eldest, Jane in 1802. She felt that eight children were not too much. They were all healthy and well fed. George made sure of that. They had only lost one due to a sudden illness a few years before.

"Poor little Agnes," Mary said to herself. She then said a prayer for her. Their farm was prosperous and money was not a problem. His small army pension and what he had saved from the great French treasure that he and his men had come across in Spain, in addition to what they received for the wool, placed them among some of the wealthier farmers in the area around Dufton.

Mary had met George just after he had arrived from up north twenty-four years before. He was a native of Castle Carrock, near the Scottish border and had moved south to work in the local lead mine over by Long Marton. George had never liked mining. He always said that "the lead would eventually kill him" so he turned to farming. The Henderson homestead up north, Stanbridge, had been a wealthy farm so after quitting the mine George had asked his father for some sheep to set up his own farm in Long Marton.

It was in June of 1800 that Mary Black first met her future husband. A small Parish gathering on the lawn of the Long Marton church was the spot where they first laid eyes on each other. He was a big strapping fellow of twenty-four years and Mary was a lovely girl of nineteen. Her sisters had teased her immediately about how she stared shyly at the newcomer. Before long that day, they both overcame their mutual shyness and conversed over a cup of strong English tea.

They had so much in common; they were both independent, healthy, and lovers of adventure. George was soon visiting the Black family in Knock on a regular basis, it being only an hour's ride up over the Fell and back into the small hamlet where Mary resided with her family.

Her father, Samuel Black, was not a farmer but a local butcher and both he and George soon became great friends and were able to strike up a deal to help George to market his sheep.

Married on June 21st, 1801 at the small Dufton church, George and his new wife settled down for a life that would see them grow old together with a loving family around them. Little did they know at that time where that love would take them.

Their first child, Jane, was born in early 1802 in the dead of winter. From then until this latest pregnancy a new little Henderson would be brought into the world about every two years. It was only during the times that George had been with the Army that no children had been born. Mary had been true to her husband and never let the many suitors she had when he was away bother her or get close to her.

George had been tempted many times while in Spain and France during the war but had also remained faithful. He had not taken part in the rape of Badajoz when so many British soldiers, drunk on looted wine, raped, robbed and murdered the local women. Scores were hanged on the spot that awful weekend. Being the Regimental Sergeant Major of the 95th he had to capture a few of his own men and had watched them hang beside so many of the redcoats. Seeing the green jacketed soldiers hanging from the gallows that day had made George Henderson very sad and ashamed. They were there to liberate Spain and Portugal from the French and now they were just as bad as they were.

Waterloo had been different, just a killing field of men and horses. No towns to liberate or plunder, just an open field to live or die in and too many died that day.

It was just after 10:00 am when George and John arrived back in the village with their huge load. Luckily the snow had not melted on the road in the warm morning sun, making it easier for them to pull the sledge to the house.

George had learned a great deal from Mary's father about butchering so they would have an easy job cutting up the meat and salting it for the long voyage ahead. Mary had been preparing stores during the winter for the trip. Each family that would travel had to bring along enough food for a minimum two months at sea. For the nine members of the Henderson family that meant a great deal of food and also forage for their animals. Mary wondered how they would all fit on board the transport ship with so many other families.

Salt pork, beef, and venison would be the staples as well as some vegetables and wine. George loved his wine. He had learned to enjoy it while fighting in Spain and Portugal and they almost had wine with dinner nowadays. That was frowned upon by many villagers in Dufton. Sometimes wine was hard to come by but George always seemed to be able to purchase enough over in Penrith to satisfy his thirst.

Dufton was a strange little village; very close knit and rumours were always rampant, especially in the local pub, the "Old William".

"Odd name for a pub," George had commented one Sunday to Mary as they walked from church to their house on the edge of the square.

Mary replied, "It is named after William Francis Frankham, a local hero at the Battle of Cape St. Vincent. He had been pressed into service by a Royal Navy frigate crew in 1795 at Maryport. The ship had stopped over on the way south to take station off Cadiz, Spain. William unlike others whom the 'Press Gang' had rounded up actually liked the Royal Navy!

"In 1796 he was transferred onto *HMS Captain*, one of the early ships that Lord Nelson had commanded during his numerous battles with the French and Spanish fleets. William ended up as a gun captain and his first and only fight was the Battle of Cape St. Vincent in February of 1797 off the coast of Portugal. He and his crew fired off some of the best-aimed shots at the Spanish fleet in the early minutes of the battle. Unfortunately he did not live to see the end. William died just like hundreds of others at Cape St. Vincent, blown to bits by a Spanish broadside. His body was just thrown over board along with the other flotsam during a battle.

"William Frankham was one of the sweetest and nicest men I have ever known. He was my uncle and in 1799 when our old pub burned down the village fathers decided to name the new pub after their one and only Royal Navy hero."

Dufton had sent many a man to war but they all had been in the Army, never the Navy. To have had one of theirs serve with Lord Nelson made him a hero to them all and the letter from Captain Nelson telling his parents and family of his tragic death still hangs in the pub so aptly named after William Francis Frankham of Dufton.

Rumours in the village had George Henderson having to leave the area because of an immense debt he owed. He would probably end up in Australia like his brother Joseph, banned to a God-forsaken land thousands of miles away, and without his family. However, the rumours were just that—rumours, holding no truth whatsoever. The real reason why George Henderson was going to Canada was his love of adventure and love of his family. He wanted them to grow up and prosper in a new land where opportunities abounded. Where land was there for those who wanted to work for it. He knew it was not going to be easy but George never took on anything that was easy. He had been a miner, a soldier, and now he was a farmer with an ever-growing family to feed. Yes, Canada would be a challenge, but challenges were what he really liked in life.

The letter came to the Henderson household just a few days before they were to leave for Maryport. Reverend Joseph Ashford in Canada had written it in late September. He was the local circuit rider for the Church of England in an area just west of Montréal. Reverend Ashford had heard from George's friends already in the area near where the Hendersons were planning to settle that he, his family and possibly others were planning to emigrate the next spring. Reverend Ashford wrote of the life in the region; problems such as cold winters and hot summers, great fishing in the lovely golden coloured lake, excellent grazing land for sheep and cattle if you had them, lack of any problems with the French residents and no Indian problems at all.

Mary Henderson had always worried about Indians after having read about them in news clippings about the Hudson's Bay Company and the North West Company. Skirmishes with Indians in that new land were far from over but from what they had read about; the local natives across the lake were quite friendly and traded a great deal with their new neighbours from England.

Ashford wrote of other Cumberland and Westmorland families already in the area now known as Cavagnal. Many names were familiar to George and Mary though none were from the Dufton or Long Marton area. Unfortunately they knew only two of the families personally. They were James Henderson and his wife Rachel Winston formerly of Aspatria on the west coast of Cumberland, not far from Maryport. The other was yet another Henderson family, Robert and his children from Hunsonby.

James was from just north of Penrith, Great Salkeld, and had also been a sheep farmer like so many of the area farmers of this area.

"It would be great to see old James once again," thought George. He had left Cumberland for Canada in 1819 but had always written at least twice a year since then to George and other from back home. Though George now lived in Westmorland he was really from Cumberland and though they were not related, George always thought of James Henderson as family.

James had written of the Sampson, Roblin and Loland families who had all settled in the area of Cavagnal in recent years. One family James had written about in his last letter was Robert Henderson and his family. They were good friends of George and Mary and had left Hunsonby the year before. George was deeply saddened on learning of the sudden death of Robert's wife Elizabeth King. She had survived the long voyage but had suffered a heart attack shortly after arriving in Canada. Robert was now left with a family of four to raise in that harsh wilderness. George thought that it would be good to see Robert as soon as he got settled in their new land. Robert would need a lot of comfort and help with his family. Luckily some were over twenty now and would soon be looking to make a family of their own if there were any available partners in the area.

Reverend Ashford and James Henderson had written to George with some details on the area where he and his family were heading so they knew what to expect. Having been to war George was not unaccustomed to severe hardships and his excellent health and great strength would be a great asset in settling in the wilds of Canada.

Chapter 2
"The Pioneer"

It was the last week of April 1824 and the port town of Maryport on the west coast of England was experiencing a boom time. Reports had come back to the various western coastal port towns from Royal Navy ships stating that the ice had broken up in the St. Lawrence River leading to Montreal and the weather at that time of the year was exceptionally warm.

With those reports now being published all across England, ship owners were scrambling to find crews to man their ships for the long voyage to the New World. With the war against Napoleon long over, there was now an excess of unemployed sailors around the country. However, the problem every ship owner was having was finding enough men wanting to sail again. After having served in His Britannic Majesty's Navy under terrible conditions, the idea of having to sail once again to the New World did not appeal to too many. But the possibility of getting a chance to set up a new life once over there did appeal too many and soon the harbours on the west coast were bustling with experienced sailors.

"It is just like the good old days," thought Captain Jonas Smithfield of the transport ship *The Pioneer*. "Lots of manpower to man the sails and work the ships, but hopefully not too many will jump ship once we land at Montréal. I have got to have a crew to come back here."

The Pioneer was not a bad ship for its age, fifteen years old. It had been in service with the East India Company for a while until its present owner, Samuel Watterson, had purchased it the year before. It was one hundred and fifty feet long and displaced just under six hundred tons. Being an ex-Navy man himself, Watterson had outfitted it with a brace of eighteen pound cannon on each side and a couple of swivel guns on the fore and aft deck railings. Such armament had been quite common with the East India Company ships plying the trade routes around the "Cape of Good Hope" to the Far East. But they were not at all common for transport ships heading to North America.

The war with France had ended and there was no longer a need to have such formidable weapons on board, according to many of Watterson's friends and fellow ship owners. However, Captain Smithfield did not mind having them on board and he often trained his crews with their use.

"No use having weapons like these if you do not know how to use them," he would say to any doubters.

"Never know who one might meet or where." Granted four eighteen pound guns were not much of a defense, but with good gun captains, they could do a great deal of damage if need be.

The Hendersons arrived two days before the ship was to leave the bustling harbour after traveling for three days across the County from Dufton. They had an easy trip and no one had gotten sick or lost on the way. Isaac Kirkbride had met them in Greystoke and had brought along his own belongings in a one-horse cart. One thing neither he nor George Henderson had forgotten was their trusty Baker rifles. It was a rare day that either George or Isaac did not take down their guns from the racks in their homes and check them out. Beside their rifles, they both had brought along a shotgun and a brace of pistols. They had both read about "the wilds of Canada" and while reports of Indian troubles in the area that they were headed for were basically untrue, both George and Isaac wanted to be safe and with such arms. They felt that would be able to protect them if necessary and certainly provide them with ample meat for the winter season.

Isaac was traveling alone as he had never married but he was still hoping to find a wife and he felt that Canada might provide him with the new life and a woman that he could love and provide for. Though he was getting on in years, maybe he could have a family life similar to what George, his best friend, had. "A family so dear to him that little else mattered," he thought.

The new settlers met on the dock beside the ship and found that there would be others similar to them on board. All were from the County of Cumberland and most, like them, were farmers. One man was a doctor. George was able to talk to two young families from Greystoke—the Grisenthwaites and the Fowlers. They told him that they too were headed for a small place just west of Montréal called Cavagnal and had been in contact with Reverend Ashford.

"This Cavagnal sounded like a lovely place," thought George, "if only they had an idea where they would be staying upon arrival there."

Dr. Grisenthwaite had heard that there was an Inn along the river and that it was very popular with the Montréal fur traders heading out into the wilderness. "Maybe we could stay there," he remarked to George.

Their new found friends from Greystoke were not as well off as they were and both Isaac and George worried about them. However, it was not up to them to worry about the others, they both had to start their own lives too and George had a large family to care for.

The Pioneer set sail for British North America on April 28th, 1824. It was a fine day for sailing. A light northeast breeze filled the sails of the ship as she headed out into the Irish Sea. Captain Smithfield was expecting a voyage of about thirty days if the weather held. Thirty days to the Gulf of St. Lawrence then about ten more up to Montréal, depending on the winds.

Captain Smithfield was a decent man, not one of those iron-fisted tyrants that many a poor emigrant would find aboard a ship bound for the Americas. Many of those tyrannical Captains cared less if his passengers made it or not; money was the most important thing to them. "Charge them for every little thing they want," that was the motto of many a transport ship Captain.

Jonas Smithfield, late of His Britannic Majesty's Royal Navy ship *Broadview*, was a small rotund man of forty-five years old. He had served during the Napoleonic Wars and had been at Trafalgar with Nelson on the *Victory* when the famous little Admiral had been killed. In those days,

Smithfield had been third Lieutenant in charge of the middle gun-deck. He had not seen Lord Nelson shot nor had he been with him when he died; only the senior officers and the surgeon had been present along with the other wounded sailors in the cockpit on the orlop deck deep in the bowels of the ship.

After Trafalgar, Jonas Smithfield had worked his way up through the officer ranks and just before Waterloo he had obtained the rank of Post Captain on the *Broadview*. He served with her until being paid off in 1821. The Royal Navy was now just a shadow of itself after the glory days in the early 1800's. But Britannia still ruled the waves even though the upstart Yankee Navy was proving to be a force to reckon with.

Smithfield had even fought a short engagement against one of their big frigates during the War of 1812, off of Cape Hatteras. He was impressed with their battle plans and seamanship and it had only been by the grace of God that his ship had beaten the bigger American ship. Since then he had crossed paths with many an American and had vowed to find the Yankee Captain who had fought so bravely against him in 1814. Smithfield was an adventurer and maybe if that Yankee were still alive they could sail together sometime and exchange memories and ideas. *The Pioneer* was a fine ship, but Jonas Smithfield longed once more for a sleek frigate.

"Maybe the young American Navy would have something for a man with his experience," he often thought. The crew of *The Pioneer* was a rowdy bunch but well behaved overall. George Henderson worried at first about his daughter, Jane, but as the spring days turned into weeks his worries left him. The crew was actually very religious, something quite unheard of on board a sailing ship. The First Mate, Obadiah Heathcliffe, told George one day that most of the crew had been with Captain Smithfield since his days on the old *Broadview*. When he left that ship in Liverpool in 1821 and headed north, fifty men followed him. He also told George that many are still on board *The Pioneer*.

George had heard of and seen devotion like this in the army as well. His small band of riflemen had been much like these sailors. They had followed their famous Colonel all through Portugal, Spain and up into France. Some had died beside him; others like himself and Isaac had been some of the lucky ones, surviving to live their lives in quiet respite, away from the ravages of war.

On the third week out of Maryport, a sudden call from the masthead alerted all those below on deck.

"Deck there, sail to the Nor' west." Captain Smithfield immediately called for identification. His lookout, being an ex-navy man had already checked that after yelling the alert. "Navy frigate zur. She looks like that new one out of Plymouth." Smithfield's men were no longer navy lads but they knew their ships and with no wars threatening them, they had any fear of the infamous "Press Gangs". Anyway, no Navy ship in peacetime would ever steal another ship's crew out at sea unless some sort of deal was made between the Captains.

"Frigate signaling zur," yelled the lookout. The First Mate read out the words of the Royal Navy ship's signal flags as they were run up. "Heave to, we are the Royal Navy Frigate, *Warspite*, we wish your Captain to repair on board as soon as possible. Signed Captain Trevor Linden of His Britannic Majesty Navy," said Obadiah Heathcliffe.

"That is odd, very odd," said Smithfield, "I have never have had this happen before. Something must be up over the horizon. Mr. Heathcliffe, prepare the jolly boat and a good crew," ordered Smithfield.

"Want to come along, Henderson?" he asked George, who happened to be standing by the rail listening and watching as the big frigate began to lower her sails.

"Sure, why not? I have not been on a frigate in ten years. It will be interesting to see how the peacetime Royal Navy operates these days."

Chapter 3
Trouble at Sea

The *Warspite* had been built in 1823 in Deptford but was based out of Plymouth, patrolling the Irish Sea for smugglers and other "nasties," as the Navy called contraband dealers. She carried a crew of two hundred and eighty eight and was armed with thirty-eight guns: twelve and eighteen pounders and two carronades on the bow. What she was doing three weeks out from Plymouth in the North Atlantic made Captain Smithfield just a little concerned. Especially since he was being stopped by her.

"Something must be dreadfully wrong somewhere," he thought, as he had never been stopped in the open ocean since leaving the Royal Navy three years before. "They better have a damn good excuse," he whispered to George, who was seated next to the Captain in the open jolly boat. It was not a ride that George was really liking: an eighteen foot open boat, six sailors on the oars, a cox'n, the Captain and himself all heading across a half a mile of swells on the North Atlantic in mid-May.

"I must be crazy," thought George. "One wrong move and we are all goners in this cold water. Some husband I would make for my wife and children—me lying at the bottom of the Atlantic and they on their way to set up a new home."

Captain Smithfield just smiled and guessed correctly what his new friend was thinking. Smithfield's smile quickly turned to a frown when he got closer to the now hove to frigate. It showed distinct signs of having been in a battle.

"But who with?" he wondered. "Britain is not at war with anyone, at least not that I am aware of just now." As the jolly boat drew closer to the frigate, the cox'n gasped and spoke to Smithfield in a strange and frightened tone.

"She's been in a bit of a tussle zur," he said.

All hands quickly turned towards the frigate and the little open boat lost headway in the four-foot swells.

"Mind yourselves," yelled the cox'n. "Let us get there first before we take a look." As the jolly boat drew alongside, the sailors were able to see the damage and some of the Navy sailors looking down at them from their battle-scarred ship.

A senior officer could be seen at the gangway waiting for the guests. Smithfield had never met Captain Linden nor had ever heard of him. Things had changed a great deal in the Royal Navy since he had left in 1821. There were many new young officers now and Linden must be one of them. However, he had heard of the *Warspite*. The frigate had indeed been in a "bit of a tussle" as the cox'n had so politely stated. Holes could be seen along her starboard beam, there was serious damage to her afterdeck, and blood stained the sides of what had been a freshly painted ship. "But where and with whom," Smithfield wondered out loud. They would soon find out as they latched onto the chains of the Royal Navy ship. It would be the first time in many a year on board one of His Majesty's ships for most of the jolly boat's crew, and Smithfield could sense their nervousness.

Captain Linden met Smithfield at the railing and wished him welcome. Linden was a tall man, about six feet in height, and very handsome, unlike most Royal Navy captains that Smithfield remembered. Most were short, fat, and middle-aged drunks. He figured Linden to be about thirty-two years old, an ideal age to be the eyes of the fleet and on one of the newest Royal Navy frigates.

Smithfield introduced Captain Linden to George, who up till then had been very quiet and had been just gazing at the beautiful warship that seemed to have been in a stiff battle—and not too long before, either.

They headed to the Captain's cabin while the crew of the jolly boat and the cox'n toured the ship with the frigate's bosun at the request of Captain Linden. Smithfield and his crew could plainly see that Linden was very proud of his new ship and wanted to show her off, despite the damages to her.

Captain Linden began the meeting with a toast to the King. He had a fine selection of port wines and claret on board. Linden apologized to Smithfield for stopping *The Pioneer* in mid-voyage, but he had needed help. Smithfield was hoping what was about to come from the lips of Linden would not come.

"I need manpower and I need your ship," exclaimed Linden. "I have fourteen dead and twenty wounded and I have got two guns out of commission. Two days ago we were patrolling just outside a thick fog bank when all of a sudden a mysterious ship loomed out of the fog bank with guns blazing. Luckily the wind was in our favour and we ran for it. Hardly had time to get a shot off. This being peace time and this our first cruise in four months, we had little gun practice—though most of these hands are old salts."

"But who and why?" asked Smithfield and George at about the same time.

"Don't know who, and I sure don't know why," said Linden. Just then, there was a tap at the cabin door. "Enter," called Linden. It was his first lieutenant, John Benson, another handsome young man of about twenty-one years old. Smithfield and George were introduced and more claret was passed around.

"I'm getting to like the Royal Navy," thought George.

Lieutenant Benson spoke quietly to the group gathered. "Two more men have died of their wounds, sir," he explained. "That makes sixteen now and more may yet die from their wounds." He turned to Smithfield and asked him, "Do you have a doctor on board your ship, sir?"

Smithfield nodded and responded in the affirmative. "Yes, actually I have two on board: one is a passenger and my own surgeon. Can I lend you one of them?" he asked.

Captain Linden whistled and exclaimed, "A ship with two doctors and us needing them. Lady Luck is with us. Now for my next request."

"Uh-oh," thought George.

Linden leaned forward and spoke quietly but very deliberately. "I need some of your men. Are any of them ex-Navy men or Marines?"

Smithfield thought for a second and considered lying to Linden. "I could lie, but he can take them anyway; it is his right as a Royal Navy Captain in trouble on the high seas. Might as well tell him the truth," he thought.

"Ninety percent of my crew are ex-seamen from the Royal Navy," said Smithfield." I have a few from the East India Company as well, but no ex-Marines. However, two of my passengers are ex-Riflemen. Mr. Henderson here is one of them. He served with the 95th Rifles, I believe, in Spain and France. He and his friend were the best shots in their regiment from what I hear tell. Ain't that so, George?"

Speaking for the first time, George told the frigate captain that what Smithfield had said was true but that he and his friend were now retired soldiers heading to North America to begin a new life. "I'm traveling with my wife and children. Though my friend is alone, he does travel with us," explained George. "We don't want no part of any fighting. We are retired soldiers. Retired."

Linden stood up and turned towards the stern windows and spoke in a slightly louder voice but still very relaxed. "I know how you feel Mr. Henderson. Britain is at peace, except for some sort of small skirmish in Burma. We are not supposed to be engaging in any battles out here in the Atlantic but you have both seen my ship. We almost got blown out of the water two days ago. And by whom? God if I know." Linden was getting more excited and this worried Smithfield a little.

"How many men can you spare, Captain Smithfield?" asked Linden.

Smithfield thought for a moment and then said, "About twenty at least, plus my surgeon. I have a crew of ninety, plus numerous passengers. None have ever been to sea except for Mr. Henderson here and his friend Isaac."

"The surgeon will be my own. He served with me on the old *Broadview*.

"My crew will need a guarantee from you, Captain Linden, that when you have no longer need of them on this voyage, they be returned to my ship as soon as possible. They are paid employees of my ship's owner and

I may have trouble convincing them to volunteer for active duty on a Royal Navy warship in peacetime, sir.""You have my word," Linden told his guests. "My written word." He then produced a written statement attesting to the fact. Smithfield smiled and told the tall captain how sly he was in preparing the document prior to his acceptance of the deal.

George whispered into Smithfield's ear as Linden turned to get more wine from the cabin's cabinet, "Tell him about your guns, Captain."

Linden turned in a flash and stammered, "You have guns, Captain Smithfield? How many, and what size?"

Smithfield smiled and said, "I have four eighteen pounders and some swivel guns and my men know how to use them very well," he said proudly.

Smithfield could see the Navy Captain thinking and starting some sort of a scheme to have *The Pioneer* help him defeat the strange warship. Smithfield welcomed the idea of having a Royal Navy ship in the vicinity if a rogue warship was patrolling the mid-Atlantic. *The Pioneer* could be the next victim and with only four big guns she would be no match for a ship that had just sent a brand new Royal Navy frigate running. "Maybe Linden's ship could escort them to Canada; at least hopefully not back to Britain," he thought.

After a short exchange of some more details concerning the upcoming exchange, Smithfield called for the jolly boat and he and George returned to their own ship.

"This could prove to be a very interesting next few hours, George," Smithfield whispered, not wanting the rest of the jolly boat's crew to hear them speaking. However, as much as Smithfield wanted not to tell his men just yet, the infamous Royal Navy rumours had already spread word of the proposals by Captain Linden to *The Pioneer's* crew that had wandered around the big frigate.

Not too many of them were looking forward to having another stint in the Navy at King George's expense. The crew of *The Pioneer* was very happy with their ship, their Captain, and his treatment of them. The last thing they wanted was to see the gun deck of a Navy frigate in battle, or the end of a cat-o-nine tails if they misbehaved. If they misbehaved on Smithfield's ship they were disciplined—but not with the infamous "cat".

Smithfield whispered to George as they neared their ship that he would muster all hand and passengers as soon as possible after conferring with his officers and the first mate. George and Isaac would be welcomed at the meeting too, since they had emerged as the civilian leaders on board the ship over the past three weeks. Their excellent military backgrounds would also help in case a battle did occur. George agreed, but only after having spoken to his family in private.

Mary was shocked and very much alarmed when George explained what had happened on board the frigate. She cried at first, but after some thought as George continued his explanation she finally agreed. Isaac entered and he too was not in a great mood. George had pulled him aside as soon as he had got back on board *The Pioneer*. George had explained to both him and Mary that they did not have much of a choice. Besides, having a Royal Navy warship to escort them to Canada could prove to be a blessing. It would seem silly to return to Maryport or even Liverpool now, turning tail because of some rogue warship. With both ships well-armed and being good, sturdy ships, they might have a combined chance in defeating this unknown enemy and continuing on their way.

One thing was certain and that buoyed everyone's hopes: both of their ships were closer to Canada than to England, and there was a strong possibility that they could meet other Royal Navy patrol ships or even some from the American Navy. Either one would be a blessing right now.

George was a little worried about Captain Linden. He seemed very agitated about having to do battle once again with the rogue warship. George had mentioned this to Isaac and Smithfield. Smithfield had noticed this too and was also worried. "The last thing we need now," he had said to George, "is to have this Linden fellow turn and run from the battle when we need each other. I wish I knew more about him."

The meeting of the crew and passengers occurred about forty minutes after the jolly boat had returned to *The Pioneer*. Captain Smithfield stood on the quarterdeck looking down on the main deck where the group was gathered. Many were talking amongst themselves; they had all heard by now about what had happened to the *Warspite*. She was still hove to about a league away from their ship. The seas were fairly calm, and the skies were clear. This, combined with lookouts on both ships, guaranteed them that the rogue warship would not sneak up on them.

Smithfield cleared his throat and asked the gathered people to be quiet. He thought to himself that this was not going to be easy but he really had no choice. They would have to help the frigate no matter what. Linden had promised them safe passage to Halifax: that should be at least six days away if the winds held.

"I have asked you all here, for we have a major problem before us," he began. "Some unknown and vicious rogue warrior or pirate has damaged that Royal Navy frigate. Captain Linden of the *Warspite* does not know who attacked him a few days ago, nor why. However, now that we are here, we too are in danger. As you know, this ship carries some armament. Not as much as that frigate—nor the unknown enemy—but some. Captain Linden has asked me to help him if need be in case he or we are attacked. I have agreed.

"That Royal Navy frigate has lost some much-needed manpower, and we have many able-bodied seamen on board. I have agreed that twenty of this crew will be loaned to Captain Linden until we make landfall in Halifax."

As soon as Smithfield mentioned Halifax, there was much whispering in the crowd gathered below him. "Quiet please. I must speak and all must hear me. This affects all of us."

"I do not want a battle any more than any of you. But a battle may occur anyway, if this rogue shows up again. We know nothing at all about where this ship is from or why he took on a Royal Navy frigate without any provocation whatsoever. However, Captain Linden has given me a sworn written statement that all volunteers that so wish to return to this ship after we land in Halifax may do so. They will not be pressed into service in his Britannic Majesty's service. If any wish to continue to serve with the *Warspite* after we land in Halifax, they may do so. All others will be free to return to this ship. This statement was signed in front of me and George Henderson while on board the frigate a couple of hours ago."

Smithfield had lied about his last sentence but believed it had been necessary to do so.

"Halifax is now our main destination, since that is the closest British port. I figure we are about six days away from there if the winds hold. *Warspite* will escort us there, as there is a possibility that we could be the rogue's next victims. I imagine him to be some sort of modern-day pirate. We all thought that the days of Captain Kidd or Blackbeard were over. I guess not.

"After we make Halifax, those wishing to continue onto Québec and Montréal may do so. Hopefully we will have another escort up the St. Lawrence, as Captain Linden will raise the alarm as soon as we land in Halifax. Halifax is the major Royal Navy port in British North America and there will be numerous warships there, I hope. We might even come across a squadron on our way in."

"Many of you are ex-Navy sailors, and that is what Captain Linden needs: experienced men. You are probably more experienced than all of his crew and I know you will be able to help him. As for who goes, that is another question. Any volunteers? I need twenty hands. My surgeon has already said he would go. Our civilian doctor will stay on board, as he has his family with him. Mr. Heathcliffe will take names of any volunteers."

As men began to file forward someone asked, "Why do we have to help the Navy anyway? Can't they fend for themselves? It is not up to a privately owned ship to provide backup to a Royal Navy warship. What has happened since the times of 'Ol Nelson. Have we gone soft?"

Captain Smithfield had expected such questions, and they did not anger him, as he too had felt the same at first. "No, the Navy has not gone soft—just a little unprepared I guess. I do not know anything about this Captain Linden over there on that frigate, nothing about his previous career, or about what kind of an officer he is. One thing is for sure: he needs manpower to work his frigate the proper way and we are his only source. If he heads off back to England and leaves us out here in the vast ocean alone there is a very strong chance that this rogue will pounce on us. Alone with just four eighteen pound guns, we would not stand a chance against a ship that had just routed a Royal Navy frigate.

"Together we may have a chance. I plan to move all of our guns to the starboard side so we can have a heavier broadside if need be. That will leave our port side empty so if it does come to a scuffle we will have to do some nifty sailing to get on the starboard side so we can use our guns. Those extra four guns will help Linden if we do come to grips with our unknown enemy. Hope-fully we will be able to get him in crossfire. There is lots of planning to do and you are well-versed in handling these guns— as most are ex-Navy men.

"I see that Mr. Heathcliffe has his full list now. I thank you men for trusting in the Royal Navy, and in me. I know that the Navy has had a bad reputation in past years but with peace now upon us I think we can trust them a little more. I myself am an ex-Navy person," Smithfield said, turning his attention more to his passengers than his crew who all knew him so well. "We have two experienced sharpshooters amongst us and they too will be helping out. Mr. Henderson and Mr. Kirkbride possess a type of gun called a rifle and it is very accurate, even, I am told, up to two to three hundred yards. They could be an asset in a close battle. If any of you passengers own weapons, please let Mr. Henderson or Mr. Kirkbride know right now. They will give you your orders and positions in case we have to do battle.

"All the women and children will be kept below decks if a battle is about to happen. Our civilian doctors will need help so if any of you wish to volunteer, please let them know. Battle wounds are not pleasant to see, but they must be attended to just like any other wound.

"As soon as we can get our volunteers over to *Warspite* the sooner we can get under way for Halifax. Mr. Heathcliffe, signal her that we are sending twenty sailors and one surgeon right away, and then we will be making sail for the port of Halifax as he requested."

"Aye, aye, sir," Heathcliffe said as he descended onto the main deck with the surgeon, who had already packed his bags for the trip across to the awaiting frigate.

Chapter 4
Disaster

Seventy-two hours had passed since the final boatload of sailors from *The Pioneer* had been transferred over to the *Warspite*. Since then, both ships had sailed westward towards Halifax and there was still no sign of the new and unknown enemy. Both Captains also exercised their gun crews at regular intervals. Smithfield was an old hand a naval warfare but had not been in a pitched battle in a number of years. He only wished that he could find out more about the frigate Captain. But how? And would it be too late if he did find anything?

It took some work to maneuver two of the eighteen-pound guns and lash them down on the starboard side of *The Pioneer* but with help from some of the male passengers, Smithfield's crew was able to do it without too many problems. Luckily his ship had been originally set up to handle an even battery of ten guns, five per side. The old gun ports were still there and were still usable.

"Too bad we do not have those extra six guns eh, Captain?" Heathcliffe had said to him while they were watching the crew manhandle the big guns across the deck. Smithfield could not help agreeing with him. He knew that his crew would make a fight of it, but what of that damn frigate Captain? Would he stand or make a run for it and leave us to the mercy of the rogue?

"Wind is picking up Captain," Heathcliffe yelled to Smithfield. "Looks as if a storm is a brewing to the Nor' west, sir. Should I take in some sail?"

Smithfield told him not to just yet, but to make sure all hands were well fed with a hot meal, then to douse the galley fires. "No need to have a chance of a disastrous ship fire in a storm or a battle," he said. "Never know when that bastard will show up."

"Maybe he has gone off to some warmer climate," Heathcliffe said in his unique monotone voice.

"Maybe he has," Smithfield said. "Maybe he has, but I somewhat doubt it. Make sure we have a good eye aloft. It will be dark soon but I want a man up there before first light. I don't want to get caught like Linden did. I do not trust that man at all. Something about our meeting with him and Henderson made me uneasy. Henderson noticed it too, Heathcliffe. What gets me is why a frigate on Irish Sea patrol was way out here."

The storm came up quickly and hit just before dark. Both ships soon lost sight of one another even though they did carry stern lights. The rain and sleet were heavy and the winds ferocious. Heathcliffe had managed to get the crew fed and the galley fires doused before the storm hit. The crew on watch reefed in the topgallants and main sail and foresail so the ship was riding out the vicious May storm at ease. One thing was certain about ex-East Indiamen, they were sturdily built for their size and could weather about anything Ol' Neptune could throw at them. The frigate would probably have a harder time of it, but that was their problem and not his, Smithfield thought.

George Henderson had not been idle as many of the other male passengers had been since the general meeting of all those on board *The Pioneer* three days before. Both he and Isaac Kirkbride had gone over their own plan of action and had checked their weapons countless times. Neither had been in a sea battle before and they were not exactly looking forward to one either. However, their past military experience was a blessing to the other passengers on board. They were to form the core of a "civilian" Marine company on board their ship.

Henderson had hoped for some help from Captain Linden on that account, especially a loan of one or two of his own bullocks, but he had been turned down immediately.

"I need all my Marines myself," Linden had said nervously. "I could do with you two but that is asking too much." At which George had whole heartily agreed. There was no way that he was going to leave his wife and family to man a Royal Navy frigate with some nervous, wine drinking and very inexperienced Captain. "Probably never has seen the muzzle of an eighteen pounder fire at him until the other day. Probably pissed his pants then yelled for the retreat. It is amazing he did not strike his colours!" Smithfield said. Like Smithfield, George also had a very bad feeling about that frigate Captain and he had told Isaac about it.

Both he and Isaac had seen cowardly Army officers in Spain and many of them had been killed by their own men as a last resort of saving their own lives and the lives of their comrades. The British Army was noted for their so-called "gallant officers" who had little or no military background or training and had purchased their positions.

Rankers like themselves had to deal with some bloody awful stuffed shirt officers who did not know a battle plan from a dart game. They all seemed to think that it was fun, but that was until the first bullets began to fly. After that, only the true officers stood with their men and fell with them too and many did that. Luckily for both Isaac and George, the 95th Rifles had some damn good officers. Too bad so many of them had met their death at Waterloo and other vicious battles during the war against Napoleon.

Besides Isaac, George had been able to muster some twenty other men with weapons. The rest were either too scared, too old or did not know which end of a gun was which. At least twenty extra guns on board would help a little if they had to do a pitched close in battle with the rogue. George and Isaac had examined the other men's weapons. There was nothing all that great but at least all could fire their guns. One man surprised both Isaac and George when he showed up with a rifle just like theirs.

George wondered if this fellow passenger had been a rifleman like him and Isaac. The passenger, Henry Irons, had been just that, but with the 60th Royal Americans, not the 95th. After having fought in Spain and in

Europe, he had remained in Britain rather than returning immediately to North America. His company had been raised in Halifax in 1811 and it had seen a great deal of misery as had George's 95th as they moved up the Iberian Peninsula to France. He was missing an ear but just having another experienced hand with a gun pleased them both. He was nominated as the Sergeant of the Company. George was named Captain and Isaac his 1st Lieutenant. George thought to himself, "After all those years as a Sergeant Major, here I am a Captain of a Volunteer Marine Company! Will wonders never cease?"

George and his two fellow riflemen drilled their company as often as time allowed until the storm came upon them. The three of them felt that they would be able to make some sort of showing if the need arose. At least no one would run away, as out there at sea there was just no where to run except below decks and the stairs to the lower decks were going to be guarded by a sailor with a short barreled Brown Bess with a bayonet.

Since Smithfield's general meeting, George had very little time to spend with Mary and their children. With the storm in full progress and all hands below decks except for those on watch, they would be able to talk and discuss their plans between themselves. Privacy was almost non-existent on the merchantman but with twenty-one fewer men on board, those having gone over to the *Warspite*, some extra room had come into being.

Mary had never stepped in front of her husband and stopped him from what he had done best, being a soldier and she was not planning to do it here either. However, many of the rest of the Company's men had wives who were not so lenient.

Some of the wives just did not understand that their whole voyage and future lay in the hands of Captains of both ships. If one or both of them failed to defeat the rogue ship they would never make it to their new home. The North Atlantic was not the place where any of them wanted to die but there was a strong possibility that many would soon die on both sides if the rogue ship were encountered before they made land at Halifax. Some were now talking among themselves of staying in Halifax rather than making yet another voyage around Cape Breton and up the St. Lawrence River, a trip of almost another 1,500 miles.

All the passengers were tired of the long voyage and just wanted to find their new home and land. The Hendersons all had similar feelings but both Mary and George both knew that if a fight was to be, then God had wished it. Also, they were both ready for it.

The storm grew worse during the night and lookouts on both ships soon lost sight of each other's stern lights. "The last thing we need is to be separated," thought Smithfield. "Neither of us can fight this unknown bastard alone unless we surprise him and that is unlikely. Hopefully," he thought, "Linden will find the rogue first and not us. I will have to come to his support as I promised. However, will he come to my support if I find the rogue first?" That thought worried Smithfield a great deal all night as he tried to get some much-needed sleep.

Below decks on *The Pioneer* the passengers were also restless as they knew that Halifax was not too far away. If only they could sight land or a friendly naval squadron before a battle occurred. Everyone on board was nervous and sleep did not come easily to most of them.

The storm abated as dawn approached and the skies began to clear about two hours before sunrise. Finally a brilliant moon shone through the clouds with its faint light. The lookouts began to scan the sea around them; it was empty. The frigate was nowhere to be seen.

As the sun began to rise Smithfield had already been up for two hours and had called the early watch to set more sail once again. No matter where the frigate was, they must head to Halifax as fast as they could. The *Warspite* was a much faster ship than *The Pioneer*, it being a sleek frigate and the other an elder merchantman.

"The *Warspite* is probably miles ahead of us," Smithfield said to George, who had joined the Captain on the quarterdeck with a hot cup of coffee for both of them. Smithfield welcomed the hot drink and took out a small flask of brandy from under his coat and poured a small shot in each cup. "That will warm your innards a wee bit better," Smithfield said to his friend as he winked at him.

"Deck there, smoke and gunfire to the sou'west. Two ships doing battle, zur," called down the main mast lookout. Men clambered to the rails on the port side to see if they could see it too, but the ships were too far for those on deck. However, every once in awhile the dull echo of gunfire drifted across the water.

"Looks as if Linden and his men have got that bastard at last," Smithfield said happily to George and Isaac. Kirkbride had just joined the other two when the lookout had called down.

"Deck there," yelled out the lookout once again, "one ship is on fire it looks like. Cannot tell which one though yet, zur, too much smoke." All those on board who were on deck could clearly see the smoke now as it rose high into the morning sky.

"Prepare the crew for battle and clear for action," Smithfield yelled to Heathcliffe. "All women and children below decks! NOW!" They had no drummer on board as the frigate would have had to beat the crew to quarters, so Smithfield's loud voice and his speaking trumpet would have to do.

"No use taking a chance on who is winning and who is losing before we get too close, eh fellows?" Smithfield said to George and Isaac. "Now you two best get your Volunteers ready also." They both nodded and left Smithfield on the quarterdeck with his bosun.

"Deck there, seems that *Warspite* is taking quite a beating, sir."

"Heathcliffe, grab yourself a telescope and tell me what is going on," yelled Smithfield.

"All guns ready sir," the first mate yelled up to his Captain. "Two loaded with round shot and two with chain." Smithfield's only chance now was to get around behind the rogue and fire all four of his guns through the unprotected stern of the warship. This tactic had been the tide turner of many a battle he had been in and a tactic proved worthy of its innovator-Lord Nelson.

"Hopefully they won't dismast me first," he thought.

If *The Pioneer's* guns could create enough havoc on the already damaged rogue they might just have a very slight chance of a second broadside. At close range Henderson's men would have to fire at least two rounds a minute to keep the enemy's heads down. They will not be expecting a merchantman to be carrying big guns, especially now that Britain is at peace with Europe and the United States nor to be carrying a platoon of sharpshooters. Smithfield's mind was racing and his heart pounding in his big chest. He was excited and his men knew it too. They had served well under him on the old *Broadview* and they were going to serve him well once again.

"Experience just may pay off this time. God knows we need some luck," he thought.

They would run their four guns out at the last minute just before they came across the stern of the rogue. She was flying no flag from what they could see. All still seemed a little strange to Smithfield but he was committed now.

"Prepare to lower all boats to pick up survivors of the *Warspite*," yelled Smithfield to his First Mate. "Must give them a fighting chance at least. Twenty of that crew does come from this ship and we must try to help them," Smithfield said to Heathcliffe who had now joined his Captain by the wheel.

George was more nervous than he had ever been and he could see that his small group of volunteers was too. "I must not let them see that I am as scared as they are," he thought. "Not exactly like Waterloo, but as damn dangerous and no place to run," he said quietly to Isaac who now stood beside him. Their eyes were glued to the battle raging in front of them, now less than a mile away.

George added by saying, "It has been so long since we have been in battle. We are supposed to be retired. I hope we remember what to do."

Isaac reminded him why they had joined the army in the first place: to protect their country and Crown from an outside threat and that is what they were about to do once again. George agreed with Isaac.

Everyone on board *The Pioneer* could see that the Royal Navy frigate was in a bad position; her men were jumping overboard to escape the searing flames that began to consume the once proud ship. *Warspite* was a doomed ship and all expected her to explode very soon, as the flames could not be too far from her magazine.

"She's struck her colours, sir," Heathcliffe yelled over to his Captain. However, all those on deck could plainly see the British battle ensign come fluttering down and hear the cheer aboard the rogue ship. Just then, a big black and white flag was unfurled off of the stern of the rogue: the "Skull & Crossbones" of a pirate ship.

"Look at the flag she is flying. A fucking pirate," Isaac whispered to George as they crouched behind some hammocks that had been strung along the side of their ship to offer some protection in the upcoming battle. All the eyes of the volunteer Rifle Company were on Smithfield as he paced the quarterdeck above them.

One of *The Pioneer's* crew yelled over to Heathcliffe saying that the pirate ship had the lines of a Spanish frigate. Whether a frigate was of British, French, Spanish or American origin, they all had certain easily distinguished traits that an experienced seaman could identify. The American frigates were the easiest to identify, as they were so much larger than their European counterparts.

But how this former Spanish frigate had become a pirate ship was yet another unanswered question.

"Too damn many unanswered questions these past couple of days," Heathcliffe said to Smithfield.

"Hopefully we will have some answers soon," replied his Captain.

"Deck there, sail to the south-east. Looks like another ship heading this way, sir."

"Just what we need, another damn pirate. Doubt she's one of ours. We are doomed just like Linden over there unless that new ship is one of ours which I hazard to doubt."

Suddenly the whole area was lit up with a tremendous explosion and the burning frigate disappeared in a huge ball of flame and smoke. Men were screaming for help in the water but the cold soon took their cries away from those listening. *The Pioneer's* boats, all three of them, had been in the water for about ten minutes now and were pulling the few survivors aboard. Many were burned but others amazingly were unscathed. Smithfield quietly whispered under his breath that hopefully the rogue would not fire on his rescuers.

Slowly the stern of the rogue came closer and Smithfield yelled to run out the guns as prepare to fire on the uproll. Four guns would not be much of a broadside, but all on board *The Pioneer* knew it was their only chance to catch the rogue napping after their glorious victory over a Royal Navy frigate.

They were only two hundreds yards apart when the officers on the pirate ship noticed the guns glistening from the side of *The Pioneer*, aimed directly at their unprotected stern. They tried to steer away but it was too late.

"FIRE!" yelled Smithfield and all four guns belched out their lethal loads. "Reload and fire at will, two with round shot and two with chain to cripple her!" he yelled.

Screams were heard across the water as the four eighteen pounders of *The Pioneer* found their mark. The devastation was as Smithfield had hoped. Guns on both sides of the ship were turned over and havoc rained supreme. Smithfield had fired on the unprotected stern of the pirate ship and his guns had sent their lethal loads the whole length of the enemy, killing and maiming scores of men. Each of the four guns had found their mark. Smithfield's insistence of practicing with his guns had paid off. Not one shot had missed the pirate ship.

"My guess Heathcliffe," Smithfield yelled as yet another broadside was fired, "is that they will be the next to strike, ha, ha!" No guns had yet fired on them from the rogue. "Linden's frigate must have done quite a bit of damage to the rogue before being set alight. Probably by some lucky shot. Linden had proved his worth after all and had not run away. Doubt he is alive though," Smithfield thought.

George and his men were firing as rapidly as they could reload and they too were having an affect on the rogue. He had split his small company into two groups, one at the bow and the other near the stern. Henry Irons was put in charge of one group and George commanded the second with Isaac at his side. Men at arms again just like in Spain so many years before.

The small group of marksmen kept up a withering fire, firing and reloading and firing again and again as fast as they could. Many had never fired on another human before, just wild game in the hills of northern England back home. However, this time they were fighting for their lives and the men were doing the best they could under the terrible circumstances.

George, Isaac, and Henry had a greater advantage over the others due to their expertise with their rifles and previous Army service. Their rifles were taking a toll of the enemy across from them. George's main objective was to kill as many of the enemy's officers as he could hit and he was killing them as quickly as he could spot them. His officers back in Spain had always told their men to kill the officers first, then the sergeants. After that, the common soldier has no leader and is confused on the battlefield and will often turn and run. Of course, there was no place to run on a ship!

George had taken a suggestion from one of the crew and placed four of his men high in the rigging of their ship so they could fire down upon the other ship's deck and at the enemy's sharpshooters in her rigging. The crewmember had been in the Royal Navy before with Smithfield and he remembered that the officers always placed a few Marines high up in the rigging during a battle. George thanked the man for his suggestion, but asked for four volunteers, as he could not order anyone up there. He had four men in no time flat willing to climb high up over the swaying deck with their guns, powder, and shot.

Suddenly the rogue was able to let off a ragged broadside at *The Pioneer.* Luckily most of the shots missed but a couple tore into the old merchantman, killing a few hands and wounding others with splinters. "The doctor will have lots of work today," George said to Isaac. "Probably never seen many wounds like these either," as they both helped carry a wounded sailor to the gangway. The surgeon had set up to care for the wounded two decks below and some of the female passengers had volunteered to help him. Mary Henderson was one of them. Hopefully *The Pioneer's* surgeon was one of those who had survived the inferno on the now blown apart frigate. He would be needed now on board his own ship.

"Deck there, more sails to the south east sir. Looks like five to six ships, some big ones too. The other one is still heading this way and making full sail. She will be here soon. Hope they are ours," the lookout yelled.

"Get a man up there who knows his ships better than that bloody idiot, Heathcliffe!" Smithfield yelled angrily. "I need reports at a time like this not stories about big ships!"

Though *The Pioneer* was equipped with four guns she was not equipped to fight a long engagement. She just did not have enough shot and powder on board. Her owners never believed she would be in the fight for her life with a ship that had just sunk a naval frigate and one of the newest ones at that.

Smithfield needed to make a quick decision but he still had three boats in the water with survivors.

"I cannot leave them," he thought. "I'll never forgive myself. Must try to get them on board. Helmsmen continue to circle the rogue, she's lost headway thanks to Linden and us. If we can get around her bow and blast her from our starboard side, might be able to pick up our boats on our port side. If we are lucky."

"Deck there, first ship is a small brig, other six are warships. One is a small two decker, two others look to be frigates but one seem to be too large and there are three sloops of war also. My God! Two of them are Yankee ships, sir."

Smithfield and Heathcliffe looked at each other and both said at the same time; "The Royal Navy with the American Navy, impossible! No way!" But anything was possible these days and that is exactly what was heading their way.

Since the end of the War of 1812 and the defeat of Napoleon at Waterloo in 1815 the Americans and the British had learned to live together in a relative state of peace in North America. They were very wary of each other, especially out west where exploration was going on at a fast pace and where the border between the United States and British North America was still very much undefined in many places. However, on the high seas things were different. Both the huge Royal Navy and the fledgling American Navy were having their troubles with pirates and slavers. Slavery was still legal in the Americas but growing less and less popular, especially in the north.

Spanish pirates based out of the numerous Caribbean islands raided up and down the American coast, sometimes as far north as Nova Scotia and out to Bermuda. The Royal Navy had a North American squadron. It was based in Halifax in the summer and at Bermuda in the winter.

It had at least four ships of the line, four or five frigates and numerous sloops acting as messengers. The squadron heading toward them had to be the one out of Halifax as with the warmer weather on the way it would have relocated by now. But why the American ships with the squadron, if they really were American ships at all?

The small American Navy was built of over sized frigates but no ships of the line. Most frigates were rated to carry from forty four to forty eight guns. However, most of them carried even more than that and these guns were usually over sized also, often-big twenty-four pounders instead of the normal twelve or eighteen pounder guns that the Royal Navy frigates had on board. A big US frigate carried as much firepower as some of the small two deckers in the Royal Navy and King George's men had found that out not too long ago.

This rogue they were fighting must be either a pirate or a slaver and the guardian of the ship that was heading towards them at a very rapid rate. "Hopefully she is not carrying any big guns," thought Smithfield. However, brigs rarely did anyway but very little had made much sense these past few days.

The Pioneer had made her way around the rogue and had kept firing the whole time. Ammunition was dwindling.

"Only enough for a half a dozen shots out of each gun left sir," Heathcliffe yelled. They could double the effect by doubling the shot on the next couple of broadsides. That could help if the guns held and did not blow themselves up. So far they had been able to battle the rogue to a standstill and Smithfield was actually winning. He could not believe it nor could Heathcliffe. They were ecstatic and hopping around on the quarterdeck as they could see a victory coming if the rogue could be blasted away with one more broadside from them. Even the small swivel guns were having some effect, blasting away as fast as they could be reloaded.

Just then, six guns on the enemy ship opened up and blasted them with full force. One gun was over turned but the other three were still operable and fired all at once. Suddenly smoke could be seen rising from the rogue in an ever-increasing fashion. Something was on fire and it was out of control.

"Deck there, the brig heading away is now being chased by the smaller of the two frigates. She is not going to get away from that one." A dull bang echoed across the water, quickly followed by another.

"The Yanks are using their bow chasers on her," Smithfield said to his first mate. "That battle won't last much longer."

"All boats are aboard sir," the bosun yelled to his Captain. "We were able to save thirty-eight men. Seventeen are our own men! Many are injured sir, but most will live I believe."

"Is Captain Linden among them?"

"No sir, he went down with his ship, killed in the last broadside from the rogue that set *Warspite* on fire."

"At least he did not see his ship die, Smithfield stated sadly. "That is one thing I do not want to have happen, see my ship die before I do."

"Aye, sir. I know how you feel, sir" Heathcliffe said.

All firing had stopped now from the rogue and those on board *The Pioneer* now watched her burn. A few men could be seen jumping overboard and swimming towards the ship that had just destroyed them.

Once again Smithfield called to his First Mate, "Lower the boats again and try to pick up a few of the survivors to find out who they are. Do not waste too much time though. She will be going down soon."

The last broadside of the rogue had not only overturned one of the eighteen pounders but had mown down numerous crewmembers and one ball had ploughed through George's small group of volunteers. Lying in a pool of blood was his best friend, Isaac Kirkbride. A huge wooden splinter from the railings had sliced Isaac open from his groin to his lower back. George had only time to cradle his dying friend for a second before Isaac died. He did not even have chance to say a word, Isaac was already unconscious and bled to death. George just sat there with Isaac's head in his blood soaked lap and cried. Others lay dead or dying around him but George was oblivious to it all. He had lost his best friend and he began to blame himself for this stupid dream of his to set up a new life in North America.

"Why? For this," he cried out loud. "Why?"

The four British warships and the second American frigate were soon upon them and began lowering boats to pick up survivors and come to the aid of the battle-scarred merchantman.

"Admiral's flag on that two decker zur," a sailor yelled over to Smithfield.

"She is the *Salisbury*, sir," Heathcliffe said to his Captain. "Out of Halifax the men say for sure."

"Probably Rear Admiral W.C. Fahie," Smithfield said. "He too was at

Trafalgar. First Lieutenant on the *Bellerophon* then and a mighty fine Officer he was. Well liked then and probably still is."

"I had heard he had been made Admiral in charge of the Halifax squadron," Heathcliffe told Smithfield. "Doing a fine job over here too I hear say. Before making Rear Admiral, Fahie served for awhile on the *Euryalus* as her Captain in the Mediterranean Squadron. Good man."

"The sloops are the *Argus*, eighteen and the *Athol*, eighteen and the *Egeria*, twenty four sir," the bosun called to Smithfield. "I believe the *Egeria* is out of St. John's, Newfoundland," the bosun added. "I saw her there two years ago. Can't identify that big Yankee frigate though."

"She looks quite new to me," Smithfield said.

Heathcliffe replied by saying, "Things must be pretty serious to have the Yanks and the Halifax and Newfoundland squadrons all join up. That pirate frigate and the brig must have been involved in a whole lot of nasty events to have this many warships after them. Maybe that is why Linden was way off his station in the North Sea and never told us. I guess he knew more than he told us after all. Rest his soul."

The first American frigate had caught the brig and was sending a boarding party over to her to sail her back to either Halifax or Boston. A bosun yelled, "By God, that Yankee frigate is the old *Macedonian*." Heathcliffe grabbed a glass and took a look as did Smithfield.

"By God," said Heathcliffe; "She is the *Macedonian*. I haven't seen her since before she was lost to the Yanks in 1812."

"Neither have I," said Smithfield.

George could not help over hearing their conversation and tore himself away from the limp and bloody body of Isaac to approach Heathcliffe and Smithfield. After clearing his voice and wiping his eyes, he asked them, "What happened in 1812?" Behind his back, a small party of *The Pioneer's* crew lifted up the mutilated body of Isaac and carried it over to the port side of the ship and laid it down beside the bodies of the other crewmen and passengers who had been killed. All would be buried at sea in a few hours after the results of the battle were examined.

Smithfield filled George in on some of the details that he remembered of the great sea battle in 1812 between the Royal Navy's newest frigate the *Macedonian* and an old Yankee frigate, *The United States*.

"The Yankee ship was a forty four gun frigate and ours was a big forty nine gun ship and only two years old. *The United States* had been launched in 1797 or 1798 if I remember right and she was the first of the big Yankee frigates to be built and launched."

"The battle," George asked, "what about the battle?"

"Oh yes," Smithfield continued. "Lasted only ninety minutes and the Yankee thoroughly whipped our ship. Over a one hundred men killed or wounded on the *Macedonian* while *The United States* had lost less than a dozen killed and wounded.

"Captain John S. Carden of His Britannic Majesty's Ship *Macedonian* surrendered to Commodore Stephen Decatur who was also a great friend of his. Decatur was reported to have been dressed as farmer rather than a naval officer. Bit of an insult to Carden I guess.

"The Yankees took over the *Macedonian* and refitted her as a thirty eight gun frigate from the rumours we heard after the war. This is the first I have seen of her since. She looks great too."

Heathcliffe added his comments to those of his Captain, "I wonder if there are any of our boys still on her?"

"I doubt it," Smithfield said. "Remember that was fourteen years ago, but there might be. We will never know now as she goes after that brig. If that brig was a slaver, the smell on board will not be too pleasant for those American sailors. Not a pleasant trip home!"

Rear Admiral W.C. Fahie was a portly fellow of about as wide as he was tall and with a beet red face. Not the same fellow that Smithfield had remembered hearing about after Trafalgar, but that was nineteen years before and the two of them had sailed many a league since then. However, despite his looks, Fahie seemed to be a nice fellow and was simply amazed, as were the five Captains who also had come on board *The Pioneer.*

It was not every day that a privately owned merchantman had the honour of hosting a full fledged British Navy Rear Admiral, let alone five ship's Captains all heaping praise on the merchant Captain.

Of course they were very sad at the loss of one of their best frigates, but what they could not understand is how a private merchant ship loaded with emigrants, livestock, and just four guns could defeat and sink a rogue they had been trying to capture for the past eight and a half months. They were embarrassed. However, the Royal Navy Captains and their Admiral were overall very pleased that Smithfield had done his duty, just as their "Old Nel" would have wanted him to do so long ago.

Smithfield had quite a lot of explaining to do over the next few hours as the six ships sailed along together towards Halifax. He insisted that they all attend burials for the eighteen dead on board his ship. Since the arrival of the other ships, Smithfield had not been able to talk to George at all and he was not aware of Isaac's death until his name was placed before him on the register just before the burial service. He looked at George with tears in his eyes and he could see how shaken George was at the loss of his best friend.

Unfortunately Smithfield did not have time to console his friend as he had to get on with the service then speak once again with the Admiral before he and the five Captains left to go back to their respective ships.

The service was short and a hymn was sung at the end as each man was committed to his grave, fathoms below. Each man was wrapped in his hammock, which was then weighed down with a cannonball or a rock from the hold. The guns had used up almost all the ammunition, so only three bodies could be weighted with eighteen-pound cannon balls. Extra shot and powder was now being ferried over from one of the British warships as the service continued.

Chapter 5
Halifax at Last!

The American frigate, with its prize brig off its port side, quickly sailed from sight as they headed south to Boston. It was an American capture and *they* would get the glory, not the Royal Navy. However, it was Smithfield and *The Pioneer's* crew who would get the hero's welcome when they entered the harbour at Halifax.

The rogue had once been a Spanish frigate just as the crewman had said to Heathcliffe before the battle. It had gone by the name of *Santa Lucia* but had been captured in a dawn raid on Havana, Cuba by a group of renegade former Spanish and French sailors. The rogue's new name was *El Condor* and she had been the scourge of the Caribbean for close to a year. Numerous innocent merchant ships had either been sunk or burned after their crews had been murdered, set adrift or just thrown overboard. Any woman found on board the merchant ships was abused at the pleasure of the crews until they too were fed to the sharks.

El Condor's Captain, a Spaniard by the name of Juan Carlos Montez, had died on board his ship as it was consumed by fire. He had been flabbergasted that a lone English merchant ship with just four guns had defeated him. However, its Captain knew more about naval warfare than he did and he would never get to meet him. That Captain was Smithfield and he was receiving this information from one of Montez's officers who had somehow survived. He would not live long, as all the survivors of the

El Condor would be hanged shortly after their arrival in Halifax. The same would hold true for the officers in charge of the captured brig heading towards Boston.

Neither the United States of America nor Great Britain had any leniency for the crimes that the crews of the two pirate ships had done. All would die, and the sooner the better, both Governments believed. What would happen to the poor, retched human cargo on the little brig would depend on the American authorities in Boston. They would probably be released and serve in and around Boston in whatever jobs they could find for themselves. They had been the unfortunate pawns in the slave trade that Montez and his two ships had been conducting as well as working as pirate ships in support of each other.

Rear Admiral Fahie would meet with Captain Smithfield again upon their arrival in Halifax. During their first meeting after the battle, Fahie had told Captain Smithfield that his conduct and that of his crew would be mentioned in his dispatches to the Admiralty back in London.

The Pioneer would be repaired by the Royal Navy at no expense to her owners. The Navy had a huge dockyard in Halifax and it was one of the best harbours in the world. Smithfield always liked landing in Halifax, but it had been a couple of years since he had last been there. In recent times, he had been sailing either to Québec or Montréal with his cargoes of new settlers for the Canadas.

Seventeen men who had volunteered to serve on the *Warspite* had survived and they were pleased to be back on board their own ship. They told of how they had come across *El Condor* at first light and though none of them had thought much of Captain Linden at first, their final impressions of him were of outstanding praise.

He had conducted himself with the utmost care and had handled the battle as well as they had seen of any other frigate Captain with a new crew, untested in battle. The twenty volunteers from *The Pioneer* had actually been a boon to Linden as they had all been veterans of numerous naval battles over the years. Sadly though, Smithfield's surgeon had not survived the inferno that had consumed the frigate. He had been trapped below during the fire and had died in the massive explosion that had blown the ship apart.

The only officer to have survived from *Warspite* was Linden's First Lieutenant, John Benson. He had been wounded above the right eye by a splinter but had stayed on deck until Linden was struck down in the last broadside that killed him and set the ship on fire. Benson had nothing but praise for Smithfield's volunteers and he strongly believed that both ships would have easily been defeated by Montez had it not been for the "chosen twenty" as he called them. He too would make a report to the Admiral as soon he arrived in Halifax.

Most of the survivors of the lost frigate were ferried over to the Rear Admiral's ship, the *Salisbury* as soon as they were able to withstand the trip in the open boats. However, some would have to stay on board *The Pioneer* until they reached Halifax. Others would be dropped overboard as they succumbed to their oozing burns.

All through the battle, Mary Henderson had bravely worked alongside Dr. Grisenthwaite below decks on *The Pioneer*. She had seen death before and wounds but none that compared to those that she witnessed on board that ship. Men were crying for help and there was little they could do. Luckily those who were the worst off died soon after they were wounded while the others suffered in the near darkness of the below deck room. Hopefully they would reach Halifax in a couple of days where these poor souls would be able to get better treatment than they were getting now.

After the battle Mary came up on deck at the hurried request of her son, John. He had seen Isaac die in his father's arms and he knew that his father was suffering a great personal loss. George was going to need some strong support in the next little while and his mother was the best support his father could get at this time. It was going to be a tough time for them all. John had tried to console his father before Mary got there but was shoved away. George was in deep mourning and John had never seen him this way. It was going to have a lasting effect on him. There was one glimmer of brightness in the whole affair, and that was that the Henderson family had come through unscathed, except for George's mental anguish. John thought his father would pull through and be his old self soon enough, but only time and the New Land would know for sure.

That New Land still seemed so far away. They had been at sea for almost a month now and it was going to be an adventure they would talk about for years. It would certainly make the London papers, and with the Americans here, maybe the New York or Boston papers as well. They would be famous! Adventure had always followed George Henderson, but this time it had brought tragedy to him. His best friend was dead, but they had fought side by side once again and their rifles had done their service once more. George was feeling a bit better as he and Mary toured the ship, examining the damage and the temporary repairs that were going on. Talking with his dear wife was helping the big man slowly get over the death of Isaac, but he knew deep down that there would always be that question:

"Why did I ask him over here when he was just as happy back in Cumberland?"

However, George also knew that Isaac's love of adventure had also drawn him to cross the Atlantic with his pal. Only fate had sealed his destiny.

The Pioneer and the warships sailed proudly into Halifax harbour just over two days after the battle that had left two ships sunk. Since *The Pioneer* was to be repaired at H.M. Naval Dockyard she docked there, whereas all other merchantmen tied up at the main commercial dockyard separate from the naval base. This surprised many a sailor and deckhand on shore as they watched intensely as the flotilla of six ships made their way to the naval base. Many were wondering why battered merchantmen were being escorted to the naval base. They thought that it was probably some smuggler caught red handed. Their queries would soon be answered as word of the battle soon spread around the dockyards like a hot summer's brush fire.

Captain Jonas Smithfield was soon the talk of all the pubs and hotels in Halifax as well as the Royal Naval base. He and his crew were heroes, but some resented the fact that some privately run ship had defeated the "*El Condor*" and sent her to the bottom when their own ships could not. But they did not know the whole story. No one in Halifax had heard of the two battles that the *Warspite* had with the *El Condor* and those two battles had weakened her drastically. Just enough for Smithfield and his experienced crew to capitalize on.

After tying up at the dock all passengers and crew were advised that they would be staying about two days while repairs were being made to "The Pioneer," then they would set sail for Quebec and finally, Montreal. All passengers were free to leave the ship in Halifax and stay there if they wished or continue on to Quebec or Montreal.

George asked Henry Irons as they watched the deckhands secure their ship to the dock, "Are you planning to stay here or continue up the St. Lawrence River?" Henry had pondered over the idea of heading up to Québec but finally had come to a conclusion.

"No. I am going to head over to the Annapolis Valley and settle down there," he said. "That is where I am from and I hope to find some of my relatives there. Hopefully there will be some land left for me to buy and farm. But first I am going to tour Halifax for a few days, find me a woman or two to fondle a wee bit," as he winked at George.

George thought about Henry and what he had said, "I haven't had much time to fondle Mary these past few days; haven't seen much of her at all. Soon though things will quiet down a bit and we will have time for ourselves and the family."

Captain Smithfield skipped down the gangway like a young sailor half his age. Obadiah Heathcliffe was not so jaunty, but he did have a skip in his walk as well. They were proud and they both knew that they would be the talk of the town in no time. Just ahead of them was the big American frigate, probably one of the first times an American warship had been into a British port since the end of the War of 1812. She was a fine looking ship with long sleek lines.

As they approached her, her Captain and another officer began to walk down their gangway. The four men met as the Americans reached the shore. Smithfield immediately introduced himself and Heathcliffe once again as they had already met shortly after the battle. But at that time it was Rear Admiral Fahie who had done all the talking and Smithfield had not really had a chance to meet any of the five Captains who had come on board The Pioneer with the Admiral. The American Captain said he was Jacob Greenshields and he had been with the American Navy since the early part of the War of 1812. His 1st Lieutenant, Samuel Ashcroft was with him.

The four chatted for a few moments then Smithfield asked

Greenshields, "What is the name of your ship and can I take a look at her? I did battle against a couple of your ships during the War but never got to board one. They always ran away from us! I did defeat one in 1814 off the coast of the Carolinas, but we lost her when a storm came u. Never did find out her name or whether she survived that vicious storm."

"She did, Greenshields," he said quietly as he led Smithfield and Heathcliffe up the gangway. "She did survive and I know because I was that Captain you defeated." Ten years had passed and both men had sailed many a mile on the Atlantic and Pacific Oceans never knowing if either ship had survived.

"My old *Broadview* lasted until 1821 when we were paid off and she was scrapped," Smithfield said sadly. "Heathcliffe here was with me most of those years as was most of the crew of *The Pioneer*. It was those old salts that defeated Montez's ship the other day."

"From what I saw of your battle," replied Ashcroft, "we all knew that they were not just merchant sailors but they had to be trained navy lads."

Greenshields finally said that his big frigate was the *Yorktown*, a new forty four gun ship, only two years old. "Named after our great victory over Cornwallis a few years ago," Greenshields added smugly. "We were attached to Commodore David Porter's West Indies Squadron until we received orders to head north to try to intercept that bastard you killed a few days ago. Porter is still down south with his ship the *John Adams*, a twenty eight-gun corvette and a handful of armed schooners. I will be heading back there in a few days after I have met with Rear Admiral Fahie again and had my ship restocked with supplies at his insistence for our mutual cooperation in this great victory that we all witnessed. The *Macedonian* will join us as we sail south past Boston.

"We are having quite a problem with pirates based out of Cuba and other Spanish possessions in the West Indies. It still amazes me that it took just new one Royal Navy frigate and a merchant ship to bring Montez to justice when all of the American east coast squadrons and the North American squadron of the Royal Navy could not do it. My hat is off to you, Captain Smithfield, and your crew."

They talked about the Battle of Yorktown that had ended the American War of Independence and granted the United States their freedom from Great Britain. It had been long before their own military careers had begun and they had only read about the battle or heard their fathers talk about it years before.

"Good name," said Heathcliffe. "We do not have a habit of naming our ships after great victories as you have done. Maybe we should. We just name streets or put up great marble monuments to remind us of our victories." The night was going to be a long one as the former enemies, now friends, began to mould an everlasting friendship.

A night of drinking was at hand and the evening was still young. They still had to make the rounds of the pubs and the officer's mess before daylight. They were heroes, and all four knew it. They would be celebrating for two long days. As they walked towards the closest pub along the waterfront, Greenshields remembered Smithfield's request to tour his big frigate.

"Captain Smithfield," he said, "you may tour my ship tomorrow afternoon, we have much celebrating to do first and I think neither of us will be in any shape early tomorrow morning to appreciate my ship."

"I agree," laughed Smithfield as the four of them headed into a pub called "The Lion's Head" on Barrington Street.

George Henderson led his family off the ship and straight to the nearest hotel along the waterfront. He was not going have his family cooped up on board *The Pioneer* while it was under repair and with a wonderful and lively town at their doorstep to explore.

Mary, though heavy with child, was anxious to see Halifax as were all the other Hendersons. George made sure that Jane was going to be coming along with them and not wander off with John and get into trouble somewhere. Halifax, like any other naval base, was no place for a decent good looking young girl to wander around alone or with her younger brother. John was a big young man but he would be no match for a bunch of whisky smelling sailors ready for a go at his older sister. George had decided that they would all stay together and explore the town as a family.

Their first stop after securing a hotel for the night was to give thanks to the Lord for their relatively safe passage to North America. Smithfield had told George of the beautiful St. Paul's Church on the Grand Parade in Halifax. The church had been built in 1750 and it was the oldest Church of England in British North America. Smithfield had told the Hendersons that the church was known as the Westminster Abbey of the Canadas.

The Hendersons walked up the steep incline from the docks to the lovely Grand Parade and there on its west side stood St. Paul's. The tired but proud family spent a few moments outside gazing up at the tall white church then proceeded up the steps. Led by George and Mary, the Hendersons quietly walked down to a front pew and settled down.

Since there was no service on at the time, the church was empty, except for the odd parishioner and an altar boy attending to his daily chores. George led his family in quiet prayer, then prayed to himself, weeping as he went. Mary knew that he was praying for his old friend, Isaac Kirkbride. After a few minutes of silence, George stood up, wiped his reddened eyes and motioned to the door. As the family filed out the door George dropped two shillings in the offering box near the entrance.

The 47th and 81st Regiments of Foot, The Loyal North Lancashires or as they were sometimes called, "The Loyal Regiments," were the garrison of British Army troops located at the Citadel. As they watched a small squad of men march by, Mary reminded George that that same Regiment, the 47th, had been her grandfather's at Québec in 1759.

"Seems they have stayed over here in the British North America since then," George added. The fifteen hundred or so redcoats had been there off and on for a number of years, only leaving for maneuvers in Cape Breton or to patrol the countryside for smugglers. There was a small detachment of Hussars and the ever present Provost to keep the peace in the region.

Henry Irons, being a native of Nova Scotia led the Henderson family around for awhile before finding a pub to pop into to wet his whistle and find that local wench he had talked about.

"Must have a fondle before leaving Halifax," he had said. Of course it had been a short tour as the first pub that they came by drew Irons in like a magnet and that was the abrupt end of the Halifax tour for the Hendersons. They would have to fend for themselves now.

Before leaving the ship, George had asked Smithfield about the voyage up the St. Lawrence. "Would it be treacherous? Would they be getting an escort ship like *Warspite*?"

"I doubt it," Smithfield had told George, "no need of an escort now that the damn pirate *El Condor* is gone and the trip is quite easy if the winds are right. Can be a real bugger in Lake St. Peter due to the shallows there and all.

"Should be in Québec in about six days and up to Montréal in about ten if all goes well. We will be stopping at Québec for one day to off load a couple of families. Don't know why, it's all French there anyway except for the garrison at the big fort. But they want to settle in the region. Maybe they are merchants. Who knows and who cares," Smithfield had said. "My duty is to get them there safe and sound and that I will." That was one thing that George knew Smithfield was telling that was true. He would get those settlers there safe and sound. He had just survived one of the toughest peacetime voyages ever by a British merchant ship with the loss of only a few hands and passengers. Until they had met with the rogue *El Condor* Smithfield had not lost one of his passengers or crewmembers to sickness or accidents. He truly cared for his ship, crew and passengers and George admired him for that.

The two days in Halifax passed quickly it seemed and soon *The Pioneer* was heading up the eastern coast of Nova Scotia bound for its next port of call, the fortress at Québec. Mary was very anxious to show here children where their great-grandfather had been when he had climbed the hill from the cove now known as Wolfe's Cove to meet the French under General, The Marquis de Montcalm in 1759.

Former Sergeant Christopher Black of the 47th Regiment of Foot, now known as the 1st Battalion Loyal North Lancashire Regiment, had often talked about his life in the army while stationed for a few years in Québec after the British victory. That battle was the second major defeat that France had experienced in just a few months; the other being the loss of the great fortress of Louisbourg on Cape Breton Island. Montréal would be the last major area to fall, in 1760, before France lost complete control of their great Empire in North America and Britain would be the new ruler of what would become known as British North America.

Christopher Black had loved the ruggedness of the land but had hated the cold winters. "Nothing like you have ever seen," he had often said to his family. "Nothing like you have ever seen or experienced. So cold that rivers freeze four to five feet thick and snow so deep that even the deer have trouble getting through. No place to settle in as far as I'm concerned." Christopher had been glad to return to his home village of Knock in the mid 1760's and that is where his granddaughter, Mary, had been born.

The trip north around Cape Breton was an easy one for *The Pioneer* as the winds were favourable and the days were warming up as May progressed. Mary was anxious to get to her new home as the birth of her child was due in a couple of months. She hoped to have a warm home for the baby when the child was born.

If only her dear little Agnes was here also to see this new land. A tear came to eyes as she thought back on how little Agnes had passed away just three years before. She had never been a strong child and when the influenza epidemic raced through Northern England in 1821, her eighteen year old daughter had been taken from them as had so many other children and elderly that winter. Luckily the Hendersons had not lost any other of their children but the loss of one was bad enough. Mary and George had decided then to try to have one more child and this new unborn one would be their first "Canadian" child and they were both looking forward to its birth sometime in August.

Their last child George, born during the winter of 1820/21, was doing well and had turned out to be a strong and healthy young child just like his older brother John had been.

"Poor little Agnes," Mary thought, "too bad she had been so frail, probably because I had been sick all great deal that year just before her birth. Must have been caused something to happen while she was in my womb, only the Lord knows for sure."

Three days out of Halifax and *The Pioneer* was ploughing through low swells in the Gulf of St. Lawrence when the masthead lookout yelled down, "Deck there, smoke on the horizon, two or three ships". Everyone on deck that heard that cry looked towards Smithfield as he turned to grab a telescope from the rack near the wheel on the quarterdeck.

"Oh no, not again," he said to Heathcliffe. "Prepare the guns and all women and children below decks." The guns had been all placed back in their original spots, two on each side of the ship, with a new one installed back in Halifax replacing the one broken during the battle with *El Condor*.

No gunfire could be heard but there was smoke for sure on the horizon as they proceeded closer to the three ships.

"Deck there, seems that all the ships have smoke coming from them. They are whalers zur! Whalers!"

"Thank God for that," Smithfield said, "Thank God."

"Stand down everyone," yelled Heathcliffe as everyone breathed a sigh of relief of not having to prepare for another battle. "Let all the women and children back on deck if they so please."

The Pioneer was a happy ship and Smithfield and his crew all enjoyed having the children on board, as long as they did not get in the way of the daily workings of the ship. His belief of a healthy ship reflected the beliefs of the ship's owner, John Watterson.

"Cannot have passengers dying on board my ships before they get to their destinations, bad for our reputation. Must have a healthy and happy ship at all times, better for the passengers and crew alike." The way Smithfield's men had handled themselves during the tussle with the rogue had proven both his and Watterson's theories.

"What is that awful smell?" Mary Henderson said to her husband. "It is absolutely disgusting." Everyone on deck was holding a cloth over their faces, even the crew, trying to avoid the gut retching smell that was coming their way over the Gulf from the three ships.

"The whalers are processing their catch and that is the smell from the tryworks on board each ship," Smithfield told the crew and passengers. "It is disgusting," he said. "Don't know how they get used to it. Helm, hard a starboard and let's try to put some distance between them and us."

"Aye, aye sir," the helmsman said and he thrust the big wheel hard to starboard.

"We will lose some time but it is better than having everyone vomiting all over the decks because of those three ships," added Smithfield.

"Deck there, thar she blows!" yelled the lookout once again. "She blows, she blows!" Suddenly whales surrounded them. Mary, with her children beside her glanced over the port side as whales of every size and shape surfaced just off the port bow. At least two dozen of the leviathans had surfaced right near their ship. Probably thinking their ship was yet another whaler the huge beasts soon sounded and disappeared out of sight in the cold green water.

"Wasn't that something?" George said to his wife. He had seen whales before during his passages to and from Spain but never so close and never so large.

Smithfield called up to the lookout to ask him what type they had been. "He is an ex-whaler out of Bristol, George."

"They be humpback whales zur," the lookout yelled down, "Some of the biggest in these here parts. Only the blues are bigger around here and they be not here right now. Wait till August or September, then you will see some big whales."

"Why do they kill them mother?" Asked Frances Henderson, "They are such beautiful fish."

"Mammals dear," George told her, "they are mammals like us; they breathe air and originally came from land so I hear tell. Thousands, maybe millions of years ago when the earth was young they left the land and turned to the sea to live."

"Did someone chase them into the sea, father?" asked little Mary Henderson.

"No, I don't think so," George said to his young daughter, winking to his wife at the same time.

George had to explain to his children that most of the whale was used. Whalebone was used for clothing and the blubber melted down for oil, some meat was consumed but it was not great tasting he had heard. "Don't plan on eating any either," he added. "Some of the whales that are killed have huge teeth and the bone or ivory as it is called is used for carvings and ornaments. Some teeth are eight inches long! And finally a part of some whales, ambergris is used for perfume, but you wouldn't know it when it first comes out of the whale, awful smelling stuff that makes you want to vomit. Ambergris is so rare that a small amount of it is worth hundreds of pounds they say."

Smithfield happened by as George was talking to his family. "Where are they from, Captain?" Mary asked him.

"Well I doubt they are American whalers, as these are British waters, probably out of Bristol or Milford Haven in Wales I guess. I hear that the Yanks already have a huge whaling fleet on all the oceans, most come from Massachusetts, New Bedford or that small island called Nantucket. Actually Yankees now man most of the British whaling fleet from those two places I mentioned in Wales. Usually the main part of the whaling fleet is far north of here, off the coast of Baffin Island and Greenland. Wonder why these three ships are so far south? At least they have found something to catch."

The change of course that Smithfield had ordered soon left the smell from the whaler's tryworks far behind and it was clear sailing the rest of the day.

Henry Irons had decided to stay on in Halifax as he had wanted and only one family had remained there too. All the others had voted to continue their trip onto Québec and Montréal. The Fowlers and Grisenthwaites were still on board and were finally enjoying the trip.

Joseph Grisenthwaite the youngest, had been the civilian doctor on board who had tended to the wounded during and after the battle with *El Condor*. He was looking forward to their new home in the hills beyond the growing hamlet called Cavagnal. George was pleased to know that a doctor would be in the neighbourhood with Mary about to have her child in just a couple of months. Both of them had asked Doctor Grisenthwaite to check her over after they had left Halifax as Mary had come down with a chill while in Halifax. Joseph had promised to send for his father and grandfather at a later date if the area around Cavagnal proved to be a nice place to settle in.

Joseph had made sure that she was all right and told her to make sure that she ate lots of chicken broth and stayed warm. The prescription had proven correct as Mary began to be her joyous self a couple of days later.

"Nothing to worry about," she had said to George, "nothing to worry about. Dr. Joseph seems to know his business and he will be an asset to our new home."

"Wonder if he will be far from where we will be settling," George wondered to himself. "Hope not."

Chapter 6
Lower Canada

The British fortress at Québec loomed into view exactly six days out of Halifax, just as Jonas Smithfield had predicted. Everyone on board was on deck to take in the magnificent view as *The Pioneer* sailed around the end of the Isle d'Orléans and all on board the ship could see the huge stone fort with its old Town of Québec nestled below. They had been able to see the fort from downstream below the island but had lost sight of it until they rounded the end of the island.

Mary was as excited as ever. "Only wish grandfather was here to see this," she said as she hugged George. "Isn't magnificent?"

"That it is dear, that it is," he said. "Must have been some battle that day back in 1759. I am glad I was not here. I have never seen a more impressive and foreboding fort than this, except for the one time I visited Edinburgh Castle while I was still in the Army."

Smithfield had already told all those on board that they would only be here one day, to unload passengers and take on a couple if any were wanting a quick trip upriver.

Only two families were getting off in Québec and unloading them would be not take too long but Smithfield had let it be known to all those on board that those wishing to disembark for the day could as long as they were back on board by dark. No one was remaining in the Town overnight.

"I want to sail before first light if possible as the tide will be right," Smithfield told George and Mary who were standing not too far from him.

"A tide here?" Mary said to George at the same time as Dr. Joseph.

"Yes he said, even though we are miles from the ocean, there is a small tide here at Québec and the water is slightly brackish."

"How do you know that father?" John asked.

"Captain Smithfield told me, son. I may know a great deal about the world, but I must admit I am not an expert on everything." And with that, he turned to hide his growing smile.

The fortress at Québec would be the Henderson's first encounter with the dominant French influence in North America. George had last encountered the French at Waterloo and his French was very rusty, as was his Spanish. But he was ready to try a few words if necessary.

"This Town is one of the oldest in North America, children," he said. "It was founded by Samuel de Champlain in 1608. Two hundred and sixteen years is not really that long when it comes to European or British history children but over here it is everything. Two hundred years ago this was all wilderness occupied by native Indians and no white people except for a few fur traders and explorers. The fur trade still goes on I am told, and there is a vast land west of our new home that is still largely unexplored."

John poked his father and quietly said to him, "Are those Indians over there watching us?"

"I guess they are," George replied. "Look Mary, Indians." With that she let out a slight yelp of fright and covered her eyes.

"Damn savages," one of the other passengers yelled across the water. "Be gone with you!"

"Hope that man is not coming to our territory, father," Jane said. "We should try to understand those poor people. We are here taking their land and this man calls them savages. Maybe he should look in a mirror and see who the real savage is."

The Pioneer docked just below the fort and soon the luggage of the two families disembarking was being lowered ashore.

"Everyone back by dark," Smithfield warned once again. "Everyone, crew and passengers. We leave on the tide in the morning."

George and his family disembarked along with all the other passengers while the crew remained on board for a couple of more hours. There would be no extended shore leave at this stop. The weary crew was going to have to wait until Montreal to celebrate their successful crossing. There was a small tavern near the end of the jetty and Smithfield was allowing the crew a couple of hours in there after the ship was readied for its last leg of the long journey.

Obadiah Heathcliffe was conferring with his Captain as the Hendersons walked toward the Lower Town of Québec. It would be a steep climb up the long stairs with all the children in tow, but the final result would be spectacular according to Mary's memory of her father's stay in the walled Town years before.

Heathcliffe was concerned with the last leg of their journey as the ship was still heavily laden and the channel through and past Lake St. Peter was not well marked.

"Don't need to run aground now this close to the end of our journey. We will need to take on a pilot if we want to be safe," he told his Captain.

"You might be right, the last time I was here the water was higher, and they must have had a lot less snow this past winter further west. We will stop at Trois Rivières and try to get one there. If not we'll just have to take a chance."

It was a long hike up to the edge of the fort for the Hendersons and the others that had come along for the afternoon walk. They all planned to have a picnic near where Mary's father had done battle with the French in 1759. There were red coated soldiers everywhere along the battlements and in the streets of the old Town.

"No more signs of those Indians we spotted from the deck as *The Pioneer* had pulled up to the dock. They must have headed for the bush when they saw us," Joseph Grisenthwaite laughed.

"I don't think so," John Henderson said as he pointed towards the western side of the Plains of Abraham. Camped on the edge of the open field were scores of Indians dressed in ragged deerskins and a variety of European-styled clothes.

"They do not look to be very savage," George said, "more like destitute to me.

"What have we done to these poor souls," Mary and Jane said together.

"Don't mind them, ladies," a young Army Officer said as he walked by, overhearing their comments. "French liquor has done them ruffians in. They get it down in the Lower Town and have been camped up here for a few months now. We cannot seem to get rid of them. Do not get too close, their smell is something awful. General Armstrong should shoot the lot of them and dump their bodies over the cliff."

Mary and Jane were shocked at this young Officer's comments and George noticed this.

"Don't you dare speak like that in front of my wife and children," he bellowed at the young Officer. "Apologize now or you will be the one over the cliff and not those Indians. Now!"

The young Officer laughed and was about to walk away when George's big hand grabbed the man by the back of the neck and lifted him off of his feet.

"I said apologize or it's you who will go over!"

"My apologies, sir—I mean ladies—but I was just stating the true facts."

"True or false does not matter," George said. "You are supposed to be a gentleman, so act like one and speak properly in front of a lady with her children." All activity had stopped around the locale where George Henderson had almost come to blows with the young upstart Army officer.

"What Regiment are you from?" George demanded.

"I am from the 15th Regiment of Foot," sir. "I am Lieutenant Horatio Peabody, sir. I beg you no wrong doing but I do apologize." All the while he was eyeing young Jane Henderson who, at twenty-two years old, was about the nicest thing he had seen in a woman in many a long month.

George noticed Peabody eyeing his daughter and warned him, "I accept your apology young man but my daughter is not interested in you I am sure. Are you Jane?"

"No father, I am definitely not. But he is actually quite handsome," she whispered to her mother.

All those around the gathering were getting on with their own concerns as Lieutenant Peabody and the Hendersons parted company. "Would you have really thrown him over the cliff father?" John asked.

"Yes I would have, without even a second thought about it too. No one insults my family and gets away with it without dealing with me first. Learn to stand up for what you believe in son, even if it means getting into a fight once in awhile. One day soon we will have a long chat when we get to our new home and I will tell you about growing up."

Mary had never seen her husband that angry before over such a small incident as what had just happened. Maybe Isaac Kirkbride's death was still bothering George somewhat. She made plans to have a good long conversation with her dear husband as soon as they had time, when they were alone with no other ears to listen in on them. *The Pioneer* was not such a place, so hopefully nothing else would happen between now and their arrival in Cavagnal.

As the small group of settlers made their way back to the dock and their ship, John Henderson noticed that two of the Indians were following them.

"Father, look behind, there are two Indians following us and they have been doing so since we left the Plains of Abraham."

"I know son," George said, "I know. We will stop and meet them and see what they want. Mary, children, hold up a minute, let's meet some real Canadians: those two Indians behind us." Everyone looked at each other and wondered what their father was thinking.

"Come here," George called to the two natives who had also stopped but had held up some seventy-five feet behind the Hendersons. "Come here," George motioned with his hand and called to them. Slowly the two natives, dressed in buckskins and each carrying a long rifle and a big knife, came towards them.

George and John both held out their right hands to greet the two young men. The Indians stopped and carefully stretched out their right hands and took a firm grip with the two white men opposite them.

"My name is George Henderson and this is my son John and my wife Mary and my family," George said in a nice soft voice so as not to scare the strangers.

"I am Sori'howane and this is Awen'rah:ton. We are Mohawks of the

Iroquois Nation. We have been here for two months now trying to see the British Governor, The Earl of Dalhousie, about land we want to hold onto near Montréal. The Governor does not want to see us; we are savages to him, useless now that the wars with the French and the Yankees are over. Can you help us? You seem to have great power over the British Army."

George laughed. "No I do not think I can help you nor do I have great power over the British Army. You saw what I did with that young Officer, did you not?"

"We did and it impressed us. No one ever does that around here, especially not us. We would be hanged immediately and our families run off this land."

"Seems there is a slight problem father," John said to George. "Do you think we can do anything?"

"I doubt it John. Remember, we have only been here for just a few hours, but have learned a great deal already.

"We are headed to a place west of Montréal, called Cavagnal do you know it?" George asked the two Mohawks.

"Yes, it is a nice place," Sori'howane said. "A nice, quiet place. There is a small settlement of our people across the river, my father's brother lives in our village there. It is called 'Kanesatake.' The settlement is located on a lovely lake you white people call 'Lake of the Two Mountains.' We Mohawks just refer to it as 'Atawene Kanetari' or the Ottawa River, as you would call it. There are two big mountains on the north shore, one of them bigger than the other, which we call 'Tionont'ekowa.' It is very sacred to our people. No white men are permitted on it."

"Are there many French in this 'Cavagnal'?" George asked them.

"Just a few I believe. Most of the French live on this side of Cavagnal near a small village called Vaudreuil. The Seigneur of the Vaudreuil Seigneury lives there and he is a pleasant man from what we have heard."

"Where did you learn such good English?" Mary asked the two Indians.

"We both served with the British Army in the your last war with the Yankees," Awen'rah:ton said. "They taught us well, yes?"

"Yes they did," Mary told them. "I am duly impressed with what our beloved British Army has done."

George had been eyeing the two guns of his new found friends ever since they had stopped to chat with them. Local inhabitants, French and English, were scurrying around the small group, all muttering something about how awful it was to see white folks talking with that Indian rabble from the Plains of Abraham. "We are not well liked here," Awen'rah:ton told the Hendersons. "A couple of our people have already died from mysterious causes and others have disappeared without a trace. We are all leaving tomorrow for our home village."

"Your guns," George said, "what are they and may I take a look at one?"

"They are Yankee long rifles," Sori'howane said, ".50 calibre and VERY accurate. Much longer and lighter than your beloved Brown Bess gun that you British use."

"Wrong there, my friend. I am ex-Army myself but I never had to use a Bess. I also used a rifle, a Baker rifle and it was of .65 calibre. It was heavier though than that fine gun of yours. Never seen anything like these, but I have heard that the Yanks have been building something like this for some time now. Too bad we do not have something like this. My rifle is great, but I would like to try one of these sometime. Too bad we cannot spend more time together, I would like to know more about you and your culture and try this gun. I like it very much."

Sori'howane smiled and said, "We will meet again, kind man. We will meet again. We will be following your big ship back up river. You will reach Montréal in about three or four days if the winds hold. It will take us much longer and we will visit other villages along the way. But we will come to visit you in your new home at Cavagnal, I promise, and then we will let you try our guns. Maybe I can get you one from my family across in New York. They are very rare and expensive up here in Canada but I can get them very cheap across in the United States. We Mohawks have ways of getting things across the border. Lots of trails that only we Indians know about. You English would rather stick to your new roads or the river rather than travel through unmarked woods. And there is lots of thick forest out west of here that no white man has seen. But we Mohawks and our brothers know the woods. Maybe I'll show you sometime later."

"I hope you do," said George. "I hope you do."

With that the two groups parted and the Hendersons hurried down to *The Pioneer*. It was getting dark and the sun was just above the horizon when the last of the settlers came aboard the ship.

Smithfield called George Henderson aside and quietly said, "Heard you had a slight confrontation with some Lieutenant up on the Plains this afternoon. That true?"

"Yes, I guess it is Jonas, but he had it coming. Spoke in awful disgusting terms in front of my wife and children."

"Take it easy, George, I know it must be hard getting over the loss of your friend Isaac, but this is a new land and a lot of people have a few rough edges. Many have not seen their own families in months, maybe years, and have forgotten what having a family is all about. I know you are a war veteran too, but Europe is different from North America. This is a wild and dangerous place and it can turn on you before you know what hit you. Be careful, and watch what you do, especially around this place.

"Québec is a tough little settlement and her soldiers are tough, especially the ones from the 15th Regiment of Foot. Luckily for all of us, we are leaving before daylight. We might have a welcoming party on the dock at first light if we are not careful. I heard that that Lieutenant you met has a bad reputation around these parts and could easily cross you when you least expect it. He has lots of nasty friends among the local inhabitants."

"I can take care of myself, Jonas, but thanks for the talk. You are right. Isaac's death does still bother me and I feel that it will be many months before I get over it. However, I have met two Mohawk Indians who live not too far from my new home and they seem to be very nice."

"Mohawks eh?" Smithfield pondered for a second, "Did they speak any English?" he asked.

"Yes, they did. Why?"

"Just wondering. Not many Indians around here speak much English; mostly Huron and a little Cree and of course French. Funny there were Mohawks all this way east. Did they say why they were here in Québec?"

"Something about land claims," George said. "I did not dwell on it too long; I was more interested in their long guns than land claims.

"They said they would visit us after we reached Cavagnal. They are also leaving at first light, though they plan to stop along the way. They did not say where exactly they were from though. However, both of them did mention a small Indian settlement across the river from Cavagnal called Kanesatake. Have you ever heard of it, Jonas?"

"Can't say that I have. I don't even know where Cavagnal is. Remember I can get you from Maryport to Montréal, but after that you are on your own my friend. Good luck, because methinks you are going to need it. But on the other hand, making friends as quickly as you did with some of the local native population could prove to very helpful in many ways.

"Them Mohawks are excellent farmers. Never expected that from some savage. Did you, George?" George was already lost in some deep thought and he turned to head down below decks without even saying good night to the Captain. George was thinking about what Jonas Smithfield had just said: that the Mohawks were excellent farmers. That could prove to be very helpful this coming summer and fall.

"Yes," he said in a gleeful manner. "Yes," he repeated and then George slapped an overhead beam as he made his way below decks to his family. Things were beginning to fall into place already, and they had just arrived in their new land.

The trip up river to Montréal was uneventful, though Smithfield did heed Heathcliffe's warning about troubles in Lake St. Peter and the Captain stopped at Trois Rivières to pick up a local pilot for the short haul up to Montréal.

"If all goes well," the pilot had told Smithfield, "we should be in Montréal in two days. I only hope dat this nor'easter will hold, giving us enough wind to fill dese big sails to beat de current.

"As you know, Smithfield," the pilot said, "de current just below Montréal is very swift and dere are many shoals dat we could run aground on. If de winds are not right some ship have to lie at anchor for days until dey get de right wind to sail into Montréal. So far dis year very few ship have made de trip from Québec to Montréal on dere own, if we make it we will be only de fourt dis spring.

"Thank goodness dat new type of ship called a steamship will be more available soon. One steamer pulled eight ship up de St. Mary's current last summer. Supposed to be more put in service dis year and next. Mr. Molson is putting up de money for dem."

Smithfield told his pilot that he had seen small steamers in England on the Thames in 1823 and that he had been quite impressed with them, except they made an awful noise and put up a great deal of smoke. "Much like those damn smelly whalers we saw recently, George." George nodded in astonishment as he had not heard of the steam ships nor had he yet seen one.

"As long as this nor'easter holds we will be fine. Terrible weather though," Smithfield said, "Nor'easters always bring this damn rain.

"The pilot has mentioned that we might see one of the new steam tugs as they are called when we get closer to Montréal. Hopefully we will not need it; it's quite expensive too I hear."

Smithfield continued on about the weather, stating that it was too late in the season for snow, but who knew with this strange country. "Why anyone would want to carve out a new home in some wilderness that still has an Indian threat is beyond me. However, I don't know what these folks have left behind them; some were pretty bad off I hear. George, you are just the adventurous type I guess. A good family and enough money from what I understand to begin a new and good life, eh? My hat is off to you. You sure came in handy this last voyage."

The French Canadian river pilot listened intently as Smithfield rambled on about their trip over and the encounter with the *Warspite* and *El Condor*. Word had been brought by fast mail packet from Halifax already spreading the wild news of how some merchant ship had defeated a huge pirate warship after it had sunk a Royal Navy Frigate. "Never expected to be on dat particular merchantman," said the pilot.

"How big was de pirate ship?" The pilot asked excitedly the now smiling Captain.

"Same size as our British frigate, it wasn't some huge three decker as some may lead you to believe, but I must agree the story gets better every time I hear it from another source. In ten years from now they will tell of how we defeated two warships after they had sunk a whole squadron of Navy ships of the line. The truth is that we had a very close call and if our poor frigate had not softened up the rogue before we got there, we would have been the ones on the bottom and not *El Condor*. Luck was with us my friend. Luck and a wee bit of Royal Naval tactics that I had learned from Admiral Lord Nelson many years ago."

The big tree covered mountain at Montréal was the first sighting the passengers on board *The Pioneer* had of their new home. The lovely green mountain rose abruptly behind the small settlement of Montréal that was nestled along the waterfront. The passengers and crew could see lovely green fields between the mountain and the Town's buildings and smoke rose from where settlers were clearing more land further east.

"Look father," cried Frances Henderson, "more Indians in canoes over there." She was pointing to a flotilla of large canoes heading downriver on the southern shore of the river. "Those are bigger than the ones we saw in Québec," George said. "Maybe they are used to haul furs from further west. Wonder where they are going though? Oh well, not my problem," he said.

"Look over there children!" George pointed to the south shore of the St. Lawrence to two large mountains rising up from the plains.

The pilot could see George pointing to the two mountains and he yelled over to the Hendersons that one had a lake on top of it. Smithfield quietly spoke to his river pilot, "Never mind being a tour guide. Get this ship safely into harbour. We are almost there and I don't want to mess it up now. This is the trickiest bit of sailing I have had to do in months, just no room to maneuver. Damn outbound ships too; they don't help matters any either."

The Pioneer finally docked opposite a numerous warehouses and taverns and a church just after noon on June 7th, 1824. Everyone on board cheered as the huge hawsers were lashed to the shore and the port anchor was dropped into the murky green water. It had been a long and trying voyage but they had finally made it.

Captain Jonas Smithfield stood by the gangway as all the passengers disembarked and he shook each and every one's hand. The last passenger to leave was George Henderson. They shook each other's hand and then embraced each other like brothers. George had a tear in his eye as he took one last look at the spot where his friend, Isaac Kirkbride, had been killed a fortnight before by the last broadside of *El Condor's* guns.

"I am not going to miss this ship," he told Smithfield. "I am not going to miss her for one second. But I will miss those whom I have made friends with; you Jonas, Heathcliffe over there, and all your great crewmembers. They are a tribute to you and your owner Mr. Watterson. I hope not too many decide to stay here in Canada so you will have enough of a crew to return. Above all, I am going to miss my friend Isaac the most. I have kept his rifle to give to my son John after we get settled in Cavagnal. But I am afraid that I am going to miss him a whole lot more after I get to where I want to settle down, he was a great friend and fighter but also a great farmer and that is the type of man we need for this new land. Damn, I miss him."

With that, George turned to wipe more tears from his eyes and he hurried down the gangway to join his family on the Island of Montréal.

Smithfield yelled down to him, "I might come and join you one day if the Yankee Navy doesn't lure me first. Good luck, friend. May God be with you and Mary."

George Henderson would never see Captain Jonas Smithfield again as both Mary and he had hoped. After leaving Montréal he sailed *The Pioneer* back to Halifax then down to Boston and met with Captain Jacob Greenshields of the *Yorktown*. Greenshields had asked Jonas to visit him in Boston if *The Pioneer* did not have a cargo to return with to England. Upon arriving, Smithfield was the one who jumped ship, not one of his men.

He turned the ship over to Obadiah Heathcliffe and told him to return to England with their ship. "Do your duty as a first rate Captain as I know you can. I am staying here in Boston and I am going to join the American Navy. I feel that I can help them with my experience and that last bit of shooting we had a few weeks ago got my blood racing, Obadiah. *The Pioneer* is now yours," Smithfield told the new Captain. "Here are all the official papers signed and sealed stating the fact that I am making you her new Captain. Good luck and good sailing."

Smithfield joined the American Navy and with his past experience along with a few good words from Captain Greenshields and Captain Jonas Smithfield, late of His Britannic Majesty's Royal Navy and John Watterson's *The Pioneer*, was given his own armed brig in the United States Navy. She was the twenty gun, *Saratoga*; ironically named after another British defeat by the American Army so many years before.

Unfortunately, Smithfield did not get to enjoy his life as a Captain in the American Navy for very long. His small ship was wrecked off of Cape Hatteras in late November of 1824 during one of the worst hurricanes so far of the 19th Century. All hands were lost and Smithfield hadn't even fired a gun in anger, though he had been prepared to do so.

Chapter 7
On to Cavagnal...

The Hendersons, Grisenthwaites, and Fowlers gathered their possessions together beside *The Pioneer*. The steady rain that had plagued their trip up from Trois Rivières had finally abated and the sun was shining in the early evening sky.

"Must find some place to store all of our baggage before we settle in for the night," George said to the small group. Dr. Grisenthwaite agreed to find a place for them to spend the night while George decided to try his rusty French on some local carters near by.

"Bonjour monsieur," George said in his strong Westmorland accent. "J'aimerais utiliser vos wagons si possible, et combien?" The two closest carters looked at each other and burst out laughing.

"One shilling each cart, monsieur," they both said, laughing as they moved closer to George. "We may be French-Canadian, monsieur, but we can speak some h'English. Many cannot—but we can. Since we work along de docks, we meet a lot of English newcomers and we have learnt quick. We have learnt that if you cannot speak h'English, you will not get work."

George laughed as he shook their hands and introduced himself, his family, and the Grisenthwaites and Fowlers.

"My name is Jean-Jacques Major, monsieur, and dis is Alphonse Séguin. I will call over anodder carter to elp with de tird family's possession. Seraphin, venez içi toute de suite, j'ai un voyage pour vous. This is Seraphin Montpetit. Unfortunately he speak little h'English but he is learning slow. He come from down river, Boucherville, and dere are no h'English der yet."

"Most of de h'English are settling west and south of here, but some stay in Montréal," Jean-Jacques explained as they all began to load the emigrants' possessions onto the three carts. Two beautiful black horses pulled each cart. John asked his father what they were.

George said, "I am not sure, but they are too small for Percherons, and of course they are not Clydes. Excusez-moi, Mr. Major," George asked the head carter. "My son and I are interested in your horses. What are they, and where can we get some?"

"Dey are what we call le cheval Canadien or de Canadian Horse. Our ancestor brought dem here over two hundred year ago from Bretagne and Normandie in France. They are de only types of horse we ave had until you h'English began arriving après 1760.

"There are a few of dose big Clydesdale horses dat have arrived with some of de Scottish settlers but most of de horses you will see out in your new home territory are dese Canadiens. Great horses for ploughs, sleighs, and buggies and of course carts. All are black too."

"By the way," Alphonse asked George, "where you go? Maybe we can get you dere. Is it west of ere on de island or south towards de American frontier?"

"Actually, it is west of here," George said, "west of the island I hear. A place in the Seigneury de Vaudreuil, a small settlement called Cavagnal."

Both Alphonse and Jean-Jacques shrugged their shoulders and said, "Never heard of it. Must be far from ere. We have only been to Lachine."

As for Seraphin, he was listening intently but had not understood much of what had been spoken, spare for a few words when Jean-Jacques had talked about their horses.

"How much will you charge us to go to Lachine tomorrow morning?" George asked Jean-Jacques and Alphonse.

"For dee tree family? Let me see." Jean-Jacques began calculating in his head. "Load ere, unload dere, three hours journey if road is good; how about three shilling each cart?"

George agreed on behalf of all three families and asked the men to be outside their hotel at 8:00 the next morning.

"Which hôtel?" asked Alphonse. "Dere are many around ere."

Just then George spotted Dr. Grisenthwaite walking towards them with a smile on his face.

"I found a nice hotel over there on the hill. The Delvecchio Inn."

"Good place," said Jean-Jacques. "It is clean and well kept. We will meet you dere tomorrow morning. I will take your livestock wit me now so you will not ave to worry about dem overnight. I do not tink de manager would like to ave sheep and two cows in his hôtel."

They all laughed and quickly parted company.

"Nice chaps," Mary said to George, "hope they are all as friendly as those three men."

"They are nice," George agreed. "However, they are looking for money and being nice does bring customers. I doubt that all the French Canadians are as nice as these three men."

"Maybe it is just a ruse to get our money and leave us stranded out there somewhere," said Robert Fowler.

Mary disagreed, saying that she thought that they were decent men and would live up to their bargain.

"We will soon find out tomorrow morning," George said, somewhat apprehensively.

The Delvecchio Inn was a lovely building made of white-washed stone and set on the eastern side of a grand square that stretched from the dockyard up to rue Notre Dame. At the top of the square there was a huge stone monument.

"The square, or market as we call it," explained the hotel manager to the three families, "is called Marché Bonsecours. Twice a week this market is filled with local farmers trying to sell their produce and wares to the local citizens. Too bad you cannot stay until we have the next one. Lots of good food and lively entertainment too. You will see what we French Canadians are really like. We are noted for having a jovial mood, but do not double-cross us, my friend—we can get nasty too."

George explained that he had finished fighting the French years before, and now he and his family all wanted to live in peace and establish a new life in their new country.

"Good luck, my friend," the manager said. "With an attitude like that you will succeed; I am sure."

Dr. Grisenthwaite asked George about the monument up the street. George admitted that he did not know anything about it but they both agreed to take a closer look after they settled into the hotel. "We have a couple of hours before dinner so we can take a quick look around the town. Never know when we will get back in here again—if ever," George explained.

The three families took up most of the rooms on the second floor. They had a grand view of the Market Square and its busy goings-on. Since most of them had never been in such a large town before, they all looked forward to their little tour.

"Dinner will be served at 6:00 PM, Mr. Henderson," the manager said to George as the large group exited the hotel and headed up towards the monument.

"Maybe it is for General Wolfe, father," John told George. "Some-how I doubt that since he never made it this far. Probably that man Maisonneuve who founded this place in the 1600's."

"How do you know about him?" asked Robert Fowler.

"The hotel manager told me while you were seeing to your luggage when we checked into the room," said George with a smile.

Jane Henderson let out a yell from where she stood with her brother John after running ahead of the group.

"It is for Admiral Lord Nelson, father."

"Ol 'Nel?" said George, "That cannot be, not here in Canada, why?" But sure enough, there fully engraved on the base of the beautiful fifty-foot high monument was the dedication and description to Admiral Lord Nelson and the Battle of Trafalgar in 1805.

"Never would have believed it if I had not seen it myself," Dr. Grisenthwaite said.

Mary was so exited that she was crying. "I wonder if Captain Smithfield knows of this?" she asked. "Oh if only 'Old William' could see this, he would be so happy."

Robert Fowler, who was not much of a talker exclaimed, "Old William, whom may I ask is that?"

Mary quickly explained how the only man to have served from her village in Westmorland in the Royal Navy had fought alongside Nelson and had died on one of his ships at the Battle of Cape St. Vincent in 1797. "There is a small pub in our village named after "Old William" Frankham. All the other men who had served King George did so like my George, in the Army."

The group toured the bustling community, taking in the sights and sounds of the lively and prosperous place. They were hearing a great deal more French here than they had heard in Québec a few days before. One thing that bothered George somewhat was the dramatic lack of British troops in the town. During their two-hour tour they had only seen a handful of troops and most of them had been officers.

"Wonder where the troops are?" John asked his father. George seemed troubled about that also, as did Robert Fowler.

"Hope there is a garrison somewhere around here in case there is trouble," the Doctor said.

Rather peaceful place though they all admitted. One well-dressed gentleman stopped the group from going too far east along rue Notre Dame. "Do not head down that way people," he stated, "not unless you are looking for trouble. Some right nasty folks down there and they do not like us English too much. Never have since we defeated them here in 1760. Murders every night or so. The troops come out at night to patrol the streets. It is generally all quiet during the day, but now is the time to get off to your hotel or wherever you are staying."

"Most of the troops are out at the barracks on Ile Ste Hélène in the middle of the river. There is a good sized fort there but it takes the garrison upwards of an hour to get here if there is trouble," the man told the Hendersons.

"The Colonel in charge keeps a small company in the town, down at the Champs de Mars. They have a small two storey garrison building there that houses about fifty men. The troops stay there for a week at a time then switch with another company out at the fort. There are usually about twenty-five men patrolling the streets at all times. At night though, there are usually more. Besides watching for crimes, they patrol as a fire watch. The garrison keeps a small fire pump down at Champs de Mars and another out in Place Viger."

Mary and the Doctor thanked the gentleman and they all turned around and headed back to "The Delvecchio" for a good night's dinner and hopefully a good night's sleep.

"So it is not such a grand place after all father," John Henderson said to George.

"Just like London or Portsmouth son, all big towns or cities are the same. Safe during the day but rough at night. Glad we have the troops here, but in civilian life they are just as bad or worse. Scum of the earth the British Army is but the best army in the world too."

"George you were not the scum of the earth were you?" Dr. Grisenthwaite asked his friend.

"No, I was not, but I was one of the few that were not. Had to learn fast though to be tough or I would have died real quick, either by the French or by my own mates."

The three French-Canadians were waiting outside "The Delvecchio Inn" the very next morning with their three carts already loaded with the three families belongings. In tow was what livestock had survived the treacherous journey from England: two sheep and a cow belonging to the Hendersons and a cow belonging to the Fowlers. Each family had brought along a hog and some chickens but these had been butchered for food on *The Pioneer* while en route. The meat from George's big stag had lasted a good part of the trip as well.

Dr. Grisenthwaite and his wife had not brought along any large animals and not being a true farmer, he planned to set up his medical practice in the new settlement. He did, however, hope to purchase some sheep or chickens after establishing a home. "I am not much of a farmer," he had once told Robert Fowler. "However, I am a good doctor and that is what this new settlement will need. I am young and not old like those Army or Navy doctors neither are nor am I a drunk like them. I will do well, I believe."

Fowler agreed with the Doctor and wished him well. "After what I saw you do for those wounded sailors on *The Pioneer* I know that I will come to you if I feel unwell," he stated. "You are a good man just like George Henderson. A good man," Robert finished off.

The trip from "The Delvecchio Inn" to Lachine took the group about three and a half-hours because the track was wet, narrow, and very rough and busy. "Many people heading to Montréal for tomorrow's market at Bonsecours," Alphonse told his clients. "Too bad you are going to miss it."

"We will come in one day," George stated, "But first we must find our new land and get settled. Maybe next year."

Lachine was yet another bustling village, lots of people down by the docks and huge piles of furs stacked along the wharves. A large group of huge canoes, called a brigade, was about to set off up the St. Lawrence River as the emigrants arrived led by Jean-Jacques Major and his two friends.

"Look dere h'English," Major said, pointing to a small flotilla of large canoes heading west on the water. "Dey are headed up past your new home and de will be deep into de upper Ottawa by de time you even get close to dis Cavagnal place you talk about. We French Canadians are great paddlers. Our voyageurs have reached right through to de Pacific Ocean. My cousin, Jacques Beauchamp, went wit Alexander Mackenzie years ago. He is old now but still a strong man. He often talk of his great trips out west with de North West Company."

"So they are still trapping for furs," Mary said as she gazed on the huge stacks of beaver, wolf, marten and fox furs that lined the edge of the wharf. Over to their right there was a Hudson Bay Company warehouse where numerous white workers and a few Indians were working. "New around here mister?" Asked a big burly and whiskered man who was standing near the piles of furs.

"Yes, as a matter of fact we are," replied George. "We are heading west to settle at Cavagnal. Do you know where we can get a boat to take us there?"

"Sure do," said the big man, "right over there," pointing to a small group of boats tied up alongside the wharf. "They cannot take you all the way there, only as far as Ste Anne de Bellevue. More rapids there. You can hire a bateau there to take you up the river to Cavagnal. Nice place there.

I have stopped at the tavern there many times. A man named Schmidt runs it. He used to live here years ago but headed west when this place got too busy. I hear he was a soldier in the last war against the Americans, some sort of German mercenary. A Hessian I think."

"The name is Angus Macleod," the big man said. "Used to be with the North West Company, now the Hudson Bay Company employs me. I am the main buyer here in Lachine and I have been doing it since the Bay took over in 1821. Traveled west for years but am getting too old for that now and my wife likes me here rather than out there. She is afraid that I will meet up with a fine squaw and diddle her once too often and settle down in the bush."

"I have had me a few squaws in my younger days. Lots of good-looking ones out there. Best are those Hurons, but God they can be dirty. Got to get them young though, fourteen to eighteen years old, after that they tend to lose their teeth and get fat and ugly. Yes, I am happy here in Lachine, going to be a grand town one day, a grand town."

George Henderson and Robert Fowler had maneuvered themselves between their families and Angus Macleod as soon as the big fellow had begun talking about his escapades with the Indian girls.

"No use letting the youngsters hear all that," George had told Robert Fowler.

"Foul mouth on the fellow," Robert had said, "but sort of interesting too. I bet he can tell us some stories after he has had a drink or two." With that they both laughed and headed over to where Dr. Grisenthwaite had walked, beside the four bateaux.

The Doctor was trying to get some sense out one of the owners when Alphonse and Jean-Jacques arrived. "We will help you monsieur," Alphonse told the Doctor. "Combien mon ami pour un voyage à Ste Anne's?"

"Quatre livres, monsieur, pour toute le monde et les animaux."

"He say four shilling Monsieur le Doctor," Jean-Jacques translated but George had understood and had already agreed. The poor Doctor had not understood a word and was glad that George was there as well or he believed they would have been charged double.

It did not take long for all the cargo to be loaded onto two of the

89

biggest of the four bateaux and the new settlers headed west onto Lake St. Louis. The brigade of canoes was already far out of sight, their short but burly paddlers setting a fast pace. "Fifty strokes a minute," Angus Macleod had told George. "That is the rate at which the voyageurs paddle at. They can cover twenty or more miles a day if there are no portages to be made. Only one between here and the Long Sault rapids at Carillon and that is where you are going today, Ste Anne de Bellevue."

The Hendersons, Grisenthwaites and the Fowlers all bid adieu to their three French Canadian carters and George paid them the balance that was owed to them as promised. "Thanks very much for all your help, you have been very kind," he said as the two groups parted. Jean-Jacques shook hands with George and mentioned that one day he might try to come out to visit them in Cavagnal, wherever that was. "That would be fine," George said "and bring along your two friends. I am sure Mr. Macleod will be able to tell you where we will be living. You would be most welcome anytime." With that, they turned and went their respective ways.

"Good luck," yelled Angus Macleod as they pulled away from the wharf. "You will need it." He laughed as he turned away and headed towards four huge canoes that were just pulling into the wharf, all loaded down with furs.

"Wonder what he meant by that?" John asked his father.

"I don't rightly know but hopefully it is not a bad omen," George said.

The trip up Lake St. Louis took most of the day and the new settlers had time to enjoy the fine spring day. The air was warm and from the bateaux they could see a few houses and the odd church nestled along the shore of the lake.

"What village is that?" Robert Fowler asked the bateaux operator, forgetting that he did not speak or understand English. "I will try to translate," George told Fowler. "Quel village est ça, monsieur?"

"Pointe Claire," the bateau man grunted. "Un village qui était Français, mais il commence d'être un autre maudit-Chrisse de village des Anglais."

"He says it is called Pointe Claire or Clear Point and it is yet another French village that is becoming a damned English one," George translated for Robert Fowler.

"He does not seem too pleased about it either," John said, over hearing their conversation.

"No, he sure doesn't," his father commented. "Maybe that is what that Mr. Macleod was talking about when he bid us good luck as we left."

"I must say added Robert, Pointe Claire does sound a trifle better than Clear Point for a village. I hope they keep the French name."

"It seems that not all the locals are as friendly as our three carters were to us Englishmen," the Doctor added. We better watch ourselves as we head westward. According to my letters, that I have received from the good Reverend Joseph Ashford last year the situation between the French and English in Cavagnal is very good and there is no civil strife or conflict whatsoever."

Robert interceded by stating that those letters they had all received last fall had been written almost a year from their present time and many things could have changed.

"Remember what that gentleman in Montréal had said about walking around at night. Not too safe. Neither is London or Manchester," George added. "I still have my rifle and John knows how to use one too and we still have Isaac's and both are loaded. I did that just before we got on board this flat-bottomed scow. I do not think they will try anything out here, but watch yourselves anyway," he said.

The bateaux arrived at Ste Anne de Bellevue just after five in the afternoon. It was still daylight and quite warm. As they arrived at the dock below the rapids, The Doctor said, "Warmest day yet and a fine one too."

Ste Anne de Bellevue was a small bustling village, located at the western tip of Montréal Island. In just a couple of days the new settlers had seen both ends of the large island. "We have probably more of the island in two days than many of the locals had seen in years," said George.

Just as there had been numerous canoes loaded down with furs in Lachine, there were many others here as well. The rapids made making a portage around them necessary. Once again all the settlers' cargo had to be unloaded from the bateaux and transferred onto others up above the rapids. George discussed portaging their luggage over the rapids themselves, saving them the added expense of hiring another carter. All the men agreed and George sent John off to find a suitable place for them to stay that night. "We cannot leave now, it will take us till dark to get everything up around the rapids," George told the others.

Robert Fowler agreed with his friend and said, "That it was a good idea. Hope he finds some place close to the dock up yonder."

"Take Isaac's gun John," George told his son. "Be careful for these fur trappers or as they call themselves voyageurs, they are a very tough lot. Please do not get into an argument."

"Do not worry father. I will not," John called back as he hurried off up the hill.

"He is a good boy, George," Robert Fowler said as they began unloading the bateaux.

"Yes he is," George said, "but I have got to watch him sometimes. A little hotheaded, but a good boy in general and one hell of a shot with one of those guns, just like his old father!"

The bateaux were unloaded in about thirty minutes and Robert stayed back to guard what goods the others could not carry on their first trip up the hill. Mary was feeling a little tired due to her pregnancy but she insisted on carrying a bundle of clothes along with the others.

As they walked up the hill, a group of voyageurs came down the hill at such a fast pace they were almost running. What amazed all the settlers was that each man was carrying two enormous packs of bound up furs on his back.

"Those packs must weigh way over a hundred pounds!" the Doctor exclaimed to the others. "Look at those men go! I guess they are all in a hurry to get to Montréal and get paid so they can celebrate another successful trip back from the wilderness."

A small stout man walking alongside the Hendersons overheard them talking about the voyageurs and, excusing himself at first, stated that, "each pack usually weighs about ninety pounds. Many a man takes a tumble on the portages far west of here. This road is their last portage and very few get hurt here. But out there," he said, pointing westward, "many a man is left beside the trail with a broken leg, ankle or a rupture. Ruptures are very common with these poor fellows. They work hard for what they get but they have opened up this country right through to the west and north to the Arctic."

George thanked the little man for his comments and they all chatted as they walked up the long hill towards the upper dock and the bateaux that were waiting passengers. "Paçifique Johnson is my name," the little man stated. "I live just over here and I run a small shop downstairs from my lodging. If you want someplace to store your belongings before tomorrow's trip west, you can leave them in my barn. The dock is just one hundred yards from my place as you can see. I will charge you only a shilling each."

That seemed quite reasonable to them all and they thanked Mr. Johnson and promised to stop by his shop in the morning before they left. "I sell everything a lady might need for her home, Johnson added, eyeing the three wives. "Especially for those about to give birth," winking at Mary Henderson.

As soon as they got all their gear stored in Johnson's barn, it took three trips up the long hill, George went over to the bateaux to try to hire a couple for the last leg of their journey to Cavagnal. Only one was still manned as the owners of the other two had gone down the hill just after dark to the local hotel.

"Combien pour un voyage à Cavagnal, monsieur?" George asked the dozing bateaux operator.

"Three shillings per family mister," the man answered back in perfect English. "It is an easy trip and I work for a man there anyway, Mr. Schmidt. He owns a tavern just across from Oka."

"Oh yes, Schmidt's Tavern," said George. "I heard about that place down in Lachine from Angus Macleod."

"You met Big Angus Macleod?" asked the young man. "How is that filthy old bastard?" Somewhat shocked by the young man's comments, George told him that Angus was fine and had advised them that would be able to hire a bateau that would take them to Cavagnal. It would be located above the rapids at Ste Anne's.

The young man on the bateau then explained that he knew Angus Macleod quite well and that his son, Iain, was a very good friend of his.

John arrived at the bateaux as his father was making the final arrangements for their morning trip. "No luck father on finding rooms for us. This is one rough village. Almost got into two fights with some drunks at one hotel and it was just luck that two Army officers helped me escape. They say they are heading west tomorrow also. They also told me that they are building a canal at some place called Carillon."

"It is west of your destination mister, the bateau operator said. "About seventeen miles upriver from Cavagnal. Those two officers are going with us tomorrow so you will be able to talk with them on our journey. I would suggest that you all stay with your goods in Johnson's barn there. It is safe and dry. Not that it is going to rain but it is safer than down in that whore of a village."

"With all the voyageurs around here heading out and back into Montréal, this last stop can be bloody dangerous for settlers like you. Especially if you have young ladies along, and I did see one, did I not?"

"Yes," George said, "she is my daughter Jane, you will meet her tomorrow."

"By the way, what is your name?" George asked the young bateau man.

"My name is John Cameron. My father also lives in Cavagnal. We have been there since 1821. Our family was from Inverness, Scotland. My father, Dugald Cameron raises sheep just south of the main part of Cavagnal, a place called Côte St. Charles but those living there call it the "Grand Côte". There is a big hill near where the Pearsons and Blackwells live and that is why we called it the "Big Hill or Grand Côte". Sounds better in French does it not?" John added.

George could not help agreeing with the handsome young Scotsman, "Just like Pointe Claire", he added. Not understanding the Englishman, John Cameron just shrugged his shoulders and wished them a good night as he climbed under some blankets and furs and quickly dozed off again.

"Nice fellow," John quietly commented to his father as they headed over to the barn to join the others.

"We are staying here tonight Mr. Johnson," George told the shop owner, "is there any extra cost?"

"No, Mr. Henderson no extra charge. Just drop by my store tomorrow and buy something for your lovely wife and daughter. You too, Doctor and Mr. Fowler. Now is the time as there is not much where you are heading and it will be cheaper here." They all laughed and agreed they would drop by in the morning before embarking on their final leg of their long, long voyage.

"Just think, George," Mary whispered to her husband, "after so many weeks away from our old home, tomorrow we will be at our new one."

"Yes, dear, tomorrow we will be there," George whispered back, "but also tomorrow is the day the work really begins for all of us. We have to build a cabin before winter and clear some land. We cannot have our child born in a tent. I saw too much of that in Spain. No my dear, we will have a cabin by August when the good Doctor Grisenthwaite thinks our child will be born. I promise you that right now." With that, they kissed and checked their children one final time before falling off to sleep.

Morning came quickly but all the Hendersons and their friends had a good night's sleep in Paçifique Johnson's barn. John Cameron was awake and waiting for his cargo on his bateau when the three families arrived at the dock. "Are all of you ready for a good day's journey to your new home?" he asked.

They all said, "Yes."

"So let us get under way as soon as we load your entire luggage on to these two boats. The other bateau will haul your livestock. The operator is Simon Beauvais but he also works for Mr. Schmidt. He is an Indian; a Mohawk."

Loading took about thirty minutes and then Cameron and Beauvais cast off the lines and the two small boats headed northwest up the Lake of the Two Mountains. A few canoes were already heading west but these swift vessels soon left the two flat bottomed bateaux far behind. There were other bateaux on the river as well as the two the settlers were on, some heading into Ste Anne de Bellevue while a couple were heading west like their own.

"More settlers I presume," John mentioned casually, not caring who overheard him.

"Where would they be going, Mr. Cameron?" Mary asked the bargeman.

"Please call me John, Mrs. Henderson," he said in his usual polite tone of voice. "Probably either to Vaudreuil or further up river to Carillon."

Mary had added that she too would liked to be called by her first name and they all agreed, no more formalities. This trip was going to be a pleasant one.

"There is a detachment of British Engineers up there building a canal around the Long Sault Rapids. They have been there since about 1819," John told them. "Those bateaux could be bringing those supplies or some of the officer's families." Looking towards the two Army officers that were on board with them, John said, "You should have headed up river with them than with us." They agreed but told John that there had been no more room on board. George spoke to them only briefly on their voyage west and that was to thank them both for helping his son the night before. The rest of the time the officers kept to themselves, not associating themselves with the newcomers on board.

"Aloof as usual," George said quietly to his wife. "We have had a great deal of excitement over the past few weeks John," George explained to their Captain as the men began to help John Cameron hoist the lone sail that would help them get to their final destination before dark.

"These little boats are not very fast," John explained. "However, they are sturdy but a damn nuisance in rough weather. Sailing should be grand today, though," he added.

"What is that over there?" John Henderson asked, pointing west towards the remains of an old fort on the western side of the narrows, a mile upstream from the dock. John Cameron told his passengers that the French built the old fort in the early 1700's.

"First settlement west of Ville Marie as Montréal was then known as. The island is called Ile Aux Tourtes. Named after all those bloody pigeons we see flying around here all the time.

"I have never stopped there to explore the island. There is supposed to be an old Indian burial ground on the island. I have even heard rumours that ghosts haunt the spot. The French and some local Indians kept some Yankee soldiers there after a raid down south. One of the white women that were taken used to live in Cavagnal until she died a few years ago. Married some local Frenchie called Surois, I think. I believe her name was Sarah Hampson and that she was from either New Hampshire or Massachusetts. Some of their family still lives in the area but they sold their old cabin to a Swiss family called Lerniers a few years ago. They live just east of the Schmidt's place and are one of the few local merchants. Decent folks too.

"The island fort was abandoned after the village of Vaudreuil was founded back in 1725 or so and with the threat of Indian raids gone now it has become a derelict."

The morning passed quickly and Mary and the other two wives on board began to prepare the day's lunch. Salted pork and bread was put on three day old bread and the combination was washed down with the strong tea that John Cameron had made on a small stove near the stern of his boat.

"Indians!" cried little Frances Henderson. "Loads of them coming this way!" She was pointing westward across the bow of the bateau.

"Mohawks, I presume," John Cameron said. "Do not worry, they are friendly to us English, but Christ, they hate the French. Probably from the small community opposite Cavagnal."

"It is called Kanesatake, am I correct?" George added.

"Yes," said John, "But how the hell did you know that? You just arrived."

George began to relate how they had met two Mohawks in Quebec a week or so before and how one had told him of having family in a small community opposite Cavagnal and that it was called Kanesatake.

"The two Mohawks said that they would visit us one day and possibly bring me a couple of the Yankee guns that they were using."

"You hope to get a long rifle!" John exclaimed. "Those are beautiful guns and *very* accurate. I have seen some of the Mohawks with them. They make your big gun look small with their long barrels and such but can they ever shoot. Deadly accurate if you get a good one."

"The Indians said that they can get them quite easily down across the border and bring them into Canada by way of some back trails and rivers." George added. "I plan to get two, one for my son and of course one for myself. I have not figured how I am going to pay for them but I will figure out a way," he added.

The four Indian canoes slowed down as they approached the loaded bateau and one of the Indians stood up in his small canoe to see if he could recognize anyone on board. Recognizing John at the sweep, the big

Mohawk called a greeting to him and wished him well. "That is Aron'hio:tas one of the Kanesatake chiefs and member of the Bear Clan," John Cameron explained to his passengers. "A real mountain of a man and strong as an ox. Smart too, so do not let him fool you. He was educated down in Boston for awhile while he was a scout for the British Army during the last war with the United States. He is a good man to be a friend of."

Jane Henderson then asked John if there were any other Indians beside the Mohawks at Kanesatake. "Not that I know of," he told her. "Used to be some Hurons and a few Algonquins years ago, but they all headed west when the Mohawks became too strong under their confederacy with the other tribes. They are called the Iroquois Nation or Six Nations but we just call them Mohawks. In their confederacy, the Mohawks are known as the "Guardians of the Eastern Gate." They are the eastern most tribe of the Iroquois Nation. Simon can tell you more though, being a member himself. I do not know which tribe guards the "Western Gate", possibly the Oneidas, Cayugas or Senecas.

"The French sided with the Hurons during the French Regime here in Canada or as it was called then, New France. Most Mohawks, being from south of the border, sided with our side down there. Naturally there was immediate hatred for one another and it led to war. As you all know, we won. The Hurons and Algonquins fled west or were killed off and many of the French leaders left immediately for France, the ex-governor being one of them, Pierre de Cavagnal de Vaudreuil. Vaudreuil was the Seigneur of this region and a very wealthy man too. His father, Phillipe de Vaudreuil, had owned the land before him. They hated the Mohawks or at least were scared of them. When the French lost in 1760 at Montreal and peace was signed, Philippe's two sons, Pierre and Rigaud, and their families left almost immediately for France. Neither of them has been back since, so I'm told.

"Rigaud de Vaudreuil had been the owner of the land just west of Cavagnal now called the Seigneury de Rigaud. It is much larger than the Vaudreuil Seigneury but it is much more sparsely settled as compared to the Vaudreuil one." John continued to say "That there is a road through Cavagnal stretching from Vaudreuil on past the Rigaud Seigneury and the village there. The road fades into the bush except for a rough horse trail at the Upper Canada border, opposite Carillon, just at the foot of the Long Sault rapids."

John Cameron had taken a vested interest in the local history as his job of transporting many new settlers into the region left him with a great deal of time to chat with the newcomers. He felt that telling the newcomers about the local history would make them feel more welcome and let them know what kind of an area they were coming to.

John continued with his local history story to his trapped audience. However, they were all entranced with his tales, especially Jane Henderson, who sat opposite him with her eyes glued to his. "I do not know when the Mohawks first settled over there in Oka," pointing towards the northern shore, "but they have been very friendly with us English over in Cavagnal the whole time."

Pointing west towards a distinct narrowing in the river about two miles west of them he noted that at Pearson's Point some of the Mohawks still come from other regions each summer to gather and fish in the bay and smoke their catches. "They stay for about two months each year and many wander around our community. So do not be surprised if you see Indians around the village from time to time. They have not arrived yet but should be here by mid-July."

"Well my friends, that is where we are headed," John announced to his passengers as he slowly turned the bateau towards the southern shore of the golden coloured lake. A large stone building with a long wooden dock stood about one hundred feet back from the lake's shore. They could see about six large voyageur style canoes pulled up on the shore with huge stocks of goods piled around them and one other bateau was tied up alongside the dock.

"Schmidt's Tavern I presume," George said to them all. John Cameron agreed as he asked them to prepare for docking.

"I will need some help getting her lined up," he added. "Damn bad place to land in with a north-west wind blowing. No shelter on this open stretch of shore. There is a much better place just west of Pearson's Point, long rocky point but the land close to shore is a swamp. If it could be filled in or a wall built around the edge, it would make a great harbour."

George asked why he did not do it. "Some old Frenchman owns the land and he just does not want to sell it at the present time and I cannot afford such a large piece of land. One day maybe, one day." With that, the four men began to prepare to dock the cumbersome bateau. The two Army officers did not even offer to help them. "We will land first," John told his passengers. "Then we will need to help Simon land his boat."

Three scruffy looking men came down to the dock to help the boats tie up. Jane gasped as she glanced up at them. They were dressed in furs and animal skins and had long filthy beards. They smiled at her but said nothing. "French voyageurs," John told her. "Ignore them but be careful. I will keep an eye on them for you," he said quietly.

"Merci Messieurs," John said to the three men as they helped tie up his boat. "Merci, bien."

"Pas de problème, Anglais," they replied and then turned away, heading back to the Tavern. Mary quickly stood up and announced to all those on board that she felt, along with the other two wives, that it should be George Henderson who should first set foot onto their new homeland. They all cheered and with that, George Henderson, formerly of Westmorland, England, placed his foot onto the rocky shore at Cavagnal, Lower Canada, British North America on June 9th 1824.

Chapter 8
Settling In

After unloading all the baggage, the three families headed up to the front door of Schmidt's Tavern. It was a fine two story stone building that looked out across the broad expanse of the Ottawa River. To the east of the tavern they could spot a small wood frame house through the trees. No other houses could be seen. "Kind of a lonesome place," Jane commented to her parents as they approached the tavern door.

Simon Beauvais had followed John Cameron's bateau into the dock. He had traveled all alone up the river with the livestock. "Simon is a good man," John had told his passengers, "but he keeps much to himself. Great with animals though. I hate having to transport livestock on one of these things, never know when one is going to try to get loose and jump overboard. Simon just has some odd way with them and most of the time the animals he transports lie down and fall asleep. He must talk to them I guess." Robert Fowler looked over towards the other bateau operator and smiled then turned to walk up to the tavern with the others.

"Better stay outside here ladies," George told his wife and the wives of his friends. "I do not think this is the best place for a woman to be, especially with those ruffians inside." George was reminding all those with him of the three men who had helped them tie up a few minutes before.

John Cameron offered to introduce George, Dr. Grisenthwaite and

Robert Fowler to Mr. Schmidt, his employer so the four men entered the tavern. John Henderson was told by his father to remain outside and keep guard over their possessions and the women. Before entering, George had John had given his son his rifle just in case. Something about those voyageurs that George just did not like. "Better to have two guns available rather than just one," he thought.

Charles Schmidt, son of the tavern's owner, William Schmidt met them as they came in the door. George had to stoop somewhat due to the low doorframe and being so tall. A quiet hush fell over the rowdy bunch of voyageurs that were sitting around a huge table covered with beer mugs and tins plates. A steaming pot of stew sat in the middle of the table and hot rolls filled a large wicker basket at one end of the table.

John told everyone not to stop talking and that these were new settlers to the area and that one was a Doctor, pointing at Joseph Grisenthwaite. With that four men jumped up and came over to Dr. Grisenthwaite at a rush. Each speaking rapidly in French and making gestures of what ailed them. "Seems you will have lots of work in these parts Doctor," commented George. "See to them while I take Robert and see about our land."

William Schmidt was also a big man but not as tall as George Henderson. Actually George was the biggest man in the room and looking out the window some of them saw an equally large young man standing beside the newcomer's luggage, holding a big gun. Many wondered who they were and but they all knew why they were there. A few of the voyageurs pointed at Jane Henderson and Sarah Fowler sitting beside their luggage and muttered something to each other.

"Mr. Schmidt," John Cameron said to his employer, "may I present Mr. George Henderson and Mr. Robert Fowler, newly arrived from England. Over there is Dr. Joseph Grisenthwaite, also from England." With the brief introductions over with, John Cameron bid his new friends adieu and left the building. As he turned to leave he told William Schmidt that he had quite a load of mail to deliver to the Catholic Priest across the river in Oka. "I am heading west to Carillon with those two Army officers. I am going to take Simon with me in my bateau." William Schmidt agreed and sent John on his way. The two Army Engineer officers had grabbed a quick pint of ale and a piece of ham from Mrs. Schmidt then they too hurried out the door, following John Cameron back down to the dock. Their trip was long from being over and they wanted to be in Carillon before night, if possible.

"Good afternoon gentlemen," William said to his two guests. "May I offer you ale before we get down to details?" George and Robert both smiled and said yes.

"I doubt they have wine," George whispered to Robert. Robert just smiled and shrugged his shoulders.

William told them both that the Seigneur in Vaudreuil had entrusted him to handle the affairs of any newcomers to the area in his absence. "Seigneur Lotbinière's Agent; Mr. André Pambrun comes by here about twice a year," he told Robert and George. "Nice man but insists on having all the papers and rents in order, or else. If you had moved to Vaudreuil, you would have had to see him in person.

"He is replacing the Seigneur Mr. Chartier de Lotbinière, since he died in 1822. Mr. Pambrun will be the acting Seigneur until one of Lotbinière's daughters reaches legal age of twenty-five and that will not be for a few years, I believe.

"That old bugger, Seigneur Lotbinière, had three gorgeous daughters. He just could not father a son and he used up two wives trying! I am sure we will have a new Seigneur as soon as his eldest, Louise Josephate, reaches twenty-five years old. I am sure she will have many eligible suitors by then."

Dr. Grisenthwaite finally finished with the four injured voyageurs and joined his two friends. Robert quickly introduced him to William Schmidt and they all settled down to some nice ale while Schmidt verified the papers concerning the new land these settlers were going to occupy.

"We already have three Henderson families here now," the elder Schmidt told George. "Maybe you know them." George admitted that he did know John Henderson and his wife Rachel and Robert Henderson as well.

"We have been writing to each other for a few years now, ever since they moved here back in 1819. The other family I may know, what are their names?"

"The widow Ann Henderson and her family. She arrived here last year," Schmidt told them, "alone and dragging four young children. She is not doing too well either."

"Too bad about the loss of Robert's wife last year," said George. The elder Schmidt was amazed how the news of Elizabeth Henderson's untimely death shortly after arriving in Canada had already traveled back to England and then returned to Cavagnal.

"Mr. Henderson," William Schmidt announced, "your new land is just west of here, less than a thousand feet, actually. You are a very lucky man. Nice land, well-treed and great river access. The cost of your new land, some sixty arpents, is just ten pounds." George smiled and got out his purse.

"Mr. Fowler, your land is a further away. I do not think you will have time this afternoon to get up there. It is Lot 9 on the Côte St. Charles Concession. I have not been up there in recent months but I am told it is good land and those that are there now do like it and all your neighbours are from England except for the Grampian family who are Americans. Your land of thirty arpents is just two pounds."

"Now for you, Dr. Grisenthwaite," Schmidt continued, "your land is about nine miles from here in the Fief St. Henry. It is a hard journey from here. It will take the better part of a long day to get there. There are few neighbours. I hope you like the Irish," Schmidt smiled, "as there is a large concentration of Irish families all around you, especially up on St. George Mountain."

"Never have had the pleasure or displeasure to know any," the Doctor replied. "I guess I will soon enough. They do have a reputation as a people that likes lots of children in their families." William smiled and added that many of the local Irish rely on midwives as many of the local settlers do, there being no Doctor in the region until now.

Schmidt continued to tell Dr. Grisenthwaite that his land would also be only two pounds and that would be for forty arpents. "It is good land," Charles Schmidt added, "I was up there last summer and there are sheep grazing all over the cleared land and lots of fresh water. There is a small stream, the Raquette River, that flows down through your property and it is full of fish. No good for drinking though as it is very grey in colour, lots of clay up past your way. Seems the whole area is either clay, gravel, or sand around here."

"There is some talk already of somebody coming here to set up a glass works. There were some men from Montréal and Boston here last summer checking on the quality of the sand. No one knows who they were and how they picked this spot but rumours have it they plan to come here in a couple of years. Could provide us with some much-needed employment. We are not all farmers," William finished off.

With the exchange of cash and the signing of the papers all of them went outside. Charles Schmidt had told his father that there were ladies outside and two of them would need a good bed for the night along with their children. William was shocked at first that no one had told him of the women and children outside but glancing over at the table surrounded by noisy and foul mouthed voyageurs he realized that his popular tavern was not the best place for civilized ladies. At least not this part of it.

William Schmidt's wife, Caroline Candwell, was a jolly lady of sixty-seven years, the same age as her husband. On noting that there were other women at her home, she slapped her son behind the head and scolded him for not telling her. "Damn you Charles and damn you William," she yelled, "we have women and children outside and all you do is drink ale with their husbands. Maybe these women would like to freshen up or have something to eat. You only think of the men folk! Damn you both!"

William and his son just shrugged their shoulders and joined the others outside. Caroline was soon busy introducing herself to Mary Henderson, Sarah Fowler, and Elizabeth Grisenthwaite while John Henderson was introduced to the Schmidt men. "No need for the gun now son," George told his son. "I think we have friends here though I still wonder about those men inside," motioning with his head to the group around the table.

"Do not worry about them George," Charles said. "They may look tough and smell awful, but they are generally very pleasant fellows. "Remember how three of them came out to help you land your boat?" Charles added. "No one asked them to do that, it is just their way of helping others. They work very hard and drink hard, but most are gentlemen and will not harm you. That I can guarantee."

George nodded but he still seemed a little doubtful about the scruffy voyageurs. The door opened and the group of French Canadians piled out the door, slapping each other on their backs and singing a joyous tune. It was a happy tune and the small group of English settlers smiled as the three canoes were quickly loaded and all of them headed off east towards Lachine. "There will be a big party in Lachine tonight," Caroline Schmidt commented. "Glad it will be there and not here or we would never get any sleep."

William told all the newcomers to come inside while he and his wife and son set up places for them to sleep that night. "We will have a big pot of fresh venison stew for supper and lots of ale and wine."

"Wine, you said wine," George said with a big grin on his face. "I *love* wine, though I never expected to get it here." Charles then went on to tell him that they have some of the best wild grapes in the whole of the Seigneury right there in Cavagnal.

"We have been making wine ever since we arrived here."

"I cannot wait till we get settled so I can make some of my own, at last," George said in an even happier mood. "I now know that I am going to like this place."

George, Mary and all their family decided to take a short walk up the dirt track behind the tavern towards their new land. Mary, being a little tired, wanted to stay back with the other children at the tavern, but George had convinced her and the youngsters to come along as well. Caroline Schmidt had noticed right away that Mary was pregnant and hoped that the new child would be a healthy one and would survive the long hard winter, less than six months away. Too many youngsters had succumbed to a cough or some other illness in that new land of theirs.

It was a short walk up the track to where William Schmidt had told George where his land would commence. Sixty arpents was a great deal more land than he had owned back in England and there was going to be a lot of work for him and his family that summer. "Look father," yelled John back to the others, "there is a cabin on our land." George had not seen the small cabin as Jane and John had surged ahead of him, anxious to see their new land.

Indeed there was a small cabin on his land and in very rough shape at that. The roof had fallen in and there was no door where one should be, just a hole. The area was overgrown with weeds, but for about two hundred feet around the cabin the area had been cleared except for three large oak trees. George then announced that they would name their new home "Three Oaks".

"Must have belonged to the previous owner," George said to his family. "Mr. Schmidt told me while we were signing for the land that the couple who lived here could not pay their debts and had to move out two years ago. The place has been empty ever since and none of the settlers arriving here until we came along could afford this section of land. Some actually did not want the land even though they could afford it. Anyway, it is ours now."

George, Mary, Jane and John all cried a little and the little Henderson children watched their older siblings and parents, wondering why they were crying. "Why are you crying?" asked little Frances "Are you sad?"

"No, dear," Mary said to her young daughter. "These are tears of happiness. One day you will understand."

Then they all knelt down while Jane said a short prayer of thanks. With that, they all entered the old cabin. "It is going to need a great many repairs," Jane said, "but it will do until we can expand. John and I will help you, father," she said, hugging George.

"No dear, you will help your mother, the baby will be due very soon now, in about two months, and Mary is going to need a lot of rest. It has been a long hard journey for us all but especially your mother. I do not want anything to happen to her now or I will never forgive myself. I have lost my best friend; I do not want to lose my wife after all we have gone through these past few weeks."

"We can do it," John said, "and John Cameron has offered his help also. When he is not working for the Schmidts of course."

"That would be nice," replied George. "He seems to be a fine young lad and I think he has taken a fancy to your sister," winking at Jane.

"I do think he is kind of nice and he is handsome," she added shyly.

"Good, then it is settled, the two Johns will help me and Jane will help Mary with the other children."

"I think little William will want to help us too, father," added John.

"That will be just fine son; he is a strong lad for just eleven years old.

Another big Henderson boy in the making." With that, they headed back to Schmidt's Tavern for a good hearty supper and a warm bed. Tomorrow was going to be a busy one for all concerned.

The tavern was quiet when they returned. No more voyageurs had arrived and that made George feel more comfortable. He just did not trust the French. It was probably from years of armed conflict against them that led to his mistrust.

After Mary and the children had retired to their rooms for the evening, George decided to have a chat with William Schmidt about the area and try to learn as much as he could in the short time they had before work began in earnest up the road.

Schmidt admitted that he had been a Hessian mercenary with the British Army and had fought against the American rebels in their War of Independence. He told George that he had been present at Bunker Hill and had witnessed a terrible slaughter there of many a good soldier. "George," he said, "I hope that I never have to witness another war, I have had to serve in two wars against the Americans and I am lucky to have survived both conflicts unscathed. War is hell, as you very well know. If you are a God-fearing man George Henderson, pray that we never have to take up arms again."

George sat for a moment contemplating what he had just heard from the old soldier. "I must admit I have never thought about it that much," George told him, "but you are right and I will pray that we never have to take up arms again to defend our country, be it here in Canada or back home in England."

Charles Schmidt joined them at the table with three tankards of ale. "I served with father during the last war," he admitted. "We were present at the Battle of Chateauguay under our local militia commander, Major Lotbinière. Our unit was the Vaudreuil Division of the First Battalion and we won a major battle that day. We were commanded by Lt. Colonel Charles de Salaberry. There were also others from here in Cavagnal and Vaudreuil including the Grampians and André Pambrun. It was grand; British, French and Indians all fighting alongside each other against the American invaders."

George told them that he still could not see himself fighting alongside

Frenchmen. However, he had met some Indians and felt that they could be trusted and from what he had heard and read that the Indians, especially the Mohawks, they were excellent fighters.

"You are correct in that statement George," William told him, "but I must admit that if you plan to live here in this country for the rest of your life, you had better start to learn how to trust the French.

"I am a German by birth and I have adopted the British way of life but the French-Canadians have a lot to teach us as well. We have to live alongside them here in this Seigneury. We have married some of them and we trade and buy goods from each other. Get to know them as they are your neighbours and can be of great help when you need them.

"That is all I have to say tonight about politics," William announced coldly, "good night and once again, welcome to our land." With that, he told Charles to go upstairs and the two Schmidts left George alone in the tavern's dining room.

George sat for awhile. Then he too decided to head upstairs to where his wife was sound asleep. "I know they are right in what they say," he thought, "and I'll promise them tomorrow that I will make an effort to make friends with the local French. We have to, we are all neighbours and neighbours have to help each other, especially in this wild land."

The months of June and July passed quickly and the long hot summer days saw George and John busy fixing up the run down cabin and clearing the land. They had quickly cleared a large patch of ground that had been covered in weeds and planted a large vegetable garden. Frances, little William, and their older sister, Margaret, were placed in charge of that project. They had brought seeds from England and had also got some corn seeds from John Cameron one day after he dropped by to see Jane.

Potatoes were not yet common in the region and Mary was glad that they had brought some with them. The corn plant was new to all of them, as it was a crop that the locals had told them about. "It is from the Indians and it tastes great. When you are finished with the cobs," someone told them, "feed them to your hogs."

Unfortunately, the Hendersons did not have any hogs, but George, with some of the money he had left, had managed to purchase two, a horse, and two more sheep. He had made a rough sort of barn that was attached to the backside of the cabin. "You will need a good place for those animals come winter," John Cameron had told him. "It gets mighty cold here in January."

George's prize Ayrshire cow had survived the long trip as had his two sheep. They were finally enjoying their freedom and the good fodder available after having been cooped up in the hold of *The Pioneer* for so many long weeks. Many a poor family had arrived with little or no money and having had to kill their livestock during the voyage from England just so they themselves could survive. The Hendersons had been lucky and had arrived with their livestock in reasonable shape and with some money left. Enough to get them to Cavagnal and to purchase more livestock as the summer wore on.

Just as John Cameron had predicted, a large group of Mohawks arrived in the small bay on the eastern side of Pearson's Point and set up camp. There were about twenty or more and each morning and afternoon the locals could see them out fishing. Each afternoon and late into the evening the women of the group would be hard at work cleaning then smoking the fish. Most were what the local French called doré. The English called them walleye because of their big round eyes. The Indians also caught yellow perch, sturgeon and catfish.

The smell of the smoking fish was evident all through the community and to many of the residents it was an awful smell. However, almost all of the locals dropped by the Indian camp to buy or barter for some of the freshly smoked fish. The Indians always loved to chat with the youngsters and trade with their parents. Since very few of the residents of Cavagnal had any great amounts of money, they would trade woven materials with the Indians for the fish.

The Hendersons also visited the camp that summer. George, having some money, was able to buy several pounds of smoked doré. It would be a great addition to their diet for the coming fall and winter.

William Schmidt was at the camp on a regular basis as he liked to buy freshly caught perch and doré and serves it to his customers. Since his customers liked fresh fish rather than the smoked variety, he had to get to the camp before the day's catch was readied for the smokehouse. "They have been coming here for as long as anyone can remember," Schmidt told George one day. "Even before the Mohawks arrived, I have heard that the Hurons and Ottawas stopped here too.

"This river is known for some large fish. I have seen some sturgeon that has been caught in the Indian's nets that have weighed over one hundred and fifty pounds. The doré often weigh twelve to fifteen pounds and sometimes they will catch a fish known as the maskinongé. It is much larger than the pike you might have seen back in England and it is a very fierce predator and can weigh up to seventy or more pounds. I have heard of the maskinongé attacking ducks, beavers, and even children swimming in this bay. The best spot for them though, is right out at the end of the point.

"Not many of us English fish out here," Schmidt told George, "Only some of the French and of course the Indians. There is a reef just west of here that has some great fishing around it as well. Too bad there are no trout here. To get trout, you have head up to where the Grisenthwaites are, along the Raquette River."

"Maybe one day I will have some spare time," George said, "and set out with a pole and line to catch some fish for supper. I used to do it in the Eden River back home in England. We would catch salmon and big brown trout all the time. Are there salmon here, William?"

"I have not seen any," William answered, "but they do catch some in Lake St. Louis I believe. Big Atlantic salmon too, some upwards of twenty pounds or more. There must be some out here, but I have not heard of any being caught. You should ask the experts over at the Mohawk camp," he added. "They would know."

John Cameron's visits came more frequently as the summer wore on and it was quite obvious that both he and Jane were deeply in love. Mary and George had spoken about the young couple many a night while lying next to each other in bed. However, they had to whisper very quietly as the cabin was very small and they did not want Jane to overhear them.

Mary's pregnancy was no problem to them either and Caroline Schmidt had recommended Elizabeth Loland as Mary's midwife if Dr. Grisenthwaite could not make it down from St. Henry in time for the birth. He had dropped by one day in late July to check on Mary and had stayed overnight despite the cramped quarters in the Henderson cabin.

He told them how he and his family had built a fine little cabin next to the small stream called the Raquette River and how good the fishing in it was. "Lots of fine fat trout and some catfish too. We have learned to smoke the trout," he told George. They too had great neighbours and one of his sons had also met a young lady, one of the daughters of the Robert Henderson family in the region.

* * *

Mary Henderson gave birth to a healthy young daughter just after five in the morning on August 21st, 1824. Elizabeth Henderson had beautiful green eyes and brown hair, very much like her mother's. At eight pounds six ounces, she was by far the largest baby Mary had given birth to and she was a healthy one at that.

Reverend Joseph Ashford dropped by in late October during his circuit tour from the St. Andrews and the Hendersons had little Elizabeth baptized. There was a grand turnout of the local population and with the fall weather being extremely warm that year, a feast was held at the Henderson cabin for all those who wanted to attend.

It was at that feast that Jane Henderson and John Cameron announced to all those present that they planned to be married. George and Mary had already known about their daughter's wishes for a few weeks but they had all kept silent until then. A May wedding was planned and Reverend Ashford promised to be there for the service.

Chapter 9
The First Winter

The first winter at Cavagnal was not too hard on the Henderson family. They had prepared well and with the help of John Cameron, the little log cabin was soon in tiptop shape for the whole family. Since Jane would be leaving the next spring to be with her new husband, no extra rooms were added before the long winter had set in.

However, up in St. Henry, life for the Grisenthwaites was not as easy. Being such a long way from the rest of the English settlement down along the river and not being a farmer, Dr. Joseph and his wife Elizabeth had not been able to get as much help to prepare their land before fall.

Though he had built a small cabin beside the Raquette River, Joseph had not found much time to seed his land for crops as George had and this worried Joseph quite a bit. He had often wondered if they would have enough food to last them until spring. Joseph had not been a farmer in England and had spent much of his young life studying to become a doctor. Now all of that book learning was hampering his new style of life.

He was lucky that his son Jacob had taken time on the voyage over to learn how to use one of the rifles on board the ship. George Henderson had been a great teacher and with the new gun they had purchased in Halifax, Jacob had been able to kill three deer and a small bear up on the mountain just west of their new home. Hopefully that meat would get them through the long winter. A neighbour, Sean O'Rourke, had shown

Jacob how to set snares along the banks of the frozen Raquette River and Jacob was able to keep his family well supplied with meat from the rabbits he was able to snare. A long trip down to John A. Marsden's store in Cavagnal to get some wire for the snares had proven very worthwhile. To keep their feet warm, the fur of the rabbits was used to line their boots. Mittens were made from the wool of the sheep they had raised during the summer and these were also lined with rabbit fur.

Joseph doubted that his sheep would last the winter, as there was little or no fodder for them. He had not thought of building a shed for them and if sheep had roamed the hillsides all winter long in Cumberland, they could do it here. He had bought them from one of the Irish families down the in valley, the O'Rourkes. His neighbour, Robert Henderson, finally told him in late October that his sheep would not last past mid-December out here in Canada. "Remember," Robert had said, "this is Canada not England. It gets *very* cold here in mid-winter and last winter the snow was over three feet deep by mid-January. Your sheep will be better off in your bellies and on your backs than starving out there on the hillside. Butcher them now," he had told Joseph. "Your good wife Elizabeth will be able to use their wool for mittens and hats for your youngsters."

Joseph followed his new neighbour's suggestion and butchered his two sheep at the end of November after the first snow had fallen and the first signs of ice along the edge of the little river behind their new home had begun to form.

Dr. Joseph Grisenthwaite and his small family would weather out their first winter in their new home with great hardships and suffering and sadness. On January 14th, their young eight-year-old daughter, Irene, died after coming down with a terrible cold that ended in pneumonia. Even her father, with all his training, could not help the young child.

Irene was placed in a small pine box and buried under a huge pile of snow and branches so the marauding wolves and foxes would not harm the little body before her family could bury the little coffin the next spring.

Robert Henderson had proven to be a very helpful neighbour and he and his daughter, Phoebe, had often visited the Grisenthwaites during the winter. Even though Robert and his family had only been there a year and he had already lost his wife, he was now a hardened veteran of the area and his knowledge helped the Grisenthwaites through that first winter and the loss of their youngest child.

Phoebe had taken a liking to Joseph's son Jacob and when they had some free time they would spend it together. They would either slide down the narrow track leading down from Robert's house on the hill that overlooked the valley, or snowshoe around the farms. The Indians of Kanesatake had told Robert the summer before about using snowshoes to get around during the winter and he had purchased three pairs for himself, Phoebe, and his eldest son, Allan. His other two children would get theirs at a later date when he could afford to buy them or try to make them himself.

Life over at the Fowler residence on the Grand Côte was somewhat easier with more neighbours to call upon. The Pearsons, Blackwells, and the Grampians all proved to be excellent neighbours and they had helped Robert build his first cabin. Neither he nor Joseph Grisenthwaite had been as lucky as George Henderson, who had found a cabin already built on his land (though it had been in fairly rough shape).

Robert had made sure that his cow had a good strong shed to pass the winter in. He had even been able to harvest a small crop of hay for it to use that winter. The Grand Côte provided all the families with a lovely view of the surrounding countryside and Robert and his wife Sarah had commented many a night on how well the hill had been named. "It surely is a Grand Côte," he had often said.

George Henderson had settled well into the local community and had made friends with all his neighbours except for one man that operated a small store about a half a mile east of his place. François Xavier Deschamps was a strange little man who lived alone above his store and kept very much to himself. He spoke very good English but preferred to be addressed in French. This bothered George a lot but he remembered what William Schmidt had told him on the day he had arrived and even though George tried to like the little man, he could not find it in him to do so.

F.X. Deschamps was quite a bit younger than George and had originally come to the area from Montréal in 1820. He had come from a wealthy family and had been able to purchase a large section of land in a wide bay directly opposite the Oka Catholic Church, which was situated about one and a quarter miles across on the north shore of the Lake of the Two Mountains.

Deschamps' family had been very prosperous merchants in Montréal and in Québec and had amassed quite a fortune before the conquest. That money was spread around the family and Deschamps' father had left young François a large inheritance at the time of his death. With the money, François had decided to set up his own store in the new territory west of Montréal.

The Deschamps family had been very close friends with the former Governor of New France and the original Seigneur of Vaudreuil, Phillipe de Vaudreuil, and his successor Pierre de Cavagnal de Vaudreuil. François' father, Maxim-Olivier Deschamps had initially scouted some land near where his son eventually purchased but had not been well enough to move his business out to Vaudreuil from Montréal.

François had decided to move after his father's death in 1818 and had left the family-run business in Montréal in the control of his older brother Louis-Phillipe and his mother. Seigneur Lotbinière had sold the land to François for the reasonable sum of forty-five pounds and thus François became the proud owner of some two hundred and fifty arpents in the eastern section of Cavagnal. He was the largest French-Canadian landowner in the area. Only John Augustus Marsden, an Englishman, owned more land.

François-Xavier Deschamps' store was usually very busy as it had almost everything a newcomer like George Henderson needed to set up and run a home in the remote area west of Montréal. Deschamps sold powder and shot for guns, dishes, bolts of material, pots and pans, nails, saws, glass bottles, and candy for the children. Deschamps, though living alone, had a lady who helped him in his store most days and she stayed in a small one-room cabin behind the main building.

Many neighbours of Deschamps had often wondered if the young girl was a slave to Deschamps or his mistress as she was rarely seen outside the store in the rest of the ever-growing community. Mary Kilkenny had arrived one summer's day a year after Deschamps had his large home and store built and had stayed ever since. Nothing was known about her and some of the English residents of Cavagnal had often thought that she was indentured labour that had originally worked for the Deschamps family in Montréal.

Mary did not speak English very well and François-Xavier had once told Caroline Schmidt that Mary's mother had been French Canadian while her father had been a British soldier of Irish background stationed in Montreal in the late 1700's. Her father had died after coming down with cholera one summer just after the turn of the century. Mary and her mother had lived a very tough and poor life in Montreal until her mother had found work with the Deschamps family. After her mother died in 1820, F.X. Deschamps had sent for Mary to come and stay with him in his new store out in Cavagnal.

George Henderson often travelled down to Deschamps' store to visit the other local men who often gathered there during the winter around the large wood stove that was set in the middle of the place. George tried as he could to initiate a conversation with the strange little man but to no avail. Joseph Shouldice, who owned a farm further east of the store also, came to the store at regular intervals to meet some of the local farmers and have a game of checkers and discuss the goings on in the community.

Deschamps did not seem to mind the locals dropping by even though they often did not buy anything. Money was in very short supply among the residents except for François himself. He, like John Augustus Marsden, was very comfortable and enjoyed most of the finer pleasures of life that the early years in Cavagnal could offer.

Shouldice had also tried to make friends with Deschamps and had failed and both he and George would often leave the store and head up to Schmidt's Tavern to see what was going on there.

William Schmidt was a jolly man and always welcomed his neighbours with a strong slap on their back and wished them well when they left. "I just hate the winters," he would say. "No voyageurs stopping by to have a hearty meal and good ale in my tavern."

"The Schmidt's Tavern," Joseph Shouldice once told George Henderson, "is known all across Canada. Best place within a day's journey outside of Montréal for a meal and a tankard of ale."

George had only eaten at the tavern once and that was that first night back in June when he and his family had first arrived from Montreal. However, he did often drop by the place to have ale with his new found friends.

Mary was quite concerned with George's increased drinking and he had often come home quite drunk. He had never been like that back in England.

"What is wrong, dear?" Mary finally asked him in late March. "Why do you drink so much?" George quickly sat down. He had not been drinking for two days so Mary thought it would be the best time to confront her husband. She had asked their son John to stay close by in case George got violent. "Alcohol does strange things to people," she had told her concerned son. He too had seen a drastic change in his father over the past few months.

"I am tired of this place," he told her. "So much work and so few friends. I try to be friendly with that damn frog, Deschamps, but he rebuffs me each time. Damn Frenchman. I am looking forward to Jane's marriage," he continued, "but I guess the main problem is that I miss Isaac a great deal."

Mary had thought that Isaac's death was the root of the problem and wondered what they could do to solve it. It was almost a year since Isaac had been struck down on board *The Pioneer* by the ugly splinter that had split him almost in half. Having Isaac die in his arms had not been very easy for George and Mary had discussed his mental stability once before with Dr. Grisenthwaite. The doctor had told Mary to send for him if she believed George was getting worse.

"Can I send for the doctor, dear?" she asked her husband. "I am worried about you and so is the rest of your family. Joseph Shouldice has told me a little about your fits of rage in the tavern and Charles Schmidt has too. Your friends care for you and just try to ignore that little Deschamps. I agree he is strange and few people like him."

George began to cry. "I love you so much Mary and our new home. I have been a terrible person and an awful father and husband these past few months. Alcohol is not an answer but only a temporary solution and I guess it is killing me slowly." George had lost a great deal of weight as the winter had worn on and he had aged a lot.

"Yes Mary, send for Dr. Grisenthwaite," he said. "Maybe he can help me and also try to send for Reverend Ashford. I am sure John Cameron knows how to reach him. We need to have a church set up here and a school for our children and the others around Cavagnal."

"Now that is like the old George I once knew," Mary said smiling and then stood up to hug her husband. They both began crying and Jane who was away at the start of the conversation just happened to come back to the cabin and spotted her parents crying.

"What is wrong?" She let out a yelp, startled to see both her parents embracing and crying at the same time. Jane then asked, "Has someone died?"

"No my darling," George told his daughter, "but someone has just been saved from dying."

"Your father has just admitted that he has had a drinking problem for the past few months and we are all going to help him get rid of it, the sooner the better." John then came in the door, accompanied by John Cameron who had been out snowshoeing with Jane.

"As soon as you can, John Cameron, can you get in touch with Reverend Ashford and have him come down here?" George asked him. "I want to organise a committee to have a church built here in Cavagnal and a school. We will get also John Augustus Marsden involved. He has lots of wealthy friends in the Government and he has an ideal spot to have a school."

"John, my son, I want you to ride up to Dr. Grisenthwaite's tomorrow morning to fetch him down here so he can examine me. Your mother and I have had a wonderful discussion and I think planning a church and a school for Cavagnal will help my problem. I miss my good friend Isaac a great deal but I must confront that myself and I now know that alcohol is not the answer. From now on there will be no ale or wine touching these lips except on very special occasions. Your marriage will be *the* one this year, my lovely Jane. That will be a celebration to look forward to."

With that, the five adults knelt down and Jane led them in a prayer of thanks.

Chapter 10
An Unexpected Visitor

The May wedding of Jane Henderson and John Cameron was going to be a glorious event for all those involved. The eldest of the Henderson children had become very popular in their new community of Cavagnal. John Cameron was already well known and also very popular. Many a local girl had wished that he had chosen one of them for his wife, but he had chosen Jane Henderson, aged twenty-three and new to the region.

John planned to continue working for William Schmidt and Jane had offered to help Caroline Schmidt in the tavern as the elderly lady had not been too well over the winter months and had to rest a great deal. Dr. Grisenthwaite had thought it was her heart that was causing her weakness. William had turned a great deal of work over to his son, Charles. So between Jane, John and Charles they planned to make the elder Schmidts proud of their work and enjoy a semi-retirement.

Charles had some ideas that he had discussed with the young couple and the three of them were looking forward in having a freer hand at the operations of the tavern.

Jane and John's wedding was going to take place on the front lawn of the tavern instead of at the Henderson's cabin as had been initially planned during the winter at an all important meeting of Mary and George. George had turned over a new leaf in his life and the upcoming marriage of his eldest daughter had him walking around the community with his head held high.

The date of the wedding was set for Saturday, May 14th, 1825 at 1:30 p.m. Reverend Ashford had been asked to come to perform the ceremony on the front lawn of Schmidt's Tavern and most of the community was to be invited. It was the first wedding in Cavagnal in two years and the first that Reverend Ashford had the chance in performing. The other weddings in the community had been either for some French-Canadians by the Vaudreuil priest or by the Wesleyan Methodist Minister, Reverend Angus Bradfield. He had dropped by the Hendersons in late October to see if they were Methodists, but on discovering that they were Church of England supporters, he had left and visited some of the other new families in the area and his regular parishioners. Most of them actually lived up on the Côte St. Charles concession and not down in Cavagnal.

"Where are you two young lovers going to live?" asked William Schmidt one day a month or so before the wedding.

Jane said, "We hope to build a small place in back of father's place, but until then, we were hoping that we could get a room here at the tavern."

"No problem, my dear," replied the elder Schmidt. "I had already discussed the possibility of your staying here with Caroline and she whole heartily agreed, as did Charles. You are both welcome to stay here as long as you want."

"What about the rent?" John asked his employer.

"Do not worry about that just now. Our wedding gift to you will be this place rent-free for a few months. That way you will be able to concentrate on building your cabin in the woods and not have to worry about the added expense of having to pay rent."

"Oh, thank you sir," cried Jane and with that she planted a big kiss on his left cheek. John shook Schmidt's hand and then went off to tend to his boats.

Simon Beauvais was waiting for John down by the river's edge. John was going to ask his best friend to be his best man at the upcoming wedding. Jane had already selected two bridesmaids but John had delayed asking Simon because they had just been too busy on the river. Spring was the busiest time of the year, especially just after the ice broke up and in 1825 the ice did not leave the Lake of the Two Mountains until late April.

Since then, hundreds of canoes and barges had been seen travelling up and down the lake loaded with various types of cargoes. Huge rafts were also seen with timber from way up the Ottawa. The rafts were too big to pull into the bay near Schmidt's Tavern, so William and Charles would send Simon and John out by bateau to see if any of the rafts needed any provisions. Most of the time they did not, as the owner of the rafts, Philomen Wright of Wright's Village, had outfitted each raft with enough food, tobacco, and whisky so they would reach Montreal unaided. After that the rafts would restock for the final leg of their trip down to Québec. However, once in awhile a raft would request some extra provisions after some had been lost in the Long Sault rapids near Carillon.

Wright, known as the "King" of the Upper Ottawa, was hiring hundreds of young men to work his timber rights in the upper watershed of the Ottawa River. His small community was at the junction of the Gatineau and Ottawa and Rideau Rivers, about ninety miles west of Cavagnal.

The rafts would be broken up at Québec and the wood loaded onto waiting ships for the trip across to Great Britain. The late spring of 1825 had delayed the flotillas for three weeks and now the river was full of traffic. William Schmidt was looking forward to a great year. Even F.X. Deschamps, in his store, "Magasin Général de Cavagnal" was enjoying a boom time and it was only the beginning of May.

"Will you be my best man, Simon?" John asked his best friend.

"Of course, John," Simon responded. "I would be honoured."

"I would like you to wear some traditional clothes also, please." Simon agreed to wear a traditional Mohawk ceremonial outfit for his friend's wedding. To be able to wear the ceremonial outfit at a white man's wedding would be a great honour, but Simon also hoped that it would not upset too many of the new English settlers in the area. He had heard that some of them were still quite nervous about having an Indian settlement directly across the river from their small community.

May 14th was beginning to look as if it was going to be a grand day for all those concerned in Cavagnal, especially the proud couple.

A large flotilla of canoes was sighted at 11:00 am in front of Schmidt's Tavern. Charles Schmidt hurried down to the dock upon seeing the flotilla turn into his wharf and helped the lead paddlers tie up the first canoe.

The first thing Charles noticed was the large British flag hanging limp off the stern of the lead canoe, and the presence of a small portly looking British Naval officer sitting in the middle of the canoe. The last thing Charles had expected was an official visit from the Royal Navy on the day of his friend's wedding. Here were at least sixty-five men fully equipped for a great expedition landing on his front lawn just two hours before the wedding was about to begin. "What am I going to do?" he thought. "I cannot send them away, it would ruin our reputation. I must find out who they are and tell them about our wedding plans here."

Before Charles could speak to the little officer, the man stood up and got out of the canoe. He announced, "I am Lieutenant Peter Fitzgibbon of His Britannic Majesty's Royal Navy, I bid you good day sir. Who are you?" Fitzgibbon added.

"I am Charles Schmidt and this is my family's tavern. Lieutenant Fitzgibbon, I bid you welcome, but I must tell you that your flotilla is quite unexpected as we are about to have a wedding here in just two hours and we are not all prepared for your group. Please forgive me, Sir." Charles was trying to think of what to do when his father, William, showed up beside him.

"Who are they Charles?" he asked his son.

"This is Lieutenant Peter Fitzgibbon of the Royal Navy. I think he is going on some expedition of some sort, father."

"We are," Fitzgibbon replied. "And a very long one too. This is my second expedition to the Northwest and we are trying to locate the Northwest Passage. We are to meet Captain John Franklin west of Lake Nipissing and then head west to Fort William and then into the North West region of your vast land.

"It would probably be more sensible to try to do it by sea, heading north in sailing ships as others have done and will be doing this summer. However, I think we can find the passage this way and I know our leader,

Captain Franklin, believes we can find the Northwest Passage by going overland. At least we can start earlier in the season than the ships can.

"We left Lachine this morning and we wish to refresh ourselves for a little while at your tavern before heading up river to spend the night at Carillon with the Royal Engineers who are camped there."

"Lieutenant Fitzgibbon," William said, "you are most welcome but as my son has told you, there is a large wedding here this afternoon. However, I think it would be a great honour if you and your men could attend, especially because you are such a famous explorer, Lieutenant Fitzgibbon."

"Oh, I am not a famous explorer," stated Fitzgibbon, "only my Captain is. He did not even come this way as I thought he would. He landed in the United States, New York I believe, and is travelling across country to meet with us near the mouth of the French River in Lake Huron. Captain Franklin left England just after Christmas and was to have landed in New York in mid-February if all went well during his mid-winter passage on the North Atlantic.

"He was to give a couple of speeches to some very wealthy Americans, trying to raise interest in this special voyage of discovery. After New York he was supposed to travel across the State of New York and then north to Penatanquishene in Upper Canada where he was to await the spring thaw. We are to meet him as I have already said at the mouth of the French River on what you call Georgian Bay, I believe. If we are not there in three weeks, he is to leave with his party and head for Cumberland House, meeting up with our advance parties. I hope I can get there in time.

"Captain Franklin is depending on these French Canadian voyageurs I have with me to get him across Lake Huron and Lake Superior and onto Cumberland House. From there we will use our own British seamen and some specially fabricated boats. Franklin does not really have much faith in these flimsy birch bark canoes, even though the French and the Indians before them used them solely to open up this vast land of yours. I guess we British prefer a more solid platform to travel on. I see you have a few bateaux on this lake and here at your dock."

"Yes, we do," replied Charles. "And though they are slow, they make excellent transport boats. But I would not want to travel to the west on one; I would prefer a canoe, like our friends over there in Kanesatake.

"The majority of our expedition landed last fall in Hudson Bay and they were to winter at either York Factory or Cumberland House or both, I am not exactly sure. Both are Hudson Bay Company posts."

"What do you think Charles?" William asked his son. "Do you think Jane and John would mind a few extra guests for their wedding?"

"I do not know, father, but I will go and ask them. John is here in the tavern now and I will send someone up to tell Jane and her father. But we do not have enough food for them all."

Fitzgibbon broke in by saying that they would not stay too long and not to worry about the food; a few pints of ale or rum would suffice. He did not want his men drunk on their first day out and they did have to reach Carillon before dark. "I am to get a handful of Royal Engineers from the garrison there to help me on our voyage. I have been in contact with a Major Sir William Cooper up there regarding surveying the shores of the Arctic Ocean in the north and he has agreed to lend me some of his troops to do the job.

"Sir William is an impatient man and I do not want to keep him waiting too long this evening as he is expecting me. However, it would be an honour for me to attend this wedding you have spoken of. Who is getting married?"

As the expedition unloaded their large canoes and the men filed up towards the tavern for cold ale, Charles and William Schmidt explained who John Cameron and Jane Henderson were. "Jane just arrived here last summer," Charles explained, "with her family. They had quite a time coming across from England. Got involved with some sort of pirate ship in a sea battle. Their ship sank the pirate ship but their escort, a Royal Navy frigate was also lost. Have you heard of that battle, Lieutenant?"

Lieutenant Fitzgibbon admitted that, of course, he had heard of the great sea battle. It had been the talk of the Admiralty for months. "Too bad about the loss of Captain Smithfield though." Charles did not know who or what Fitzgibbon was talking about and just let the comment pass by.

"I hope I can meet the young lady," Fitzgibbon added.

"Do not worry Lieutenant Fitzgibbon, you will certainly meet the young couple," replied Charles.

The guests began gathering just after 1:00 p.m. on the front lawn of the tavern. The weather had held and the day was warm and sunny, ideal for a spring wedding. Reverend Joseph Ashford had arrived the day before and had held a short rehearsal that evening. All had gone well and now the time had come for the real thing.

The guests travelling the furthest were Dr. Joseph Grisenthwaite and his family, and Robert Henderson and his family from the Fief St. Henry. Robert Fowler had made it down from Côte St. Charles with John and Rachel Henderson and of course Dugald Cameron, father of the groom. Dugald was a big hearty Scotsman who loved the taste of whisky and always wore a kilt for special occasions. This would be the most important occasion of his new life in Canada and he had prepared for many an hour to look his finest.

At six foot six and weighing over three hundred pounds, Dugald Cameron was the largest man in the region and not a person to cross swords with when he was angry. However, he was a jolly man and he was going to play the bagpipes for his son's wedding. Of course, who would argue with a man that big anyway?

Simon Beauvais had arrived earlier in the day and had changed into his native clothes in a room in the tavern. When he emerged from the tavern just before 1:00 p.m., many of the gathered guests gasped, not recognising him at first.

For Lieutenant Fitzgibbon, it was his first close-up view of a Canadian Indian in full dress regalia. The ones he had seen in Lachine were shabbily dressed in white men's clothes or ragged buckskins. This Indian was well dressed and impressed the young Lieutenant. Fitzgibbon immediately approached Simon and asked him who and why he was there.

"I am the groom's best man and best friend," replied Simon, in perfect English that was laced with his heavy Mohawk accent. "I live across the river with my people but I work here for the Schmidts and with my friend John Cameron, the groom."

Fitzgibbon asked Simon many more questions before Simon was called over just before 1:30 p.m. to stand beside John at the makeshift altar in the front of the tavern. Simon whispered to John just as the ceremony was about to commence that he was glad to get away from the young Naval officer as he had started to be a nuisance with all his questions about him and his people and their customs.

Since there would not be enough chairs for everyone, the benches from inside the tavern were brought outside and set up in rows, much as it would be in a church.

"We definitely need a church in this area Reverend Ashford," Dugald commented.

"Yes, we do my good man," the Reverend responded. "With your ever growing community I strongly see the need for the building of a church very soon. More weddings, baptisms, and unfortunately, burials will be taking place each year and you people need a place of worship."

"Now some of us are of the Church of England while others are Methodists like me," Dugald continued, "but it doesn't matter, either way, we need a church. Can you help us?"

"Yes I will help you, "Ashford continued, "but first you must form a church board Committee. George Henderson has already spoken to me about this and he is also very interested in getting a school opened up.

"John A. Marsden has the perfect location for the school and church being at the intersection of the Côte St. Charles Road and the King's Road. We could have a church built at a later date and Marsden has already agreed to help. I think George spoke to him last month about it."

Dugald agreed with what the Reverend was saying and told him that after the wedding was over and the reception terminated, he would gather a group of citizens for a quick meeting to lay the groundwork for a Church and School Board Committee. It was the best time to have such a meeting since so many local families would be present. Many families had already quietly spoken about setting up some sort of school for the numerous children in the area. Some of the adults even wanted to have a chance to learn to read and write. About seventy five percent of the adults in Cavagnal were illiterate.

The wedding went off without any problems and the bride and groom paid their respects to all their guests, including Lieutenant Fitzgibbon. "I must bid you hello, congratulations, and a quick adieu, fair couple," he said, "for I must be at Carillon before dark or the Royal Engineers will have my hide." He kissed Jane Henderson Cameron on both cheeks and just before turning to leave, he pressed a small leather pouch into her quivering hand.

He then gathered up his entourage and headed off up the lake at a brisk pace. Just before leaving the dock, Fitzgibbon yelled back to Charles Schmidt, promising to stop by on their return trip in two years. However, Fitzgibbon did tell Charles that the expedition might return to England by Hudson Bay. Only Captain John Franklin would be able to make that decision, since he was in charge.

Jane looked into the pouch as they all waved to the huge flotilla of big canoes as they quickly paddled out towards Pearson's Point. In the small leather pouch were twenty-five shillings. A large sum of money, especially for anyone in Cavagnal, but a much cherished wedding gift from someone they had met just an hour before.

Turning to George Henderson, Charles quietly said, "he and that Captain Franklin are going to get themselves into big trouble one day heading up into that cold north land. Only those Eskimo savages know how to live up there and God only knows how they do that. You would think they would like the warmer climates like us."

"God works in mysterious ways, my good friend," George said. As he said those last words, the last canoe disappeared around the end of Pearson's Point.

The wedding reception was a gala event with Dugald Cameron playing his pipes non-stop for most of the afternoon. Someone had brought a violin and another mouth organ. Though the musical instruments were not exactly matching in their sound, the music was fine enough for dancing and dance they did.

Mary and George had not danced since leaving England the year before and like everyone else, they were a little out of practice at first. But by the time the party was ending, everyone including the Hendersons were swinging around and keeping great time. At one point, Charles Schmidt said that more dances should be held in their small community, and everyone agreed.

Even F.X. Deschamps seemed to be having a great time. He had brought along his housekeeper, Mary Kilkenny, and the two of them were dancing as much as the others.

Mary kept to herself quite a lot, and she was not usually seen around the community except when she was out with her landlord and boss. Many of the local residents thought that they would eventually get married, even though their backgrounds differed so much; he was a patriotic French Canadian and she was from a mixed Irish and French background. Anyway, she was just as welcome at the wedding as anyone else in the community, even F.X. Deschamps.

Jane Henderson had not spoken to Mary very often but when they had, Jane found that Mary was a very likeable girl and both were about the same age. Jane thought a lasting friendship could evolve. That is why she had asked her to attend her wedding and to bring along F.X. Deschamps if she wished.

Some of the more devout Methodists frowned somewhat on the liberal flowing of ale and spirits at the wedding and they headed off early, but no one cared too much. The Methodists kept to themselves up on Côte St. Charles and they had already laid plans for their own Church. Both factions had agreed that the community needed a place of worship.

While the wedding reception was coming to a close and the women were helping Mrs Schmidt with the cleanup and the bride and groom had left for their honeymoon in their partially built cabin, a small group of men gathered inside the tavern to discuss the plans for setting up a Church Board. Present were George Henderson, John A. Marsden, Dr. Joseph Grisenthwaite, William Schmidt, James Henderson, and of course, Reverend Joseph Ashford.

Marsden operated a small store at the intersection of the Côte St. Charles Road and the King's Road. It was so centrally located that all had initially agreed that his place would be the site of the first services of the newly founded Parish of Vaudreuil of the Church of England. Services would be held here until funds had been accumulated to build a proper church somewhere in the area. Since the building was large enough for a church, it was quickly decided that it could also be the site of for a school.

There was already a small school up on Côte St. Charles in the home of the Grampian family. They had been up on the Côte since the Seigneur had first opened it up for settlement back in 1811. The Grampians were Americans but had decided to devote their allegiance to King George instead of the American President, and had decided to leave New Hampshire and follow other Loyalists up to British North America.

James Henderson's children and others on the Côte were already attending the Grampian's little school. However, that school was over three miles from Marsden's building and it would be out of the question to send small children so far, especially in winter. Marsden's place was even three miles west of George Henderson's place and other homes situated around Schmidt's Tavern. So it was decided that Schmidt's Tavern would also be a school. It would serve the few families in the eastern part of the community and the school would be held at one end of the Tavern's dining room. Since it was still a popular spot for voyageurs, concern among some members of the board was for the poor influence these roughback woodsmen would have on young children, especially young girls.

Charles and William Schmidt quickly thought over the problem and they decided to build an addition onto their building to house the school in a separate wing away from the main tavern. "I heartily agree on your proposal," Reverend Ashford told the meeting. "I think we can all accept their concession." George agreed, as did Marsden and the others.

Reverend Ashford said that he could help them for a few more years as a circuit rider but what they needed was a resident minister. The Methodists had already voiced that they would be soon building their own church somewhere on Côte St. Charles and a resident minister would be coming to live there. "The sooner we get your own church," Ashford continued, "the less chance you lose some of your potential parishioners over to the Methodists."

"Never!" James Henderson spoke up loudly.

"Don't bet on it sir," Ashford continued. "I have seen it happen over here before. Just up river at Carillon, the Methodists built a church for the soldiers a couple of years before we did at Cushing and we lost many a family until our own church was built. The families came back all right, but for a period of time my services were held before a very small congregation. People like the comfort of a real church so the sooner you get yours in operation and built, the better."

Marsden agreed to have some pews built and to try to find an organ. He was a wealthy man, owning a great deal of land and had numerous connections in Montréal and Québec. "I guarantee that we will have an organ here in Cavagnal by September or my name isn't John Augustus Marsden."

With that, the meeting adjourned and all the men gathered up their families and left for home. Before leaving, all the guests thanked the Schmidts for their kind hospitality and generosity for holding such a wonderful wedding. It had been the highlight of the spring and many hoped that it was a good omen for the coming summer. Of course, George and Mary were the proud parents of the bride and everyone was very happy for them also. They left arm in arm with the rest of their large family for the short walk up the King's Road to their own home. All of Cavagnal would sleep in peace that night.

Chapter 11
Religion and Education

The summer of 1825 was a busy one in the growing community. Plans were laid for the building of a church in the western section of the small village but until funds were obtained, Marsden's store was going to have to do. The Methodists up on Côte St. Charles could not gather enough funds either and continued to use their circuit rider, Reverend Angus Bradfield, from Côteau du Lac to administer their services.

Down in Cavagnal, the French Canadians were also having problems. Though their community was much larger than the English community, having settled in the area much earlier, not one new French family had settled in the area since F.X. Deschamps had arrived in 1820. However, until the English started talking about having their own churches and schools, not much thought had been given by the French Catholics.

F.X. Deschamps had become the leader in the French community of Cavagnal even though he had been in the community for only five years. Though he and George Henderson did not see eye to eye with each other, they tried to put their differences behind them when Deschamps met George one day at Schmidt's Tavern. Marsden also happened to be there and the three agreed that education and religion were going to be priorities of both sides of the community, French and English, and they should all work together to achieve that goal.

"I cannot believe what I am hearing or seeing," William Schmidt said quietly to his son as they both watched the other three men talk about religion and education.

"It is quite ironic father," replied Charles. "Here we are in a tavern and they talk about religion and education, French and English together."

"Times are changing son," William added. "Just think, a few years ago those two men would have killed Deschamps as soon as they had laid eyes on him. Wars change men, and hopefully we have seen the last of war for a long time."

"I cannot see us having a Catholic church here in the near future," Deschamps told the two Englishmen. "We French are not united enough. With the big Parish of St. Michel de Vaudreuil just down river and another one with a strong influence west of here in Rigaud, I believe it will be many years before we have a resident priest here at Cavagnal. However, I have to support your ideas about a school for the local children. I cannot help you build a church, except in supplying certain necessities, and I cannot help you financially. If word ever reached my family in Montreal that I had helped build an English church, I would bring a great dishonour to the rest of my family and would forever be an outcast. I cannot risk that. I hope you understand, George and John."

Both George and John wholeheartedly agreed and they fully understood the Frenchman's predicament. "But as for the school, I can help and I will support you both," Deschamps added. "If you cannot use the Tavern here, why not my store?" It was a good idea, but the English residents had already agreed that the eastern school would be at Schmidt's Tavern.

"I have an idea," said Marsden. "Why not have a French school in Deschamps' store? He has agreed to let us use it, so why not organise a community school board for both the French and English. We already have one English school up on the Grand Côte and two more English schools planned. Why not join with the French and all work together?"

Both William and Charles Schmidt were flabbergasted; they both could not believe what they were hearing. Two former British army men who had fought and hated the French for years were now planning a joint venture with one that was very much despised in the English community.

George stood up and stretched his weary muscles. He too could not believe what he was hearing. However, even though he did not really like Deschamps, Marsden's idea was a great one and he voiced his approval. "This calls for a round of drinks," George told his friends. "I know I am not supposed to be drinking, but this calls for a celebration. One round please Charles," he called.

F.X. Deschamps agreed to Marsden's idea as well and promised to try to persuade his fellow citizens to go along with the joint project. "If only Isaac could see us now," George thought, "I bet you he is turning over in his watery grave hearing this," he muttered quietly. "Me, George Henderson working together with the French. Will wonders never cease?"

John Marsden raised his tankard of ale and called for a toast. The four others raised theirs as Marsden spoke some carefully chosen words, "To Cavagnal and our new found French and English community spirit. May it live forever!" With that, the five men quenched their thirst and all shook each other's hand.

There would be lots of plans that needed going over and several more meetings would need to be held, either at Marsden's or Deschamps' store. "I hope the rest of the locals agree with our project," Deschamps said to the others.

"I think they will," replied George. "We are all living here in this new land and striving to make a meagre existence out of the wilderness. Civilization is slowly coming and we all have noticed the influx of new settlers, even since my arrival last year."

"The French will continue to attend the Vaudreuil church whenever possible, but with so many children in the area and more arriving each month, we all have to agree that education is a necessity for all the residents, young and old."

Marsden added that the community was most fortunate in having a Community Cemetery that was situated about a half a mile west of his store. He said that this spot would be the ideal location for a new church when and if it was ever built.

George told them that the question was not if, but when. They all agreed. Deschamps had not known of the Community Cemetery since most of the Catholics that had died over the past five years had been buried in Vaudreuil. He asked his friends to tell him more about the small cemetery.

"Before you arrived," Charles Schmidt told him, "many French Canadians were buried in the little cemetery that was donated by my father and John Whetstone in 1817. Before that, anyone who died was normally buried over at Côteau du Lac in the Fort's cemetery. William and John had initially said that the cemetery would be a free one for all Protestants, but some Catholics have been buried there. They were usually married to an English person of Protestant heritage therefore they were accepted into the Community Cemetery.

"There is one problem, however," Marsden added. "We have no school teachers. The Grand Côte School is doing well with their teacher, Mr. Grampian, but he cannot and will not be able to handle three schools. As for a teacher for the French school, what do you think François? Who can you get and from where?"

Deschamps smiled and said, "No problem. My sister Juliette is a nun in Montreal and would be willing to come out and teach. I wrote to her last year about this and she agreed then, so I am ahead of you in that respect."

"Good. That is settled," Marsden added. "But as for the English speaking population, does anyone have an idea who we can hire to be our teacher? George had been quiet most of the time but finally came up with a wild idea.

"While I was at sea last spring, I met a fine young 1st Lieutenant in the Royal Navy by the name of John Benson. He seemed to be a very capable man with a great future in the Navy but his wound that occurred in our battle with the pirate ship proved to be more serious than he thought.

"He was wounded over the eye and that has caused him to lose the sight in it."

"So," Marsden said, "Nelson had only one eye and look what he did."

Deschamps could not help replying in a sarcastic tone of voice, "And look what it got him: death at Trafalgar." The Schmidts immediately felt an increase in the tension in the room with that last statement, but George calmed the situation down by stating that though Nelson had died in battle with the French and Spanish at Trafalgar, Napoleon's idea of invading England had been laid to rest.

"Anyway, so much for history," interjected Marsden. "What about this Benson fellow, have you been in contact with him recently George?"

"I have," stated George, "a few times. He had to retire from the Navy, not so much because of the loss of his eye but for what it did to him mentally. He is not crazy, he just lost his confidence and he could no longer command a King's ship. With the Admiralty's permission, he has retired and is now at Halifax.

"He is well educated and I think he would make a fine teacher for one of our two new schools. I know that I can convince him to come here." The three committee members agreed, as did the Schmidts who were still listening.

"Now for the last teacher," Deschamps added, "is anyone around here qualified?"

"My wife is," said William Schmidt. "She is well educated and now that she is retired from the Tavern, thanks to John and Jane Cameron, she will probably love to do it. And you all know how she loves children. Let me run upstairs right away to ask her."

The old man went upstairs and soon came down with his wife Caroline. She spoke first at the bottom of the stairs, "Of course I will be your new teacher! I would love to! This is just the perfect place to teach. My health has improved and I feel that I can handle the job."

With that, the meeting broke up and Deschamps, Henderson and Marsden all headed home while Charles and his father cleaned up the Tavern. There had been no travellers that day so the cleanup only took a few minutes.

"Father," Charles, said to William, "I think we are going to have to hire some people to build us a better wharf."

"Why?" asked the elder Schmidt.

"There is some talk amongst some of the more recent west bound travellers that some man in Montréal is planning to have a small steam boat operating on the river between St. Anne's and Carillon next summer. He is Captain De Hertel and the boat is being built right now in Montreal."

"That should really open up this region and that west of here," William added. "I agree we will need a new and much bigger wharf. See to it tomorrow, Charles. Maybe you can hire some of Simon's friends from across the lake and some of the young lads such as John Henderson."

"He is busy on the farm father," Charles added. "However, I know Simon's friends will come. Remember how they helped us build our present wharf?"

"Yes I do," replied William. "Those Mohawks are great friends to us here in Cavagnal. I foresee a long and friendly relationship with them, as long as someone does not feed them liquor."

"I hear Deschamps has been doing that recently," Charles added.

"Bloody Frenchman. Everything for money; that is his way. I wonder how he expects to make a profit by having a school in his store. I am sure he has some plans, knowing him," William added. "We have to all work together on this school project and not let personal feelings get in our way. I am pleased to see that George Henderson has come around and is now talking with him in a peaceful manner. Remember last winter, Charles?"

"I do, very well. It got quite nasty at times. I am pleased George has stopped drinking. It was killing him. Doctor Grisenthwaite definitely helped him as did Reverend Ashford and his dear wife Mary. She really is a strong woman, having to raise all those children and having to have to put up with George's terrible fits of rage last winter. This school and church committee have made him a new man and he is showing it, thank God."

Chapter 12
A New Friendship

As 1825 turned from summer to autumn and progress to begin the three new schools rapidly advanced, a new and long lasting friendship began to mould. With meetings being held each week for the "Cavagnal Amalgamated School Committee," two of its prime organisers, John Marsden and George Henderson, began to form a strong and deep friendship.

Marsden mutually shared George's dislike and mistrust of F.X. Deschamps and they discussed their feelings at length over many a cup of tea or coffee. George's heavy drinking was now long behind him and he was feeling more like his old self than ever before. Mary Henderson had been a great support to her beloved husband and with all their children doing well in their new home, especially little Elizabeth now fifteen months old, life in their new homeland was turning out better than they had ever hoped.

One night in October, while discussing a plan about how to get John Benson to Cavagnal before the winter locked in the Ottawa River with a heavy ice pack for six months, the two school committee members began to reminisce about their days in the British Army.

George had casually mentioned that his old friend Isaac Kirkbride was the best shot in their regiment. "What regiment was that, George?" asked Marsden. George was quite surprised, as he had thought that most residents of Cavagnal had already heard of his exploits in the Rifle Brigade in Spain and France under Wellington.

"Why the 1st/95th Rifles of course," George replied. "I did not know that you were not aware of my service under Wellington so many years ago."

Marsden replied, "That I guess I have never really had a chance to get to know you since you moved here last year—and the distance between my store and your farm has proven to be a great hindrance."

"I know you were in the Army also, John, but where and when did you serve?" asked George.

With Marsden's immense land holdings in the region and his great wealth, which he was not ashamed to discuss, George figured that Marsden had held a position much higher in rank than his own of Sergeant Major.

George began by stating, "I was a Sergeant Major with the 1st/95th Rifles in Spain and later in France. My last battle was supposed to have been at Waterloo until our infamous encounter with the Spanish pirate last year off of Nova Scotia."

"Maybe we were at a few of the famous Peninsular battles together," Marsden replied, "because I too served under Lord Wellington in Spain and later at Waterloo, which was my last battle."

"I was at Ciudad Rodrigo, Badajoz, and Vitoria—and many other smaller skirmishes," George said.

"So was I," answered Marsden. "So was I. However, it seems that our paths never crossed. At Badajoz I watched your gallant commander storm the breach with a decimated company and lead the way for the rest of us. Were you in that company George?"

"I was," George responded quietly. "I was. What a mess that was."

George continued by stating that the initial attack was so bad and the "Forlorn Hope" never had a chance. "However, with Wellington's persistence and refusal to pull back to regroup, the repeated attacks up that breach finally wore the men right out, as you probably know, John.

"When we finally made it in and won the battle, Wellington's commanders were not able to control their men—thus "The Rape of

Badajoz". It was awful, as you know. Did you ever make it into the city, John?"

"Yes, but not until the next day and after the hangings had begun. Too bad Wellington had to do it but those hangings of his own men curtailed future problems later on. We lost only thirty-three men that day since we were in reserve until near the end. What about you, George? Did your company lose many men?"

"We lost one hundred and forty three and seventy-five or so were wounded or went missing," he replied. "Very high casualties for our already badly depleted battalion.

"After losing our Regimental commander at Ciudad Rodrigo and the loss of over two hundred men killed or wounded and seven others to the hangings, our little Rifle Brigade was reduced to just a shadow of its former self. We asked for men from a reserve Brigade in England but they did not arrive until mid-1813.

"By the way, which regiment were you with John?" asked George.

"Well I was originally in the Royal Navy and served at Trafalgar on board *HMS Téméraire*. I was Captain Harvey's clerk. I was able to earn a few extra pounds with our prize money and bought myself a commission in the army. I had seen enough of the world in the navy, so where did I end up? Spain and Portugal as a damn foot soldier!"

"I was originally with the 77th Regiment of Foot raised in East Middlesex. We were brigaded under Picton and fought for the first time at El Rodon in 1811. Were you there George?"

"No, I was on a scouting party further north at the time," he added.

Marsden continued his own personal account by saying "I was initially a 2nd Lieutenant but when there was a chance to be transferred into Beresford's 2nd Elvas in early 1813, I took the chance. Being from a not-too-wealthy family, I had been destined for a lowly life as a 2nd or 1st Lieutenant in the 77th. In the 2nd Elvas, I was immediately promoted to Major. Within a month I was a Lieutenant Colonel, then after Vitoria I was finally promoted to a full Colonel. None of these were brevet ranks, so I was able to hold the rank as the war progressed into France.

"This has provided me with a substantial pension these past few years and with the treasure we found after Vitoria, I have done quite well for myself."

"That treasure helped me as well," George added.

"A Sergeant Major's pension is not all that great but the extra funds that famous treasure brought to many a good man including ourselves have enabled me to live a comfortable life in England and now here. Unfortunately not all of us used the money as wisely as we both did."

"I agree," Marsden said.

The treasure they both spoke of had been for Napoleon's courts while in Spain and Portugal. It had been put on a large pack train hurrying away from Vitoria after the French defeat there in June 1813. It was captured by the victorious British troops.

George's 95th Rifles and Marsden's Grenadier Company in the 17th Regiment of the reformed Portuguese Army (2nd Elvas) were the first two British line regiments to arrive on the scene. Both were serving in Alten's Light Division that day. The French guard put up a meagre attempt of trying to defend their valuable cargo. But after the severe defeat earlier in the day, the French soldiers did not have the heart or the willingness to try and protect their precious cargo for their beloved Emperor. The French soldiers were killed, captured, or just ran away from the British onslaught.

Wellington's Provost Corps arrived too late to save most of the treasure. It had been looted by the common soldiers and many of their officers, George Henderson and John Marsden among them. Millions of pounds of Spanish and Portuguese gold and jewels were lost but enough was saved by the Provost Corps for Wellington that the loss was hardly noticed.

"Old Nosey" was able to pay off the immense Army debts, return some to the rightful owners and keep some himself. No soldiers were punished for the looting as no Spanish homes or citizens were directly involved. Had there been, more hangings would have occurred as Wellington strictly forbade looting the local population. However, the treasure had been in the hands of the French at the time of its capture even though it was of Portuguese and Spanish origins.

George would not tell Marsden how much he had received that day but he did tell him that it had been enough to make his retirement life in Dufton quite comfortable. Marsden on the other hand had done well, largely due to his rank in the army. He had invested his money wisely and when he had come to North America in 1820, he had purchased a huge tract of land in the 1st Concession of the Fief Cavagnal for only two hundred pounds.

This was just a pittance of what he had in his account and John A. Marsden was by far the wealthiest Englishman in the whole Seigneury, probably wealthier than the Seigneur himself, down in Vaudreuil.

As the two old soldiers talked, they discussed their exploits after Vitoria, particularly Waterloo. George recounted his regiment's action at Quatre Bras, two days before Waterloo. George had once again served with the 1st/95th under Kempt at both Quatre Bras and Waterloo. Kempt's 8th Brigade forces were under the direct command of General Sir Thomas Picton and everyone had extreme confidence in the General even though he had numerous rough traits. But that did not bother his men on the battlefield. He was an excellent field commander; one of Wellington's best.

At Quatre Bras and Waterloo, Marsden explained that he had served with the Light Division in Alten's 3rd Division. "Unfortunately for us," he told George, "whereas you served under General Picton, our commander was that damn youngster, The Prince of Orange. He had more of my men killed with terrible orders at Quatre Bras than anyone else did and he almost lost the battle for Wellington at Waterloo.

"I had switched back into the regular British Army after we had left Spain and I joined up with 2/73rd under Alten. I served as a Colonel throughout our march north from the Spanish border and into Waterloo," Marsden explained

"How I was not killed at Quatre Bras along with all my men, I do not know. However, I did watch as the 2/69th was mauled when The Prince ordered them to break square even though the French cavalry was advancing on them. I even saw the French capture the King's colours that day. What a terrible loss that was to the 69th. I had to threaten many a man with death, as many of them wanted to shoot the "Gallant Prince" themselves. We were all very pleased when he was wounded at Waterloo and carried from the field. I would not be surprised if one of our own men did actually shoot that bastard. He sure deserved it."

Marsden remembered how his immediate superior, General Alten, had been struck down at Waterloo by a French bullet. However, his men had more respect for him than the Prince of Orange's men had for their leader. Marsden and a couple of other Colonels had then taken over command of what remained of their regiments and were able to stem the tide of British losses and help save Wellington's beleaguered right side.

Marsden knew that George must have been on Wellington's left since he had served under Kempt that day. George related how they had taken a terrible loss in the beginning of the battle while positioned in a sandpit out in front of the main British lines.

"We lost a great many men in that pit, but I was one of the lucky ones, I guess," George told Marsden. "Some of the men who had been with us from the beginning down in Spain and Portugal died in that miserable sand pit. When we pulled back to regroup, over half of us were left to die or were already dead. I was glad to see Picton's men as they held the ridge and provided us with a withering cover fire as we retreated up the hill to regroup."

"You know John, I have never spoken to anyone except to my late friend Isaac Kirkbride, about what happened. It is sad to think about it, but I am glad I can talk to someone who really understands what happened on those two terrible days. Thanks for being my friend, John. I really appreciate it."

Marsden and Henderson had both been there, but their paths had never crossed until their lives had come together in Cavagnal so many years later. Both men had survived the hell of Quatre Bras, Waterloo and the endless struggles in the Peninsular War and now they were serving together once again. However, this time it was for the betterment of their community, not the world.

"What do you think of F.X. Deschamps, George? I am quite concerned about his political ideas and certain connections he has with some very unfavourable men of this area, especially down in Vaudreuil near the Seigneur's home."

George was quite taken aback at first with Marsden's question and thoughts as he thought that he was the only one who was concerned about F.X. Deschamps. "I have not liked that little weasel since the first time I met him," George told his friend. "I know we are all working together right now on setting up a proper school system for our little community. I was quite surprised that Deschamps would have anything to do with us, since there are so few French speaking residents right now here in Cavagnal."

"You are right, George," Marsden said. "I am amazed that F.X. decided to help out. He has some very powerful friends in Montréal and there are already rumblings about an uprising sometime soon. My contacts with the British garrison in Montréal have told me that. They have seen and heard of numerous clandestine meetings going on in certain homes of wealthy and very influential Frenchmen in Montréal and Lachine. The soldiers have already seized many weapons from some of these French Canadians or "Patriotes" as they now call themselves.

"George, I would watch Mr. F.X. Deschamps with a very close eye and please advise me on any strange happenings at his store. Maybe his housekeeper, Mary Kilkenny, could help us spy on him. Do you know her very well, George?"

"No I don't, but my daughter is becoming quite friendly with her."

"You live much closer to him than I do and I understand that you shop there from time to time."

"That I do, John, that I do. I would go to your place, but it is, as you know, three and half miles from my place, whereas that weasel's store is only less than a mile from my house.

"I will watch him for sure and let you know if I spot anything strange. I will also ask Jane to speak to Mary about her boss, too. I do not really think they will ever get married as some local residents believe. If you do not mind, I will also ask Joseph Shouldice to watch him as he is there more often than I am these days."

"Good. That is settled," John told his new friend. "We will do well together. I am planning to be the new Justice of the Peace in this area if I can get permission from the Seigneur's Agent and Governor Dalhousie when he is in Montréal next summer. Will you be my assistant, George? I will need a Sheriff and you would be the right person I think."

"Sheriff?" thought George. "I never thought I would become that. I will talk it over with Mary and the children and get back to you in a few days, John. Does it pay anything?" Marsden told him it would pay about fifty pounds a year and that would help anybody in these hard times, especially a man like George with a large family.

"Sounds good, John. I will see you in a few days with my answer."

On arriving home that day, George was in one of his old but all too few great moods. He had the prospects of a new job, he had a great new friend in Marsden and things were working out so well in their new home in Cavagnal.

"Mary, John Marsden has asked me to become his Sheriff when he gets elected as the local Justice of the Peace next summer. What do you think, dear? It would pay fifty pounds a year."

"My, George. That money would be great to add to our meagre wages now. But is it dangerous?"

"I do not really think so, dear. What dangers have you seen in this area since we moved here last year? There has been no crime at all and everyone is paying his or her rent to the Seigneur as far as I know. However, I imagine there are a few not doing too well. I would not want to have to pass a foreclosure on one of my best friends in my duties as Sheriff.

"Let us think about it over the next few days and discuss it with Jane and John."

"By the way George," Mary said, "John wants to talk to you about some trip he and a few friends want to take next summer.

"The boys are over at Schmidt's right now working on that new wharf for the new steam boat that is expected here next summer. Some lads from Kanesatake are here and talking about heading west next spring. I think you had better go and talk with them, especially that son of yours."

"I will do that right now," George said quietly, all the time wondering what adventure his eldest son had in mind for the upcoming summer of 1826.

George pondered the loss of his eldest son in some wild adventure in the woods of Canada. It would leave him without his right hand man at home. Little William would only be eleven by next summer, too young to be of any use on their small farm. With Jane now married and working at the Inn, his eldest children left at home would be Frances, fifteen, and Margaret, twenty. If John did head west, he would need some more help on the farm and around the house. "Too bad those two Indians we met in Québec never came to visit; they would be a great help around here. I wonder if Aron'hio:tas knows them? I will go over to Kanesatake tomorrow after talking with John and ask him if he knows how to get in touch with Sori'howane and Awen'rah:ton. I would really like to have a couple of their long rifles they promised me when we met in Québec."

George found his son down by the river working with Simon Beauvais, Charles Schmidt, John Cameron, and a couple of Indians from across the river in Kanesatake. The six young men were hard at work constructing the new dock in front of the Tavern. Charles Schmidt had received news that a new steamboat would be on the river by the end of May 1826, and to entice it to stop at his famous Tavern, a new and very sturdy dock had to be constructed.

The owners of the steamboat would be sending a survey party around before the ice took over the Ottawa River to check on potential sites for landing. All the residents of Cavagnal knew that Schmidt's Tavern was the most logical spot in the area on the south shore of the Lake of The Two Mountains to have the new dock but one could never be sure what F.X. Deschamps had in mind either. Rumours had it that he was also trying to have the steamboat stop at his small wharf.

The main thing that favoured the Schmidt location over that of Deschamps' was the deeper water off of the Tavern. It averaged six feet, and off of Deschamps' store it was only three feet in wet weather and in dry weather, it was down to two. Charles Schmidt was sure that the steamboat would be stopping at his new wharf after making the passage across from Oka and Vaudreuil before that.

The owners of the steamboat promised a trip from Ste. Anne de Bellevue to Carillon in just three hours. Unfortunately, it would probably put many a bateau man out of work and that is why John Cameron and his friends were thinking of a trip west that coming summer. George Henderson was soon to get an earful of high adventure and wild exploration west of Cavagnal, in the upper reaches of the Ottawa River system.

Chapter 13
Education Begins

Retired Naval 1st Lieutenant John Benson arrived in late November 1825, just before the ice took hold of the Lake of the Two Mountains for yet another long winter.

The School Committee greeted John Benson at Schmidt's Tavern and making the official welcome speech was George Henderson. He had not seen John, of course, since they had parted company in Halifax the year before. However, he had made a lasting impression on George and Mary and they had kept up their friendship, writing to each other whenever possible.

John Benson was to receive a yearly salary of twenty pounds, equal to that of Mrs Schmidt, F.X. Deschamp's sister, and what was already being paid to Mr. Grampian up on Côte St. Charles. Eighty pounds was a lot of money for the small community to afford but all those involved believed it was necessary to keep the schools provided with a good qualified teacher and provide the ever growing community with the education that was so needed.

John Benson was to be billeted at first in Marsden's store with Marsden and his wife. "I want to find a small place for myself as soon as possible," Benson told his friends upon arrival. "I appreciate your hospitality but I want to make a real go at being a good teacher for your children and I feel that being on my own would be better so I can study and plan my lessons."

George and John Marsden both agreed that was no problem. "I am sure you will be able to find a piece of land close by the school," Marsden told him. "However, not until spring because winter is almost here and you will be staying with my wife and me until then."

"Agreed," Benson told him, "but only until spring. I will do some scouting around in the next few weeks for a nice quiet place. How far is it from this place called Schmidt's Tavern to your store Mr. Marsden?" Benson asked his new landlord and employer.

"About three and a half miles I believe, we will take my buggy. We will find you a horse or a horse and buggy soon enough."

"I would like to set up a meeting with all the other teachers as soon as possible," Benson told Marsden on their trip up to his new home and school house. Marsden told him that he would do that as soon as possible. "We should be able to start school just after Christmas if all goes well. I am glad that there is already a school in operation. That way we will be able to pattern some things after Mr. Grampian's curriculum. I would like most of all to meet him," said Benson.

"That will be easy, John," replied Marsden. "Mr. Grampian comes down to my store once a week for supplies and the local news. Nice man and an American by birth but a real loyalist. His family fled the Colonies a number of years ago and settled on the "Grand Côte", as we call it, just after the Concession was opened up for emigrant settlers in 1810. I think they arrived in 1811. He and his father and brothers are very dedicated community workers and I know that you will like them. Mr Grampian was a Hessian mercenary during the Revolution and remained there for a period but was not well liked by the Americans for reasons that are quite easily understood. He left in 1780 and arrived in Halifax then ended up here as I have already said in 1811.

"Besides a Swiss family near Schmidt's place who arrived here in 1801, the Schmidts who arrived here in 1804, and that strange William Whetstone who arrived a year later, the Grampians are one of the earliest English settlers in the area. They are, of course, the earliest settlers on the Côte St. Charles Concession.

"You know Lieutenant Benson, there are a number of settlers here in Cavagnal now that are not of English backgrounds. I have never really thought about it until now. There are Germans, Swiss, Irish, Scottish, Americans, and of course the French. A real melting pot of nations in such a small area."

"May I ask you a personal question, John?" Benson asked his new friend.

"Sure, what is it?"

"Why did you call Mr. Whetstone strange? It is an odd way to comment about someone whom I have never met. What is wrong with him? Or should I wait and find out for myself?"

"No, I will explain some of it, but you will judge most of what I say about Whetstone when you see him and that should not be too long. He visits my store at least two or three times a week. All I can say is that he is a very good friend of Mr. F.X. Deschamps. Deschamps has some very strong connections, we believe, with a small group we call "Patriots" in Montréal. They are dedicated to the destruction of the British Government rule here in British North America, especially Québec. I do not trust either man."

Marsden was pleased with his first encounters with Lieutenant John Benson and he told George Henderson about this and congratulated him on his suggestion of hiring Benson as the new schoolteacher.

"I am a little worried though, George," Marsden told his friend one day during the long winter of 1825.

"About what?" George asked.

"I do not think there will be enough young students here in Cavagnal and up on the Grand Côte for all three schools to survive. As for the French school down at Deschamps' store, who knows what will happen. There hasn't been a new French-speaking family move into this area since F.X. Deschamps five years ago. I cannot see how his school will continue."

"I know his sister is very qualified and comes highly recommended by those who have met her," George answered. "However, I see your point John. How many French families are there in Cavagnal right at the moment, and with children at that?"

"At my last count in July of this year, there were only four French families but with a total of seventeen children. George, those four French families have more children of school age than Mrs Schmidt has in her whole school. But I cannot see how Deschamps' school will last. Those four families are far too poor to help pay their teacher's salary of twenty pounds a year. At least in the English community there are close to one hundred families who can pay for the three teachers we have hired. Luckily the four teacher's salaries will be subsidised somewhat by a grant for the next few years from the Government in Montréal which has seen it worthwhile that we begin education in this area. "The Government will be giving our school board, now known officially as the Cavagnal and Area School Board, a total subsidy of thirty five pounds a year for the next five years.

"That is great, John," George said to his friend. "Do you think they will support you and me as well when we become the law in this area next year?"

"I hope so George, at least our salaries will be better. However, in these rough times I would not say no to thirty five pounds a year, especially if I had a family to raise like the Lolands or you yourself do George. That fifty pounds you will be receiving beginning in July of next year should set you up in this community as a man of great importance and wealth."

Early in October, George had decided that he would take on the job as the Sheriff of Cavagnal. "With your army pension, your salary, and what you have left from the war in Spain, I think that you will do just fine in this community, George Henderson. I see you getting more land and progressing nicely as a man of leadership as the years go by. Good luck my friend."

"Thanks John, but that is not until next summer. What about now? Do you think we can keep these schools going through this winter or should we shut them down? It is very hard for the children to get through the deep snow each day. Should we have a month or two off this winter and continue the school session into June and July with August off as another vacation period?"

"Good question, George. We will have to get a meeting together soon with the School Board and the four teachers and see what they have to say."

"As soon as possible, I think, John, as soon as possible. I know my children are having it easy as they do not live too far from Caroline Schmidt's school, but I hear that up on the Grand Côte the children are having a very rough time getting to school and it is just the beginning of January.

"Let us set up next Saturday as a date for a meeting. It should be here, John, as it will be easier for Grampian to get down here from the Grand Côte. You are more central than anyone is. I will bring up Sister Juliette and Caroline Schmidt with me in my sleigh. Can you get a hold of the others on the Board and have them here for say 11:00 am on Saturday?"

"I will do that George," replied a smiling Marsden. "And you can chair the meeting!"

Saturday, January 14th, 1826 was a warm and sunny day with temperatures just above freezing. "A perfect day for a sleigh ride, don't you think George and Sister Juliette?" Caroline Schmidt asked her companions as the three of them headed west along the trail towards Marsden's Store.

"Yes, a fine day it is. Too bad we have to spend it inside at yet another meeting, but this is something that has to be solved now as we must think of the safety and health of our children."

"I totally agree with you," Sister Juliette said in broken English. "I have already had one child die this winter from pneumonia and two others are also very sick. If we decide to close the schools for a period this winter, I think many young lives will be saved."

"I hope you mention those points at the meeting, Sister Juliette," George told her as they headed up the last hill before Marsden's Store.

Solomon Grampian was already in Marsden's Store when George Henderson, Caroline Schmidt, and Sister Juliette Deschamps arrived just before 11:00 am.

"Did you have a nice ride up along the river road, George?" Solomon asked.

"Yes it was nice especially with these two fine ladies to accompany me." Both ladies laughed loudly at that and Sister Juliette broke out in a rosy red blush.

Not many men had seen her since her arrival and had she not been a member of the Order of Grey Nuns in Montréal, she might have made some man a very proud husband. Not only was Sister Juliette a strong woman for her age, but she was a very beautiful one too. She would make many a young man turn his head and stare after she became better known in the community as the months progressed.

"My brother François Xavier will be along shortly," Sister Juliette told John Marsden. "He is up seeing his friend William Whetstone whom I believe lives just west of here. Am I right?" she asked.

"Oh yes. Mr. Whetstone lives not far from here," Marsden replied in somewhat of a sarcastic tone of voice. Sister Juliette looked at him, not understanding what he meant.

George whispered to Sister Juliette that many in the area thought Whetstone was a bit strange and a radical, but explained that he himself had never met the man and still had not been told by Marsden why people thought Whetstone was strange. "One day I guess we will find out."

F.X. Deschamps arrived just after 11:15 am and with that, the meeting came to order. Sister Juliette, Caroline Schmidt, Lieutenant John Benson, and Solomon Grampian had all previously met on a couple of occasions in early December. They had discussed their curriculum, trying to match their ideas and lessons as closely as possible. It had been very difficult for Sister Juliette because her curriculum was mostly based on religious studies of the Catholic Church rather than a strong emphasis on mathematics, geography, grammar, and spelling. But the English classes did, however, study the Bible to a great extent; just not as intensely as the French school.

Of course, Sister Juliette's classes were all in French while the other three schools were all in English. However, this meeting was not to discuss curriculum, but the future of the four existing schools.

Grampian announced that he had more than thirty children five years before but now had thirteen on the best days. "Since winter has set in and because of sickness, I have, on average, eight to ten children on any given day." Lieutenant Benson had been teaching for only three weeks but his classes were almost full with a total of twenty-five children each day. Sickness was low among his children but a couple were presently very ill with pneumonia and he was not sure if they would survive. "Dr. Grisenthwaite is supposed to come down to look at all the children this coming week," he announced. "I hope he will be able to check Mrs Schmidt's classes as well as Sister Juliette's."

Caroline Schmidt told him that the Doctor would be most welcome and Sister Juliette agreed. Caroline also mentioned that Doctor Grisenthwaite would be able to stay overnight at their Tavern as it would be too much for him to ride all the way back up to St. Henry the same day.

Sister Juliette then announced that she had already lost one of her children to pneumonia and was worried about three others. Caroline Schmidt's report was like Lieutenant Benson's; good attendance since late December when her classes had begun and no children were off sick, yet.

"With the decline in Solomon's classes," Marsden began, "I see a trend in us bringing all the children into once central school in a few months. No one should be let off as a teacher. That would not be fair, as three of you have just been hired. But with already declining enrolments this winter, maybe it would be best if we consolidate a couple or all of the three English schools into one central one. What do you think?"

"Where would that leave Sister Juliette?" George and Caroline asked simultaneously.

"Unfortunately alone, I guess," Marsden said quietly.

"That is not fair at all!" F.X. Deschamps said loudly as he jumped to his feet. "We all agreed to set up an education system here in Cavagnal and already, just weeks after it has begun, you are threatening to dismantle it and separate it completely. I will not stand for this at all! Come my dear sister; let us leave these damn English with their big ideas. I see that they do not really want anything to do with us French Canadians. They will soon learn otherwise, I am afraid."

With that, F.X. Deschamps grabbed his sister by the arm and took their hats and coats and headed out the door in a hurry. Sister Juliette did not even have time to raise her voice in protest and George was not even sure she would have if her raving brother had let her voice her opinion.

"Well, he does not surprise me one bit," Marsden announced finally, breaking a long period of stunned silence among the remaining members of the School Committee. "It is only twelve noon and we have now have one less school to worry about. What do you want to do, my friends?"

"Well," said Caroline Schmidt, "I think we should approach the Deschamps and try to get them back. I think you were too harsh in your ideas and had no right to speak that way. I see that you really do not like the French and are glad that they have gone their own way. I do not like the way F.X. left with that threat, "they will soon learn otherwise." I wonder what he meant by that comment?"

PART II

Chapter 14
West to Fort William

The winter of 1825-26 finally had its back broken by mid-March. It had been a very difficult period with many young children dying of the influenza epidemic that had swept the area in late January and then again in mid-February. Just two of the schools finally reopened on April 1st but there were young faces missing from the already small attendances. Some families had been decimated with the loss of two or three children each.

John Benson's school in Marsden's building had lost four students out of a class of twenty-five. Caroline Schmidt's classes were down by six from fifteen and up on the Grand Côte, the small school that had originally only thirteen students was down to just four. Most had died in January while others passed away in late February.

Grampian's school was one of the area schools that had to close that fateful winter. The other was Sister Juliette Deschamps' school in her brother's store. Of her eight children, only two remained. F.X. Deschamps had angrily left that meeting that proposed the closing of the area schools on account of the cold and sickness.

His sister had kept her school open until late February but had finally closed the small school when all of her students ended up sick one day. By the end of the week, she would have only three left alive and in just three weeks she would have only two of her original eight young students left alive.

Even the adults of the community were not immune. Several senior residents passed away in January, and in February, eight more died from the ravages of the influenza epidemic. Poor Dr. Grisenthwaite was powerless to help as the local residents fell victim to the sickness day after day.

He had heard that the influenza epidemic had killed hundreds in Montréal and in Québec as well. Rumours had abounded that it had arrived from the United States on the last ship to make it up the St. Lawrence before the winter's ice took a firm grip on the great river. Unfortunately, by the time the river had begun to freeze solid, the influenza epidemic was already rampant around Montréal, especially in its poorer neighbourhoods.

Funerals were held almost every day in and around Montreal. Out in Cavagnal, Vaudreuil and even Rigaud, the local clergy, were kept busy with almost as many funerals as services of worship. Over in Kanesatake, however, the epidemic did not take hold at all and only a couple of people became sick. These were white residents who lived near the Catholic Church in the village of Oka, just east of the Mohawk village.

By mid-February, word of the lack of sick people in Kanesatake became well known on the south shore of the Lake of the Two Mountains and John Cameron crossed over to the native village to see what was keeping the residents so healthy.

"We are taking some of our herbal medicines," Simon Beauvais told his long time friend.

"Can we get some of them for our residents?" John asked Simon.

"I am sure we have lots but it will not help those who are already sick," he said, "only those who are reasonably healthy. And I guess there are not many of those over in Cavagnal right now, eh John? However, I will ask Chief Aron'hio:tas for permission to give you what you need."

"Thanks very much," John said to his good friend. Simon continued by saying, "Actually there are quite a few of us who are healthy; much healthier than we expected to be after this terrible winter. The herb we take is Echinacea. I take it just as I feel that my nose is becoming congested. It prevents the cold, which as you know leads into your influenza sickness after a few days.

"We have been taking this herb for as long as I can remember, John and it works for us. The Hurons have no access to it as they are not as civilized as we are, nor do they practice farming. Therefore they contract your white man's diseases more than we do.

"I will give you a large parcel of the Echinacea if you come back tomorrow," Simon told his dear friend. "I will have to gather some up from our supply and treat it by burning some sweet grass under it."

"What will that do? John asked Simon.

"I cannot tell you my brother; Mohawk secret!" Simon winked at his friend and just smiled.

"I will be back tomorrow afternoon, Simon," John said. "Hopefully this damn epidemic will be stopped soon. I am afraid that many more will die. We have already lost many children and the schools are all closed."

Sister Juliette's brother, F.X. Deschamps, was devastated and one day in March he headed up to meet Marsden and George Henderson to apologize for his actions back in January. They had not spoken to each other since that general meeting when he and his sister had walked out.

George and Marsden graciously accepted his apology and offered their assistance in trying to restart his school once again in the fall. He declined and said that his sister would return to Montréal as soon as the river opened up for navigation. He told them that the French school was closed in Cavagnal forever, or at least until there were enough students to make it worthwhile.

With no French-speaking Catholic families moving to the area in recent months and none expected in the coming months, the outlook for education in the French community that existed in Cavagnal was very dim. Both George and Marsden and John Benson offered Deschamps space in Benson's classes for the two remaining French speaking students and for any others who arrived that summer.

Deschamps thought it over for a short period and he agreed to ask his sister to see if she would stay on and work with John Benson in Marsden's school. Both George and Marsden thought that would be a great idea and they would also see if Mrs. Schmidt would also like to consolidate her school with Marsden's since her classes had also been drastically reduced.

It would mean longer travel for many students in the eastern part of the community but a central school at Marsden's store was the best idea and surprisingly, the idea came from F.X. Deschamps!

A notice would be sent to all families in the region by special courier offering the one central school in Marsden's store. He even promised to have an extension built on the eastern side of the store and have the classes there and upstairs as well. His wife had also agreed to share their home with the combined school. Marsden was already in the process of building a large mansion just across the road.

The Echinacea from Kanesatake turned the tide of the Cavagnal influenza epidemic and word was passed down to Vaudreuil and up river to Rigaud soon afterwards. Seigneur Lotbinière's agent, André Pambrun, was pleased at how the enterprising Englishmen in Cavagnal had defeated the dreaded epidemic and he sent word to Montréal after more of the amazing wonder herb was acquired for Vaudreuil and Rigaud as well.

However, the Mohawks of Kahnawake had also been using Echinacea and they gave some of their supply to the citizens of Montréal. Unfortunately, there was just not enough of it around and hundreds more died in Montréal before the spring arrived.

John Cameron, Simon Beauvais, and a couple of other young men arrived at the Henderson's cabin just before 9:00 am on a warm May 5th, 1826. They were there to help John Henderson convince his father to let him travel west with them to Fort William, at the western end of Lake Superior. Eleven young men from Cavagnal, Lachine, and Kanesatake would be heading west in a large canot de maitre that Angus Beauvais had made during the past winter. Angus had been asked by his son, Simon, and John to build the big canoe as John had landed a job hauling some goods for big Angus Macleod in Lachine. They had to be delivered to Fort William by early August.

If they arrived any later, there was a good chance that they would not make it back east before the winter set back in. They had not really planned to come all the way back to Cavagnal that fall anyway. John and Simon had learned that Ruggles Wright was opening up another timber right for his father just north of Wright's Village and that they would probably be able to find work there for the fall and winter seasons.

George had heard rumours of the planned expedition from the

Schmidts as John had already told Charles Schmidt that he would be leaving them in a few days. Actually he had recommended George as a replacement worker for the Schmidt family boat lines.

"Father," John Henderson began as his friends waited anxiously outside, "I would like to have your permission and, of course, mother's as well to head west on this expedition with my friends. We will be paid well. We have been promised sixty pounds. That is more than I can make here this summer and we hope to get hired on by Philomen Wright in a lumber camp for next fall and winter. I will be back in the spring, just after breakup. Can I go?"

Mary joined her husband's side and listened to her eldest son explain what would be involved in their long voyage west. "I have seen the huge canoe," Mary said. "It looks very stable and it is the same as those that we have seen stop by the tavern, is it not?"

"It is," George added. "It is about thirty five feet long from what I have seen, and at least five feet wide. I know Angus Beauvais would not send his eldest son west in a rotten old canoe. Angus is known around these parts as the best canoe builder alive. His work is even envied by the Indians over in Kahnawake, near Montréal.

"Angus Macleod has hired the others, I understand," George said to his son. "I liked Angus from the minute I laid eyes on him two years ago when he found us that boat to sail up Lake St. Louis. A little rough around the edges but he was once a voyageur, as you know. I will need you around this place this summer John. However, your mother and I know what you want to do and we have heard rumours about this voyage for some time now. It is hard to keep a secret here in Cavagnal, especially after you have heard that Charles Schmidt is looking for two men to replace his two best men as they head west for a year.

"You may go, John, but be careful. It is a completely new world out west of here and much of it is largely unexplored. There are not as many canoes on the rivers these days as there used to be what with the amalgamation of the North West Company and the Hudson Bay Company back in 1821. You know what can happen if you get hurt out there, miles from any help. You have spoken to many a voyageur that has dropped by here at Schmidt's Tavern for a well-earned break and a good meal.

"You will cross many swamps, rapids, and very rough terrain just getting to Lake Superior. Then it is many, many miles on an inland sea. Hundreds of men have been lost to that huge lake. It is said that a powerful Indian spirit by the name of 'Nanabosho' watches over the lake from his bed near Fort William. They say he is guarding a huge silver deposit at the head of Lake Superior. Be warned: DO NOT try to get any of that silver or the spirit of 'Nanabosho' may turn on you."

"Thanks for the advice and permission to go west. We will be with some very experienced canoeists from Kanesatake and Lachine. I figure that with all of us in great physical condition and only one of us is married, John, we should have a safe trip if the weather holds, especially on Lake Superior.

"Angus Macleod is even sending his own son, Iain, along with us, so he must really trust us. We even have a huge Frenchman by the name of Joseph Desormeaux from Lachine. Many a man around Montréal fears him but from what I am told, he is really a warm-hearted sole. However, he has a quick temper and is always ready to defend the honour of the French Canadians.

"My friends, I can go," yelled John to his friends outside the door. John ran out and they all began dancing around slapping each other's backs and hollering. John Cameron expressed his gratitude to his father-in-law and promised to keep a close eye on young John. John would be the youngest of the voyageurs and be one of only two from the group who had not already been west of Rigaud, situated at the western end of the Lake of the Two Mountains. The other was Allan Henderson from St. Henry.

John had traveled west to Rigaud the year before to visit one of the Roblin families who were living near the village. It had taken George and him two days on their horses. It had rained for quite some time and the bridge over the Raquette River had been washed out and it had taken them a few hours to find a decent ford on the river that was safe enough. Neither John nor his father had been west by boat, not even to Carillon to see the Royal Engineers hard at work on the boat canal.

John asked his friend, Simon, to make ready the canoe for an early departure, hopefully by May 12th. They would have to take the empty canoe down to Lachine from Kanesatake, load it up, and then bring it back upriver the next day. "I will also send word to Angus Macleod with the next group that goes by, so he can make ready all the materials that will be hauled west by us. It should take us two and a half months to head west. We should arrive just in time for the rendezvous if we are lucky. I am told by Angus Beauvais who used to work for the North West Company that the rendezvous at Fort William is not an event to be missed.

"George," John asked his father-in-law, "did you know that Fort William is the largest settlement west of Montréal?"

"I did not," George replied, "but it does not surprise me, from all the reports I have heard these past few weeks about the place."

John added, "I hear it used to be an even bigger place before the amalgamation in 1821. Sometimes there were over two thousand people staying in and around the fort. Its importance is waning now but it is still a very important link to the western side of this continent."

Mary asked John, "Where did you get all this information about such a far and remote place as Fort William?"

"Why, from all the voyageurs who stop by the tavern each year. They have told me lots of wonderful stories about the place and about the hardships they have encountered along the route and the beautiful scenery as well."

Eleven young men would be heading west in the next week. Three would be from Cavagnal and St. Henry; two would be from Kanesatake, and the rest from Lachine and Montréal. John had been able to contact the two carters who had helped the Hendersons back in 1824 when they arrived in Montreal.

Jean-Jacques Major and his partner Alphonse Séguin had met John one day just after the ice had made travel down river to Lachine possible. They had all met at Angus Macleod's wharf, and on hearing that John was from Cavagnal, the two Frenchmen had asked him if he knew anything about a big Englishman by the name of Henderson who had hired them in 1824 on their way west. John, of course, said yes and he told them that he was married to Henderson's daughter, Jane. They both remembered well. "She is a very pretty lady," they told John. "You are a lucky man."

"I know," John said proudly.

After chatting for awhile with them and remembering how well George had spoken of the two men, John asked them if they would be interested in a trip west. They immediately agreed and Angus Macleod said he had no problems with them since he had known them for a few years and they had been very reliable men and hard workers.

Along with Simon Beauvais there would be his cousin, Joshua Gabriel, who also lived in Kanesatake and had traveled west up the Ottawa many times while in the employ of the North West Company. He remembered when the great river was known as the Grand River or Grande Rivière as the French Canadian voyageurs had called it. It had only been known as the Ottawa River since the end of the Napoleonic Wars in 1815 or so.

The French Canadians now called it La Rivière des Outaouais or River of the Ottawas. The Ottawas were a tribe of Indians who had once lived upriver but had long since been pushed west by the Mohawks. The Ottawas had replaced the Hurons as the middlemen in the fur trade of eastern North America after the Hurons had almost been annihilated by the powerful Iroquois Confederacy. Joshua was not sure when the name changed and did not really care as the Mohawks of Kanesatake knew the river as "Atawene Kanetari" which also meant "River of the Ottawas".

Besides John Cameron and John Henderson from Cavagnal, there would be Allan Henderson from St. Henry. John had met him a few times but it was John Henderson who had suggested the big strong lad from the area south of Cavagnal know as St. Henry.

Allan was a neighbour of the Grisenthwaites and had helped the young Doctor build his cabin just after he and his family had moved to St. Henry upon their arrival in 1824. There were rumours spreading around the two communities that Allan's sister, Phoebe, would soon be marrying Jacob Grisenthwaite as they had fallen deeply in love. Both John Henderson and John Cameron planned to ask Allan for more details as they paddled west.

From Lachine there would be two of Angus Macleod's best voyageurs. He had hired them just to keep an eye on the inexperienced men that he was sending west. They would be Louis Lévesque and Théodule Bertrand. They had been voyageurs for about ten years and been to Fort William each year. Most of the time they just remained at the big Fort, resting up for the long trip back east. If they were lucky, they also enjoyed some good times with some of the Ojibwa women who were always just outside the Fort. Only Théodule had ventured west of Fort William, into the land of the Plains Indian. That land was the open prairie grassland where the mighty Sioux, Crow, Blackfoot, Cheyenne, and others lived a nomadic way of life following the great buffalo herds.

It would be a trip of almost fifteen hundred miles by canoe and to send a group of young men who had never been to Fort William would be silly and reckless. Angus needed to have his cargo arrive safely as it was worth hundreds of pounds and it was expected to arrive in time for the rendezvous. That is why he had included Louis and Théodule as the most seasoned canoeists other than Joshua Gabriel.

Angus could have hired the best voyageurs in Montreal and Lachine to make the special trip, but since Iain had known of John Cameron's wish to see the west and his experience in boat handling, Iain had convinced his father to hire John and his friends from Cavagnal. Iain had also told his father that they all would stay the next winter north of Wright's Village in a lumber camp. Iain did not mind that, but he would make sure the money that they would receive for their trip west to Fort William would be sent to him from Wright's Village before they headed into the bush for the winter.

Iain would have a special courier waiting for them on their return voyage from Fort William. They planned to be in Wright's Village by late September if all went well. Long before ice up, anyway. That would give them time to tour the various lumber camps and pick one to their liking if that were possible. Big Joe Desormeaux was the only one who could help them there.

They all had agreed to try their hand in the lumber camps of the Wright family north of Wright's Village, situated at the junction of the Ottawa and Gatineau Rivers. The Wright family had a huge lumber mill set up there using the powerful Chaudière Falls to drive their saws and gristmill. There was even a church in the small settlement and a hotel. John had heard that in 1826 there were over a thousand people living in or around the settlement.

None of the young men had ever worked in a real lumber camp except for big Joe Desormeaux. He was the oldest of the group at thirty-seven. He had been the one to convince the others of trying to tough it out for the next winter, as the money would be good, especially if they were working for the Wright family.

Ruggles Wright had taken over most of the control of his elderly father's business. He and his five brothers were the wealthiest lumber barons west of Montréal and they were opening up the Ottawa Valley region for more settlers. Their plan was to clear the land and as they cleared the land more settlers would arrive. The Wrights would make money selling them the land and then they could hire the settlers on to help clear more land during the long winter months.

John Cameron had spoken to many of the raftsmen as they traveled down the Ottawa River from Wright's Village to Montréal and on to Québec. They all talked about life in the bush and the hardships they faced, but they all seemed to love their work. This romantic talk had led John to talk about a stay in the camps and Joe had given his stamp of approval as he had already been in the camps for numerous past winters.

Chapter 15
The Ottawa River

Angus Beauvais was able to complete the big canoe a week before the trip was to begin. It was a standard canot de maitre, thirty-six feet long and five feet wide. Since this trip was a very special one and the crew mostly raw recruits, the big canoe would not be as heavily loaded, as it normally would have been. Angus remembered the early days of the North West Company when these canoes traveled as a brigade of four to twelve at a time loaded with upwards of seventy packs of at least ninety pounds each.

For this special trip they would be hauling only thirty packs of about seventy pounds each plus twenty packs of food and other supplies for the eleven men.

Louis Lévesque would be the steersman in the stern while Théodule Bertrand would be the bowman. Both were very important spots in a canoe and it was the bowman who would pick the routes through rapids, especially when they would be heading down the French River from Lake Nipissing to Lake Huron.

In the middle of the canoe were big Joe Desormeaux and Iain Macleod. Being the two largest men on the trip, they were going to need the most leg room that was available and that was in the centre of the canoe.

Besides Louis and Théodule, the most experienced canoeist was Joshua Gabriel. He had traveled up the Ottawa on many occasions and had also traveled down into the United States of America to visit other Mohawk villages that were situated along Lake Champlain and Lake George in New York State. He had traveled on some of his trips up the Ottawa in a canot du maitre while he had been working with the Northwest Company. However, when he went to the United States, Joshua traveled in a much smaller native style birch bark canoe of just eighteen feet.

Probably the person most upset with the great voyage was Jane Cameron. Having been married for just over a year, the last thing she wanted was to be alone in their new home. Though she kept busy working at Schmidt's Tavern, Jane had expressed her concerns to her husband.

"I do not want to stay alone while you are off on this adventure of yours," Jane told her beloved husband.

"I wish that you would ask the Schmidts if you can stay with them," John replied. "I am sure they let you stay in the room we were in just after we were married, my dear.

"I do not plan to take any chances and I will be traveling with some very experienced men. I trust them because their reputation precedes them thanks to Angus Macleod."

"John," Jane said softly, "I think we are going to have a family."

"What? When? How?" John said loudly, then he hugged his lovely wife as he had never done before.

"I said we are going to have a family soon. I think I am pregnant," Jane repeated. "I do not know when, probably sometime next winter, December or early January. As for how, well I will let you think about that," she said with a sly smile on her face. John thought for a second, then they both burst out laughing.

"Have you told anyone else?" he asked.

"Just mother, father does not know yet, but I think he should before you leave with the others."

"Let us tell him now Jane," John said, as he danced around their little cabin.

"I was not planning to come back till spring, but I will leave just after Christmas from the lumber camp and be here before New Year's Day. I will ask Charles Schmidt to head up to get Dr. Grisenthwaite. I think it would be wise to have him check you as soon as possible, especially before I leave. That would really set my mind at ease, knowing that you are in good health to begin with."

"I agree," replied Jane. "I was hoping you could do that. I only realized that I was pregnant last week and after talking with mother, we both agreed upon it. I do not care whether it will be a boy or girl, only if our baby is born healthy. Too bad it will be during the winter, but sometimes we cannot plan on the date of a birth I guess.

"We are both young," Jane continued, "and hopefully there will be many more children born to us as the years go by, but first let us pray for a healthy first child and your safe trip west to Fort William and return."

"God bless us both," John said as they hugged and kissed each other one more time; this time much more passionately

George Henderson was working on some tools outside his cabin when John and Jane Cameron skipped to the front of the Henderson cabin. Both were humming a tune and both of them had huge smiles on their faces.

"What makes you two so cheerful?" George asked the young couple. "How can you be so happy, Jane? Your husband is about to embark on a very long trip and be away for almost a year."

"He will not father. John will be back at New Year's," Jane told her astonished father.

"What for?" asked George. "What is so important about New Year's around here?"

"Mr. Henderson," John got very formal for a moment and it brought a frown to George's brow. "Mr. Henderson, you are going to be a grandfather around New Year's Day, that is why I am coming back."

For once George Henderson was left speechless. He just stood there for a moment then began to cry. Mary hurried outside upon hearing her husband weeping like a child. Mary realized why he was crying as soon as she saw Jane and John and she laughed and then too she cried with her big husband.

"I thought it would never happen," he said, wiping the tears from his eyes and blowing his nose. By then, all the other Henderson children were gathered outside, as many had never seen their father cry before. "These are tears of joy, children," he said. "They are not tears of sadness. Your sister is going to have a baby next winter; a new life in this new land." The trip down river to Lachine was uneventful, as the canoe was almost empty except for some mail that John Marsden had asked John Cameron to take into Lachine for him. The canoe was also only partly filled with the "voyageurs" as only John Cameron, John Henderson, Allan Henderson, Simon Beauvais, and Joshua Gabriel were on board. All the rest would meet them at Angus Macleod's dock in Lachine.

John Henderson was looking forward to seeing Jean-Jacques Major and Alphonse Séguin once again. They had not seen each other since John and his family had traveled with them from Montreal to Lachine back in 1824 when they first arrived.

The Mohawks had voiced some concerns about traveling with so many French Canadians on the trip but John Cameron reassured them that all were good men and hard workers too. Since both Théodule and Louis had worked as voyageurs for a number of years, often with natives from Kahnawake, John was almost sure that there would be no animosity amongst the crew.

However, a long trip through the wilderness in a small boat can change many a man. "Only time would tell," John Cameron thought to himself. "I hope no one gets hurt, so far from help and a doctor. One bad slip on a portage could spell disaster to inexperienced travelers such as we are," he thought.

They knew that the trip down to Lachine would be an easy one and with the canoe almost empty and Joshua at the stern, the men decided to run the rapids at Ste Anne de Bellevue rather than carry the big canoe around as would normally have been done. The spring runoff was still in force and the river was running very high. There had been a severe snowfall up north and the streams were still filling the Ottawa River and its tributaries with the spring melt water. The short run down the rapids would also give the lads from Cavagnal their first taste of what it would be like later on in the summer up on the mighty French River. "There would be lots of white water and rocks to worry about then," explained Joshua to his fellow paddlers.

Angus Macleod met the canoe and its excited crew at his dock when they arrived just after noon. The cargo they were hauling consisted of numerous bundles of mail for Fort William's inhabitants and special orders to the Montréal Agents of the former North West Company who were still employed at the Fort by the Hudson's Bay Company.

They were to learn that their employment was soon to be terminated and all would have to return to Montréal if they wished. All business would now go through either York Factory or Churchill Factory on Hudson Bay. Fort William was to continue to exist but with less importance than before.

Besides the mail packs, the big canoe was of course hauling supplies for the forty or more days it was going to take the young men to reach Fort William. They wanted to reach it before the big Rendezvous in July. It was rumoured among the men on the docks in Lachine that the 1826 Rendezvous would be the last one at Fort William. It promised to be the most important event of the hinterland that year.

Traders, trappers and Indians from all over the mid-west would be converging on Fort William for a week's worth of fun and hell-raising and drunken good times. There would be shooting competitions, hatchet and knife throwing competitions, canoe races, foot races, and wrestling matches. With big Joe Desormeaux along for the ride, Louis and Théodule were hoping to win some money at Joe's expense in some wrestling matches. However, Joe was not aware of this at their departure time.

Heading west up Lake St. Louis, the now heavily laden canoe and its crew stopped by the famous shrine at Ste. Anne de Bellevue to pray to Ste. Anne who guides all voyageurs. All of the men, including the three Englishmen from Cavagnal and St. Henry and the two Mohawks, joined their French-Canadian brethren at the shrine and prayed. They were all in this trip together and it did not take much convincing by Théodule to have the Englishmen and the Mohawks join them. Iain Macleod did not have to be convinced since his father, Angus, had told him many times about the shrine.

"Off we go," announced John Henderson, as the eleven men loaded their canoe above the rapids at Ste. Anne de Bellevue and headed off up the Ottawa River. At first they had thought that they would spend the night below the rapids of Ste Anne's but with the weather so fine and their paddling going so well they all decided to head as far west up the Ottawa as possible.

It was a calm day and they hoped to reach Carillon by dark, after a short stop at Schmidt's Tavern to say goodbye to everyone there.

Since George Henderson had accepted Charles Schmidt's offer to work part time at the Tavern in place of John Cameron, George was to keep a sharp eye out for the lone canoe heading west along the south shore of the Lake of the Two Mountains.

He spotted it while he was loading up one of the Schmidt's bateaux for a run down the next day to Ste. Anne de Bellevue then over to Ste. Eustache on the north eastern shore of the lake on the following day. George had brought his trusty rifle with him and fired off a round as the canoe headed into the dock.

In no time at all, there was a crowd down at Schmidt's dock. Jane Cameron was among them and John leapt from the canoe and almost fell into the river as he reached to hug his wife. They had only been separated for a little more than twenty-four hours, but it had felt like a lifetime now that Jane was pregnant.

"I am having second thoughts about going," John announced to his friends.

"What?" bellowed Joe Desormeaux. "You better not let us down now John. We need you. This canoe is supposed to have twelve men and we are only eleven. Without you it will be very tough on all of us, especially your young friends here who have never worked as an engagé voyageur."

"Alright," John said, "I will go, but it is not because I need to or really want to. However, I will be leaving you all just after Christmas because my wife Jane is expecting our first child around New Year's."

"No wonder you want to stay," Joshua said, "by all means. I think it would be best if you did stay here with your wife. But if you are still willing to come along, you know you are most welcome."

"Thanks," John said to his friend. "I will join you as I know Jane will be safe here in Cavagnal with her family and with the Schmidts. Anyway, Dr. Grisenthwaite has already told us that she is very healthy and should have a safe pregnancy. He will be checking on her regularly and with so many women around here, she will be well looked after I am sure."

"What is an engagé?" Jane Cameron asked her husband. Iain Macleod spoke first, explaining that an engagé was basically a labourer who was hired by the North West Company to transport a canoe and its cargo from Montreal to Fort William and return with the canoe and a load of furs.

"We are not really true engagés as we are not working for either the North West Company or the Hudson's Bay Company, but for my father, Angus Macleod. However, the term still applies and is used by many of the old voyageurs from Montreal or those that know of their ways such as big Joe there."

After a short round of ales for all the crew and some more hugs and kisses by family members, the eleven adventurers were off up the river once again. They hoped to average about forty strokes a minute if all went well, but with four of the eleven not being experienced paddlers, a more realistic thirty strokes a minute was settled on for the first few days. By the time they reached the upper Ottawa River or Lake Nipissing, it was hoped that the whole crew could do forty to fifty strokes per minute, sending their big canot de maitre along at a steady six knots.

John Henderson wondered why they had two long poles in the canoe, but as they headed out around Pearson's Point he soon found out. Louis Levesque called from the stern, "alright you milieux, set up de sail." Not knowing what he meant, both John and Allan Henderson just watched as the others scrambled with the long poles and a sheet of canvas. Soon they were sailing along at a steady clip up the Lake with Louis acting as the steersman, or the gouvernail as he called himself.

"I will soon teach you young lads de way of de French-Canadian voyageur," Louis yelled to the three Englishmen in the middle of the canoe. "By de time we get back ere to Cavagnal next summer, you will all be fluent in French and Mohawk or my name is not Louis Lévesque," he said laughing.

After rounding the north side of Carillon Island, the milieux dismantled the sail and mast and the crew set once again to paddling. Joshua started to speak to Simon in their native tongue, but Louis shut them up quickly. "No talking while we paddle my lads. On dis trip you will obey me. We talk when we stop odderwise we paddle and only paddle."

"However," Théodule reminded his friend in the stern that he may be the gouvernail, "I am de avant or bowman and I will lead you. Sometimes I will lead you in song and we voyageurs know lot of songs, don't we Iain and Louis."

"Yes, we do," they announced and with that, the three of them began a rousing song. Alphonse and Jean-Jacques knew the songs as well and they too joined in and shortly after big Joe Desormeaux did too, his big deep voice heard above all of the others.

The two natives listened for awhile then joined the chorus and in a short time all on board were singing loudly and laughing as they headed towards the Royal Engineers encampment at Carillon. Théodule reminded his fellow canoeists that only he would start the singing. That was the tradition of the voyageur. If they were to travel west to Fort William they would all have to share the workload and obey the unwritten rules of the French-Canadian voyageur.

That night, as they rested by the campfire below the Long Sault Rapids, they reflected upon their second day's trip. Allan was simply amazed at all that he had seen since leaving Lachine. He had never been west of Cavagnal except for living in St. Henry. He had never visited the small French village of Rigaud just west of his home, though it was closer than Schmidt's Tavern.

All of the men except for the seasoned travelers were astonished at the amount of work that the Royal Engineers had done with the new canal at Carillon. The new canal was supposed to be open by 1827 if all went well and it would save the travelers the rigours of a portage of over eleven hundred paces. One less portage to carry two ninety pound packs was a welcome spot for any voyageur anytime.

Chapter 16
Friends Return

A few days after the intrepid adventurers had left Schmidt's Tavern, two canoes were spotted heading up the river and in towards the Tavern. They were smaller ones than the huge canot de maitre that had taken the young lads west to Fort William.

"George," yelled William Schmidt, "look at those two canoes heading this way. I have not seen that one on the left on this lake before. Those Indians are not from across the lake in Kanesatake, I am sure of that. However, the other one looks like Rotonni's canoe."

"Beats me," George responded, "I wonder why they are coming here and not heading over there first. Strange to have Indians head here rather than to head over to one of their own settlements, unless they are not Mohawks. Could they be Hurons?"

"I doubt it," Charles responded. "Not with Rotonni with them." He had just joined his father and George at the dock. Rotonni was well known in Cavagnal. He had helped the Schmidts build their new dock for the new steamboat that was soon to start plying the Ottawa River.

"We are Mohawks from Ganienkeh in New York and we are looking for a big white man by the name of Henderson," one of the men called to the men gathered on shore. "I believe you already know our cousin Rotonni from Kanesatake."

"Holy Christ! They are looking for me," George whispered to his friends. Both Charles and William were taken aback at first as they had never heard George take the Lord's name in vain. "I wonder," he said out loud. "No they couldn't be."

"What is it?" Charles asked.

"Well, I met two Mohawks two years ago while in Quebec and they promised to visit me one day. They said they would bring me a Pennsylvania long rifle from the United States. I wonder if they are the same Indians.

"I am George Henderson," he yelled out to the fast approaching canoes. He could see five or six people on board one of them. Rotonni had only met George once though he had worked around the Schmidt's place a few times, otherwise he could have easily pointed out the big man to the newcomers from Ganienkeh. Two were men and two others were women and there were at least two children from what he could see. "Who are you?"

"You met us two summers ago in Quebec. I am Sori'howane and this is Awen'rah:ton and these are our families. I have your two rifles and we have come to visit you, as we promised."

"I did not recognize you from such a distance," George said to his guests as they landed their canoe on the beach at Schmidt's Tavern. "We met only for a few short minutes two years ago and many things have happened here since then. I wish my son was here to see you once again, but he has just left on a trip out to Fort William with some friends.

"Welcome, my friends. This is Charles and William Schmidt; they operate this fine Tavern and boat company. I am working for them part time since my son-in-law went west with my son and one of the Schmidt's workers from Kanesatake, Simon Beauvais."

Rotonni greeted his former employer, Charles Schmidt, and then he introduced his cousins from south of the border. They were dressed in traditional clothing of the Mohawk nation while Rotonni was dressed in buckskins with a white man's hat on his head. Having worked over in Cavagnal, Rotonni had learned the white man's language as his cousins had while serving with the British Army as scouts. Though they were from different parts of the land, all three had a very similar accent, very distinguishable from those of the white men. Charles recounted that all of the natives he had encountered in Canada and the United States spoke with the same heavy accent, though when they spoke their own dialects, there was a vast difference in the languages.

Charles had once told George that Algonquin, Huron, and Mohawk warriors could easily carry on a conversation amongst themselves as they all knew a common sign language that had been passed onto them by their forefathers. Though their spoken languages were different, the three nations had fashioned a visual language that was supposed to range all across North America. It was common to all native tribes with very little variance from region to region.

As the natives unloaded their canoes, Charles Schmidt advised them that they could leave them on the front yard of his Tavern. There was no room at the Tavern as some travelers heading down river had stopped in for a night's rest and some of the Schmidt's famous food.

"You are all going to stay with me and my family," George told his guests. "How long to you plan to stay?" he asked Sori'howane.

"We are not sure. How long can you put up with us? We will be here at least until the fishing season begins on the Point over there." Sori'howane was pointing to what the local inhabitants called Pearson's Point.

Charles was amazed that these strangers already knew about the local Mohawk's annual usage of the sheltered bay of Pearson's Point as a fishing village. Maybe Rotonni had told them, he thought.

"My cabin is just a few hundred feet up the road from here, my friends. How long have you been traveling?" George asked Serkhaenten.

"We left our village of Ganienkeh a little more than two weeks ago. We stopped for a couple of days in Kahnawake before heading up here. Rotonni was over in Kahnawake when we dropped by and he said that he would accompany us here as he was leaving anyway."

As they all approached the Henderson's cabin, the young voices of George's children could be heard by the visitors and they all smiled. "I hope all our children will be as good as friends as we already are," George said to Ohaeknownten.

"I believe they will," replied Sori'howane.

The two Mohawk families agreed to stay with the Hendersons for a few days, but they refused to stay in the cabin; it would be too small for all the Hendersons and their guests. George, Sori'howane, and Awen'rah:ton quickly set about erecting a lean-to next to the cabin that would offer the Indians some protection from the weather. "I do not know where you could have stayed if you had arrived last winter," George told his two friends.

"We had a very tough winter here in Cavagnal; many of our residents died from a terrible influenza epidemic. Unfortunately, most were young children."

"We heard that Montréal suffered as well," Awen'rah:ton told George. "We kept much to ourselves last winter in Ganienkeh and none of us died."

"Where is this Ganienkeh you speak of?" George asked Awen'rah:ton.

"It is a small Mohawk community just south of the border between the United States and your country. It is not far from Lake Champlain, the big lake that was once our main highway for trading and raiding between our lands south of the border and here in what was then New France."

Awen'rah:ton continued by saying that the big lake connected the mighty Richelieu River in Lower Canada to Lake George further south, then with a couple of portages you could reach the great Hudson River that leads right down to New York City.

"I thought you said you lived not far from Montréal."

"We did," Sori'howane told George, "but we had to move last summer when I killed a white man near Chambly. We were on a hunting expedition when this Frenchman came out of the woods we were in and tried to claim two deer we had just shot. After an argument, he pulled a knife and attacked me. I defended myself and was able to kill the man before he was able to hurt me."

"Did you report this to the authorities?" George asked him.

"I did not have to. They came after me one day in our home a few miles from Kahnawake. Another white man had seen the fight from a concealed place and he had told the authorities that we had murdered the man. It was his word against ours and of course, your white man's law believed him rather than us.

"We were able to flee with our families that night to the United States.

I had not been home that day but my son was and he told me about the visitors and that they would return the next day with warrants for Awen'rah:ton's and my arrest.

"Our families have been in the United States ever since and we just took a chance to come a visit you. We cross the border regularly, visiting family in Kahnawake but we never go near any white settlements.

"I wish you had not told all of this, Sori'howane, I am soon to be the local Sheriff here in Cavagnal and I am a very good friend of the Justice of the Peace, John Marsden. However, I believe you and I will not turn you in. I have never heard of any warrants that are out for you and Awen'rah:ton and therefore it is just a story you have told me and we will forget about it."

"You are a fine man, George Henderson," both of the Mohawk warriors said at the same time. "And a good friend too," they added.

"Let us eat first then see those two guns that you have brought me."

"Agreed," said the Indians and with that, the three men went inside to join the others around the table.

Mary Henderson had been able to set up a fine meal in a very short time with the help of Jane and Frances. The two native women stood back and watched as the three white ladies worked at a fast pace, cutting up pieces of ham and pork and laying out a fine feast for the large crowd. "I am glad that I was able to bake some bread this morning," Mary admitted to her daughters.

"Nothing like fresh bread with pork and ham and some hot beans to go with it all, eh girls?" They all agreed and a sumptuous meal was ready at the table for the Hendersons and their guests before long.

Rotonni had been invited to the Henderson's with the others but had refused, saying that he wanted to get back to Kanesatake as he had been away from his family for a few days and wanted to see them as soon as possible.

"Does he know about what happened?" George asked Sori'howane.

"I do not know," he answered. "I doubt it. It is not talked about in Kahnawake very much, and many residents have forgotten about it already."

"We just have to be very careful that no one finds out around here," George reminded his friends.

"We have a very patriotic young French Canadian here in Cavagnal who hates the Natives with a passion and does not really like me, either. We are watching him and his friends as they could prove to be a problem if their patriotism gets too strong. They are very anti-British and would love to have Lower Canada returned to French rule.

"What is his name?" asked Sori'howane.

"François Xavier Deschamps. He operates a small store about a half a mile east of here. His sister used to operate a small school but had to close it this winter when most of her students died from the influenza."

"We will remember that name," the Mohawks said in unison. They all began to eat.

After the sumptuous meal, George pushed back his chair from the table and said, "et me see those special guns that you have brought me."

"I was able to get two nice .50 calibre Pennsylvania long rifles for you and your son," Sori'howane told George.

"It is too bad that John is not here to see them," Mary said to her husband. "I think he would like them even better than your old rifle."

"I know he would," George said. "I like them too. It is going to be hard for me to give up my trusty Baker rifle but it reminds me too much of the hardships that we have gone through—what with the war, the battle two years ago, and the loss of Isaac. We came here to Cavagnal to begin a new life and these new guns will help me forget the old days a little. It is time to hang up the old rifle over the fireplace and leave it there."

Mary reminded her husband, "we are not expecting any more wars here now, so I think the Baker fired its last round when you shot it off the other day to let all of us know that John's canoe was about to land down at the Schmidt's dock."

"I believe you are right, my dear," George told his wife. "Unless we need it in an emergency it has fired its last round."

Sori'howane then began to show George how the new rifles were made and how they could handle. "They are so long," George told his friends.

"Just over sixty inches," Awen'rah:ton announced. "And they are very accurate. In the hands of trained marksmen like you, they can hit a target regularly at 400 yards."

"The .50 calibre bore is smaller than any I have ever seen," said George. "The big Bess is .75 calibre and weighs a hell of a lot more than this."

"These are so finely made. What beautiful lines and wood they are made of," commented Mary. "A real piece of fine craftsmanship."

"These are made by German craftsmen near Lancaster County, Pennsylvania, but there are many fine gunsmiths all over the United States now. The men of the frontier settlements in Virginia and Kaintuck are using these now more since the last war with your homeland," Awen'rah:ton told them.

"Trade with England was stopped during the last two wars and the Americans had to adopt a smaller gun as lead was scarce. They found that the smaller calibers—.45 and .50—were just as deadly as my big .65 calibre Baker and a hell of a lot more accurate than the old Brown Bess," George told his family and guests. George was proud of his knowledge of guns, as he had learned a great deal during his long years in the army with the 95th Rifles.

"The wood is American curly maple and it makes for a beautiful stock and forepiece. The barrel is octagonal. There are two sets of triggers on each gun. Setting the rear trigger first eases the pull needed to fire the gun when you squeeze the front trigger. It makes the gun much more accurate," announced Sori'howane.

"Now let us try them out," announced George.

"I brought some .50 calibre bullets with me," Sori'howane told George. "However, you will have to make more yourself."

"Deschamps sells powder," said George. "But so does Marsden, and I would prefer to buy it from him than that damn Frenchman. I will get some as soon as possible. We will have to get a mould made for the bullets, though, as there are no .50 calibre guns around here. Not that I know of. Most of the guns that are sold to the Indians by the Hudson's Bay Company and to the local white settlers are big smooth bores, often ex-military guns. I do not know of any small bore rifles such as these around here."

"We could have brought you some .45 calibre guns as well, but I thought you would prefer the larger .50 calibre," Sori'howane said. "Many of the American settlers use the smaller .45 calibre guns, even to hunt bear. We prefer the bigger .50 calibre since it hits harder and is just right for deer, bear, and even moose. Both Awen'rah:ton and I think you will like these two guns."

"How much do I owe you for these two wonderful guns?" George asked his Mohawk friends.

Sori'howane responded, saying, "I was able to buy them during a visit to southern New York in the late fall of 1825 and they have been in my camp since then. They were not expensive, just five pounds each. They are expensive compared to your trade guns that are more common up here but they are much better."

"I hope," said Awen'rah:ton, "that ten pounds is not too expensive for you."

George had the money out from his purse in no time and he gave it to his friend. "There you go," he said. "That is full payment—and you are welcome at our dinner table as long as you want to stay."

The two Mohawks thanked him and put away the money into their clothes as they all walked outside to try the new guns.

"William," George asked his young son, "go put up some targets on those old stumps behind the cabin, please. Put them at various distances too." The young lad ran out and hurriedly gathered up some various old things that could be used as targets: a couple of large mushroom tops and an old bottle that Mary had thrown out back the year before.

George watched attentively as the two Indians showed him how to load the guns. "Just like your big military gun," they said, "but longer and more accurate.

The two Indians then took careful aim with the two long guns and fired at the targets that young William had set up for his father. The two mushroom tops exploded into small pieces as the bullets hit home. The range was about seventy-five yards, they estimated.

"Great shooting!" exclaimed George. "Looks like you have been practicing with them."

"Actually, we have not. This is just the second time we have fired them. The first was last fall on the way home when we saw some deer and killed three with just four shots. We had our guns with us and were able to get four quick shots off before the herd disappeared into the forest."

"Now it's your turn, George," Sori'howane announced, winking at his friend. "Let us see what the great ex-British Army marksman can do with his new gun, made in the United States of America."

"You are being a little cynical," George said to his friend, but Sori'howane did not understand what he meant and just shrugged his shoulders as he began to load the second gun.

"Just aim as you would your big gun. Set the rear trigger first, then slowly squeeze the front trigger." There was a quiet hush over the area as George did as he was instructed. There was the ever-present puff of smoke at the lock of the gun, then a rapid boom as it fired. The bottle that William had set up on a stump about a hundred yards from the shooters exploded in a thousand pieces as the bullet struck home, dead centre.

"What did you do to that bottle, William," asked his father? "I filled it with water like John does sometimes when he practices. It makes it more fun to see the water and glass blow up like that."

"At least we know I hit it," George laughed. "It is a fine gun. Let me try the other one, too."

This time he took aim at a target that William had set up even further back behind the cabin and once again he was able to hit it dead centre. "Wonderful guns," he said, as he shook the hands of his two Indian friends. "I am sure they will get lots of good use here in Cavagnal. Thank you once again. And thank you especially for honouring your word and coming here even though you are wanted by the law. It was a great chance that you have taken, my friends."

As the spring turned to summer the two Mohawk families began to become well known in the small community of Cavagnal, and felt quite at home. Since Mohawks from Kanesatake were a common sight in Cavagnal, a few more were just more local Indians to the local white population.

On George's recommendation, backed up by Charles Schmidt, both Sori'howane and Awen'rah:ton stayed clear of F.X. Deschamps' store. When they needed supplies they went up to John Marsden's place. He was more receptive to their needs and he also told them about Deschamps' hatred of what he called "dirty, stinking Indians".

Chapter 17
A Volunteer Militia

It was rumoured that some of Deschamp's family had been taken prisoner and tortured by Mohawks during the late stages of the war that saw France's control of New France disappear with the battle of Quebec in 1759 and the loss of Montréal in 1760. F.X. Deschamps had often cursed the very presence of the Mohawk village at Kanesatake and no Indians were ever welcome in his store, no matter how desperate they were in need of supplies. Whether the rumour about F.X. Deschamps' family was true or not was another question. No one in the community really cared; he was not well liked at all. Joseph Shouldice was one of the few Englishmen who got along with Deschamps to any degree. The one Englishman in the settlement who was well known to be a great friend of F. X. Deschamps was William Whetstone.

Shouldice got along with Deschamps but Joseph would readily admit that they were not really good friends. On the other hand, William Whetstone and Desjardins were the best of friends. They were soon to be brothers-in-law as well.

Many of the residents of Cavagnal had thought that F.X. Deschamps would marry his housekeeper, Mary Kilkenny. However, in April of 1826, Deschamps announced that he would be marrying the young daughter of another local merchant, John Mark Lerniers. Mary Charlotte Lerniers was twenty-four years old and had fallen deeply in love with the strange little

French-Canadian merchant. Her father had been the earliest English settler in Cavagnal, having arrived from New Brunswick, via Montréal, in 1801. Mary Charlotte had been the first person born in Cavagnal of English descent back in 1802.

John Mark Lerniers had a French-sounding name but he spoke very little French, having been born in Nova Scotia and grown up in southern New Brunswick. His family was of Swiss background. His father had been a mercenary with the British Army in the early years of British settlement in Nova Scotia.

William Whetstone had married another one of J.M. Lerniers' daughters, Mathilda, a number of years before and they already had three children. Whetstone's father John had been an officer with the Queen's American Rangers during the American War of Independence but had moved to Nova Scotia after the British had lost their final battle at Yorktown. He had resigned his commission and had moved to in Cavagnal in 1805 with his family.

The Whetstone family was one of the wealthiest families in Cavagnal and they rivaled John A. Marsden with their wealth and influence. They operated a gristmill and large saw mill near the Grisenthwaite's place, utilizing the water from the Raquette River to supply power to the two mills. Both mills provided the Whetstone family with a good, steady income and they provided an important service to the southern part of the Seigneury.

Why William Whetstone began to like F.X. Deschamps was anyone's guess. They were from very different backgrounds and the only thing they had in common was that they were to be brothers-in-law.

After the marriage of F.X. Deschamps to Charlotte Lerniers in July 1826, a very strong bond of friendship grew between William Whetstone and F.X. Deschamps. Charlotte was quite jealous of having Mary Kilkenny around the store and she was soon moved out to the back storage building where she was set up with a small room to live in. She had lived there before upon first arriving in Cavagnal but had moved into Deschamps house when the cold of her first winter in Cavagnal had forced Deschamps to take pity on her. His new wife would have no other young woman in her house and she made Mary fully aware of her feelings.

"I cannot stay there any longer, Jane," Mary told Jane Cameron one day in early August. "I want to leave but I am afraid to. Charlotte hates me but her husband treats me good and I have enjoyed working for him, even though he is a little strange at times. He has never beaten me as some people in this community believe and he does pay me enough."

"I wish you would see about getting a job here in the Tavern with the Schmidts," Jane told her friend. "I will not be working much longer, what with me soon to be a mother. Try staying with Deschamps until the late fall then come here. Let us ask Charles and Caroline right now if they will hire you when I stop working."

The Schmidts readily agreed to take care of Mary Kilkenny that fall and offered her Jane's job in the Tavern. Jane would allow Mary to stay with her in her cabin until John returned just after Christmas. She could then probably stay in the Tavern as Jane had done just after she and John had been married.

By the early fall of 1826, the friendship of William Whetstone and F.X. Deschamps was already rock solid. "I cannot figure how they get along so well," John Marsden said in early September to George Henderson. "I agree with you," George told him. "Joseph Shouldice told me they are from such different their backgrounds." Whetstone is down at Deschamps' about four times a week and many times there are horses and buggies tied up down behind the store.

"Shouldice often sees strange men heading westward from Vaudreuil and once he followed them and they all ended up at Deschamps' store. They were not buying goods, but all went upstairs by a rear entrance."

"George, can you ask Mary Kilkenny to keep an eye on what is going on there, please?" Marsden asked his friend. "As the Sheriff of Cavagnal I do not want you to cause any problems with a very powerful and influential French Canadian, F.X. Deschamps, but I believe he is up to no good. We have all heard about his connections with some so-called Patriotes in Montréal and I think he is trying to organize some patriotic group here in Vaudreuil."

"I wonder why he has picked Cavagnal to try that," said George, "if that is really what he is doing? And why include Whetstone?"

"The Whetstone connection really bothers me too," Marsden said.

"That is one part of the puzzle I have yet to figure out. Maybe Mary Kilkenny can find out about that, too. See what you can do, George. This could all be a threat to our local security if a patriotic group starts up here in Cavagnal under the leadership of F.X. Deschamps. You know how he dislikes us English, even though he likes our money.

"I will check with the Seigneur's Agent, Mr. Pambrun, down in Vaudreuil and see if he has heard anything," announced Marsden. "We are good friends and I do not think that he would want any uprisings occurring in the Seigneury before we have an adequate leader. As you know, George, he is only temporarily occupying the position until old Lotbinière's daughter comes of age and gets married. Her husband will then become the new Seigneur. However, God only knows when and who that will be. I just hope it will be soon."

In early October, while Mary Kilkenny was visiting Jane Cameron, George had his first chance to speak to her about what he and Marsden had been discussing a few weeks before.

"I do not want to frighten you, Mary," George began, "but Mr. Marsden and I believe that F.X. Deschamps is beginning some sort of clandestine Patriotic operation in his home. Do you know anything about this, and about who actually is involved?"

Mary announced that she was quite aware of what had been going on but had been frightened to speak to anyone less she would be silenced, possibly permanently. "I have known about the meetings for a many months," she told George. "I think the men come from Vaudreuil, Rigaud, Ste Marthe, and Pointe du Moulin. I have even heard of some coming out from Ste Anne de Bellevue. I think they had certain connections with other Patriote groups down in Montréal and over on the south shore of the St. Lawrence River."

Mary continued by saying that she had served the meetings as a servant, bringing them hot food, wine and even hard liquor. Some had stayed overnight, only to leave just before sunrise so that the local residents would not see them.

"The meetings began in early May and continue to be held at least three times a month. Most of the time they are here at Deschamps' store but some have been held in Vaudreuil as well and once in Rigaud. Of course I did not attend those," she said.

Mary Kilkenny continued to tell everything she knew about the Patriotes to George, Jane, and Mary Henderson. George had made sure that none of his children were close by when Mary Kilkenny began to talk, since the fewer persons that knew of this very alarming news, the better, especially if those persons were his own children.

George held off on his most important question until Mary had nearly finished. "Do they have any weapons?" he asked her in a subdued tone.

"Oh yes," she announced, "hundreds, it looks like." George almost fell off his seat.

"I was afraid of that," he said, "very much afraid. Is there any ammunition and powder?" he asked.

Mary replied that she had seen numerous kegs being unloaded in August and it took at least two men to carry some of them, though other kegs were not as heavy.

"I estimate that there are about six of the heavy kegs and at least ten of the other ones," said Mary.

"That is almost enough powder and shot and enough guns to start a small war. It could begin right here in Cavagnal, too," George announced to the three women. "Something will have to be done about this, and soon. Too bad the young men have headed out west. We could do with their help if a battle starts here."

"At least we have Mr. Marsden and our two Indian friends," announced Jane.

"True, but four of us would be no match for such a well armed party such as Deschamps'. I must advise John Marsden right away. I will take Sori'howane and Awen'rah:ton with me."

"Maybe we could get some help from Chief Aron'hio:tas and Rotonni and their people over in Kanesatake," said Mary.

"Not a bad idea, my dear," said George. "I will remember that and ask our two friends what they think of that as well. Thanks, dear."

George Henderson, Sheriff of Cavagnal, met with the Cavagnal Justice of the Peace, John A. Marsden, a week later. Marsden had been in Montréal for a few days and George had to wait until his return before a meeting could be set up at Marsden's residence. George had received no further information concerning the Patriote's actions at F.X. Deschamps and from what Mary Kilkenny had told him, the clandestine meetings had stopped for the time being.

"This is very serious," Marsden told George, after listening to George explain all he knew about Deschamps' actions. "I have heard rumours in Montréal that there is a very strong Patriote movement that is growing in Lower Canada. Governor Dalhousie down in Québec is very worried. A couple of small arsenals have been broken into already and numerous weapons have been stolen along with kegs of powder and shot."

"Maybe some of that stolen property is here in Deschamps' store," added George.

"It could well be, George, but we are only going on hearsay from Mary Kilkenny and have no real proof. We just cannot go barging in on Deschamps without some hard proof. If Mary can get us some proof, then we might be able to do something," said Marsden

He then continued by saying that if Mary could get one of the guns out of Deschamps' cellar, that would be proof enough, especially if they are British military guns.

"I will ask her," George told his friend, "but I cannot promise anything. Mary is about to leave Deschamps' place and move into Schmidt's Tavern. We have only a couple of weeks before that happens."

"Why is she moving out?" asked Marsden.

George explained that Jane would be having her baby around New Year's Day and Dr. Grisenthwaite had told her that she must not work anymore after the end of October. "She asked Mary to replace her and Mary has agreed. Deschamps' wife, Mary Charlotte, hates Mary, and Mary is very uncomfortable working there. She is also quite scared of F.X. Deschamps; she thinks he may kill her if he finds out that she has told us about the meetings and the stores in the cellar."

"Most locals know about the meetings anyway," George added. "At least those of us who live near Deschamps' store. Joseph Shouldice has been there when the strangers have started coming in."

"Did Deschamps give any explanation?" asked Marsden.

"Shouldice told me that Deschamps said that they were friends of his and they were planning a Roman Catholic Church here in Cavagnal. Shouldice even saw what looked to be a Priest there one day.

"He also told me that the Priest from Ile Perrot has been known to be outspoken on the behalf of the wishes of the Patriotic movement here in Lower Canada, so it could have been Curé Paquette of Ile Perrot who Shouldice saw that night."

"Sounds like a cover-up to me," Marsden said. "However, the Roman Catholic clergy could be involved and that could prove to be even a greater problem than just the initial one of having the Patriotes in the community."

"So, what are we going to do?" asked George. "Form our own militia and confront them or just lie low until this blows over? Do we let the Army know? At least there are some troops up at Carillon."

"Remember those are Royal Engineers, George, not the line troops that we are used to. They will be armed, as you should know, but their priority is to build and protect that canal. I do not think they could spare even a few troops to come down here and help us.

"Then there is the garrison over at Fort Côteau. They are line troops but I imagine they will be involved with the Patriote problem over in that region, especially around St. Martine and St. Louis de Gonzague." Marsden continued by saying that he would advise them of the possible troubles in Cavagnal but he held little hope of obtaining even a platoon of the soldiers from the Fort that was situated south of Cavagnal along the banks of the St. Lawrence River.

"I think it will be up to us to form a militia and advise the Seigneur's Agent in Vaudreuil as well as the Governor in Québec. I am sure they will be able to provide us with some weapons."

"I hope so," said George, "because most of the weapons we have here in the community are quite old. Even my old rifle is fifteen years old now.

"As for military training, there are just a handful of us who have served before. Besides you and I, there are the two Schmidts, John Benson, the Grampians, and maybe a couple of others. Whetstone did too, but it seems he is on the Patriote's side and that is one thing that really bothers me," George added. "Why and what does he have against the British Government here in Lower Canada?"

"I know one thing," Marsden said, "I am not going to ask him. That would just raise suspicions and we do not want them to realize how much we already know. They could do something before we are ready. I suggest we organize a meeting of all the residents of Cavagnal as soon as possible. We have got to learn how we stand in terms of manpower, military training, and weapons and powder. I have good access to shot and powder but the weapons are hard to come by, unless we get some from the arsenal in Montréal."

"I will get right on to organizing a meeting," said George. "I do not think it should be here, as Whetstone's house is just up the road. I will try to get Ebenezer Grampian to hold the meeting at his place."

"Good, said Marsden, "let me know as soon as you get that done and then we can send a rider around to let all the residents know. We should be able to get at least fifty or sixty men under arms. That is about what Deschamps has, I believe."

George Henderson was able to persuade Ebenezer Grampian to hold a meeting in his old school room one day in late October, about a week after he and Marsden had discussed the situation. The Grampian residence was located about three miles due south from Marsden's store and it was situated on the crest of the hill that was called the "Grand Côte".

Built in 1811 by his father, Solomon, the house was a lovely log cottage with a low sloping roof. It had served as the original area school prior to the setting up of the local school committee that past winter. Now closed, the schoolroom served as a Sunday meeting room for the Methodist congregation of the Grand Côte twice a month when the circuit rider from Côteau du Lac arrived for his service. The Wesleyan Methodist minister, Angus Bradfield, would stay at the Grampian house on Saturday evening; hold an early Sunday service, then head off to St. Henry for a late afternoon service. Reverend Bradfield would usually hold this service at the Robert Henderson home and stay there that evening, enjoying a wonderful meal before heading home to Côteau du Lac on Monday morning.

George had sent word to Dugald Cameron to organize the residents of Côte St. Charles, while the same message was sent to Robert Henderson in St. Henry to organize his area residents and ask them to attend the meeting at the Grampians. George and Joseph Shouldice would handle the Cavagnal residents. For those families living west of Marsden's store, John Marsden would contact them himself—all except for Whetstone.

On Sunday in the last week of October, over one hundred men arrived at the Grampian's house at 11:00 am. George Henderson and John Marsden had never thought that so many men would be available and that concerned. They were both very happy to see the turn out, but they also quickly realized that the old school room would be too small for such a crowd. They both discussed the problem with Solomon Grampian and it was decided to hold the meeting in the back yard.

Ebenezer Grampian hitched up his team of horses and he had them bring his large wagon around from the barn so the speakers, Marsden and George, would have a platform from which they could address the large crowd.

Some of the men had even brought their guns, though they had not been told too. George had examined some of the settler's guns before the meeting began and he told Marsden that he was not too impressed with what he saw. "There is a collection of some old shotguns, a few old Hudson's Bay trade muskets, a few pistols, and some old cut-down Brown Bess muskets," he told Marsden. "Nothing that amounts to very much and, as you know, these men are all farmers and there are only a few with any formal military training. If we want to go up against Deschamps Patriotes, this group is going to have to be trained and some new weapons acquired."

Marsden told George that he had already written to the Seigneur's Agent and the Governor in Montréal asking for some muskets, powder, and shot, and to tell them that he was organizing an official Militia unit in the Seigneury of Vaudreuil. They would be called the "Vaudreuil Loyal Volunteers". George told him that he liked the name and that he would handle the training.

"I knew you would, George," Marsden said. "Now let us get this meeting under way. Gentlemen," Marsden called to the large group of farmers who were now gathered around the side of the Grampian's wagon. "Thank-you for coming today. We seem to have a serious problem arising in our small community and we may have to prepare you for military action."

Sean O'Rourke called out from the middle of the crowd, "Why do we have to defend our lands and homes? Where is the British Army when we need them? There is a group of them just seventeen miles away in Carillon and about a regiment at the Fort in Côteau du Lac."

Marsden had thought that he might get some opposition from the Irish community from St. Henry, but he was prepared. "I know how you feel, Sean," said Marsden. However, this group of rebels, known as Patriotes, is against anything that is connected to the British Crown and for now, Ireland is still part of Great Britain and you are all here. We have to join together here in Cavagnal, Côte St. Charles, and St. Henry if we want to survive at all.

"This Patriote group is quite large from what information we have so far, but from what I have seen here today, we are about as large. How many here Ebenezer?"

"There are one hundred and seventeen men from the ages of fifteen to seventy," he answered. "That includes your two Mohawk friends from the United States of America."

"Chief Aron'hio:tas of Kanesatake has already promised us twenty or thirty warriors if we need them, all we have to do is send him a message by canoe as soon as we do," Marsden told the gathered men.

"I have written to the Governor and the Seigneur's Agent requesting more modern weapons, powder and shot; have told them that our group will be known as the Vaudreuil Loyal Volunteers; and that we will be ready to help the other Militia in the region around Montréal if we are needed.

"George Henderson here has volunteered to handle the training. For those of you who do not know him very well, he is a retired Sergeant Major of the 95th Rifles and has numerous years of service for King George in Spain and France. I myself will be your commander and I would like to know how many others of you have had some military training. I know the Grampians have and the Schmidts too, but I am not sure of the rest."

Two of the O'Rourke men from St. Henry raised their hands and announced that they had been with the Royal Irish Fusiliers and had served for six years. Joseph Shouldice even announced to George's surprise that he too had served in the Army, with a cavalry unit, but had not seen any action as the war with Napoleon had ended before he was shipped over to Belgium. "When the war ended, I deserted and came here to Montréal," he announced.

"That is fine, Joseph," George told him. "I will not fault you for that."

After an hour of further discussions it was decided that the men would meet at least three times a month for regular training and drill practices. All agreed that the Grampian farm was the best spot.

There were still some grumblings from some of the farmers on why they should have to arm themselves when the army was so close by. Marsden had to choose his words carefully so as not to scare off any of the men. He succeeded; only five decided not to join, mostly due to their health and sicknesses in their families.

In closing, Marsden told his audience that since other Militia units were paid an allowance each time they met for drills or were called to duty he would try to get the same allowance for the Vaudreuil Loyal Volunteers. "How much do the others get?" asked Robert Fowler.

"From what I have heard and seen written in the Montreal Gazette," Marsden responded, "the organized Militia units are allowed two shillings-sixpence for each day they are on duty." There were cheers all around when the men heard that. It seems that Marsden had saved the best for last.

"They are all poor farmers," Marsden whispered to George. "This money could help many of them with their debts and build up their confidence. It could prove worthwhile for all of us if Deschamps does plan to do something drastic. I just hope that no one gets killed, on either side. It could have lasting results for many years to come."

Chapter 18
The Voyage Continues

The young canoeists from Cavagnal and Montréal stopped at Wright's Village to verify that they would be able to spend the winter in one of the many lumber camps that the Wright family operated north and northwest of their settlement. The young men were amazed at the size of the community. Joe Desormeaux told them that when he was there the year before there had been reported to be over one thousand people living in and around the area.

"I guess this is the largest community west of Montreal, except for Fort William," exclaimed John Cameron. "I never expected to see this, so far west of Cavagnal. Look, they even have a big gristmill and a large church. That is even more than we have back home."

"Maybe we can get someone around our area to set up a lumber mill, other than Mr. Whetstone," said John Henderson.

"I wonder if the area is already too developed for it to be worthwhile," said Allan Henderson. "I have seen what Whetstone has already done in our area and there is not too much prime timber left. At least not enough for a big operation that the Wright family is used to."

Joe agreed with Allan and stated that in 1824 alone, the Wrights had sent over twenty large rafts of timber down the Ottawa River to Quebec, and from there most of it went overseas.

"If someone could open up a sawmill in our area and have the wood available for home building rather than the logs we now use, that would be good," said John Cameron. "I have heard from Solomon Grampian that his cousin down in the United States has told him of new sawmills that are now being set up in their old hometown of Charleston, New Hampshire.

"Trees are cut but then the logs are cut by a big circular saw rather than being squared off. Lots more of the tree is used and nice planks are a result. The planks make building a home a great deal easier and make it more pleasant to live in. They are even making floors from the planks. Imagine no more dirt floors!"

All the men laughed at this and discussed the possibility of them setting up such a mill with the money they hoped to make that coming winter, working for the Wrights. John Cameron said to his friends, "The end of the square timber trade is not far from now. I have already heard from Lieutenant John Benson that the Royal Navy is about to cut back its fleet in Halifax by at least half. There is just no demand. There will be great unemployment all over the lands that Britain controls unless an alternative to the square timber trade is found.

"From what the Grampians have told me, it is due to the rapid American expansion into Pennsylvania, Ohio, and Kentucky, and other regions west of New York and Boston. The lumber business will be the way to go in the very near future. In the mean time all we have up here is the big timber trade."

The area near Wright's Village had been covered in prime timber, especially huge one-hundred-foot-tall white pines. Now the big timber trade was looking elsewhere, especially up into the Gatineau Hills, as the area north of Wright's Village was referred to. The hills were known all across eastern North America as the best place to find work. Only New Brunswick and northern Maine had more lumber camps in operation. However, these two areas had been settled years before the Wright family had set up their village at the junction of the Ottawa, Rideau, and Gatineau Rivers.

The upper Ottawa River basin was now being developed as well by numerous big timber cutting firms besides the Wrights and they were starting to stake claims from the Lièvre River east of Wright's Village all the way up to the Madawaska, the Bonnechere, the mighty Dumoine, and finally up the Petawawa River. "This area is going to make many a man wealthy," Ruggles Wright told John Cameron and his friends when they stopped by to see about their fall employment.

When old Philomen Wright saw big Joe Desormeaux, he immediately recognized him from his previous employment in 1824 on the Upper Rideau and was pleased that he had brought along some of his friends. "I will find you a fine place to work, Joe," Wright said to the big Frenchman, "but as you know I offer no favours and you are only paid after your work is done—or you can quit. I hope to have over one thousand men in the bush this winter and you boys are most welcome."

The young men thanked the old man and then went to the small church in Wright's Village to offer their thanks to the Lord before continuing up the Ottawa towards the mighty Mattawa River where they would then turn west towards Lake Nipissing.

The trip on the upper Ottawa was quite easy for the eleven young men. They made good time, even though most had never worked as voyageurs. The first few days had been tough on the young men from Cavagnal and all of them had developed serious blisters on their hands. However, the Mohawks had come prepared with some special salve and the two men from Kanesatake soon had the four young Englishmen in fine shape and paddling as furiously as the others.

Big Joe Desormeaux and Iain Macleod had found the cramped canoe tough on their long legs, but after a couple of days they found that if they sat on a canoe thwart they would be able to paddle in comfort. All the others kneeled in the proper manner of a voyageur.

Théodule Bertrand explained to the four English lads that most voyageurs were less than five and a half feet tall. "A good voyageur can haul two ninety pound packs on a portage den paddle another ten mile before resting," he told them. "A canoe is a small cramped boat and big men are not comfortable in dem," Théodule continued to tell the boys from Cavagnal. "Big Joe and Iain are strong on land but we short guys are more dan a match for dem in dis canoe."

As the big canoe passed the mouth of the a small river, about twenty five miles west of Wright's Village, the voyageurs spotted two large canoes ahead of them pulling into the shore. "We will stop ere for de night," announced Louis Lévesque from the stern. "We can see who dese lads are at de same time. I tink they maybe a little lost."

The big canoe pulled in just beside the two other canoes and the men soon saw that their fellow paddlers were not voyageurs at all but Royal Engineers from the British Army. "Having trouble?" asked Théodule from the bow.

"Just wondering which river this is," announced a man that John Cameron guessed was an officer and the party leader.

Théodule told him that it was known around there as the Mississippi River.

"We cannot be that far west already!" exclaimed one man in the engineer's canoe.

"You are tinking of dat big river in de west," announced Louis. "Dis is de Canadian Mississippi. It is cleaner and a hell of a lot smaller."

"Where are you from?" asked John Cameron. "And where are you going?"

"We are from Fort Henry in Kingston and we are looking for the Madawaska River, replied the officer. "I am Lieutenant John Walpole, of His Majesty's Royal Engineers, Third Battalion. I am making a plan to see if a navigational canal on that river would be feasible. Do any of you know where it is?" he asked.

Théodule announced in his broken English that the mouth of the Madawaska was just up river, about six or seven miles. "You might as well stay ere wit us tonight before heading dere."

"That would be nice," said Lieutenant Walpole. "There seems to be plenty of room here on this beach for all of us."

The three canoes were soon emptied of their goods and a small camp was set up. The British Engineers were a tough looking group of twenty men. They were quite loaded down with their instruments for surveying the land. Simon noted that their only guide was a young French Canadian who quietly admitted that he had been up the Ottawa River only once before and that he was not really sure where he was.

"Trust the British Army to get lousy guides," admitted Joshua. "They can never see past the end of their stuck-up noses and get good advice when they need it. It is amazing that they win so many wars."

"I agree," said John Henderson. "My father has some real horror stories from his days in Spain and France. Many a time, he told me, that his men were ready to kill their officers rather than be slaughtered like sheep. They figured they could do the job better themselves than be led by a bunch of store-bought drunken officers."

"Did many officers get killed by their own men?" asked Allan Henderson.

"My father says yes, but he never killed one himself."

"I wonder if dat was de same in de French Army," asked Théodule.

"I do not know," answered John, "but I imagine it is common with all armies all over the world when the men cannot trust their leaders."

"May I speak with you, sir?" John Henderson asked the Royal Engineer's Lieutenant that evening.

"Of course you may," replied the young army officer.

"My father has told me that his brother is at Fort Henry serving with the British Army. We have been here in Canada for two years now but have not heard from him. Do you know him?"

"Well son, what is his name?" asked Lieutenant Walpole.

"He is John Henderson and he was with the 68th Regiment of Foot as far as I can remember."

"I do not know him but maybe my Sergeant does. Sergeant Bell, please come over here," Walpole called.

"Yes, sir?"

"Do you know of a John Henderson with the 68th?"

"Yes, sir, I remember him. Why sir?"

"This is his nephew, also called John Henderson. John is from down the Ottawa and has been here since 1824. His family has not heard anything from his uncle since they left England. Do you know of him, Jock?"

Sergeant Jock Bell was a big burly Scotsman but had a gentle demeanor. He began to tell John what had happened to his uncle.

"I am sorry to report young lad but Corporal Henderson has been dead for about three years now."

John slowly sat down and bowed his head.

"We never knew; father will be deeply saddened on learning this. He was hoping to visit him one day soon. What happened, Sergeant?" John asked quietly.

"There was an explosion of one of our big guns on the south rampart during some routine drills in December of 1823 and your uncle and two other men who were with him were killed instantly. They are buried in the fort's cemetery just outside the walls. He was a good man, from what I can remember of him. It was not his fault, either. One of the men on the gun crew made a mistake with the powder charge and three of his fellow soldiers paid for it with their lives. The soldier at fault was court-martialed tried and hanged for that mistake. Your uncle had been the acting gun captain that day because his Sergeant was sick, if I can remember correctly.

"I was watching some American ships that were entering the harbour at Kingston when the explosion occurred. The gun was a big twenty-four pounder and as you probably know it will make a large noise when it shot off but when one like that explodes, the noise is deafening. Shrapnel injured numerous men in the area around the gun and even some down on the parade grounds were injured as well.

"A small fire started in one of the barracks below the gun when some red hot shrapnel fell on some crates and barrels that were piled outside. Luckily we have a small fire pump and that quickly put the fire out before we had an even worse disaster."

"What kind of soldier was he?" asked John.

"I guess you should ask one of the men who served with him," said Sergeant Bell. "Hey, Arthur, come over here and meet this young lad from down the river."

With that, a young soldier of about twenty-five came over and sat down beside Sergeant Bell and John Henderson.

"This is Private Arthur Jones of the 68th Regiment of Foot, John. Arthur, please meet John Henderson. He is the nephew of Corporal Henderson who was killed three years ago. You served with him, right?"

"That is correct, Sergeant. I knew Corporal Henderson very well. He was a fine man and very well liked by those in the Regiment."

"I guess Lieutenant Walpole had forgotten that you knew him, him being an officer and all that. He has more important things to think about and remember than what happened to a Corporal in another regiment over three years ago."

"He was a good man and a very dedicated one, too, especially to his friends and of course to the regiment. You and your family should be very proud of him. As I said before, he was well liked and he could have easily been a sergeant and if he had been in the right place. He would have made a great officer, I think. Too bad he was not from the right place in society. You know what I mean, don't you, John?" asked Arthur.

"Yes I do," answered John. "I am pleased to hear that he was well liked, father will be pleased too—but also deeply saddened. His other brother, Joseph Henderson, is in an Australian prison."

"I remember John speaking of him, and your father too," said Arthur. "John was always very proud of your father, his elder brother. But he was also very ashamed of his other brother. It must have been a very serious crime to have been banished to Australia."

"It was," John answered. "He robbed a local Church and the preacher just after a Sunday service. Then he raped the preacher's young daughter. It was only because of my father's influence in the County of Westmorland that the Justice of the Peace in Appleby sent Joseph to Australia for life rather than having him hanged in the square in Appleby."

"It seems your father had quite the distinguished career in the army," Arthur Jones announced in a voice that was a lot louder than what he had been speaking to John in. It seems that he wanted to impress his fellow soldiers that were with him on the trip up to the Madawaska River.

All the heads of the Royal Engineers turned at once and a few of them came over to listen. John was a little embarrassed but he had to admit that what Arthur Jones was saying was correct.

Jones was only one of two men of the 68th Regiment of Foot who were along for the expedition, all the others were members of the Royal Engineers, 3rd Battalion. Even Lieutenant Walpole and Sergeant Bell came over to where Jones and John had been talking. The latter two had gone off to discuss the next day's voyage up the Madawaska and how far they hoped to get.

They had learned from Louis and Théodule that the Madawaska was a fast flowing river in its upper reaches but after they got past the falls that were just upriver from the its mouth, the river was an easy paddle until they reached a region about sixty miles upstream. It was from there that the river narrowed and began to flow very fast.

"I do not know why you want to verify wedder de Madawaska is navigable or not," said Louis. "Any voyageur from Montréal knows dat it is but dere is nothing up dere except trees. All de beaver have been kilt long ago." Just as he mentioned trees, Louis realized what he had said and stopped. He immediately knew what the British were planning and he just smiled as the young Lieutenant did too.

"So," asked one of the Engineers in a sarcastic tone of voice, "who was and what did your father do in the British Army?"

"No one special, and nothing much," answered John.

"Not exactly correct," John Cameron and Simon Beauvais both said sarcastically. John Cameron calmly told them that his father, George Henderson, Sergeant Major of the 95th Rifles had fought in just about every major battle throughout Spain and into France and lived to tell his tales, even after being at Quatre Bras and Waterloo. He then organized a make shift rifle platoon on board the ship he was coming over on, in 1824, and between him and the ship's captain they defeated a Spanish pirate off the coast of Nova Scotia and sank the ship, too.

The young Engineers, their sergeant, Lieutenant Walpole, and the two men of the 68th sat with awestruck looks on their faces.

"Is it true?" asked Lieutenant Walpole.

"Every word," said John Henderson. "Every word."

"None of these men has ever seen any real action," announced Sergeant Jock Bell. "That includes Lieutenant Walpole. I was in France during the occupation after Waterloo but I never saw any of the real fighting. All the rest of these men are recruits that only joined after 1820. I joined in May of 1815 but was not shipped to France until July, a couple of weeks after Waterloo."

John Henderson began his story by stating that his father had joined the army and had been shipped off to the war in Spain almost immediately after his very basic training. "The 95th Rifles were looking for sharpshooters and my father was a great shot, so he volunteered for the Rifles. They were a new concept in the British Army, from what I can remember. None of the men were issued with the old smooth bore Brown Bess muskets but had the new Baker rifle.

"I have one with me on this trip. However, my father is now waiting for a nice Pennsylvania long rifle from some Mohawk friends we met in Québec in 1824. I hope he gets it. Our old rifle has seen lots of action and needs to be replaced soon."

"So where did your father see his action?" asked the Lieutenant.

"He was at Vitoria, Badajoz, and Ciudad Rodrigo—and other less-famous battles. He was once slightly wounded in his left leg but some work by some Spanish maggots cleared that up nicely. Luckily the bullet had just grazed him but infection had set in. The maggots are not used over here, I see. However, I have seen some leeches being used.

"After he got into France he was at the battle of Toulouse. Then he made his way north to Belgium. I think he was under Picton's control at Quatre Bras and at Waterloo. His unit was almost wiped out in the sand pit near the start of the action at Waterloo but he and his captain and a few other men were able to get out. Many a good man that had been with them from Portugal to Spain and up into France were left dead in that lonely sandpit.

"He had one good friend. No, that should be a great friend, whom my father was with during most of his enlistment. He even came over on board the ship with us but as fate would have it, he was killed during the battle with the Spanish pirate ship, the *El Condor.*"

"You were on the ship that sank the *El Condor?*" exclaimed one of the young Engineers. "We have heard a great deal about that famous battle, even way up in Kingston. I never thought that I would meet someone who was involved in such a famous battle. From the reports of the sailors on the Lake Ontario Royal Naval Squadron, your battle is one that sailors will be talking about in years to come."

Lieutenant Walpole then stood up and raised his tankard of rum. "Gentlemen, let us raise a toast to this young man and his father for the glory they have brought to Britain and King George." All of the men, including the French Canadian voyageurs and the Mohawks, stood up and raised their full tankards as John Henderson sat there smiling and looking somewhat ashamed. All he could say was thank you as he wiped some free flowing tears from his now very red eyes.

The next morning the two groups split up as they arrived at the mouth of the Madawaska River. "This is where we leave you, my friends," Lieutenant Walpole told the young voyageurs from Lower Canada. "Good luck on your way west and have a safe passage. We will leave you now and head up this little river. How far we go will only be known to us in a few days, I guess."

They all shook hands with each other and then the young adventurers broke into another French Canadian paddling song as they headed out into the fast-flowing Ottawa River. "We have some tough going from ere to Lake Nipissing," announced Louis, "but when we get to de 'Rivière Creuse', we will ave at least thirty mile of easy paddling. However, before dat, we will earn our pay, eh Théodule?"

"Oui, mon ami. You are correct and after dat is de mighty Mattawa River," announced Théodule. With that, they set off at a brisk pace.

The trip up the Mattawa River was very difficult. There were many rapids and swamps to pull through. Allan Henderson had twisted his ankle after slipping on a moss-covered rock on the last portage before they entered into Lake Nipissing. At first, John Cameron had thought that it was broken and that they would have to leave him at the first Indian settlement they came across, but Louis had looked at it and told them all that it was just a sprain and that he would be able to rest it as they paddled across the big lake and then down the Rivière des Françaises.

Allan was glad of the rest and, though his ankle was hurting, was still able to paddle as strongly as the others. When they had to portage a couple of times along the French River, big Joe Desormeaux put Allan on his back and carried him over the portage.

The young lads had been able to get across Lake Nipissing in good time because the winds were right and they were able to put up their sail. They had not used it since the first day, back on the Lake of the Two Mountains.

"If de winds are right as dey are here on Lake Nipissing," announced Théodule, "we will be able to do some great sailing in La Baie Georgienne."

"We will stop at Manitoulin Island for a day or two and visit a Huron village dere," Louis told the men one day as they headed up the north shore of Georgian Bay.

Simon and Joshua looked at each other and smiled. "Why you two smile?" asked Louis. Simon turned to Louis in the stern and told him that the Hurons on Manitoulin Island had originally lived at Kanesatake before they moved west when the Mohawks became too strong in the area around Montréal.

Joshua continued by saying that it would be best for all of them if the Hurons did not know that Simon and he were from Kanesatake.

"They will know that we are Mohawks right away, but let them think that we are from Kahnawake or down in the United States. There is still no love between them and us, even after these many years. Our tribe almost wiped out the Huron nation completely and this small community here and one near Québec are all that is left from the once-powerful Huron nation."

Simon added some more details by stating, "if the Hurons of Manitoulin find out that we are from Kanesatake, we could be very easily robbed of all our goods and possessions and sent back east with, if we are lucky, just our canoe. I would recommend that we stay there just one day and then head west."

"That sounds fine by me," announced John Henderson. However, Théodule interjected by saying that they would stay two days. "We need to ave a short rest and Allan needs to ave his ankle checked. Dere is a Jesuit missionary on de Island and he will be able to look at it. He is well train in wilderness medicine."

Allan's ankle had swollen up quite a bit over the last few days while they paddled and sailed the north shore of Georgian Bay. Théodule was worried that the ankle might be broken after all and it could get infected. "If dat ankle gets infected, you might lose your leg or your life, especially way out ere. We must stop," announced Théodule.

"Agreed," said Simon, "but please do not mention Kanesatake."

"Dat is fine with me," said Théodule. "Neither Louis nor I will as long as no one else does. We all want to get through dis adventure safely and arrive in Fort William in time for de Rendezvous in early July."

Chapter 19
Bad Luck!

Father Antoine Demers of the Jesuit Mission on Manitoulin Island had taken a good look at Allan's ankle and had told him that the ankle was definitely broken and that he thought some infection had set in.

"I will have to use leeches and he should not leave here," the old Jesuit Priest told Allan's friends.

"I want to go west with the others," Allan protested.

John Henderson put his hand on his shoulder and told him, "no, Allan, you must stay here with the Jesuits. We cannot risk having that leg get gangrene out on Lake Superior. The pain or the infection will kill you."

"You must think of the rest of us too," announced John Cameron. "We want you along but if you get sick out on Lake Superior, we will not be able to help you as this good Priest can here. We will pick you up on our return voyage and by then you should be fluent in French and maybe have a Huron girl as your bride."

"That is not very funny, John," Allan replied. "But you are right, and I will stay. I just do not want to miss the Rendezvous and all the fun up there in Fort William."

"We will be back by late August if all go well," announced Louis. "We will not forget you and I promise dat we will bring you someting from de Rendezvous, eh, mes amis. Une jolie jeune Ojibwa ou Sioux si possible!"

They all laughed except the Priest who was crossing himself and saying a hasty prayer of forgiveness for Louis.

"Bon, that is settled," said Father Demers. "You will all stay here tonight then do some trading if you like with the Hurons tomorrow then you may leave. It is not a long voyage to Fort William from here, if the winds are right. However, if you get caught out on that lake in a storm, may God and Sainte Anne be with you."

Allan Henderson was left in relatively good spirits though his ankle was getting worse by the hour. Father Demers had noticed a slight reddening of his calf muscle and around the knee but did not tell the young boy. He guessed that it would not be long before the young boy was dead. Father Demers prayed for Allan's salvation and was sad that he could not do more for the young boy.

Allan Henderson died three days after his friends had left him with the old Jesuit Priest on Manitoulin Island. Allan's fellow voyageurs would not learn of his death until they arrived back in August. However, Father Demers did send word of Allan's death east with the next brigade of canoes that were heading for Montreal. The leader or bourgeois of that brigade kindly advised Father Demers that he would stop at Schmidt's Tavern and leave word there for Allan's parents.

"I know the Tavern well," the bourgeois told the old Priest. "It is the most famous Tavern west of Ste Anne de Bellevue and east of Wright's Village."

Allan Henderson was buried in the Jesuit cemetery at the mission on Manitoulin Island in early July of 1826. A simple cross marked his grave. On the cross, the Priest had one of his workers carve the following inscription in English. "Allan Henderson, A Young Adventurer from Lower Canada, July 1826."

John Henderson and his fellow canoeists headed west from the Huron village and in a couple of days were making their last portage. The St. Mary's River is a fast flowing river that drains Lake Superior into Lake Huron. The North West Company had a small trading post set up near the height of the rapids and the men from Cavagnal and Lachine stopped there for a short rest before heading out onto the mighty Lake Superior.

Louis explained to his fellow voyageurs of the tremendous battles that had gone on between the North West Company and the mighty Hudson's Bay Company that were based out of Churchill Factory up on Hudson's Bay.

It was open warfare out here in the bush, he told them. Joshua Gabriel agreed and recounted how he had seen more than one empty canoe floating down a remote river in the hinterland, no canoeists to be seen, and all the furs gone. Each company was as bad as the other was and scores of men were killed each year.

The Hudson's Bay Company was noted for its well-planned ambushes out along the Methy Portage. "In one year dey even took over Fort William for a short period of time," Louis told his friends. "Théodule and I once came across a brigade dat had been wiped out by some Bay employees. All dere furs had been stolen, de four canoes had been sunk and de men all scalped."

"How do you know it was white men dat had killed de voyageurs?" asked Jean-Jacques Major. "The murderers were probably Indians."

"Indians would not have sunk the canoes," answered Simon. "We are smarter than that."

"Simon is right," said Théodule. "It was de white men. Dat was de worst case of out-right murder dat I ever saw in de bush. I am glad dat de two companies ave amalgamated now, at least de war est fini-finished."

"Are there many problems out west, past Fort William with unfriendly Indians?" asked John Cameron.

"Yes," replied Louis, "in particular de Sioux, Cree and de Cheyenne. Of de three, de main one we Canadians ave to worry about are de Cree. De odder two tribe stay mostly across de very much-undefined border with de United States.

"The western Indians, like dere eastern cousins, cannot relate to de border between two nations dat dey cannot see. During de buffalo hunting season de tribes move all across de western plains, following de great herds."

"Ave you ever seen a buffalo, Théodule?" asked Joe Desormeaux.

"I have seen a few just south of Fort William and once when I went west to de land of de Bitterroot Mountains, I saw a herd dat took over tree days to go by. What a mess dey made of de prairie and de smell was awful. Owever, de meat is very good, better dan our beef any day.

"Do you think we will see any?" asked John Henderson.

"I doubt it. De bush up ere along de north shore is too tick for dem. Dey are a grazing animal," answered Louis. "What we will probably see are caribou and more moose dan you ave ever seen before. We will ave to be very careful on our return trip. By de time we get onto de French River and east along de Mattawa and Ottawa Rivers, de moose rut will be on and a big bull moose in love is not an animal you would like to meet on a portage."

"Will we see any Indians from out west?" asked Jean-Jacques. "Besides the Ojibwa from around the Fort dere should be some Cree and maybe a few Sioux. Dey come up from de south to trade with de British," explained Louis.

Théodule told them of meeting some American Army soldiers under a Major Henry on the northern part of the Missouri in 1823. He had stayed over the winter in a small fort that they had to build in a hurry after an early winter had set in near the mouth of the Yellowstone River. Henry had reported having some troubles with the Sioux and Arikara Indians that fall and over the winter. He lost five of his men during a wood-cutting expedition and two others during a mid-winter hunt for some buffalo.

"When I and a few odder men from Montréal and Fort William came upon de beleaguered American soldiers, they were in a bad way. De young soldiers were terrified of anything dat moved and or looked like an Indian. We had been in de bush for quite sometime, living with some Cree and de poor soldiers tought we were yet anodder bunch of raiding Indians, bent on taking dere scalps.

"Dey were very surprised when one of our men approached dem and spoke h'English to them. We were loaded with furs and were in de process of heading to Fort William for de big rendezvous. It was my one and only time dat I stayed west of Fort William and was able to call myself un gars du nord."

"Alphonse, were you ever un gars du nord?" asked Louis.

"No not really, I only stay one winter in Fort William and traveled in dat region for short trips while waiting for de spring to come. I had been sick one August, after de rendezvous. I was not able to head east with de last brigade before de winter set in."

"Too much of the company's liquor?" laughed John Cameron.

"Partly, but it was mostly dat I ate some bad mushrooms and dey made me very sick. I den developed a rupture from de coughing. Luckily it healed well enough for me to continue east dat next spring but for a couple of years, I was not able to work as a voyageur because of de pain it caused me."

All the while the men had been talking they had been sailing gently up the north shore of the great lake.

"Is de water always dis cold?" asked Alphonse.

"Yes, it is," replied Théodule. "If we capsize now, none of us will last very long in de cold water. Actually de water on de southern shore is even colder. Only a few American traders go dat route and of course all de Canadians stay on dis side.

"We may see some bateaux out on de lake as dey head east from Fort William down to Sault St. Marie and over to de post at Isle St. Joseph. Dey ave to leave dere heavy boats above de rapids and all of de equipment and cargo is transported around de rapids by portage den loaded onto eider canoes or more bateaux for de ride over to St. Joseph's."

"I can see de day when de canoe will be no longer be used on Lake Huron and Lake Superior," announced Louis. "De end of de canot de maitre is near at hand and with de amalgamation of de two big companies five years ago we all have seen a vast decline in de amount of fur making its way down de Ottawa to Montréal. 1826 will be de year of de last great rendezvous at Fort William and I am glad dat Alex Macleod has asked us to go dere wit his last cargo."

"The world is changing and we have seen many a great change around Montréal and Lachine," Iain Macleod told his friends. "At our dock we are seeing more and more people heading west as settlers rather than as explorers, trappers, and hunters. Ever since the fusion five years ago the whole area around Montréal and the lower Ottawa River has changed.

"As we all know the age of the steamboat is upon us and soon the noisy boat will be taking our cargoes up river, and men like my father will be just a part of history that people hopefully will talk about in years to come."

"You are right," announced John Cameron. "My employer, Charles Schmidt, had a new dock built last year in preparation for the coming of the steamboat on the Lake of the Two Mountains. I guess I will have to look for another job too and that of the bateaux man will be part of history as will be the men of the brigades of canoes in their canot de maitre."

"Out west de Fort William de canot du nord will still be used as dere are so many rivers dat cannot take a big bateau, but who knows for how long?" said Théodule. "I feel dat de fur trade as we know it will soon be quite different."

Théodule amazed his friends with his knowledge of the fur trade. He continued by saying, "Les castors will no longer be king. I tink more of the finer pelts will reign as de type of furs to trade. Furs from de marten, fox, lynx and maybe even de buffalo hides will be king. Buffalo hides are too heavy to be hauled by canoe, the Americans are now using keelboats on de Missouri and Mississippi Rivers and they can haul hundreds of pounds.

"De American soldiers we saw in 1823 on de Yellowstone had arrived dere in keelboats, not canoes. Dey were able to haul cannon and hundreds of pounds of shot and powder in dem. You not see us Canadians hauling cannon in dese fragile canoes, do you?"

Iain mentioned that he was quite concerned about the rapid expansion of the Americans into the west. "They seem to want to take over the entire continent."

Simon and Joshua both said they agreed with Iain, as did all the men on board the canoe.

Iain continued telling his friends that his father had been with the Canadian Corps of Voyageurs during the War of 1812 and had been present at the capture of Fort Michilimackinac. "He told me that they scared the living daylights out of the American troops at the fort." All of the others laughed at his last comment. "The British regulars were outnumbered by the unruly voyageurs and Indian allies and the Americans all thought that they would be murdered after they surrendered the fort.

The voyageurs all got drunk, as did the Indians, and the British troops had to send the Americans quietly away or there may have been a massacre. It was quite funny from what I was told by my father. He had never seen so many young Yankee troops so scared in all his life. General Brock had wisely chosen the wild voyageurs and Indians of the north for the job. There were only about forty or fifty British troops that day and the fort was taken with just a few shots exchanged.

"The poor Americans left the fort in such a hurry that they just had time to take enough food for a day or two. The British troops let them go after dark as not to upset the Indians and voyageurs. Even the British were worried that a massacre would occur. They had some fast talking to do the next morning and it was only by letting the voyageurs and Indians sack the fort that the British troops got away with not being killed by their allies.

"The drunken orgy lasted three days after that and the unit was disbanded just six months after it was organized. The poor British Army officers just could not control and discipline the unruly voyageurs." Iain ended his account of the battle by saying that, "They had more luck with the Indians!"

Chapter 20
Fort William

The gates of Fort William were a welcome sight for the ten weary men from Lower Canada. The big fort lay near the mouth of the bronze-coloured Kaministiquia River. The river was the east-west communication route for the western brigades of canoes that supplied the fort with furs from the vast western regions of the country. The deep sounding boom of a cannon being shot off announced their arrival and numerous men and women and children were seen hurrying down to the big dock that was just in front of the big wooden gates.

"Before we land, just a word of warning to all of you," said Louis. "We are all engagés according to dose at de Fort, except for Théodule. If you meet one of de Scottish management people, and we will at de dock, you must call him mister. Never call him by his first name, as dat is an insult. Even de lowliest clerk must be called Mister So-and-So. All you h'English boys will be staying with us as you are all just engagés like de rest of us. Iain may be able to stay with de bourgeois as dis load does belong to his father. I am not sure, dough, and I radder doubt it since he is paddling like de rest of us. Dat is something a real bourgeois would never do."

"I would rather stay with my friends," Iain told Louis.

"Yes, I h'understand, but out here we go by dere rules and once de head Factor finds dat you are Angus Macleod's son, you may ave to stay wit de hodder bourgeois and gentlemen."

Louis continued his lecture as they slowly paddled up to the main dock. "I should ave told all of you dis yesterday but wit dat stiff wind we had to fight, I had my mind on odder tings. Théodule will be staying at de Guide's House. Dough both of us have been de main guides of dis trip and dose on land will see dat we are experienced voyageurs, but he being de bow man, will get de chance to stay in de Guide's House inside de fort and will be de only one of us who will be able to eat and drink in de big hall.

"Therefore, Simon, Joshua, Joe, Alphonse, Jean-Jacques, and the two Johns and I will be staying wit de other engagés. We will find out about Iain soon enough. I do not tink we will get much sleep over de next couple of weeks as des engagés are all here for the big rendezvous. Dis has been a trip of adventure for you all, but to de others here dis month, it is de end of an era.

"Do not be surprised to see many things dat will shock your eyes. There are few women here so many of de men will be dancing wit each odder. Many a man will die here over de next few weeks as de party can get a little out of hand. I have even seen men scalped by some jealous voyageur or Indian as one took a special liking to his squaw.
"Stay away from most of de women. They are usually full of disease and very dirty and de ones dat are not are already spoken for, usually by de gentlemen of de Fort. Only very few white women make it dis far and dey are de wives of de senior management. Many of de young clerks already ave wives. Owever, the loneliness of dis fort has made many a good husband turn to two of de many vices dat are common here; an excess of liquor and an Indian girl as a companion. Do what you want, but beware. There is a gaol ere and I do not tink Mr. Macleod would like to ave his crew thrown in dere while dey are ere, especially his son," he finished, winking at Iain.

All of the men on the big canoe nodded their heads in agreement, though Jean-Jacques and Alphonse did mumble a few words with each other about the prospects of diddling one of the young Ojibwa girls that they had heard about while on Manitoulin Island with Father Demers.

As the big canoe pulled up to the dock, all of the voyageurs noticed a couple of very well-dressed gentlemen walking out of the gates and down to the dock. "Do not speak unless spoken to," whispered Théodule to all the others.

"Iain, introduce yourself," Louis whispered to their employer's son.

The lead gentleman doffed his Paris Beau hat and introduced himself as the Chief Factor of Fort William, Mister Robert Thompson. The other man introduced himself as the Fort's chief clerk, Mister Thomas Duckworth. "Who are you and where do you hail from?" asked the Factor.

"I am Iain Macleod of Lachine, and I bring with me a load of mail for you, Mister Thompson. We have been on the water since late May. Have we missed the rendezvous?"

"No. It does not begin until next week, by then most of the western brigades should be here. Have you seen any other brigades heading west?" Iain responded that they had seen only one other canoe brigade since they had left the mouth of the St. Mary's River.

"That brigade landed two days ago. Why were you so slow?" asked Mister Duckworth. "We would have appreciated the mail a lot sooner." John Cameron looked at big Joe Desormeaux and smiled.

Alphonse, who was standing behind big Joe, whispered in his ear, "Dis young Mister needs to ave his tongue a little shorter, metinks." Both Joe and John began to laugh but quickly stopped when the Factor asked them what was so funny.

"Nothing really, Mister Thompson," answered John. "We both noticed that it seems strange to see such well dressed gentlemen so far from Montréal. We are not used to that. Actually I am quite impressed."

"Thank you," replied the Factor. "Who are you?"

"I am John Cameron from Cavagnal."

"Never heard of it," the Clerk said in an abrupt and sarcastic tone.

"He was not talking to you, Mister Duckworth," the Factor wryly told the young Clerk. "That is on the Ottawa River, is it not?"

"Yes, Sir," John said. "It is a small English community and my friend John Henderson and I have come along for the chance to see the west before the fur trade stops. There were three of us from Cavagnal but we left our friend at the Jesuit Mission on Manitoulin Island because he had a broken ankle. We will pick him up on the way back east in August."

With the final introductions over, the ten young men from Lower Canada hauled their big canoe out of the water. As half carried their cargo, the others carried the canoe through the gates and over to the canoe repair shed at the back of the huge fort.

"There are over forty buildings here," the Factor announced proudly to the newcomers. "We will probably not meet again, so I just wish to thank you for this very important load of mail. It confirms my suspicions that this fort has seen its last real important year as a cog in the wheel of the great Hudson's Bay Company. Iain Macleod, you have brought us some sad news, but it is part of history and you should consider yourself part of that. Tonight I will toast your name at the main banquet in the Great Hall."

"Will I be invited, Sir?" asked Iain.

"No you will not, being a simple engagé like the rest, you are not permitted and not even I can change the rules, even for such an important event. Enjoy yourself, Iain, as it will be very doubtful that our paths will ever cross again, even though this fort is so small. We gentlemen do not and will not associate ourselves with the lower classes even though some of you are as well educated as us.

"I am impressed with that John Cameron and his friend, John Henderson. Why are they along with you and the other engagés?" asked the Factor to Iain.

"They wanted some adventure and a chance to make some good money. Getting sixty pounds for the round trip and a chance to make even more in the lumber camps of Philomen Wright brought them along. They are good strong workers and they have done well."

"Well, thank you again," Factor Thompson said to Iain Macleod. "Good bye and enjoy your stay. Stay out of gaol." They shook hands and parted their ways, never to speak to each other again. That was the way of the life of a voyageur and the Factor in the employment of the mighty Hudson's Bay Company.

As the young voyageurs split up for the day and went off on their separate ways to explore the huge fort, Théodule warned them all not to get into trouble and remember to address any of the management by Mister.

The engagés soon found their quarters, which were already very crowded. They were location just outside the fort's twelve-foot wooden walls. There were tents and lean-tos set up all along the western side of the fort. All the best sites had already been taken.

"I saw a small encampment outside de walls on de eastern side," announced Jean Jacques. "Maybe we can set up a tent over dere."

"It would probably be quieter, too," laughed Alphonse. "The only ting we will ave to contend wit will be des maudits chrisse des mouches noir. Dere are clouds of dem here," he said.

"None here," yelled an engagés who was relieving himself in one corner of the campsite.

"Too much smoke from our pipes and our campfires," yelled another. "Get out in the fresh air where you belong."

"Uh-oh," John Cameron thought, "we had better leave now before big Joe loses his temper."

"Hey big man, with those long legs did you cut holes in the bottom of the canoe and walk here?"

"Restez tranquille, Joe," Alphonse said to the big man who was already rolling up his sleeves and getting ready to hit the next man who spoke.

"We will all be leaving now, Joe," John Cameron said as he pulled the big man around by his left arm and led him away.

"Sorry John, but I do not like being teased."

"Get used to it now, Joe," Jean-Jacques told his friend. "We are ere for just two weeks and I do not want to spend any time in any Hudson's Bay Company gaol. Dese men are known for dere teasing and dey will pick on someone who is vulnerable."

"They really do not mean any harm, I hope," said John Henderson.

They all found a nice spot to the right of the main gate and just outside the walls. "When the rendezvous begins in a few days, the area main square inside the fort will be so crowded, you will be glad you moved over here," said a grizzled old voyageur camped next to the lads from Lower Canada.

"Dis is my sixteenth rendezvous and dey ave all been wild times," the old man told the new campers. "My name is Henri LaRivière and I am from de Cumberland House." The young men from Cavagnal and Lachine introduced themselves and then began to set up camp.

Théodule had better luck in finding a place to stay in the guide's quarters. Their cabin was smaller than that of the management's but the guides at the fort were rated as a lower class, just above the engagés. Usually there would be just one or two guides per brigade and for the lads from Cavagnal and Lachine, Théodule had been their only guide on the trip.

Louis admitted that he would have liked to been staying in the guide's house too but since their trip had consisted of only one canoe de maitre, rather than the usual four or five in the typical brigade, they could not justify having more than one guide.

Henri turned out to be a veteran voyageur about forty five years old. He was not exactly sure when he had been born. "I am one of de oldest ere this year. Most of de men are much younger but I can match most of dem in a day's paddle." Henri told the new campers that he had been a voyageur for over twenty five years and he could well remember the good old days of the real voyageur and the stiff competition between the North West Company and the Hudson's Bay Company.

"I ave not been in Montréal in close to ten years," he told his neighbours. "Has it changed very much?" Jean-Jacques Major, being from Montréal, told him that Montréal was growing rapidly each year and there were ships of all sorts arriving each day with new settlers.

"Dere is even a small bateau à vapeur or steam boat now on de fleuve St. Laurent." Not realizing that Henri did not know what a steamboat was, Jean-Jacques had to excuse himself and took time to describe the smoke-belching, noisy, but powerful boat.

Henri just could not visualize a ship with a fire on board at all times and not burning down to the water line and how that fire could move the ship, especially with no sails. They all laughed but then realized that Henri was quite serious and the young voyageurs quietly apologized to him.

The last great rendezvous at Fort William began on July 18th, 1826. There were close to two thousand men, women, and children in and around the great fort. The children were those of the local Ojibwa tribe that had benefited greatly over the years from having such an important site located right next to their village. Many a voyageur had fathered a child by one or more of the local Indian girls. There was a dramatic cross culture to be seen and heard among the locals. The Ojibwas spoke their own language but many of them had included various English and French words, thus making the local dialect quite difficult to understand, especially for someone from outside the territory.

The last few bateaux that had arrived had brought numerous kegs of watered-down rum and other spirits such as gin, wine, and ale. The liquor was free-flowing and everyone was drunk from almost dawn till dusk. John Henderson and his friends had been warned by Louis Levesque about things that would shock them. They never expected to see such drunken debauchery as they were now seeing at Fort William.

"I think Reverend Angus Bradfield would curl up into a ball and die if he saw what we are seeing here this week," John Cameron told his good pal, John Henderson. "I cannot believe how much these people can drink." John Cameron had worked for the Schmidts at their Tavern for a number of years and he told his friends from Kanesatake and Cavagnal that even he had never seen so many people intoxicated for such a long period of time.

Théodule and Louis were having just a fine time celebrating the rendezvous like all the others. The Indians from Kanesatake held back a little but did try to enjoy themselves. Alphonse and Jean-Jacques stayed most of the time with Théodule and Louis while big Joe Desormeaux kept close to the two Johns.

Joe had grown to trust the two Englishmen and he had thanked them for not letting him get into a fight on their first day over at the main voyageur camp.

"Want to make some easy money?" John Cameron asked Joe and John Henderson during the fourth day of the week-long rendezvous.
"But of course," they both announced. "But how? We are not card players like the others."

"But you are big and strong, Joe, and John here is an excellent shot with that rifle of his. Let's see what we can find," said John to his friends.

They gathered together with their Mohawk friends and headed out towards the back of the fort where games of chance were being held. The Mohawks had shown their skill with the tomahawk during the voyage up from Lachine and everyone knew how strong Joe was. "There must be a wrestling match sometime this week," John Cameron told his friends.

Henri LaRivière had overheard their conversations and had followed them around to the west side of the fort. He also told them that there would be a wrestling match later that day. "The best games are over dere," he told his new friends. "Bet what you can but be warned dese men of de nord woods, les gars du nord, are a tough lot and dey may cheat on you, so beware."

John Henderson had not used his rifle since shooting a deer along a portage on the French River. However, he had kept it clean as his father had taught him and he was sure that poor old Isaac Kirkbride would still be proud of the big gun. John had practiced a great deal since inheriting the gun after Isaac had been killed on *The Pioneer*, two years before.

Both John and his father, George, were undefeated in local shooting matches in Cavagnal. Actually it was only George's failing eyesight that let his son win once in awhile, though sometimes John was not sure of that and often wondered if his father had just let him win the odd time to make him feel better.

Looking around at the other guns, John Henderson did not spot another rifle. Most were old trade muskets, often just old Brown Bess muskets that had been cut down. He did not even see one of the long Yankee rifles that he and his father had seen down in Quebec in 1824.

"I wonder if those two Mohawks ever showed up at Cavagnal," he thought to himself. "That would be the gun to have here."

The first targets were set up at fifty paces and each of the five men entered had two shots each. If there was a tie, more shots would be fired until the tie was broken, then they would shoot at one hundred paces, then one hundred and fifty. John knew that his gun was deadly accurate to over three hundred paces so he was quite confident of winning the whole event.

In the meantime, Simon and Joshua had found a spot where they could compete with other natives and some voyageurs in a tomahawk-throwing competition that also included as an a knife-throwing event.

Big Joe Desormeaux would watch the others compete and make sure no one cheated against his friends. They had agreed to watch him when he entered the wrestling match later that day.

John found that he was up against some stiff competition, even though the guns of the voyageurs were no match for his well-oiled weapon. He beat all comers at fifty, one hundred, and when it came to one hundred and fifty paces the others did not even enter. They all realized that this young lad from Cavagnal with his old army rifle was too great a shot even for the best marksmen from the north. John Henderson, the rookie voyageur from Cavagnal, was crowned the best shot at the Great Rendezvous of 1826. He was given forty shillings for his prowess.

Simon and Joshua, on the other hand, were having more trouble winning than John had. They were good at the tomahawk throw but since the knife throw was included in the same competition, they had more trouble. Neither had been used to throwing a knife as much as the other voyageurs had and though they tied in the tomahawk section for top place they both placed last in the knife part.

As a consolation prize, the two Mohawks were given a small keg of rum to share with their friends if they wished. Word was soon spreading around the fort like a fast-moving prairie brush fire that the last canoe to arrive at the fort from the east was full of some very tough competitors who were excellent shots and tomahawk throwers.

The final competitions of the day were the tests of strength and big Joe Desormeaux was ready for that. So were his friends. The money that John had won was bet on big Joe in his final match of the evening. He had already thrown, punched, and wrestled four men out of the makeshift ring, all in less than two minutes each.

All of his friends were there, including Théodule who had left the grand banquet early when he had heard of the match between some big Frenchman from Lachine and a massive Scotsman from Fort Chipewyan. The Scotsman, Sean Mowat, stood a few inches taller than Joe and out weighed him by at least twenty pounds. However, Joe had learned his fighting trade in the streets of Montréal and in the lumber camps. Sean Mowat had never fought a man as large and possibly as mean as him. His opponents had all been half-starved Indians or the smaller voyageurs and who normally were no more than five-foot-five in height.

The match was to be of unlimited time, the winner would be declared when the other could not answer the bell. It began right off from the start as a messy and bloody fight. Joe had not lost his temper while battling the first four opponents but it did not take him long to lose it with Sean.

To begin the fight, instead of trying to wrestle Joe, Sean just lunged at burly the Frenchman and bit part of his lower left ear off. With blood now gushing all over Joe's huge neck, he let out a blood-curdling scream and came at Sean like a charging bull moose. He was unstoppable. Sean thought that he could just side-step the huge Frenchman but Joe was quicker on his feet than the Scotsman had thought. Joe had learned to be extra quick on his feet while working the spring log drives in the woods of Québec.

Joe caught Sean with a huge right fist that sent him flying onto his back. When Sean tried to get up, one of Joe's big boots was on his neck and Joe quickly flung himself around behind his head and with one quick snap of his huge forearms the big Scotsman lay dead of a broken neck in the middle of the ring.

The fight was declared fair by the two judges, though one of them vomited beside the ring as he heard Sean's neck crack like a dry twig. Joe was exhausted and sad. He had never killed a man in a fight before, but had maimed scores.

"I hope nothing serious comes of this fight," John Cameron whispered to Théodule who was standing next to him at ringside.

"I do not tink anyting will. It was a death fight from de beginning; I guess everyone knew it except maybe you and John, and big Joe imself."

"I did not want to warn you in case you convinced Joe to back out and den dat would ave made tings very nasty around ere. As it was, de fight was fair but dirty but dat is de way tings are out ere. Only de tough will survive and Joe has proven dat he is de toughest man in the Canadian bush west of Montréal."

"One more ting," continued Théodule, "Sean Mowat had never been beaten in a fight in de past ten years. Actually it is too bad dat de two big men never really got to know each odder. I tink dey might ave made good friends."

"I am not sure about that," John told Théodule. "I am not so sure."

Joe Desormeaux had to join numerous other injured men in the fort's small hospital. Applying some hot spruce gum on the wound quickly stopped the bleeding. However, Joe would have an everlasting reminder how he became known as the strongest and toughest man in the Canadian bush: he would have one ear lobe fewer than most men. But at least he was alive and now famous.

All of Joe's friends had bet heavily on the big man and all had won substantial amounts of money, furs, guns and liquor. Jean-Jacques even won an Indian girl from one voyageur who had dragged along the young girl to the fight and bet her and his gun on Sean Mowat. He lost both.

Poor Jean-Jacques did not know what to do. He was over 1,200 miles from his home and his wife and two children and now he had a young Indian girl of no more than fifteen years old to care for. "I would try to give or sell her or even bet her on some game or competition dat you cannot possibly win," Louis told his beleaguered friend.

"I will do dat later, in a few days," was Jean-Jacques' answer. "But first I am going to enjoy aving a nice young girl around me." With that he winked at Louis and Alphonse then he led the young girl off to his tent.

The girl was one of the most beautiful young things he had ever seen and though she was very young, Jean-Jacques had learned that the voyageur had been with her for over a year, after he had saved her from certain death at the hands of some American fur trappers near Lake of the Woods. They had already killed her parents and younger brother, Jean-Jacques learned, and now she was an orphan. She had meant everything to the poor voyageur but in his drunken stupor, he had even wagered her and his gun on the fight that big Joe had won so easily.

Jean-Jacques enjoyed the young girl for a few hours, then realized his mistake, even though she had submitted to him with ease. "I hope his wife never find out," thought Louis as he turned and headed back to the party. Jean-Jacques' conscience got the better of him later that night and he went searching for the young girl's real lover. He found the man in the cantine salope, still drunk and very full of remorse. "He is on the verge of suicide," said another voyageur in the cantine. "Ever since he lost the girl."

After trying to talk to the drunken man without success, Jean-Jacques brought the girl into the cantine and handed her to the man. Not wanting to offend both of them, Jean-Jacques bet the man that he could have the girl back if he beat him in an arm wrestling match. The man agreed though it seemed that he did not really know what he was saying. The match was set up and one of the other patrons volunteered to act as the referee. Jean-Jacques knew that he could easily beat the man, even if he had been sober. "I ave to make dis look real," he thought. "We will make it de best two out of tree," he announced.

The match commenced with Jean-Jacques easily taking the drunk in just a few seconds. "Looks like the man from Montréal is going to have that whore for good," came the comment from across the cantine. Jean-Jacques looked up but quickly ignored the comment. Deep down he felt sorry for the young Cree girl. The next two matches were more evenly matched as the man began to realize what was going on. He had seen this true love and during the final arm wrestling match he put up a very stiff fight and Jean-Jacques found it was not easy to let the man win even though he wanted to. No one in the bar knew that Jean-Jacques had let the man win and the young Cree leaped into her man's arms and kissed him lovingly on his dirty beard. Jean-Jacques smiled and left the two together in the cantine as he quietly slipped outside.

Théodule had left the games as well after big Joe had won and he returned to the Grand Banquet Hall, where yet another party was going on. The servants were dishing out huge helpings of moose and venison stew that were garnished with potatoes, carrots, and other vegetables that had been grown in the Fort's large garden.

While he was sitting at one of the tables, a young clerk sat down beside him and began to chat. "I am Stephen Thompson and I am a recording clerk here at this fort." It did not take Théodule long to realize that the young clerk was very drunk. He was slurring his words as he tried to talk with Théodule and another man across the table from them. Stephen grabbed at a passing servant for another glass of claret. He yanked at the poor man's arm so hard that he spilled all of the glasses onto Théodule's back.

"I am so sorry, Sir," the man said to Théodule, while wiping up the mess with a now blood red cloth.

"You fool," yelled Stephen, "I will have you whipped-for this."

"Calm down," Théodule told Stephen, who was now standing up and attempting to kick the servant. Théodule told the man to get out right away and to make himself scarce.

Turning around, Théodule was facing a very red-faced Stephen Thompson who had drawn a knife from under his belt. He lunged at Théodule, who easily stepped to one side. With one quick hit with his big fist, the young clerk was out cold on the floor. "Good work, Sir, that could have been a bit nasty I say." Not knowing who had said the words that seemed to support his actions, Théodule turned to face the Chief Factor, Robert Thompson himself.

"I saw the whole episode from the other end of the table and that drunken clerk you just put onto the floor was out of line. Good work."

"What will appen to Mister Thompson now, Sir?" Théodule asked the Factor, all the while remembering to call the Clerk he had just knocked out, Mister Thompson.

"He will spend the next couple of days in our gaol and hopefully that will teach him to hold his liquor. However, I guess you do not know that Mister Thompson is my son, do you?" Théodule felt a lump in his throat as the Chief Factor explained that the young clerk he had just knocked out really was his son. "Do not worry, guide or whatever your name is, as I said, I saw the whole thing and my son was out of order. Around here I am the law and whomever disobeys it will answer to me, even if that person happens to be my only son."

"My name is Théodule Bertrand, Sir," Théodule answered in a quivering voice. "I appreciate your fair justice and I will obey it too. I have already warned my friends about staying out of your gaol."

"I hope they do. I hope they do too, Mr. Bertrand." With that the Factor returned to the head of the table and continued his animated conversation with a couple of young ladies and another well-dressed gentleman. He acted as if nothing had happened at all.

Chapter 21
Homeward Bound

The last great rendezvous at Fort William ended as quickly as it had begun in late July. One complete week of seemingly endless drinking, carousing, and partying came to an abrupt end when two kegs of black powder exploded outside the main gate. Eight men were killed instantly and at least a score were injured. The cause was not found but the Chief Factor's son, Stephen, was one of the men killed that day. He was also the prime suspect as the person who had caused the horrible explosion.

Stephen Thompson had made many enemies that week, even though he had spent two of the seven days in his father's gaol. After getting out, he threatened to destroy his father and all those involved in putting him in gaol, especially Théodule Bertrand.

Stephen had felt that he had been shamed in front of his fellow workers and who he thought were his friends. Little did he know that he had very few, if any, friends at the fort. Being the Factor's son he had expected to have a certain respect from the other clerks and senior management. He did not. They felt he should be treated like any other clerk, which he was. Factor Robert Thompson had warned all of the management of his wishes that his son needed no special treatment. Unfortunately, Stephen could not accept this. His excessive drinking spells did not help the matter.

Mr. Duckworth once told Robert Thompson that he had often seen

Stephen in the cantine salope and out in the Ojibwa camp trying to get some rum or other spirits when the Grand Hall had been closed for the evening.

"He will end up dead from either the liquor or by someone's knife if he does not watch himself," was his father's only comment. "He is thirty years old and must take care of himself. I am only his father and an old man. I do not need the extra worries of an intoxicated son besides the problems I already have at this fort," Thompson had told his Chief Clerk, Thomas Duckworth.

The massive explosion had thrown Théodule and a couple of other men out into the Kaministiquia River but they had not been injured. Other men closer by, though, had horrible injuries and some had been burned quite seriously.

No trace was ever found of Stephen Thompson, except his knife which had his name engraved on it. His body had been completely blown apart. There was just a red heap of twisted cloth and mangled meat, showing the others that there once had been a living human in those awful remains.

A large funeral was held at the fort two days after the explosion for the men who had died that terrible day. Fort William did not have a chapel; with the weather being so fine that week, an open-air service was held in the main square.

Chief Factor Robert Thompson led the service from the main balcony of the Great Hall. A Wesleyan Methodist missionary who had been out in the North West country among the Blackfoot tribes trying to convert them to Christianity assisted him.

Reverend Thomas Longstreet had arrived from the west in a brigade of canoes that were coming to the fort for the rendezvous. He had tried to hold a couple of services during the rendezvous but without much luck. Only a handful of men had turned up at his impromptu service. John Henderson and John Cameron had been two of them, even though they were both followers of the Church of England.

Every man and woman at the fort was in attendance at the funeral. Eight men had been killed outright during the initial explosion but three others had since died of their injuries, mostly severe burns and broken limbs. Théodule had only suffered some bruises and a few scratches and he considered himself very lucky. Some of the other men who had been blown into the river had received broken ribs and legs. John Cameron had jumped into the river to save one man who was on the verge of drowning. John Henderson helped his friend pull both the drowning man and Théodule out of the cold, murky water.

A couple of prayers were said at the funeral and a clerk played a lament on a set of bagpipes. The men tried to sing a hymn but most just mouthed the words. Most were French Canadian voyageurs and many had not learned to speak English yet with any real fluency. Factor Thompson's wife led a small makeshift choir made up of four other women from the fort, wives of the senior management, as they sang "Ye Servants of God". There was hardly a dry eye in the fort.

Henri Larivière had told John Cameron and the others from Cavagnal that the terrible explosion had been the worst disaster ever to hit the fort in its long history. There had been stabbings, gun shot wounds, and a couple of fires, but never had there been a deliberate plot to kill or maim, or even to destroy the fort. "Stephen Thompson was a sick young man," Henri told his eastern friends. "I am glad dat he was killed in de explosion. Odderwise his father, Factor Thompson, would ave had to put his only son on trial for murder den carry out de execution. It would ave been too ard on de old man. It is better dat Stephen died in the explosion."

The young men of Cavagnal, Lachine, and Montréal loaded their big canot de maitre with enough provisions and supplies to get them back as far as Wright's Village. "We will stop on Manitoulin Island to pick up Allan," said Théodule. We should be back at Wright's Village by late September if all goe well." "Just in time to head into the bush," big Joe Desormeaux said with a wide grin.

"Allons-y!" said John Henderson and with that they all laughed and pushed away from the dock. They had laughed because though John had been listening to the French Canadians for many weeks now, as they conversed in their lovable language of the bush and rivers, he still had not mastered it as well as John Cameron had and his speech was still very thick with his native Westmorland accent. It was quite humorous to listen to and each time poor John tried to speak to the French Canadian voyageurs in their native tongue, he had them laughing so hard their stomachs ached and they often had tears in their eyes. "Stop now," they would tell John, "or we will die laughing." It was a standing joke in the big canoe and Henri Larivière laughed too as he waved goodbye to his new friends from the east.

The way east went well and Théodule and Louis soon called for the sail to be set and in short order the big canoe was cruising along at a fast pace, faster than any of the now-seasoned paddlers could have maintained for any long period of time.

They arrived at Manitoulin Island just short of two weeks after they had left Fort William. Father Antoine Demers had been expecting them and he had already prepared Allan's things for them to take back to Cavagnal if his friends so wished. Father Demers had been asking some of the eastbound brigades if they had seen a lone canoe leave Fort William heading east. None had until a small brigade of four canoes had stopped by the mission to say a short prayer before the men headed into the North Channel of Georgian Bay.

"We saw a lone canoe leave just before us," one of the brigade members told the Jesuit Priest. "However, after the second day out from Fort William we lost them in a storm. I hope they made it but we ourselves lost one of our canoes and all those on board. The storm blew up so fast behind us that we did not have time to find a good safe landing. Twelve good voyageurs were lost."

"I too will pray for their souls and those that are heading this way, on the way home to Montreal and Lachine," said the aging wilderness priest. He had been working among the Hurons for close to fifty years and though he was now well over seventy years old, Father Demers was as fit and as strong as many a man twenty years his junior.

The young adventurers arrived two days after the brigade that had advised Father Demers of the storm out on Lake Superior had left Manitoulin Island. "We got eld up in a terrible storm," Théodule told the old priest, "but we are ere. Where is our friend Allan?"

Father Demers asked the young men to come into the chapel and sit down. John Henderson began to sense that something had gone wrong, but he was not ready for what the old Priest was about to tell them all.

"I regret to inform you that your good friend Allan passed away just a few days after you left here last month."

"What? Why? How?" John Cameron and Iain Macleod both said aloud at the same time.

"He died of gangrene and blood poisoning. I tried everything that I knew how to treat such an injury and even had a Shaman from the Huron nation come and try, but he was too weak.

"Your friend was very upset that you left here without him. He knew that he was very ill but he did not want to let onto you, his dear friends. I believe that he may have died of a broken heart, if that is possible. But the infection in his blood was what really killed him."

John Henderson finally spoke, though with tears streaming down his face, "Could you not have taken his leg off Father?" he asked the old Priest. "I thought of that but by the time we realized that the leg was dead, the poisoning had already spread up into his groin. He would never have survived the shock, I am afraid. He died peacefully, however. The Huron Shaman had given him an herbal drink that eased the pain and Allan just slept away, three days after you left. It was very sudden, but he did tell me before he died that he was sorry for the pain and suffering his death will cause you, but he thanked all of you for letting him come along. Until his accident he told me that he had been having a wonderful and very exciting time."

"Where is he buried?" asked Simon Beauvais. "I had Allan buried in our cemetery beside the mission and I even had a small cross placed on his grave. Come, I will show you his grave and we will say a prayer for him and for all of you and your voyage back home," said Father Demers.

"I do not know how poor Robert Henderson is going to handle this, having just lost his wife a couple of years ago," John Cameron told his pal John Henderson and the others gathered beside him at Allan's gravesite.

"I know," John Henderson continued, "he is lucky to at least have Phoebe with him at home but Jacob Grisenthwaite and she will soon be married. Maybe Robert will find another wife, though there are not too many available women right now in Cavagnal or St. Henry."

"Quiet please, gentlemen," Father Demers said to the ten young men who were now in a semi-circle at Allan's grave. "Father, we are gathered here this bright fall day to pay tribute to a gallant adventurer and brave young man. Allan Henderson was from Lower Canada and he met his fate along some well-traveled portage not far from here. He suffered a great deal in the following days but let no person know besides himself and You, Oh Lord. I hope he finds a special place amongst the other gallant voyageurs that have preceded him and those that will follow. Amen."

Father Antoine Demers continued by saying a short benediction in Latin and French for the French Canadians that were with the four men from Kanesatake and Cavagnal, all of whom were members of the Church of England or Wesleyan Methodists.

John Henderson had picked some wild flowers while waiting for the short memorial service to begin and when Father Demers nodded his head, John placed the flowers on his good friend's grave.

All the men had tears freely flowing from their eyes and John Henderson was sobbing uncontrollably as they turned and headed back to the mission. "Thank you Father, you have been wonderful and a very kind man," Iain Macleod told the old priest. "I know that Allan's father and family would be pleased to see how well his son and their brother had been treated out here so far from home, both in sickness and in death."

"It is my duty to serve all the children of God," Father Demers told the men. "Just my duty. I only wish I could have done more for the young man, but he was just too sick."

John Cameron then spoke on behalf of the rest of the mourning voyageurs. "We made some money while we were at Fort William and we have decided that we would like to give you some of that money for your mission here on Manitoulin Island. It is to help with supplies and whatever you need it for," John told the astonished priest.

"I do not expect anything from any of you," Father Demers told them in a subdued voice. "However, I will accept it on behalf of the Jesuit Mission here and I am sure it will be put to good use. We always need something, especially with winter just around the corner. With that, John Cameron presented Father Demers with a small leather pouch that carried seventy-five shillings. It was only part of the money the men had won, betting on Joe Desormeaux's wrestling match with Sean Mowat, but Father Antoine Demers did not have to know that.

"We must be off at first light," Théodule told the others as they entered the mission's wooden walls.

"I will provide you with a good meal and a warm place to sleep this evening," Father Demers told the voyageurs, "after that you must leave at first light. I cannot have you around too long, even though you have been very kind to me with this fine gift. However, I am expecting many more canoes soon and the fall gathering of the Huron nation is about to begin. I do not really think that they would appreciate having a couple of Mohawks on the island during that celebration."

Joshua and Simon both looked at each other and smiled. "We could be upset with that comment," Joshua told the priest, "but we understand and we do not hold any bad feelings with your wishes."

"We would not want them around our special tribal celebrations either," Simon said. "There are still many of us who despise each other and we want no more trouble on this trip, which has already seen too much tragedy and death."

"I agree," said Iain. "Thank you, Father for everything you have done. I will report back to my father when I reach Lachine and I will recommend that you get some much-needed supplies next spring from our warehouse in Lachine."

"Thank you, Mr. Macleod," Father Demers said as he shook all the young men's hands. He then left them to their meal and a good night's sleep. Just before leaving he told them that he would see them before they left the dock the next morning and that he would give them what possessions Allan had when he had died.

Father Antoine Demers met the ten young voyageurs from Lower Canada as they loaded up their canot de maitre just after five the next morning. "Good luck and God be with you, my friends," he told them as they all took part in the Sacrament of Holy Communion at the dock. "This is something I do with each brigade that stops by here on the way east," he told the men. "Promise me that you will stop in Ste Anne de Bellevue to give one final word of thanks to Ste Anne before you finish your voyage in Lachine."

They all promised him that and as they pushed away from the dock, Father Demers waved goodbye to the intrepid young men from Lower

Canada. "They have all seemed to have matured a great deal in the past few weeks," he thought. "They seemed to be just young lads when they stopped by here in early July. Now they are all men. They must have witnessed some rough things up in Fort William. Oh, well, at least they are safely on their way home now." With that Father Antoine Demers turned and walked slowly up the steep gradient to his mission.

Chapter 22
Cavagnal at Last

The trip back up the French River, through Lake Nipissing and down the Mattawa River, went smoothly for the intrepid paddlers. They rested well each night and as they made their way east towards the Ottawa River a strange silence settled over the canoe.

"We are not a appy group of voyageurs," Louis announced to his fellow canoeists as they cleared the Mattawa River and headed southeast on the mighty Ottawa River. "What is wrong?"

After a long silence, all of the men brought in their paddles. They floated gently down with the current with only Louis guiding them with his long steering paddle in the stern.

"It is about time we discussed what we are going to do when we reach Wright's Village," John Cameron told his friends. "We have all gone through some very rough times over these past few weeks and I, myself, would like to go home. As you all know my wife is expecting our first child towards the end of the year and I promised her that I would be there.

"With the loss of Allan—something that we never really anticipated—I am now more inclined than ever to head straight down the river to Cavagnal."

"I agree," said Iain. "My father's wishes were to transport his cargo to Fort William and then return when we wanted to next spring, after spending this coming winter in the bush with the Wright's operation.

Allan's death has definitely changed us all, especially, I believe, our two comrades from Cavagnal who knew Allan so well. My vote is to head right down river and return to our normal lives, if that is possible. How do you others feel about this?"

Both Simon and Joshua agreed that they too would like to return to Kanesatake that fall. The extra money from the work in the lumber camps would be nice but they all had made some unexpected extra money during the rendezvous that more than made up for what they would probably make in the lumber camp that winter. It was also a great deal easier. Everyone agreed with the two Mohawks on their last comment but big Joe Desormeaux was not so easy to convince.

"I ave been a bucheron for many years," he announced. "I want to be one for awhile yet and dis winter will give me a good chance to set up a very good friendship with de Wright family, if I go. Dey like me and I like dem very much. I ave no immediate family to go home to like all of you do. I wish to stay in de upper Ottawa Valley and work dis winter. I am sorry for de loss of Allan, but he is now gone and we cannot bring him back. I am sure he would want us to make our own choices and dat is what we are doing right now. My wish is for you to let me off at Wright's Village in de next week or so and I will work dis winter for Mr. Philomen Wright's company. I will stay de winter and maybe return to Montréal in the spring with de big timber drive. Maybe I will find a good wife in de area around Wright's Village and settle down dere. Only God knows for sure."

One after the other, the other men on board the big canoe voiced their opinions. Louis continued to steer the big craft as they discussed their problems and futures.

Both Alphonse and Jean-Jacques said that they had families and they would really like to be with them at Christmas and that they, like the others, had made enough money with the gambling at the fort to get them through the winter and set themselves up with another carting business in the spring.

John Henderson was one of the last to speak. He had been the closest friend to Allan, during and prior to the trip itself. "I feel that I would like to stay with Joe and experience the life in the lumber camps this winter but I would be forgetting my promise to Father Demers to deliver Allan's things to his father and sister and explain to them personally what happened to their only son and brother.

"My father will not be expecting me but I am sure that he, mother, and my brothers and sisters will be very glad to have me home this winter. I wish to head home with John and you others too. I am sorry, Joe, but I hope you understand our wishes." The big man slowly nodded his head and smiled, but did not utter a word.

The last to speak were Louis and Théodule. They too had decided a few days before, between themselves, to continue down river to Lachine and turn the big canoe over to Iain's father, Angus Macleod. Though Angus Beauvais had built the huge craft, Angus Macleod had purchased it as soon as he had seen it upon its arrival, prior to their departure from Lachine in May.

"We will head down de river wit you odders and maybe we will find a job on de river next summer guiding de new steam boats up de Ottawa or St. Lawrence", Louis said.

With that, the nine paddlers picked up their well-worn maple paddles and started up a steady rhythm of fifty strokes a minute. Théodule began a well-known voyageur's song and soon they were all singing gently and smiling as they headed down the Ottawa River towards Wright's Village.

They arrived at Wright's Village a few days later and big Joe Desormeaux gathered up his few possessions and left his good friends. He would work the next few years for Philomen Wright and become a true legend in the Canadian bush. Joe tangled with many a man later that winter and over the next few years as a group of Irish ruffians caused quite a ruckus in the area around Wright's Village and later Bytown, across the river.

Joe Desormeaux fought many a tough battle with the Irish immigrants but finally settled down and found a nice woman in Montreal. He raised a family of sixteen in a large house on de Bullion Street.

Paddling the big canoe down the Ottawa from Wright's Village was easy for the nine men from the east. They would have only one more portage before reaching the vast Lake of the Two Mountains and the little settlements of Kanesatake and Cavagnal. That portage was at Carillon and they were over that in just under an hour since their cargo was so small on the homeward bound voyage. They gave a quick salute to the Royal Engineers who were still working hard on the new canal that would soon bypass the awful Long Sault Rapids. Then they continued on down river.

No one was expecting to see any of the adventurers at all before the next spring. The only exception being John Cameron, who had promised to trek overland by snowshoe and dog team just before New Year's Day so he could be at home when his wife Jane gave birth to their first child.

The big canoe had seen the men through scores of rapids and miles of quiet lakes and rivers and had weathered the terrible storm out on Lake Superior with only slight damages. It had been expertly repaired at the canoe repair shed at Fort William and the paddlers had no serious leaks or tears in the fragile craft as they had headed east towards Montréal.

As they came around Pearson's Point in late October, smoke could be seen rising from the eastern part of the community. John Henderson said to his friends that it looked it there was a house on fire, or possibly a large shed. "It looks as if it is down towards Joseph Shouldice's farm," he said to John Cameron.

"Paddle as ard as you can," Louis called to his fellow crewmembers. "Maybe dey can use some extra help." They slipped by Schmidt's Tavern without anyone seeing them and pulled into the bay just east of Deschamp's Store. They could hear people yelling as they pulled the big craft up onto the beach.

They had arrived home two days before the beginning of November, 1826. Unfortunately no one was there to greet them as most of the community of Cavagnal was at Joseph Shouldice's farm. John Henderson had been correct when he had said to his friends on the canoe that the smoke seemed to be coming from the area of the Shouldice farm.

A fire was burning fiercely in the large two-storey cabin and it had already spread to the cow shed. The nine young men ran up the slope to the fire and pushed their way through the small crowd that was gathered watching the roaring fire. John Henderson quickly realized that neither he nor his friends could do anything to help as the fire consumed the log cabin and cow shed with growing intensity.

"John!" screamed Jane Cameron as she turned to see her husband standing beside his friends. No one in the crowd had recognized the young men with their beards and unwashed faces and ragged clothes, even though they had been standing with the others watching the fire now for close to two minutes.

The whole crowd turned, including a red-eyed and soot-stained Joseph Shouldice. He was leaning heavily on George Henderson and it seemed that he had been injured in the fire. "My God son, what are you doing here?" George asked his son, slowly moving over to greet him. John Henderson could only see his father's good friend, none of his family was present. His wife of twenty years, Alice, and their three children were no where to be seen.

"We decided to come home this fall," John told his father. "It has been a long trip and not without much hardship and tragedy. We all made it back except for Joe Desormeaux and Allan. I will tell you more later. What happened here? Where is Joseph's family?" John asked his tired-looking father. Mary was no where to be seen and John asked his father right away when he noticed that his mother was not there either, where she was and if she was in good health.

"Mary has taken Alice away to our place," George explained. "The three Shouldice children are still in there," he said, pointing the inferno before them.

"Oh, Jesus, God have mercy upon them," was all that John could say. Jean-Jacques, Alphonse, Louis, and Théodule all made the sign of the cross on their chests when they over heard George's last few words. Simon, Joshua, Iain and John Cameron just bowed their heads in silent prayer when they, too, heard the shocking words of George Henderson.

Joseph Shouldice was now sitting up against a large tree and he seemed to be in a trance. He just stared at the fire as it darkened down as the fuel was consumed.

It began in the chimney, George told his son and the others. Joseph was in the barn with his wife trying to shoe their horse when they heard screams from the upstairs. They had left the children in bed this morning as they had all been sick with a cold.

"Joseph said he tried to go upstairs with a bucket of water but he was driven back by the flames and smoke. We saw the smoke from out on the lake where I was working with Charles Schmidt and Rotonni. We grabbed our horses after landing at the dock and as we raced east at a gallop we yelled for help. Even F.X. Deschamps came. He must be still here somewhere."

Simon nodded his head at Deschamps, who was standing talking to some other men on the far side of the burning buildings.

"We had about fifteen men here in no time, but with little water, there was not much we could do," George continued. "We were able to get the two cows and the team of horses away from the shed before it caught on fire. I am afraid we will soon be searching for the bodies in the rubble."

"Poor little Sarah, Elizabeth, and Jacob," was all that John Henderson could say. "We have arrived home hoping for a warm welcome and this is what we see: more tragedy. This summer will long be remembered as one of triumph and tragedy."

"Where is Allan?" George finally asked his son and John Cameron.

"We had to leave him on Manitoulin Island," John explained. "He is dead."

George staggered back and put his head into his hands. When his face came up a few seconds later, it was streaked with tears.

"What more can happen to this small community and poor Robert and Phoebe and the others. Do they know yet?"

"I am not sure, Sir," said John Cameron, "we only found out ourselves a few weeks ago as we headed home.

"Father Demers said that he had sent word east with the first brigade that left his mission and the bourgeois had said that he knew Schmidt's Tavern well and that he would leave a message there for Robert Henderson and his family. I guess if none of you know, then the message never reached here. Maybe the bourgeois forgot or his brigade never made it back. Father Demers had hoped that his message would have gotten through by now."

John explained that had Allan never made it to Fort William. "He fell on a portage near the end of the Mattawa River and he broke his ankle. Even though he was very sick, he never told us. We left him at a Jesuit Mission, under the care of a Jesuit Priest, Father Antoine Demers.

"Father Demers told us that Allan died just a few days after we left him. Blood poisoning, he said. It seems that the break in the ankle had caused some infection to set in and, even with some help from a Huron shaman, Allan died. He is buried near the mission and that wonderful priest even had a marker erected over Allan's grave. We visited it on the way home. It was shortly after that we all decided to come home this fall, all of us except big Joe Desormeaux. He is now working for the Wright's in the Gatineau region, north of Wright's Village."

"How is mother?" John asked his tired-looking father as they returned to care for Joseph Shouldice.

"She is fine, son, and actually all of the family is healthy. Just look at your sister, she is large now with her child, but she is very pleased to have John home so soon. We all are and we will need you too. Things have changed greatly here in Cavagnal and in the Seigneury since you all left here back in May.

"I will explain to you after we get this remaining fire out and help with the recovery of the bodies."

With that, George and the others organized a bucket brigade, using the water from the creek that flowed slowly through the eastern part of Shouldice's farm.

They decided to let the fire in the cow shed burn itself out, as the main goal was to try and find what remained of the young Shouldice children. They were quickly located in the back of the now ruined cabin but they were burned beyond recognition, almost incinerated.

The little bodies were wrapped up in some sailcloth and carried away from the cabin and the others. George asked Charles Schmidt to send for Reverend Joseph Ashford, as he would be needed for the funeral as soon as possible. Charles called on Rotonni as he and his brother Harvey had the fastest canoe in the area, and it would not take them very long to reach St. Andrew's East. "We will have him back here by tomorrow," Rotonni promised Charles and George as he hurried off, stopping just for a second to shake hands and hug his cousins, Joshua and Simon.

Chapter 23
Happy New Year!

After the fire was out, the voyageurs returned to their beached canoe and then headed upriver to Schmidt's Tavern, where they unloaded Allan's few possessions as well as those of John Henderson, Simon Beauvais, Joshua Gabriel, and John Cameron. Iain then told his four friends that he and the rest of the crew would take the canoe down river to Lachine that day, if they could make it past Ste Anne de Bellevue before dark.

"Why not stay here?" asked Charles Schmidt. "Your room will be free as our welcome back gift to all you intrepid and gallant men."

Iain looked at the others and they all nodded their heads.

"It has been many months since anyone of us has slept in a warm, comfortable bed—and one that was clean, too," announced Iain.

They all laughed and commenced to unload the big canoe for the second to last time. Louis and Théodule had no intentions of portaging it one more time. They were going to run the rapids at Ste Anne de Bellevue and be home before noon the next day.

Jane Cameron and Charles Schmidt provided the voyageurs with a hearty meal of roast bear, potatoes, and carrots.

"This is the best meal we have had since we left Father Demers' Jesuit Mission on Manitoulin Island," they announced. By eight o'clock that night all of the men were fast asleep in their clean beds at Schmidt's Tavern.

After many lonesome weeks, Jane was now able to sleep in a warm bed next to her beloved husband. They had not had much time together since his arrival. John had a tough time trying to explain to Jane that he just had to spend one last evening with his dear friends before they parted company the next morning.

Jane understood, but was wide awake when he crawled into bed late that night and began to stroke his beautiful wife and her swollen abdomen. In just a few weeks they would be parents for the first time.

Shortly before six o'clock the next morning, and after a hearty breakfast of bacon and eggs and some hot coffee, the last leg of what had been a real adventure for all of the young men, began. Louis, Théodule, Iain, Jean-Jacques, and Alphonse all said that they would be able to handle the now almost empty canoe by themselves. Joshua and Simon had decided to leave the evening before after their meal and had returned home to Kanesatake and their families.

The two young men from Cavagnal shook hands with their traveling companions and agreed that they had had a wonderful time. They also agreed that it had been a real learning experience for them all, especially Jean-Jacques, Alphonse, and the two Johns from Cavagnal. They regretted the loss of Allan but his death had been an accident and they realized that no one could be blamed. It had just been an unfortunate episode in what had been a great trip. They all hoped that big Joe Desormeaux would have a good winter in the bush.

With the good-byes said, the big canoe and its five crew members pushed off from the Schmidt's dock and before long Théodule had the men singing one of his many favourite French Canadian songs that had guided them along during the previous months of paddling.

Just as they had promised, Rotonni and his brother Harvey were back shortly after one o'clock that afternoon with Reverend Joseph Ashford from St. Andrew's East. It was going to be one of the saddest days in the short history of Cavagnal. Every resident of the small riverside community, plus score of others from St. Henry and Côte St. Charles, were in attendance for the funeral of the three Shouldice children.

George Henderson had organized a group of six men to dig the a grave in the small community cemetery that was located about a half a mile west of Marsden's store. It was a tranquil little clearing that had a wonderful view of the Ottawa River from the high bluff on which the cemetery was located. The three little bodies, or what was left of them, were placed together in one small pine coffin.

Reverend Ashford held a graveside service the next afternoon. The service had to be held outside by the grave, there still being no church in the area.

"We have to have a church built here soon," whispered John Marsden to his good friend George Henderson during a lull in the service between hymns. "This would be an ideal location, too."

Dugald Cameron had brought his pipes and he played a lament as well as "Amazing Grace". During the last of the hymns, "They are in Peace", both Alice and Joseph Shouldice collapsed due to the strain of having their only three children lying before them in their little coffin. John Cameron and Rotonni grabbed Joseph as he went down and John gave him a stiff shot of brandy that seemed to rouse the grieving man. The brandy soon began to work and Joseph was able to resume his position beside his wife at the edge of the grave. Alice had been caught by Mary Kilkenny and she too had been given a shot of brandy which quickly revived her as well.

The service lasted about forty-five minutes. During the service, Reverend Ashford called upon all the good citizens of Cavagnal, St. Henry, and Côte St. Charles to band together and form a building committee for a new house of God.

"I will find you a good minister," he promised the congregation. "All you have to do is build him a fine place of worship."

The coffin was lowered slowly into the cold, sandy ground, and as the large congregation turned to head towards the Schmidt's, John Henderson and three or four other young men began the task of filling in the grave.

It had been the worst tragedy ever in the region. Not even John M. Lerniers, who had been in the area for almost twenty-five years, could remember when so many people had died at the same time. The whole community was in mourning. Even F.X. Deschamps had shown up along with William and Charles Whetstone, though they had not been expected to. Their isolation in the community had grown larger and the newly arrived voyageurs were soon going to learn from George Henderson about what they had missed while traveling to Fort William and back.

Those in attendance were all invited back to Schmidt's Tavern, where a huge feast had been put together by many of the women of Cavagnal, Côte St. Charles, and even St. Henry. The women of Côte St. Charles had already built up quite a reputation as the ones to call on in times of need or celebration, as they were able to provide such wonderful pies, cakes, and other special treats from their excellent farms.

Côte St. Charles, of all the settlements around Cavagnal, had the best arable land. The farmers up there, such as James Henderson, Dugald Cameron, Solomon and Ebenezer Grampian, the Pearsons, and the Blackwells, had well-established farms that all produced fine crops of hay, oats, and even corn as well as huge vegetable gardens with squash, pumpkins, potatoes, tomatoes, and other essential vegetables.

While most of the residents of the region were at the Tavern that late fall afternoon, Reverend Joseph Ashford once again called on all those present to band together and form a proper building committee for their new church.

"You have organized your schools, not without hardship, but they are working. Now is the time to get together and really get some work done on attempting to build ourselves a church. Whether it is a Church of England or a Methodist, this community needs a church—now. However, I would like to see a Church of England here, of course."

"Besides our church," George told his son and John Cameron, who were standing next to him both eating piece of apple pie, "we have had some major troubles with our friend down the road, F.X. Deschamps."

John Cameron said that he had heard of the problems from his wife, Jane. However, John Henderson had been too busy talking with his brothers and sisters to have had time to find out what had occurred during the summer and proceeding weeks that fall.

"What has happened, father?" John asked the big man.

"Ever since you left, we have had major concerns about what has been going on down at the Deschamps' store. Even Mary Kilkenny has recently moved out because she feared for her life after what she found out for Mr. Marsden and me. As you both know, I am the new Sheriff in this area and Mr. Marsden is our new Justice of the Peace. Well, during the late spring and all through the summer we suspected some very covert operations were going on during certain nights at Deschamps' place.

"Joseph Shouldice, bless his poor broken heart, kept an eye on the place, but our main spy was Mary. She kept us informed all summer and when Deschamps' wife threatened her one day last week, she moved in with Jane and she is now working here at the Tavern.

"We never expected you boys back until either late December and or the spring. Your arrival with both Simon and Joshua is a Godsend. We have raised a Militia of just over one hundred men, which is called the Vaudreuil Loyal Volunteers and approved by the Governor himself. Aron'hio:tas has even offered us as many of his warriors as we need to help defend Cavagnal. We told him that we would help him over there if the need ever arose.

"By the way," George said to his son and John Cameron, "just after you left our old friends that we met in Québec arrived here with our two new guns." Both John Henderson and John Cameron were glad that George had finally received their much-dreamed about Pennsylvania long rifles and they both asked him about them and the visit of the two Mohawk warriors.

According to George, Awen'rah:ton and Sori'howane had left for the United States a few weeks ago but they said that they would be back and probably settle over in Kanesatake in the next couple of years. They had spent all summer with their relatives and friends down in the bay at Pearson's Point, fishing and then smoking their huge catches.

"The guns they brought us are magnificent and are more accurate than I ever dreamed they would be. I am glad, however, that you were able to bring back old Isaac's big rifle in fine shape after your long trip." John Henderson explained how it had served them well and how well he had done in the shooting competition at Fort William during the great Rendezvous back in July.

George then continued to give his son and John Cameron the intricate details of what had occurred that summer and during the early part of the fall. "Luckily," George explained, "we have not yet had any open violence. The air may have cleared for the time being as the clandestine meetings seemed to have ceased, at least here in Cavagnal. However, we have heard from various other Militia groups in and around Montréal and Québec that the Patriotes, as they call themselves, have quite a large following already. The Governor has written to Horse Guards in London for a regiment from the regular Army and a detachment of light cavalry. From what Marsden has told me, a large army contingent of is supposed to be arriving in the spring. I hope the troops are not too late."

Both John Henderson and John Cameron were quite shocked at what George had just told them. They both told him that there were no rumblings at all in Fort William nor on the way back in the other outposts they had stopped at. "No word was even mentioned of a potential uprising in Wright's Village," John Cameron told his father-in-law, "and that place is just upriver from here."

"Maybe it is because all the men are so well employed by that good American, Philomen Wright, that they just do not have the time or willpower to cause any problems there," explained George. "Remember, John, Wright's Village is a privately run village, owned by one man, Philomen Wright, his word is law up there and no one wishes to anger the largest employer in the upper Ottawa Valley, especially if he is paying you good wages."

"I guess you are right George," John Cameron told his friend. "I just hope everything blows over and we can live in harmony. We made such great friends with those men from Lachine and Montréal this past summer on our trip; I would not want to see us having to fight against them."

"I agree," John Henderson added. "However, they are very dedicated French Canadians and I could see them all, except of course for Iain Macleod, joining the Patriote cause in their area."

"In the meantime, what are we going to do about rebuilding Joseph's house and barn?" asked George.

"I cannot see us getting a barn up in time for winter but at least a sturdy cabin can be made in a few days, if we get a group of men together," explained Charles Schmidt, who had now joined his three good friends beside the roaring fireplace.

Most of the other guests had now left. Many would have a good one to two hour ride in a buggy or on horseback that cold afternoon. "Looks like snow," Charles said to his friends as he looked out over the Lake of the Two Mountains. "It is not too early, but we do not need it just yet. Some of the men do not have all their corn in yet."

"I will post a sign at Deschamps', Marsden's, and Lerniers' and in here," said Charles, "asking for all available manpower and material. We can start next week, say Wednesday? I will tell Joseph in the morning, he has gone upstairs to see his ailing wife and try to comfort her. I am glad Reverend Ashford will be staying this evening as those poor people are taking this loss very hard.

"I do not think Joseph will ever be the same, what a tragic loss to them and all of us. I am glad that Dr. Grisenthwaite was able to help Alice Shouldice with her burns and depression. I know Joseph welcomed the salve that Rotonni was able to get from the Shaman in Kanesatake for their burns. It has helped a great deal, no infection has set in."

The signs that Charles Schmidt had put up in the community once again drew a large crowd of able-bodied men. William Whetstone kindly donated a large wagon load of cut timber from his sawmill in St. Henry and F.X. Deschamps brought a whole keg of nails from his store. Others brought glass for the windows, furniture and clothing as well.

"Surprised to see us?" Whetstone asked John A. Marsden and George Henderson who were supervising the whole operation.

"Yes and no," Marsden answered. "That aside, we are all very glad to see you both here. I guess we all know where we are needed the most and now is the time to put our differences aside and work together and help this poor family get over at least part of their terrible tragedy.

"I agree," said Deschamps, "so let us stop talking and get to work, we have a got a cabin to build."

George and John Marsden looked at each other smiled and fell in behind Whetstone and Deschamps as they began hauling wood to the area where the old cabin had been. Some of the young boys of the area had cleared the old burned out rubble from the stone foundation a few days before so the workers that Wednesday had a clear spot to build the new Shouldice house on.

Fifty men had shown up that day and by late afternoon there was a fine new cabin for Alice and Joseph Shouldice to live in for the upcoming winter. Alice was still deeply depressed and had many fits of crying that day as she watched her neighbours build a new home for her and her husband.

"It will be a long lonesome winter," Joseph told George Henderson as the last windows were installed. "However, we will attempt to start a new life. Both Alice and I are young enough to try for more children and we have decided on trying to start a new family as soon as possible."

"You are one tough character Joseph Shouldice," George Henderson told his old friend. They had grown very close over the past two years since George had moved to the area. George had largely credited Joseph for helping him get over his serious drinking problem two winters before. George had known what deep depression was like, after the loss of his daughter Agnes five years before but mainly from the loss of his best friend, Isaac Kirkbride on board *The Pioneer*.

"Many of us thought that you and Alice would move away from here," George told his friend.

"We had thought about it last week, just after the fire and funeral. However, we decided that this is our home. No use running away from the old memories. We will try very hard to make a go here in Cavagnal and hopefully by this time next year there will be a new little Shouldice in this fine new home you and the others have built for us. Thanks very much George," Shouldice said to his friend, hugging him as he said it. "You are a fantastic man."

Jane and John Cameron's first child was born on January 5th, 1827 in their little cabin just west of Schmidt's Tavern. Dr. Joseph Grisenthwaite was present as was Caroline Schmidt and, of course, Jane's mother Mary Henderson. Duncan George Cameron was healthy young boy of eight pounds ten ounces and though it was Jane's first child and a big one at that, the birth went very well.

"I thought it would be tougher than that," Jane said in a tired voice to her mother and Caroline Schmidt.

"We are all glad that it was not," they both exclaimed.

"I have seen too many young girls go through hell with the birth of their first child. Many a local woman has died at childbirth in these parts," Caroline told Jane and Mary.

"Too many young babies have also died at birth or shortly afterwards as well. I am sure the good Doctor can vouch for that, here and over in England as well. I understand that the Irish families up in St. Henry have been calling on him quite regularly these past couple of years."

"Please change the subject, mother and Caroline," asked a weary Jane. "I do not want to hear anymore about death; only love and caring and that is what Duncan is going to receive.

"You are so correct," said Mary Henderson, "I am so happy that both you and Duncan are doing so well, already. You will make a very good mother and Dr. Grisenthwaite has told me that your strong young body will just perfect for lots of other children if you and John so wish."

"We do mother. Oh we do, but first we plan to have this one grow up a wee bit before another one comes along, if that is possible," winking at her mother and Caroline Schmidt.

George Henderson and Dugald Cameron got roaring drunk that evening over at Schmidt's Tavern. It was the first grandchild for both of them and even though Duncan would carry the Cameron name and not the Henderson name, it did not matter to George Henderson one bit. He was now a grandfather and very proud of it. However, Dugald Cameron was letting everyone know who was Duncan's paternal grandfather. He had ridden down from Côte St. Charles on the afternoon of the birth, playing his bagpipes the whole way.

When he got to Marsden's store, he stopped in to announce to those there what had happened. He played a couple more tunes, to everyone's delight, grabbed a jug of rum from Marsden's well-stocked shelves and then headed off east to see his grandson and brother-in-law.

By the time Duncan reached Schmidt's Tavern he was well on the way to becoming very intoxicated. More tunes were played on the bagpipes and then both he and George celebrated some more with more rum and wine.

George had not been drunk in a couple of years and at first a few of the local patrons were worried about his inebriation, remembering how violent he had become many months before. But this time George was not melancholy and this was a grand celebration and both he and Dugald Cameron were letting everyone know how proud they were of their grandson.

Dugald Cameron did not return home that night but had to spend the night in Schmidt's Tavern as did George Henderson. It was the first time he had not been home at night since he had arrived in Cavagnal back in 1824, except for the odd boat trip he had done for the Schmidts down river to Ste Eustache while John Cameron had gone west to Fort William the summer before.

Charles Schmidt had sent Joseph Shouldice over to tell Mary Henderson that George would be staying at the Tavern that night and he was fine but just too drunk to be moved. He told Mary that it had taken six men to haul the area's two largest men upstairs to the rooms that Charles Schmidt had provided for the very inebriated men.

Charles Schmidt and Mary Kilkenny were to be Duncan's selected Godparents. Since Mary had begun working at the Tavern in late October, rumours had swept Cavagnal that she and Charles would be married that coming summer. Jane had introduced Charles to Mary prior to her beginning work there at the Tavern and Charles had taken an immediate liking to her.

Their engagement was announced shortly after Duncan's birth in early January and a wedding was set for mid-June. John and Jane Cameron planned to have Duncan christened the day after the wedding so no one in the area would be able to complain that the Camerons had chosen an unmarried couple as the young baby's Godparents. It was a longstanding custom in the area to have Godparents that were married to each other and not just single adults. Having the christening the day after also made it easier for Reverend Ashford. He would not have to make two trips across the river from St. Andrews too close together.

Both the wedding and the christening went as planned and everyone in the region once again had a grand time. It was a party reminiscent of Jane and John's own wedding two years before. The only thing missing was an unexpected arrival of a large party of Royal Navy explorers.

Those Royal Navy explorers did arrive, however, in late September 1827. "Look there, yelled John Cameron to Simon and Rotonni one afternoon during the last week in September. "Look at what is heading around Pearson's Point and coming this way," he called to his friends who were up by the Tavern fixing a broken window.

They came down to the dock where John was standing and watched in amazement as at least eight large canoes and two bateaux silently but swiftly approached their dock. "Rotonni, John told his friend, "run up to the Tavern and tell Charles, Jane and Mary that there will be a large crowd of men arriving momentarily and as yet I do not know who they are, but they look official, especially with that flag flying from the lead bateau."

The large flotilla arrived a few minutes later and as John and Simon tied up the two heavily loaded bateaux the canoes were beached on each side of the big sturdy dock. "It is John Cameron, is it not?" called a bearded Naval officer from one of the bateaux. "Yes, John answered, who are you?"

"How quickly they forget," announced the dirty and bedraggled man. Others in the boat laughed.

"I am Lieutenant Peter Fitzgibbon, of His Britannic Majesty's Royal Navy. You do not remember me visiting your wedding?"

"Of course, I do Lieutenant. It is just that you look so different now and it has been over two years since we last met and I was very busy that day. What brings you here?"

A short and quite plump man stood up beside Lieutenant Fitzgibbon before the Lieutenant could answer.

"I am Captain John Franklin of His Britannic Majesty's Royal Navy and this is my expedition. My Lieutenant told me of your kind hospitality to him and his crew two years ago and he insisted on stopping by here on the final leg of your trip down to Montreal and home to England this fall."

"Welcome, Captain Franklin, all of you are most welcome," John told the portly middle aged Naval officer. "I have sent word up to the Tavern that a large flotilla was approaching so they should be almost ready for you and your men, Captain Franklin. Will you be staying the night or heading down river to Montréal?"

"I would like to stay here if it is possible. How many rooms do you have?", asked Captain Franklin.

"We have seven", answered John, "not enough for your large party but more than adequate for yourself and your officers I am sure."

"That will be just fine," replied Captain Franklin. "My crew will bivouac outside as they have done for the past two years. One more night in the open air will not harm them. We have gone through many hardships during these past few months. They will find this most welcome, especially with your highly renown food. Can you serve us all tonight? We are one hundred and twenty men."

John and Simon looked at each other and smiled. "Charles is going to soil his pants when we tell him that they will be serving one hundred and twenty men tonight for supper. Do you think this Franklin fellow has enough money?" whispered Simon to John.

"I hope so or we will have a lot of dirty dishes to wash. Remember it was us that welcomed them and told them they could stay here."

"Not us," laughed Simon, "you did John. You did!"

Charles Schmidt was very surprised when he looked out his front door and saw the large crowd of men approaching his Tavern. "Jane, quick are the pots of stew ready yet?" he called to a now very busy Jane Cameron in the hot kitchen.

"Soon, Charles, soon. "Just give me a few more minutes," she called from the steamy kitchen.

Charles greeted the famous explorer as he came through the door of the equally famous Tavern. "We have heard about this place as far west as Cumberland House," Captain John Franklin told his host as they both shook hands. "I hope the food is as good as it smells." Franklin had stopped just inside the door and gazed around at the large dining room, all the while taking in deep breaths of the smell of good home cooked food that was being prepared just a few feet from him in the large kitchen.

"Your meals will be ready in a few minutes Captain Franklin," announced Mary Kilkenny as she handed the senior naval officer a tankard of ale.

"Most of my men will eat outside if that is fine with you, Mr. Schmidt," Franklin told his host. "My officers and I will eat in here."

"There is room for thirty at a time, Captain," Mary told the portly man.

"No, I insist they will eat outside and I will be inside with my fellow officers."

"How was your expedition?" Charles Schmidt asked Lieutenant Fitzgibbon when they both had a minute alone.

"It was very tough," answered the weary naval officer. "Very tough indeed and not without many setbacks and tragedy. We should have used your Canadian birch bark canoes out west rather than the heavy wooden boats we had brought from England. Carrying them over the portages tired many an already weak man. It was only after some difficult times with Captain Franklin that we finally discarded them on our return voyage from the Coppermine River and Arctic coast and settled for the easier handling and much lighter north canoe or as you call it, canot du nord.

"We lost many men due to scurvy during the past two winters and as you can see many of the men are very thin and undernourished. This meal you will be providing us will be the best one we have had since leaving Fort William almost two months ago.

"Some of the men died due to an encounter we had with some not too friendly Eskimos last fall off the coast of one of the islands we were camped on for a few weeks. They struck one afternoon while twenty of our men were on a seal-hunting trip. Fifteen of our men were killed and butchered on the spot. The other five escaped by hiding in some rocks and had to endure watching their friends being cut up alive as they had been only wounded by the arrows and spears of the Eskimos. Some of the survivors went crazy afterwards and three committed suicide soon after we sent out a rescue party. The remaining two have never been the same and we sent them home by ship from Churchill Fort earlier this past summer.

"Our heavy boats lasted until we got back to Cumberland House then we able to finally get the nice light canot du nord that are so well adapted to the western streams and rivers. Some of the men were on the verge of mutiny, I think, if Captain Franklin had not finally purchased the canoes for our trip back here. At Fort William we exchanged them for the bigger canot de maitres which you see here with us today. We were able to hire two bateaux at Wright's Village for this final leg of our long voyage.

Charles continued to sit quietly as the weary traveler recounted his story to him. "We have had a hard trip these past two years but I think Captain Franklin will want to return, but next time it will be by ship. He believes that he can find a passage through from Baffin Island to the western coast and the Pacific Ocean even if it kills him. He is a very determined man and wants to find the North West Passage before anyone else; be that American, British, French or Norwegian."

"I hope he does, for his sake," added Charles. "He does seem to be a nice man, though a little bit arrogant."

"You are right on that last comment," said the Lieutenant. "But he means well and he does try to treat his men fairly though he demands a great deal of them. That is why these men are all volunteers, including myself.

"The voyageurs we hired in Montréal went only as far as Cumberland House. From then on it was our own Royal Navy sailors. They were suited and trained for work on the high seas and a large warship, but not to work in the tight confines of a canoe or a long boat for any extended period. I think that is why many wished they had never volunteered for the expedition and why they almost mutinied."

"Was the whole two year expedition worth the monetary cost and the loss of life it caused?" asked Charles.

"I believe it was," answered Fitzgibbon. "We charted hundreds of miles of coastline and though we had terrible losses from the cold, natives and general hardships; most expeditions are similar in nature. Whether those expeditions are down south, to Africa or north into your frozen wasteland, I definitely believe we always benefit from them and we are much better for it."

"I guess you are right," Charles answered back. "However, I guess I am so settled here in Cavagnal that I cannot see why you do it. It cost our Government in London so much, and for what? The far out chance that you might find a quick passage from the Atlantic Ocean to the Pacific Ocean. I find it hard to believe that it is worthwhile at all."

"Well that is your opinion and you are welcome to it Mr. Schmidt." Charles turned to see Captain Franklin standing behind him.

"I am sorry Captain, but I have been listening to your Lieutenant here and I am just offering my opinion as you seem to have overheard, accidentally." Charles had ended his sentence with a cynical tone.

"I understand your feelings Mr. Schmidt," Franklin added. "However, you must realize this expedition was partially paid by you as well as those in England and though you have your rights to voice your opinions. I would hasten to say that your opinions would not go well back in the Admiralty. I understand you were born in what is now the United States of America."

"Yes, I am an American by birth but my family came here to British North America soon after my birth. My father had fought as a Hessian in the American Revolution. I know too well what happens to those who are too outspoken, especially opposing what our famous Government decides back in England. But you have your rights too Captain Franklin and I must admire your stamina and foresight and spirit of adventure for leading an expedition such as this."

Charles had hoped that with this last sentence he had won over the stern Captain and had appeased his speculations that Charles could be a potential rabble rouser, causing trouble for the British Crown in the region. Of course, Captain Franklin would never know or probably could have cared less that Charles was a very active member of the local Volunteer Militia unit that had been raised the previous year.

The matter was dropped and Captain John Franklin asked his senior officer to accompany him to the other side of the Tavern where they could have a private conversation and enjoy their last meal in the frontier.

Charles then told Mary that most of the men would be eating their meal outside. Mary shrugged her shoulders and said that would be fine. "I will have Simon and John set up the tables outside," Charles told his wife and headed off outside to see that everything was going okay out there.

John was worried about his wife inside with so many men and they not having been near another white woman in almost two years. Charles saw John looking towards the Tavern and guessed correctly what he was thinking. "We better both be inside with the women, John," Charles told his friend. "Simon, Rotonni and these men can handle the set of the tables out here. I am like you and am worried about my wife as well." They both smiled and headed inside to help the two ladies with the meals for the officers.

Jane had been baking some bread that morning and afternoon in the large woodstove in the kitchen and it was still warm. In her large cast iron pots was the Tavern's famous moose and venison stew laced with carrots, potatoes, onions and good thick gravy. George and Rotonni had shot two deer and a large moose two weeks before up on St. George Mountain and had hauled them back in the back of George's big wagon.

Captain John Franklin had been quite correct about Schmidt's Tavern and the great food that it was known for all across North America. Voyageurs had been stopping there since it had opened in 1798. They had spread the reputation of the food and how initially William and Caroline Schmidt had been such great hosts right through to the west coast. Now Charles Schmidt and his young staff of Jane Cameron and Mary Kilkenny Schmidt were running the Tavern and its reputation was still thriving though fewer and fewer brigades of canoes were now traveling the Ottawa River.

The amalgamation of the North West Company and The Hudson's Bay Company in 1821 had drastically shifted the trade of furs from Montreal to Fort Churchill on Hudson's Bay. A few local traders like Angus Macleod of Montréal still financed some brigades but these were growing fewer and fewer each year.

The boats seen most often now on the Lake of the Two Mountains were the large bateaux transports that John Cameron had been using and huge rafts of logs heading down river from the area around Wright's Village.

None of the proposed steamboat traffic that had been promised months before had yet materialized. Delays in the construction of the new boats had set back their arrival on the Ottawa River.

With more and more emigrants arriving to the area each summer, these new steamboats would help them reach Cavagnal and other points west with a greater ease and safety than the slow and unreliable bateaux.

Captain Franklin turned out to be a jovial man and Lieutenant Fitzgibbon was pleased to see how well Jane and John Cameron had done since their marriage two years before. "I hear you already have one child Jane," said Fitzgibbon as he and the others sat down to a hearty hot meal.

"Yes, he was born last January and he is called Duncan George Cameron, after my father George Henderson and John's great-grandfather Duncan Cameron."

"Charles," asked Jane, "is there enough stew for the crowd outside or do they need more?"

"They are already calling for more," said Charles "and more ale as well."

"Give them as much as they want, Mr. Schmidt," Captain Franklin told his host. "This food is so good and my men have not had such a feast since they left Fort William many weeks ago.

"We did not stop at Wright's Village for any longer than it took us to make the portage around the falls and hire the two bateaux. I was hoping to reach Montréal tomorrow afternoon but methinks we will be delayed leaving here tomorrow morning. I know I will," he laughed. "A toast to our fine hosts and King George," said Franklin. All of the officers in the Tavern as well as all the men outside then stood up and raised their tankards and took a long drink of their ale as they toasted King George and the Schmidts and their staff at the little stone tavern on the banks of the Ottawa River in the remote community of Cavagnal.

Captain Franklin, Lieutenant Fitzgibbon and the other one hundred and eighteen men of the Franklin Expedition left about ten the next morning. Many of the men had a great difficulty in getting themselves up but the smell of hot coffee and bacon and eggs cooking over the open fire soon had them all up and preparing to leave.

The staff at the Tavern had been up for a few hours and had set up a cooking area outside the Tavern's front door so the large group of men could be served a hearty breakfast before leaving for towards Lachine and Montréal. One hundred and twenty men were served their last hot meal in the hinterland of British North America under a chilly but sunny sky and then they set off down the river, singing the famous Royal Navy song, "Hearts of Oak".

Just before leaving, Captain John Franklin handed Charles Schmidt a leather pouch, heavy with coin. After the canoes had pulled away from the dock, Charles emptied the pouch and counted out one hundred shillings. "Best day we have ever had," he said as he smiled. With that Charles, Mary, John, Rotonni, Jane, Simon, Caroline and William all waved goodbye to their famous guests.

"I wonder if we will ever hear of him again?" commented John Cameron.

"I doubt it," said Charles. "Those expeditions of his are too expensive and I imagine King George can find a better place to spend his money than having some arrogant naval officer tramp or sail all over the frozen north trying to find a channel through all that ice and snow for their big ships."

With that they all turned and headed up the slight slope to tackle the huge clean up of dishes and refuse that had been left by the Franklin expedition.

Chapter 24
More Trouble

George Henderson missed the visit of Captain John Franklin that fine fall afternoon in Cavagnal. He had been up at Robert Henderson's farm with John Marsden and Joseph Shouldice. Robert had sent word down to Marsden and George that he had found a body floating in the Raquette River the day before. Since George and Marsden were the local representatives of law enforcement in the area, they had left that morning for the two hour ride up to St. Henry from Marsden's store. Joseph Shouldice had asked to come along since he had not been up that way in over a year and had not spoken to Robert Henderson since the funeral of his three children.

Robert had dragged the body out of the river and with the help of Dr. Grisenthwaite they had placed it in Robert's small icehouse until George and the others arrived.

"It is a body of a man about forty," announced Robert when they arrived that afternoon. "He seems to have been shot in the back with a shotgun. Never seen him before, either."

"It looks as if we have a murder on our hands," announced John Marsden. "The first one in our little community."

Joseph Shouldice took a good look at the man and immediately said that he knew him. Everyone stopped talking and looked at Joseph.

"Well speak up man," George told his friend.

259

"He worked for Charles Whetstone, William's notorious brother, in the lumber mill just over there, past the Grisenthwaite's place. I believe his name was Gaspard Séguin and he came from over in Ste Marthe. He was not married and he was the manager of Whetstone's mill."

"If someone was going to commit a murder, why would they just dump the body in the river?" asked Marsden. "I would have stashed the body somewhere more remote than this."

"Maybe," announced George, "whoever did this was not able to do just that and maybe had to dump the body in a hurry, hoping that the river would carry it downstream and it would snag up under some branches."

"There is a huge beaver dam not far from here," Robert told his friends, "but not many people know about it, especially anyone from way over by the mill. It is on my property and as far as I know, only the Doctor and his family and my daughter Phoebe know that it is there."

"I will have to get in touch with the authorities in Montréal," John Marsden told the others. "This will be my first real important duty since becoming the local Justice of the Peace. This is a little more serious than the odd land transaction or robbery that I am used to. I wonder if it has anything to do with Whetstone's connection with F.X. Deschamps and the Patriote movement? Charles is just as bad as his brother with their deep involvement with those damn Patriotes."

"I hope not," George told the others. "This could prove to be a very serious turn of events and cause some rumblings in the now seemingly quiet Patriote movement in this region."

"There are few English workers if any up at the mill," Robert told the others. I think one of the O'Rourke's works there, but only part time. Most of the men come from the village of Ste Marthe."

"Therefore, most are French Canadians, right?" asked George.
"That is correct George," Robert told the local Sheriff. "Of the twenty five or so men at the mill, only Stephen O'Rourke is not a French Canadian. Stephen has a wicked temper, as do most of the O'Rourkes, but I do not think he would do this."

"Can you send someone over to Ste Marthe to this man's family and tell them to come and get the body, Robert?"

"I will send my son", interjected Doctor Grisenthwaite. "Jacob is a good lad and he has been over there a few times with me."

"Good. We will head over to the mill to ask a few questions," announced Marsden. "They might not appreciate us visiting them but I am sure that this poor devil has been missing at least a couple of days."

"From the look of the body I think he was in the water about three days before Robert found him," announced Dr. Grisenthwaite.

"I am glad you had him on ice for a while, at least, and that the weather is cool. This Séguin fellow needs to be buried soon. He does not smell too nice! I think it would be better if Jacob took my wagon and the body instead of having someone come and get it," the Doctor told the others. "The sooner this man is buried the better."

"Agreed," said John Marsden. "Jacob will leave as soon as possible with the body of Mister Séguin and deliver him to his family, if there is one, or drop him off with the Parish priest in Ste Marthe. At least he will get a decent Catholic burial there."

Marsden continued by saying that he, George, Shouldice, and Robert would go over to the mill and talk to some of the workers there, then head back and speak with Charles Whetstone as soon as possible.

George Henderson had never visited either Whetstone's large lumber mill on the side of the hill in St. Henry nor his large house that was in a newly settled area west of Cavagnal that was known as Choisy. It was about three miles west of Marsden's store. He was not sure if he was going to like either visit. The three of them, known leaders in the English community, were now investigating what looked like a murder of a well-known French Canadian citizen of Ste Marthe who was also employed by one of the main supporters of the local Patriote movement, Charles Whetstone.

John Marsden had quickly taken on Joseph Shouldice as George's Deputy when they decided that the death of Gaspard Séguin had been a murder and that they would need the extra help. Shouldice gladly accepted his new position. He also explained that he had seen the Séguin fellow a few times while buying wood at the Whetstone mill and it had had been the poor man who had loaded his wagon.

The only thing that George, Marsden, and their new deputy, Joseph

Shouldice, did not know was that Séguin had been a major opponent of the Patriote movement and was not at all well liked by those who worked with him at the Whetstone's lumber mill—or by those in his own village of Ste Marthe.

Gaspard Séguin's family had been long-time supporters of the British crown and had thought many times of moving down to the mainly English communities of either Côte St. Charles or Cavagnal. Gaspard had fought alongside the British regulars at Chateauguay and Chrysler's Farm during the recent war with the Americans and,as a result the Séguins had received a large land grant from the British Governor in Québec. Séguin had saved the life of a British Colonel at the Battle of Chrysler's Farm, and at the Battle of Chateauguay he had captured a whole platoon of American soldiers with only his brother, Emile, helping him.

Since that time the Séguin family had prospered as landowners in Ste Marthe and though Gaspard worked for Whetstone in the lumber mill, he did it to make extra money so he could purchase more land and cattle. He had great plans for the small community of Ste Marthe but unfortunately this all came to a tragic end in late September of 1827.

The Justice of the Peace for Cavagnal and area, John Augustus Marsden, and his two Sheriffs did not have much luck with their investigation over at Charles Whetstone's lumber mill. No one would speak to them in English and with George's limited French they soon found out that no one at the mill was willing to discuss the disappearance and then-obvious murder of their manager.

"No use staying here," announced Marsden to the other two. "We might just end up like that Séguin fellow if we do not watch ourselves." George had brought along his new rifle but had left it in the wagon, not thinking that he would need it. They were there to investigate the death of Gaspard Séguin, not to cause a disturbance and any uneasy feeling among the very partisan Patriote followers. The only thing that Marsden, George, and Shouldice knew about the mill was that it was crawling with Patriote sympathizers and they would probably not be well liked at all.

They were correct and left after having spent only fifteen minutes in the noisy place. Everyone had ignored them except for one fellow who seemed to be in charge. It did not even seem that Gaspard Séguin was being missed. No one cared and no one would talk about his disappearance, let alone the recovery of the body by Robert Henderson the day before. It was if Séguin had never existed nor had ever worked at the big mill.

"Next stop will be the Whetstone residence," announced Marsden.

"I hope we get some better results there," George told his friends.

"I do not think we will," Joseph Shouldice said in a quiet tone. "Look," he continued and pointed back to the mill. George and Marsden turned and saw that most of the mill workers were outside the mill and watching them wind their way slowly down the road in the heavy wagon.

"There goes a fast rider over there through the woods on our left," Shouldice said to George and Marsden.

"I bet you anything," George said, "that rider is off to tell Charles Whetstone of our recent visit and our probable visit to his place. That rider will be there long before us. Whetstone will have time to think of what to say before our arrival."

John Marsden was visibly angered by what had transcribed over the past few hours in St. Henry and was quietly thinking of how he was going to handle this crisis in his normally peaceful community.

Over the past few weeks the Patriotes had almost curtailed their operations in the region and it had seemed that the need for the Vaudreuil Loyal Volunteer Militia had been all in vain. However, now with this murder, things might change and the Militia might yet be called to action. Jacob Grisenthwaite was able to deliver the body of Gaspard Séguin to his brother Emile in Ste Marthe late that afternoon and by dark he was back at his home along the Raquette.

He immediately told his parents that he was heading into Cavagnal on their horse as he had found out some very important information while he had been in Ste Marthe.

Emile Séguin had told Jacob what he thought had happened to his older brother and how Jacob should warn John Marsden and the others in Cavagnal.

Jacob arrived at John Marsden's store just after ten o'clock that night and collapsed into a chair after entering the dimly lit building. Marsden, George Henderson, and Joseph Shouldice were all still there and could not believe their eyes when they saw the young Grisenthwaite walk into the store.

He was exhausted and needed a shot of rum and a hot meal before the others could make any sense of what he was trying to say. His mind was racing a mile a minute but his tongue was messing up the words as they came out of his mouth.

After a few minutes Jacob was finally able to piece his words together in a manner that the others could finally understand him. "Mr. Séguin's brother, Emile, whom I found in Ste Marthe, believes that it was the men from the lumber mill who had killed his brother. It seems that both Gaspard and Emile are strong supporters of the British Government here in Lower Canada and against anything that would cause the overthrow of that Government.

"The Séguins are not at all popular in Ste Marthe and now with the death of his brother, Emile will be moving down here to Cavagnal as soon as he can. Gaspard was not married, but Emile is and has a large family, some even have English names such as Joseph, Sarah, and Alfred. Emile is actually married to an English lady by the name of Gray. She is from over on the south shore of the St. Lawrence, Georgetown I believe."

"Well that settles that," announced Marsden. "We know that we have a murder. Now we have a reason but unfortunately we do not have the person or persons who committed the deed and I do not think we will ever find them. It is more than likely that Charles and or William Whetstone were involved somewhere and maybe even F.X. Deschamps."

Jacob learned from the others that they had already visited with Whetstone at his home in Choisy. As expected the fast rider had arrived much sooner than the slow-moving wagon that Marsden, George, and Shouldice were in and the stranger had time to warn Whetstone about their impending visit and what had transcribed up at the Whetstone lumber mill in St. Henry.

All Charles Whetstone had to say when Marsden and the others arrived at his door was that he did not know anything about what had happened to Gaspard Séguin. He was sorry about his death and he would send the family a sum of ten pounds as a partial compensation for their loss.

Whetstone admitted that he had known Séguin had been missing for a few days but he thought that he was off hunting up on the mountain. "He often hunted in the fall," Whetstone added. Marsden's visit lasted about fifteen minutes, then he and the others left to go back to his store for a couple of glasses of rum and to think of what to do next. It was while they were pouring their third glass of rum that Jacob arrived.

George and Joseph decided to stay that night at John Marsden's store since it was quite late by the time they had finished their meal and talked with John and Jacob about what they were going to have to do in the upcoming weeks. George and Joseph only found out about Captain Franklin's visit the next day when they arrived home from their investigation.

Gaspard Séguin's murder went unsolved that fall. He was buried in Ste Marthe just before his brother and his family moved to Cavagnal. Emile settled a new section in the west of the concession that was being opened up by the Vaughans, one of the newly arrived families from Alston in eastern Cumberland.

Emile and his family left their farm in Ste Marthe and moved their furniture and other possessions in the two wagons that they owned. They brought their horses and fourteen head of cattle with them as well. Emile was able to convince a neighbour in Ste Marthe to buy his house, barn, and property for twenty pounds. It was far less than what it was really worth but Emile had decided to leave and get out as soon as possible. They would have to start a new life once again down in Cavagnal.

Isaac Vaughan had been able to purchase a large section of land from the Seigneur's Agent, Mr. Pambrun, and had set up a sheep farm. When Emile Séguin arrived a few days after his brother's funeral in Ste Marthe he spotted the sheep farm of Isaac Vaughan and stopped in to see if he needed help tending the herd. Isaac admitted that he did and Emile was hired on immediately.

John Augustus Marsden was very upset that neither he nor George Henderson were able to solve Séguin's murder, and he was even more upset when he had to report his findings to the Government in Montréal.

Murders were fairly common in Montréal but out in the settlements on the edge of the hinterland only one or two murders or suspicious deaths were reported each year. Séguin's murder in the Seigneury of Vaudreuil was the only one reported in 1827 and, unlike most of the others in the regions around Montréal, it went unsolved.

The threat of more trouble with the Patriote movement never materialized that fall, and life in St. Henry, Côte St. Charles, and Cavagnal returned to its normal quiet style as the residents prepared for yet another long and cold winter and another new year in their newly adopted home.

The Vaudreuil Loyal Volunteers were disbanded just before the 15th of December, 1827, on orders from the British Army commander at the fort on Ste Helen's Island in Montréal.

PART III

Ten Years Later—1837

Chapter 25
Progress and Change

Ten years had passed since the initial rumblings of a possible rebellion in Lower Canada, but during those ten years only some very minor incidents had occurred throughout the colony. No actual rebellion had taken place. The scare of an uprising in Cavagnal in 1827 had been long forgotten.

The ever-growing community of Cavagnal had greatly expanded in both size and population. From a backwoods community that had a population of a little more than three hundred in 1827, the population now stood at close to six hundred. This figure included all those who lived in St. Henry and Côte St. Charles. However, most of those who had arrived were from either England or Scotland. Very few were of either direct French or French-Canadian descent.

The few French-speaking settlers lived either in the western section of the community or east of Deschamp's store. Most of the new French settlers had set up farms or businesses in either Vaudreuil or Rigaud, close to the existing Roman Catholic churches. Cavagnal still had neither a Protestant nor Catholic Church for the residents to worship in.

The year 1837 began on a happy note, with John and Jane Cameron's fourth child being born in January. Andrew Iain Cameron weighed in at six pounds four ounces and he was the smallest of all babies that Jane had given birth to.

Jane had always been a healthy woman and that strength helped her during her pregnancies. Neither she nor her children had ever suffered any serious illnesses. John had survived the births of his four children almost as well as his wife. His initial nervousness had given way to helping as much as he could around the house now that there were so many young mouths to feed.

The arrival of the steamboats on the Ottawa River a few years before had greatly increased the work he had to do at the Tavern, especially since the deaths of Caroline and William Schmidt in 1827 and 1828. They had died just months apart of each other. Caroline had died of a severe heart attack in December 1827. William had contracted a serious case of pneumonia in February 1828 and had succumbed to it even before Dr. Grisenthwaite had been able to arrive down at the Tavern. William had been very depressed after the sudden loss of his dear wife and had become ill shortly after her death.

Charles Schmidt had thought of selling the Tavern but both John and Jane Cameron had convinced him and Mary to hang on to it as it was still a very popular stopping off spot on the Ottawa River. The food continued to be as good as it had ever been, even though the brigades of canoes were almost non-existent. The steamboat trade with the scheduled stop at their wharf added as much or more revenue to the Tavern as the canoe brigades had years before.

George Henderson was now sixty-one years old, but even though he had slowed up somewhat, he was still a very healthy man and Sheriff of the community of Cavagnal. There had been very little crime in the community and he had even thought of giving up the job. However, the money that he received each year had helped improve his lifestyle and that of his family in Cavagnal.

Mary Henderson aged as nicely as her husband. Excellent health had blessed them both. All of the family was doing well. George and she now had only three of their eight children living at home. Margaret had left two years before for Montréal, where she now worked as a dressmaker.

Frances had also moved out of the old homestead and was now married to Simon Beauvais and living in Kanesatake. Their marriage had caused quite a stir amongst the strict Anglican community of Cavagnal.

However, George had quickly quietened the rumours and the terrible comments some of the locals had passed around shortly before and just after the wedding.

George had announced that he would withdraw from the local Church committee and also withdraw his funds that were a backbone for them forming a building fund. Simon Beauvais had been part of the work force of Cavagnal for many years and even though he was a few years older than Frances, that did not matter to either Mary or George.

Simon and Frances were happy and their young daughter, Isabel, had brought the two communities even closer together than ever before.

William Henderson had left the house that he had helped his father build when he was ten years old in 1824. He was now working as a deck hand on the new steamboat that was plying the river every day. *The Deux Montagnes* was based at Lachine, where William had moved in 1835 to be closer to the docks and the main warehouse.

Over the past few years more and more English-speaking settlers had arrived in the community. The lack of French-speaking emigrants had caused F.X. Deschamps to openly voice his opinions, which had largely gone unnoticed. Though he was little more than a thorn in the side of many of the settlers, he was also an important local merchant; and though the English settlers despised the little man, they had to frequent his thriving business as it carried so many of the little things they needed to make their tough lives a little more comfortable.

Arriving in 1834 had been a family from Kirkoswald whom George had known many years before while still in England. Thomas Grantham and his wife Elizabeth Fraser arrived with three young adult children and had settled in Choisy, not far from Charles Whetstone's home.

George had written to his cousin, Thomas, a few times over the years since he had been in Canada and had finally convinced him to emigrate. Thomas had lost his first wife to consumption in 1823. He had three young children at the time and, with no mother to care for them, Thomas had delayed his trip to Canada until he had found a new wife and step-mother for his three children. Elizabeth Fraser was from Lazonby. Thomas had known her for many years and she was just what he needed:

a beautiful, loving, and caring wife whom his three children came to love as their new mother.

Thomas had been a carter in Kirkoswald and John Marsden hired the big man to transport goods from the two steamboat wharves in Cavagnal to his store and various places around the community. Thomas' two sons, William and Peter, also helped their father while setting up a productive dairy farm. His daughter, Elizabeth, helped her stepmother around the farmhouse and on the small farm alongside her two brothers.

They had brought two Holstein cows along with them and enough money to purchase a fine Holstein bull calf in Vaudreuil from Regent Castonguay. Thomas had heard that Regent had a good herd of Holsteins and that he would probably be willing to sell one of his bull calves.

It was the beginning of what was to become one of the finest herds of dairy cattle in all of Cavagnal. The Granthams had always had Holstein cattle back in Kirkoswald and they were the only ones in Cavagnal with them in 1837. All of the other English settlers were raising either Ayrshires or Guernseys. The French-Canadian settlers commonly had small herds of their hardy black Canadienne cattle.

Since George Henderson's arrival in Cavagnal in 1824 from Cumberland, England numerous other settlers from other parts of Cumberland had arrived. Many had been sheep farmers in England and they initially tried to do the same in Cavagnal, St. Henry and in Côte St. Charles. Only a few were able to raise a good herd of sheep but most had serious troubles with the local wolf and bear populations that tended to kill off many of the young sheep.

"If I had two pounds for every sheep I have lost to those damn wolves up in St. Henry, I could buy this whole Seigneury," said Richard Golding one day in 1835. "I have lost so many that I will have to sell off the rest to anyone who wants them and try my hand at something else."

Poor Richard had arrived in 1832 from Culgaith, in Cumberland, with his wife and nine children. They had settled on lot 15N in St. Henry, next door to Isaac Vaughan. Isaac was also a sheep farmer, but he had been able to purchase a couple of large dogs. They kept the St. Henry wolf pack at bay most of the time.

George and John Henderson were summoned up to the Golding's

farm one day in early 1837. Richard had heard that both of the Hendersons were crack shots with their Pennsylvania long rifles and he had hoped that the two men could kill off some of the marauding wolves in the area.

"I will pay you the most I can afford—sheep, wool, meat, or wood— if you can just get rid of these damn wolves," he pleaded to George and John.

"We will try, but we cannot promise you anything," George told the distraught farmer.

That spring, George and his son were able to kill only three wolves and one large male bear. All four were killed as they prowled close to the Golding and Vaughan farms. All George had asked for in payment was half of the bear meat after they had butchered it. The skins of the three wolves were not in their winter prime and they were all discarded except for the tails, which were nailed to the back of Richard's buggy.

The St. Henry wolves continued to be a nuisance all through 1837 and both the Goldings and the Vaughans continued to lose sheep to them. It was only after John Marsden was able to locate some poison that the pack of wolves was killed off.

George's two Mohawk friends, Awen'rah:ton and Sori'howane, had stayed around Cavagnal for a number of months after bringing George his two new long rifles from the United States. They had made many friends with the white settlers of Cavagnal, but when F.X. Deschamps had found out what they had done on the south shore of the St. Lawrence many months before, they fled back to the United States.

Deschamps called for the resignations of George Henderson and John Marsden as the local Sheriff and Justice of the Peace, knowing that they had been close friends of the two Mohawks from New York. Deschamps believed that the two men—whom he hated most in the community, though especially Marsden—had knowingly harboured the two Mohawks from the Lower Canada authorities in Montréal. Unfortunately for Deschamps, he could not prove his accusations and George and John Marsden remained in office. George had never told John Marsden what his two Mohawk friends had actually done, but he did have to explain the situation when Deschamps' claims began to grow louder by the week.

It was under Marsden's guidance that George had decided to persuade Awen'rah:ton, Sori'howane, and their families to return to the United States as quickly as possible. They left one afternoon while Deschamps was in Montreal trying to rally more support to his claim. With the two Indians now safely in the United States and out of touch of the British law in Lower Canada, Deschamps' claims could not be proven.

He had informed his two friends that he had told Marsden, since they were both involved in the law and order of the community and he trusted Marsden. They accepted this and they also accepted, though regrettably, to leave their new-found home but they did promise to return if their friends in Cavagnal ever needed their help, no matter the circumstances.

Chapter 26
Storm Clouds

On a clear spring day in early June 1837, John Marsden dropped in to
see George Henderson.

"How many men can we get under arms if we need them?" Marsden
asked his long time friend.

"I imagine a few more than we had back in 1827, but not many more.
I would guess about one hundred and twenty at best."

"That is just twelve or so more than we had ten years ago," Marsden
replied.

"I know," said George. "I think I know why you are asking me. Has it
anything to do with our two Patriote friends, Whetstone and
Deschamps?"

"Yes," answered Marsden. "Whetstone has purchased a small printing
press and it was delivered to his home last week. My son, Stephen, saw it
being unloaded from Thomas Grantham's wagon. Thomas had his two
big sons with him as the press was so heavy, Stephen said. He had been
walking down from visiting Cornelius Gannon when the Granthams
pulled up in front of Whetstone's house.

"Stephen said that Peter Grantham had whispered to him that he had
heard in Vaudreuil, where they had picked up the press, that Whetstone
planned to print and circulate a newsletter pushing the Patriote cause in
the Vaudreuil Seigneury and the rest of Lower Canada."

"We cannot do anything right now," replied an astonished and intrigued George Henderson. "However, let us just keep an eye on our two friends and if something does come from this newsletter. If we see another possible rebellion arising, I will call out the men once again.

"It has been ten years since we last mustered. Many of the men are too old now to shoulder arms and fight a battle if the need be, but those old soldiers of the Vaudreuil Loyal Volunteers have fathered many a fine son. They are the young lads we will need this time as they are just about the right age now."

George continued by saying that he had read a copy of the *Montreal Gazette* with Joseph Shouldice at Schmidt's Tavern the week before and he told Marsden that there was once again talk of rebellion in Montréal and in some of the south shore communities, such as Chambly and St. Hyacinthe.

"The troops stationed out at the fort on Ste Helen's Island have been put on a semi-alert status as there already have been some fire bombings of some homes of some prominent English politicians in Montréal and Lachine. It is too bad that the 24th Regiment of Foot is no longer stationed over at Fort Côteau," George continued. "They have to be some of the best troops that the British Army can field."

"I agree," said Marsden. "But they left about four years ago, did they not?"

"Yes—but they were replaced by a Canadian Militia battalion that does not have the battle experience that the 24th did. I have heard a rumour that the Royal Canadian Rifle Regiment may be placed there, but that will not be for a few years yet. They are still at the Citadel in Halifax, according to the last letter that I received from my old friend Henry Irons. It is too bad that I cannot convince him to move up here. He was in Spain and at Waterloo with the old 60th Rifle Regiment."

"I remember them," Marsden commented. "They were a great Regiment. Did you meet this Mr. Irons over in Europe or on your way over here?"

"I met him on board *The Pioneer*. He was beside me when Isaac died in my arms," George told Marsden.

George had not thought of his old friend for many months and the mere mention of his name and that awful battle thirteen years before brought tears to his eyes.

"I guess you still miss him, eh George?" asked Marsden.

"Yes, I do. It is just that I have not thought about him too much lately. Both he and Henry. We two would be more than a match for that damn Whetstone and Deschamps and their rowdy Patriots. Right, John?"

"Awful odds, George. The last time Deschamps raised a force of Patriotes, they numbered about one hundred or more, if I remember right."

"Correct. Twenty-five to one, great odds for four well-trained men who were led by Lord Wellington. Old Nosey would be proud to see four of 'His' lads battling the French to a standstill once again."

"Wait a minute, George," said Marsden. "Think now, my friend. Your friend Isaac is dead, Henry is in Halifax, and we are not all that young anymore."

"Age is only in your mind, John. I feel great. With our experience, I know we can beat these bastards when the time comes."

"Let us just hope that once again the great battle or the small skirmish will not arrive and we can continue to live in peace."

"I must agree, John. However, we must be prepared if these newsletters prove to be as real as Peter Grantham has said."

"George," began Marsden. "Can you do a very quiet survey of all the English settlers here in Cavagnal, Côte St. Charles and up in Côte St. Henry?"

"Sure I can," answered George. "I will contact Joseph Shouldice to help me."

"No, said Marsden. "I do not want anyone but us knowing about this potential problem. Take your time but try and get the survey done by next week, if possible."

"Fine," said George, wondering to himself what prompted the secrecy. Maybe Marsden knew more about this potential uprising than he is letting on. "I will have your survey for you by the weekend—if not sooner. My crops are all in and I was planning to visit Dr. Grisenthwaite this week at any rate. I will just drop by all the homes on the way up there and come back by Côte St. Charles the next day. I still have the list of those who were in the militia back in 1827, though some of the older men have now died."

"I just want to say one more thing," Marsden said to his friend before he left to head west to see his ailing wife, Harriett. "I have received direct orders from Governor Gosford to re-enlist our Vaudreuil Loyal Volunteers as soon as possible. He is shipping some new guns to us next week if he can arrange it, and he has asked for a standing militia of about one to two thousand men in and around Montréal. He really expects trouble this time and has asked me to have our militia in place by the end of the month. Can we do it, George?"

"Sure we can do it. We did it back in '27, and we can do it again. I have heard rumblings of discontent that have been fed to me from Simon Beauvais over in Kanesatake. He has seen large groups of men and arms heading towards St. Benoit along some back trail that cross over the Indian lands. They have been challenged but scared off the questioning Mohawks with gunfire. No one was injured but the Indians across the river are just as tense as we will be if this gets out of hand.

"I have also heard from my son William that there are regular meetings of the Patriotes over in Ste Eustache. His steamboat, *The Deux Montagnes*, makes a stop there once a week and he has seen many men get on and off, carrying guns and kegs of what are probably shot and powder. I am afraid that we could be in for a long hot summer of uprisings if this gets under way. I hope that the Governor has asked for more troops from England or Halifax."

"I have heard that Sir John Colborne had recently moved his headquarters from Québec to Montréal, and that troops would be heading here from England, Halifax and Upper Canada," replied Madsen. "However, Upper Canada cannot spare too many British regulars, as there seems to be troubles up there as well, not far from York. Some gentleman called William Lyon Mackenzie is stirring up trouble there as well."

"Fine," said George. "As soon as we get our list of men available, we can call a meeting at your place. There will be no need to be as clandestine as we were back in 1827. I will get a message off to Awen'rah:ton and Sori'howane tomorrow asking them if they can make it up here as soon as possible. They have always said that they would come back here to help us if the need arose and I think now is the time."

"Good idea," Marsden announced. "With that, I will leave for home. Dr. Grisenthwaite is supposed to arrive around noon to see my poor wife. I hope it is not pneumonia. She has not been well for about five days now."

"Tell the good Doctor that I will see him shortly," George told Marsden.

"Good luck," George called to his friend as Marsden's buggy pulled away from the front of the Henderson's house.

"What was all that about?" asked Mary Henderson as she walked around from the back of their home. "Was he here long?"

"About forty-five minutes, I guess," answered George.

"You could have at least told me. I wanted to ask him about Harriett. I heard that she has been quite ill."

"He mentioned that Dr. Grisenthwaite was coming down around noon to see her. John thinks it might be pneumonia again. I am sorry I did not call you, Mary, but what he had to tell me was so important that I completely forgot. Anyway I thought that you were out in the back field planting with Elizabeth and little George."

"We were, but we have been out in the back yard for the past twenty minutes. George's little dog wanted to play. We were throwing a stick and it was retrieving it each time.

"What is wrong dear?" Mary asked. "Are we in for more trouble?"

"I am afraid we are. Remember back in 1827, how Deschamps was getting together a large band of rebels?"

"Yes, of course. How can anyone forget that?" Mary answered. "However, nothing ever happened and we have lived in peace and harmony ever since."

"Well, this time it is for real and already Governor Gosford has called for more troops from Halifax, Upper Canada, and even England. He has asked for a standing militia of up to two thousand men in and around Montreal and that includes us once again.

"It seems that the Whetstones are once again involved as Thomas Grantham recently delivered a small printing press to William's house along with numerous boxes of paper and bottles of ink. Marsden thinks that Deschamps and he have something planned for the region and he has asked me to take names of all those that can serve in our Vaudreuil Loyal Volunteers once again."

"Oh, George," Mary exclaimed. "You are sixty-one years old! You are not the young soldier you once were. Remember your health."

"My health is fine. You know that as well as I do," he answered. "I know I am not the young warrior that once fought from Portugal through to the heart of France and up to Waterloo, but both Marsden and I both have the best knowledge of anyone here in Cavagnal and we know how to lead these men into battle. Tactics have not changed since Waterloo and—with the new weapons the Governor has promised us—we should do all right. As long as Deschamps and Whetstone do not call on assistance from the Patriotes across the river in St. Benoit or Ste Eustache.

"Marsden is counting on the troops at Carillon. They may have finished the canal years ago, but the Governor has been wise and kept a small company there to maintain and guard the canal. Sir John Colborne's has a crack regiment in Montréal to keep an eye on St. Benoit and Ste. Eustache. Personally I think we will have to keep an eye on the docks, steamboats, and ferry links in Vaudreuil and Ile Perrot. Guard duty rather than actual fighting. I think the British line regiments will be doing the fighting."

George continued discussing the matter with his wife as they entered their home. "I will make us a cup of tea and we can talk some more," Mary told her husband.

"That is great. Do you have any of those great scones that you made the other day?"

"Two left and they are both yours, my dear," Mary said with a warm smile. As she turned to put the heavy iron kettle over the fire, she smiled to herself and saw how the George's anticipation of once again seeing active military duty had perked up his morale.

George had been feeling somewhat depressed in recent weeks. There had been very little for him to do as the local Sheriff and, with crime in the area so low, he had felt that the position was almost redundant. Mary had seen the change in him over the past winter but now with the renewed threat of a real armed rebellion on the horizon, George's morale and look had already improved—even in just the few minutes since John Marsden had left their house.

"I think we can raise a militia of about one hundred and twenty," George said to Mary as they sat at the kitchen table sipping their steaming cups of tea. "Most of the men who were with us back in 1827 have settled down with families, and some have even moved away to Upper Canada. Even so, the boys from up in St. Henry and Côte St. Charles will surely come to us. I wonder how many men Deschamps and Whetstone have on their side?"

"Do you think Thomas Grantham will help?" Mary asked.

"I imagine he will. He has two good strong lads and both are excellent shots, from what I have heard.

"What is William like?" asked Mary. "I have met Peter and he seems to be a dreamer and a prospective wanderer. He told me one day, while I was at Marsden's store with Alice Shouldice, that he was considering moving to Upper Canada to join a militia regiment there. He had read in the *Montreal Gazette* of the troubles up around York and he was thinking of heading west."

George was surprised with Mary's knowledge of Peter Grantham's wishes, but he smiled and thanked her for the information.

"I am sending for our two good friends down in Ganienkeh, Awen'rah:ton and Sori'howane," he said. "I think they will be a definite asset to us if we do actually have an armed rebellion."

"It will be great seeing them once again," Mary said. "I do not think of them as any different from any of us, though many still do. I guess certain attitudes among the whites will never change when it comes to having to deal with the native populations of this great land."

"I agree," said George. "However, we will not talk about that right now. I have a great deal of work to do and I have to get started right away. I asked Marsden if I could get Joseph Shouldice to help me but he said no. He did not want to not arouse the population too much right now. I think John is wrong this time, but I must go along with his wishes. At least for the time being."

Chapter 27
The Recruitment Ride

George began his ride through Cavagnal, Choisy, Côte St. Henry, and Côte St. Charles the next morning. He estimated that he would have to visit about one hundred and fifty homes in the time he would be gone. "I will be gone for about three days," he told Mary. "I have told both Jane and John what I am doing and they promised not to tell anyone. They will check on you as well."

"You know that I will be fine," Mary told her beloved husband.

"I know that, but nevertheless they will be here for you. After I get going, word will soon spread around the community of what is happening and you never can be to sure of what those bastards Whetstone and Deschamps will do. Remember how poor Gaspard Séguin was murdered back in 1827, and how I linked it to Whetstone's lumber mill in St. Henry. If word gets around that Marsden and I are raising an armed militia once again, I know that both Whetstone and Deschamps will be very angry. They may even try to stop us. There is no telling what they may do."

"You mean they may try to kill you now?" asked Mary.

"Yes. Or burn us out. Who knows what else? I have loaded all of our guns. They are primed and ready to fire. You know where the extra powder and shot is, and George Jr. knows how to fire and load as well. My old army rifle may be too heavy for him—but at least the shotgun is not.

"I am taking my brace of pistols and my long rifle, so please do not worry. Maybe William Grantham will ride along with me as I head up towards St. Henry. It would be nice to have some company, especially up there."

"I am sure Sean O'Rourke will ride with you as well," Mary replied.

"I hope so. The three of us should deter most any ambush that Whetstone could possibly set up. Marsden said that he wanted me to go alone, but after I have visited a few homes along the way, word will get around the community faster than I can travel. I doubt that John thought of this. As I pass his place I will tell him that I will try to get William and Sean to come along with me.

"I may be sounding a little too pessimistic," continued George, "but in times of armed rebellion or insurrection, you can never be too sure of who your enemies are. Many can be your next door neighbours, which is exactly the case we have here. At least at Waterloo I knew who was with us and who was against us; here it is a different matter. Hopefully, we will be able to sign up some of the French Canadian settlers as we did back in 1827. I know that not all the local French Canadians are in favour of this rebellion. However, if they are, then we English are in big trouble."

Mary hugged and kissed her husband before he headed off to visit all of the English farmers, merchants, and settlers in the area directly linked to Cavagnal.

About half-way between George's home and that of John Marsden there was a small creek that flowed gently through the rolling landscape. The land on both sides of the creek belonged to Richard Blackwell, brother to Joseph Blackwell of Côte St. Charles. Richard had arrived from Skirwith in Cumberland back in 1829. His brother had arrived a few years earlier and had set up a farm next to the Pearsons at the foot of the Grand Côte. Richard already had a large family and George was sure that he would be able to convince him to join the Volunteer Militia.

Just a few hundred yards west of Richard's large farm lay a number of small cabins belonging to numerous French Canadian families. George was worried about Richard's safety if these French-speaking residents became members of the Patriote following.

The creek had been named after the previous owner of Richard Blackwell's farm, Henri Vivirais. Since he had moved away many years before and with so many English-speaking emigrants in the area, the name of the creek had been anglicized to the Viviry Creek. It had its headwaters not far south of the lower side of Joseph Blackwell's farm on Côte St. Charles.

Thomas Roblin owned the land where the creek began, but it was mostly a deep swamp with numerous patches of dangerous quicksand and was not worth much. Roblin had already lost three or four head of cattle to the unforgiving quicksand.

By the time the creek meandered down through the fields and bush to the area near Richard Blackwell's farm, it was a fast flowing brook, full of nice speckled trout. In that area it was known unofficially as Blackwell's Creek, not the Viviry Creek.

By the time George reached John Marsden's store on that first morning of recruitment, he had already spoken to fifteen families and had received promises from twelve of the landowners that they would join the militia. Most had served back in 1827 and were more than willing to sign up. The pay would be the same, a fact which intrigued them greatly.

George gave a short report to Marsden at his home—informally referred to as "The Wilderness"—then continued up the King's Road towards Thomas Grantham's house in Choisy. Marsden had jokingly asked him if he would be stopping at William Whetstone's place to see if he would be interested in joining the militia. "Highly unlikely," replied George. "I just saw a copy of the first issue of the Patriote newsletter that bastard and his slimy friend, F.X. Deschamps, have produced."

Marsden seemed shocked, since he had not seen anything as of yet. "It came out this morning," reported George. "I got a copy of it from Odilas Sabourin. It was only in English and, as you know, Odilas can barely speak any English, let alone read it.

"I wonder why they are putting out an English-only newsletter for the Patriote cause?" asked Marsden.

"Maybe it is to scare us and get some of the fence-sitters on their side before the actual armed revolt begins. Anyway, at least we now know why they got that printing press in recently," replied George.

"Any word from the Governor on those arms?" he continued.

"For heavens' sake, George," exclaimed Marsden, "I only sent the letter the other day! Give him a chance. I am sure there are more pressing matters closer to Montréal than ours. If I have not heard anything by next week, then I will travel by steamboat into Montréal to try and see him or Sir John Colborne. Hopefully I will be able to get some new arms for us."

"Yes," replied George. "Those old Brown Bess muskets that we had back in 1827 are now obsolete. I bet even the Patriotes have rifles now. I wonder if Deschamps still has all those muskets in his cellar. Too bad Mary Schmidt was not working there anymore."

"You are right," said Marsden. "However, with no inside connection we will have to assume that Deschamps still has a large cache of arms, powder, and ammunition."

"A good fire at his store would sure let us know in a hurry," laughed George.

"Yes, but it would be that would be a tragedy for all those local settlers that need Deschamps store for supplies. Even though he is a lousy little man, his store does serve a valid purpose here in our community."

"I will have to agree with you on that," stated George.

George continued west from "The Wilderness" and arrived at Thomas Grantham's farm around two that afternoon. He noticed that there was quite a commotion going on as he rode into the front yard. Elizabeth Grantham was crying while Thomas had his second son, Peter, in a big hug. George noticed that Peter's big bay mare was already saddled and loaded down for what looked like long trip.

"Oh, hello there George," called Thomas' other son, William. "You just caught us in the act of saying goodbye to Peter."

"What do you mean?" George asked as he dismounted.

Thomas announced that his son was leaving for the small Glengarry village of Williamstown in Upper Canada to join the local militia there. He had heard that there was to going to be trouble in Upper Canada as well as in Lower Canada and that there were going to be two militia regiments raised around Glengarry, one as a Highland Regiment and the other as a Cavalry Regiment. Peter, not being of a Scottish background, had decided on the Cavalry Regiment.

"I have nothing against our fight here in Vaudreuil, but I want to be in a Cavalry Regiment and theirs is the closest. I think we are to head west towards York in mid-July."

"Whatever suits you," George told the young lad. "Best of luck. We could have used you here, but I am sure that your father and brother will join our Rifle Regiment."

They all shook hands and Peter Grantham rode off towards Williamstown, Upper Canada. He would only return three times over the next sixty years for the funerals of his parents and brother William. Peter advanced quickly in the Upper Canada Militia and resigned in late 1839 with the rank of Captain.

"Will you join me in my ride around the area?" George asked young William Grantham.

"If it is alright with you, father, I will." Thomas Grantham smiled and nodded his head.

"I do not want you to get my son lost out back in St. Henry now, Henderson."

"You do not have to worry. I know this area very well. However, I must warn you that we may meet some scalawags who intend to harm us. I plan to ask Sean O'Rourke up on St. George to accompany us as well. He is a big strong lad and an excellent shot."

"Good idea, George," Thomas told his cousin. "When do you plan to muster the militia?"

"Early next week—if all goes well. Marsden should have some news by then about our new weapons."

"See you there. I trust you will be Marsden's right-hand man in this, George?"

"Yes, I am. However, I will need some good officers and sergeants. Have you any formal military training?"

"I cannot say that I do," answered Thomas. "Neither has my son, but we are willing to learn from the best."

George laughed and mounted his horse. They had wasted too much time and he wanted to get to the O'Rourkes before dark. George planned to stay with them that night.

The trip up towards the O'Rourke home was uneventful and, with only a couple of farms to visit, George and William arrived at the O'Rourke home just before four o'clock that afternoon.

"I have eighteen men so far," George announced to Sean O'Rourke. Will you join me?"

"Of course, but only if I can serve as an officer this time," he announced with a sly wink towards William Grantham.

"Agreed," said George. "You will be my second Captain. Joseph Shouldice is my senior Captain, though he does not yet know that."

"You have not yet been east towards Vaudreuil on your recruiting mission?" asked Sean's wife Maureen.

"No, not yet," responded George. "It is too dangerous, and I thought that it would be best to visit the outlying areas to warn them first. I am afraid of some reprisals coming east from Rigaud or Ste Marthe if we are not careful.

"With so many farms out here set so far apart from each other, a small roving band of Patriotes could cause quite a bit of trouble without us knowing about it until one or two days later, back in Cavagnal or up on Côte St. Charles."

"Maybe some of the families should band together as added protection," Sean suggested to his two guests.

"Not a bad idea," announced William. "But where?"

"The best place would be Robert Henderson's farm near the Raquette River. He has a large barn and, with his stone house, he could hold off a small army for God knows how long," replied Sean.

"That could be just what we are up against, I am afraid," announced George. Sean took a step back then sat down. His face had turned pale.

"A small army is what we could be easily up against," George said again. "I have sent for help from my Mohawk friends in Ganienkeh and our friends over in Kanesatake. Rotonni, Simon Beauvais, Joshua Gabriel and, of course, Chief Aron'hio:tas and all the others have already told John Marsden that they will come across if we need them and we may yet."

"Damn," exclaimed Sean. "Just like at the Battle of Chateauguay, except it will be the English Militia and the Indians against the French once again. Just as it was back in '59, English against French."

"Seems that history may repeat itself," replied George. "Hopefully, for our sake, the history we are about to make will be identical to that of 1759 and we win once again."

Sean, Maureen, and William all nodded their heads in agreement.

By the time George, William, and Sean had arrived the next morning at Robert Henderson's large farm situated below the sandy bluff that ran south of the Raquette River, the news of George Henderson's recruitment ride through the Seigneury had preceded him and his two partners.

Robert met the three riders with Dr. Grisenthwaite and his son Jacob, who had married Robert's daughter in 1830. "We are ready to ride with you right now," announced Robert. "The good Doctor will once again be our Medical Officer if you so wish."

"I do," replied George. "However, we do not need you ride just now. Just give us some water for our tired horses and a cup of tea and we will be on our way."

"Just a small warning," announced Jacob Grisenthwaite. "I saw a small group of riders pass by here early this morning. About five men, I think. They all were carrying guns across their saddles. I watched them with father's telescope. They did not see me watching them, but they did point towards this farm as well as ours. Unfortunately they were too far for me to hear what they were saying."

"Thanks for the warning, Jacob," Sean said to his longtime friend. "Can you go with us, just to even things up?"

"That is why I am here. I have my rifle and it is ready to fire."

"Great," George announced. "I was not going to ask you along but now that we know of a possible ambush up ahead, we might as well have you along. Will you be safe here, Robert?"

"Do not worry about me," he replied. "Phoebe is as a good shot as her husband and I think we can care for each other. We managed without difficult until this fine young man came along and rescued her from my grip."

Robert seemed to have taken the sudden losses of his only son, Allan, and his wife Elizabeth quite well. He had been without both of them now for close to ten years, and having Jacob marry his only remaining daughter had brought a new spot of light into a man that had been fading fast with sorrow.

"Your father-in-law seems all fired up and ready to take on the whole Patriote cause," George told Jacob.

"He is, and he will take them all on if things get out of hand around here. Unfortunately, I forgot to tell your father to move his family over here as soon as possible."

"I will ride back and tell him."

"No don't bother. Isaac Vaughan's farm is the next one we are to visit and he can head over and pick up your parents on his way to Robert's place."

Chapter 28
Ambush

George and his fellow riders rode slowly east, all the while watching the bush in front and to the sides. Their guns were loaded and primed and they felt that they were ready for any surprise that might occur.

Both William and Jacob were new to the possibility of being shot at. Only George and Sean had served in the military before. Even though their service had come many years before, they were able to coach their friends in what they should do as they rode towards Côte St. Charles. On-the-job training was not what George had hoped for but the chance of their being ambushed in this remote area of the Seigneury seemed to be quite good, even more so since some armed riders had been seen earlier that day heading south by Jacob Grisenthwaite.

George was hoping to reach Isaac Vaughan's large sheep farm before they ran into the five riders. They were not so lucky. As the four men rode to the trail that led down through the bush towards Isaac's farm in the area known as the Fief, the blasts from five muskets broke the silence of the afternoon. Almost immediately George and Jacob were lying on the ground, their horses shot out from under them. Jacob was yelling that he had been hit.

Seeing the smoke rising from the trees and knowing that the men who had fired on them would either be reloading or racing away on their horses, Sean O'Rourke decided to make a drastic decision and charged the area where the shots had come from. William Grantham followed him, not knowing exactly why. He was just following someone he trusted.

George started to yell at Sean to stop but halted in mid-sentence as he grabbed his long rifle and took careful aim at one of the men who had just ambushed them.

The man had broken clear of the woods and was riding away as fast as he could. George aimed a little high over his back and slowly squeezed the big gun's trigger. The puff of smoke it gave as he fired concealed the death of the man riding away. It was the first man George had killed in over twenty years.

Jacob was lying under his horse and bleeding from a nasty wound to his left leg. The bullet had gone through his leg and into his horse. It was still alive but in bad shape. George grabbed his pistol from his dead horse and shot Jacob's mount, putting it out of its misery.

In the meantime, Sean and William were still riding after the attackers who now had fled like their unfortunate cohort. Sean reined his horse to a sudden halt and took aim at one of the riders. His Baker rifle barked and another man dropped, dead. William had also reined his horse and had fired almost simultaneously as Sean. His aim was not as good as Sean's and the rider was only slightly wounded and was able to stay in the saddle.

William had never fired a gun at another human being in his life, though he had killed many deer and a few bear since arriving in North America in 1834. However, he had not taken any time to consider this fact; they had been attacked and one of them was seriously wounded, and they were on the offensive.

George went over to Jacob and with a little luck was able to pull the young man out from under his now-dead horse. As he attended to Jacob's wound he thought about what had just happened. Two horses dead, one man wounded, two others dead, and three who got away—though one of them was wounded. Perhaps the rebellion had begun.

George looked down at his two big hands and they were trembling. So too were his knees. He had not felt that sensation since lying in that awful sandpit on the side of the hill at Waterloo. That damn pit where so many of his good friends had died in June of 1815. So long ago, he thought.

Well it was June, 1837, now, and he was once again defending himself from the French. They had been lucky, he thought. Jacob would probably live. The bullet had gone right through and with Isaac's farm not too far from there he was sure that Jacob could be patched up enough to be able to make the ride back to Dr. Grisenthwaite's in Isaac's wagon the next day.

Sean and William were over looking at the two dead men who had ambushed them. Sean yelled that he recognized one of them but the other he did not know. William did not recognize either man. Both men had been shot in the back and George now wondered how this would affect his stature if the word that got back to Whetstone and Deschamps told a different story than what had actually occurred.

Luckily, George was not alone. He realized that with three witnesses, his version of the fight would stand up in court—even if Whetstone and Deschamps tried to challenge it.

The rebellion was not officially under way, but already blood had been spilled. George took the saddles of the two dead horses and stashed them under some branches just off the trail. He and William would come back for them after they got Jacob to Isaac's farm.

The ride down to Isaac's took about twenty minutes and though it was uncomfortable for Jacob, the young lad was in quite good spirits. He had been in the first gun battle ever to occur in recent memory in the whole of the Seigneury of Vaudreuil and though he had been wounded and out of action right from the beginning, he had been there. It was exciting to him even though he had not fired his gun.

However, both George and Sean were more subdued. They had quickly realized that they could have easily been killed and no one would have known about it for days. Their bodies could have been hidden like poor old Gaspard Séguin's had been ten years before, dumped in the Raquette River after he had been brutally murdered.

"We now have major problems around this area," Sean said to George. "What those five men tried to do was attempted murder."

"I agree," George said. "We are going to have to get this ride over with as soon as we can, let Marsden know what has happened, and organize a general assembly of all the members of the Militia as soon as possible. The man that you recognized was one of Charles Whetstone's foremen at his lumber mill, right?"

"I always suspected him in Gaspard's murder," said Sean," but I never could prove it. My son, Stephen, told me about his problems with him and that is why he quit the mill shortly after Gaspard's death.

"I never told you about this, George, as there just was not enough evidence. I guess we will never know. That was one great shot you made with that long gun of yours. He must have been over two hundred yards away when you fired."

"Thanks Sean, but I had to do what I had to do. He was the first man I have killed in over twenty years. I guess that is about the same for you, right?"

"Not exactly, George," Sean replied. "I killed a few British soldiers awhile back before coming to this country. After leaving the British Army, I joined an underground group of dissidents that was striving to rid Ireland of British rule. We did not succeed, and I came over here to escape prison and probable death. It has been my well-kept secret until this moment. Even my wife does not know."

"I will not tell anyone, Sean. But it does not surprise me. I still remember your comments back in 1827 when we had our meeting to form the original Vaudreuil Loyal Volunteers and you wondered why we just did not call on the troops up at Carillon and, I think, Fort Côteau. I sensed a slight animosity towards the Crown then but never said anything. I had forgotten about it until just now."

"That was then and this is now," Sean said. "We have to go back for those two bodies and then head over to Côte St. Charles as soon as we can. Isaac can take care of Jacob and see that he gets over to the Doctor's home tomorrow morning. We must warn the others."

"I agree, but you will do that," said George. "William and I are going to gather the bodies and the saddles and bring them back to Cavagnal. I would like to know who that other man was that you shot. By the way, damn good shot too. Have you had that rifle very long?"

"I have had it since 1830; I picked it up at Fort Côteau during a boxing match with the Army champion one day. I won! You have one as well, am I correct?"

"Of course. Actually I have two. Well, my son, John, has one and I have another one back at the house. Best guns I have ever seen or used until this beauty came along." George was patting his Yankee long rifle as he spoke.

George and William headed back up the hill to the small clearing where the deadly ambush had taken place. They put the two bodies in the back of the wagon that Isaac Vaughan had loaned them. Meanwhile Sean O'Rourke traveled as fast as his horse could carry him over to Côte St. Charles. His mission was to spread the word to James Henderson, Ebenezer Grampian, Dugald Cameron, Joseph Blackwell, and all the others over on the Grand Cote of what had just happened. George had reminded him, though, that their main mission was to recruit men for the revived Vaudreuil Loyal Volunteers and not to spread a general panic throughout the region.

As George and William headed back to Cavagnal with the two bodies, George shared his thoughts with young William Grantham.

"You know, William, this ambush might be a blessing in disguise and really hurt the Patriote cause in this region."

"Why do you say that, George?" asked William.

"Well we were on a recruiting mission based on pure speculation. Now that this ambush has occurred, we have a greater chance of raising a good-sized militia."

"I think you are right," William told the older man. William had grown to like and admire the big Englishman from the eastern section of Cavagnal. "I bet that whoever sent those five men out after us never expected to see any of us alive again. That could have been the end of the Vaudreuil Loyal Volunteers. However, since we survived and two of them did not, everything now changes in our favour."

"Yes, I believe that as much as you do, William. I imagine that Sean will get every able bodied man up on Côte St. Charles. I hope he will because we are going to need them. Whoever set that ambush up has a very good line of communication and we do not yet even know who the Patriote sympathizers are and who are not. We will have to be very careful from now on. Even at our general muster in a few days we may have spies among us."

It was a little past eight in the evening when George and William arrived at Marsden's store. There was already a small gathering of men in front of the store and, to George's surprise, they all carried weapons. John A. Marsden, Justice of Peace for the area known as Cavagnal, met the two men as they got off the wagon.

William's horse had been tied to the back of the wagon. As the day had grown warmer William's horse had become quite unruly. The smell of death in the warm afternoon caused the poor animal to pull and yank at the rope that tied him to the rear of the wagon. As they proceeded with their grisly cargo from the scene of the ambush to Marsden's place—where George had hoped that the unknown ambusher could be identified—George finally asked William to ride the horse alongside or in front of the wagon.

"It might be better if you rode point in case someone tries another ambush to steal these bodies back," he suggested.

Luckily, nothing happened, and the two of them arrived with their now ripe cargo in good form.

"Sean O'Rourke arrived an hour ago," Marsden said to George as he stretched his tired legs. "These men are from the Grand Côte and they are about ready to torch William Whetstone's house and that of F.X. Deschamps as well if we do not do something first. We have a mob here, not a militia. George, I need your help."

Poor old Marsden was red in the face and sweating profusely.

"Listen up men," called George as he climbed up onto the wagon seat. "We are a militia and not some unruly mob bent on revenge. I know it is hard to accept that we have been ambushed and one of our good friends and neighbour has been shot and wounded. However, we did kill these two and wounded another.

"We have to identify these men and advise their families so they can get a Christian burial."

"No way!" yelled a man from the back of the crowd.

"Why not?" asked George. "Just because they tried to kill me and the others with me? Does that mean they are not entitled to a decent burial?"

"They are trash!" yelled another. "We should just dump their bodies into the river as they did with that poor Séguin fellow years ago."

"No!" answered George. "That would make us as bad as them. We are decent men here in Cavagnal and we want to live in harmony with everyone, French, English, or Indian. Hopefully this upcoming rebellion will be short-lived and we will get along with our lives as we have in the past few years."

There was some subdued grumbling among the men before the two men who had yelled the comments pushed forward through the crowd and extended their right hands to George and Marsden. "You are right and we are wrong," said one. "Go ahead, bury these poor men. However, after that we can get on with really forming a crack militia unit."

The two leaders shook their hands and then everyone clapped. They gathered around the foul-smelling bodies.

Sean had told George that he recognized one of the men but in the aftermath of the ambush he had forgotten to tell George what the man's name was. He did now.

"That is Jean Claude Rouleau. He was a foreman at Charles Whetstone's sawmill in St. Henry. My son, Stephen, knew him well. He is a man that really hates the English. He hated Stephen as well until Stephen explained the difference between the English and the Irish and our equal hatred of English rulers."

The other man was unknown to all of the local men who examined the body. "He must be from either Vaudreuil or Rigaud," said Sean. "I would guess Rigaud as it is closer to Whetstone's mill and we all know that there is quite a large Patriote backing there."

"It seems we are somewhat surrounded and with our backs to the river," Marsden commented, breaking his long silence.

"We seemed to be," replied George. "At least on three sides. Remember, we still have our friends, the Mohawks, on the other side of the river and they are very willing to help us.

Aron'hio:tas has already promised at least thirty warriors and I do not know how many my good friends Awen'rah:ton and Sori'howane will bring with them from Ganienkeh. They should be here in at a week or two, permitted they can get safely across the border."

"How many men do you think will join the militia?" asked Marsden.

The crowd had quietened down somewhat since George's speech, which seemed to please him.

"I expect between one hundred and ten and one hundred and twenty-five," announced George. "The eighteen men present have already signed up and I have not even spoken to any of the settlers east of my own place."

"Great," announced Marsden. "I will write to the Governor immediately and let him know that we have a good standing militia of over one hundred men. When do you expect to start training them, George?"

"I want to begin tomorrow, if possible. That is, if we can get the word passed around. Who can take these bodies to Rigaud?"

"I will," announced Thomas Grantham. "I have fairly good relations with the citizens up there and they know me quite well. I will see the Priest at the church and leave the bodies with him. Father Charette is a fine man and he will take care of them, Patriotes or not."

"I hope you will take someone with you Thomas," announced George, "preferably not William, your son."

"No. I was not planning on doing that," said Thomas. "Hopefully one of these men will accompany me.

"I will," said Ebenezer Grampian. "I am known up there like Thomas is. They know that I am a decent man. I also know Father Charette."

Thomas and Ebenezer took the bodies of the two Patriotes to Rigaud the next morning. Unfortunately, the unknown man remained that way, as neither Father Charette nor his assistants at the Catholic Church in Rigaud recognized him.

Chapter 29
Battle Preparations

Two days after the ambush, John Augustus Marsden sent a special letter to Sir John Colborne, Commander of the British Army in North America at his new headquarters at the old fort on Ile Ste Hélène in the middle of the St. Lawrence River, south of Montréal.

The letter stated that he had raised a standing militia for the Vaudreuil Seigneury of one hundred and twenty men and that he would need funds for their salaries, modern weapons, and winter clothing.

Twelve days later there was a response from Colborne. Though he was very pleased with the number of men Cavagnal would be able to provide him in terms of a standing militia, he would not be able to provide the militiamen with new weapons. All that he could offer would be some old Baker rifles. Most of the militia units still had to use some well-used old army muskets.

Through Marsden's connection with the ruling British Government and his past record as an outstanding army officer he was been able to obtain one hundred and twenty Baker rifles, each complete with sling, ramrod, bayonet with scabbard and belt, a cartridge box with belt, and a supply of extra flints.

When Marsden read the short note from Colborne, he thought that George Henderson would be pleased to know that his command would be armed with the rifle. Marsden had only used the now obsolete Brown

Bess during his tenure in the British Army during the Peninsular War and at Waterloo.

Colborne had also said that he would be providing the Vaudreuil Loyal Volunteers with army greatcoats and fur hats for the coming winter. He expected that the Patriote movement would make their attacks that coming November and December. That meant that they had a few months to train and equip the new militia.

As for the militia salaries, Colborne had written that the Vaudreuil Loyal Volunteers would be receiving the same amount as they had back in 1827, two shillings sixpence per day of service.

"That will be a welcomed boost to the local economy," thought Marsden. "Those poor settlers sure need the extra cash and this will help many of them get through the winter by paying off many of their debts, mine included."

The summer remained quiet, except for the regular drills of the militia and scores of rumours that abounded in the region and word of ever growing tensions throughout Lower Canada that was published in the *Montreal Gazette*.

By mid-November the Patriotes had already held a mass rally in Vaudreuil where F.X. Deschamps, and William and Charles Whetstone had addressed a large and heavily armed crowd numbering close to three hundred men, women, and children.

One man who seemed to have more control over the large crowd than anyone else was Hyacinthe Chaput. He was from the Parish of St. Michel de Vaudreuil and had worked as an accountant for the Vaudreuil Seigneur, Robert Unwin Harwood. When Harwood had found out that his right hand man was a Patriote sympathizer, he had fired him. Harwood from then on kept silent on most matters concerning the Seigneury of which he was in charge. Officially, he was supposed to be the person in charge of the Vaudreuil Loyal Volunteers, but not being a military man he had asked John Marsden to handle the military protection of his Seigneury.

William Whetstone's small printing press was working overtime. Every two or three days a small double-sided broadsheet was published and delivered throughout Cavagnal by some of Whetstone's hired men.

The *John Gripe*, as it was known, regularly criticized Marsden and his followers and called them puppets of the British, especially Governor Gosford. Many of the locals who had known Marsden for many years started to comment openly about some of the paragraphs that they were reading in the *John Gripe*.

What was turning into an open war of words between William Whetstone and John Marsden (with Whetstone winning most of the battles) changed drastically on November 20th, 1837. F.X. Deschamps made a dramatic ride through Cavagnal. When he began that morning he had two other men with him. By the time he had returned to his store he had close to fifty armed men following him.

Luckily for the local English population, Deschamps' former housekeeper, Mary Kilkenny Schmidt, happened to be in Deschamps' store when the Patriotes arrived en masse. Mary did a rough count of the men, hurriedly left the store, and ran back to her husband's tavern. Charles Schmidt had once again become a member of the local militia. When he saw Mary running up the King's Road to their home, he wondered what had happened.

Charles had been in the cellar of their tavern when the fifty mounted Patriotes had ridden past his place. The thundering of the many hooves of the horses had caused the ground to shake but Charles thought it had been another earthquake, similar to the one they had experienced earlier that week.

Mary could hardly speak, and Charles had thought that some passerby had molested her.

"Men! Scores of mounted and heavily armed men!" was all that she could say before she collapsed in a fainting spell.

Charles knew that Mary had been at F.X. Deschamps store and that she was still nervous about going there even though she had not worked for Deschamps in over ten years.

When Mary came to a few minutes later, Jane Cameron was standing beside her with a wet cloth in her hand. Jane quickly explained that Charles and John had left the tavern to warn George Henderson about the mounted Patriotes down at Deschamps' store.

"Father will know what to do when he finds out," Jane told her dear friend. Jane thought to herself that probably her father would not be able to do too much right away, since the members of the Vaudreuil Loyal Volunteer Militia were still scattered all over the Seigneury at their homes or farms. It would take at least a couple of days at least to round them up, arm them, and make a battle plan.

Jane was right. George cursed out loud upon hearing that F.X. Deschamps had fifty or more mounted and armed men down the road from his place.

"I cannot muster the militia in time to meet them," he thought. "I am glad that Charles and John are racing west through the community, alerting all the English residents. Hopefully Marsden will come down here so we can plan our strategy."

But F.X. Deschamps had no intention of doing battle with the local militia volunteers. All he wanted to do was to scare the local English population. His plan worked amazingly well. The local English settlers were terrified of his "cavalry" and many headed for the bush in and around Cavagnal as soon as they received the word of the presence of a cavalry unit in the region.

Infantry dread attack from a cavalry unit, especially if they are caught out in an open field or road. There is often no time to form a square, the ideal protection against a massed cavalry charge. Unfortunately, for the leaders of the Cavagnal militia, John Marsden and George Henderson, they had not trained their men to form a square while under attack from a cavalry unit.

Neither Marsden nor George had foreseen the possibility of having to face a mounted unit of Patriotes. Deschamps had outfoxed them, and it angered them both.

Luckily for the citizens of Cavagnal, the day after Deschamps' triumphant ride through the community close to forty Mohawk warriors, led by Chief Aron'hio:tas, braved the cold Ottawa River and canoed across to Cavagnal, landing at Schmidt's Tavern. With them was Awen'rah:ton and Sori'howane and ten more warriors from Ganienkeh, New York.

This added force gave a significant advantage to Marsden's militia. He now had close to one hundred and seventy-five armed men, many of whom he and George Henderson had been training thrice weekly behind the Henderson homestead.

Their rifles had arrived a couple of weeks before along with fur hats, woolen army greatcoats, and enough ammunition to hopefully sustain a lengthy campaign which no one really expected.

George was elated to see that his local militia unit would be using his all-time favourite rifle rather than the old and now obsolete Brown Bess. The British line Regiments would be using a newer model of the Baker rifle, but he still admired the older and just-as-trustworthy model that he and his son owned.

He was not sure what the Patriotes would be using for weapons. George and Marsden had both guessed that the enemy would have a wide variety of civilian weapons and others stolen from a couple of British arsenals in Montréal and Québec.

One thing about the weapons that the Vaudreuil Loyal Volunteers would be using was that they would utilize a common ammunition, a .65 calibre round ball. The Patriotes, on the other hand, would have a problem supplying their men with enough of the correct ammunition for they odd assortment of guns—one disadvantage of having a semi-organized rebel army.

George was not sure if the guns, ammunition, and powder were still in Deschamps' cellar, and there was no way he could find out. If they were, it would be a big advantage for Deschamps' Patriotes. However, the weapons had been brought there in 1827, so maybe they had already been distributed to more radical areas where the Patriote movement was more active. Places like Ste Eustache, St. Benoit, and St. Jerome. Two of the places, St. Benoit and Ste Eustache, were across the Ottawa River from Deschamps' store. St. Jerome could be easily reached in a few hours by riding north from Ste Eustache.

Aron'hio:tas' warriors were either armed with a bow and a quiver full of razor-sharp arrows or Pennsylvania long rifles that they had purchased at Ganienkeh. Awen'rah:ton's warriors were armed with the very accurate long rifles, as well as a very sharp tomahawks and an equally sharp scalping knives.

George had hoped that his two blood brothers from Ganienkeh

would show up, but he never expected them to bring ten more warriors with them. He hoped that they did not have too much trouble getting into Lower Canada from the State of New York.

"Where will we put all these Indians?" Marsden asked George after meeting with Aron'hio:tas and Awen'rah:ton.

"We will have to put them up in either the Schmidt's Tavern—which I do not think Mary will like—or in my barn. It is large enough for them and they are quite self-sufficient."

"Then they will stay there," announced Marsden. "Is that alright with you, Aron'hio:tas and Awen'rah:ton?"

They both smiled and nodded their heads and admitted that they would prefer to stay close to their good friend George Henderson. All George could say was Nia'wen (thank-you) to his two good friends. With that they left for George's house.

F.X. Deschamps and William Whetstone had seen the arrival of the flotilla of canoes from Kanesatake and they both quickly realized that their small Patriote unit might not be enough to cause any real threat to the English settlement.

"Can we get more men?" asked Whetstone.

"Yes, I believe there are about thirty five in Rigaud who will support the cause and another eighty or ninety in Vaudreuil," replied Deschamps. "That would bring us about even with the English, and if we can get some from St. Lazare and Ste Marthe we will have a superior force to these damn Englishmen."

Simon Beauvais, Rotonni, Harvey, and Joshua Gabriel had been among the thirty warriors that Aron'hio:tas had brought from Kanesatake. George had hoped that the presence of the fierce Mohawk warriors would act as a special threat to the Patriotes since he knew how many of the local French Canadians feared the Indians from across the river.

The Mohawks had always had great relations with the English settlers ever since they started moving into the area forty years earlier. However, many of the French settlers either feared or did not understand the ways of the Native Americans.

F.X. Deschamps was one of those who both feared the Indians and did not trust them. However, he did respect their fighting skills and because of that called for extra help from the Patriote supporters in Vaudreuil and Rigaud. He was not able to get any more men from either St. Lazare or Ste Marthe, as they had already been sent to support the Patriote cause south of Montréal. Even the Village of Vaudreuil could only supply half of what he needed, forty-five men.

Thus, by November 21st, 1837, the battle lines were set in the Seigneury of Vaudreuil. John Marsden had a substantial combined force of English settlers and Mohawk warriors, while F.X. Deschamps had a slightly smaller force of well-armed Patriotes from Vaudreuil, Cavagnal, Rigaud, and possibly Notre Dame de L'Ile Perrot.

Only time would tell when the two opposing forces would confront each other.

Whetstone's little newspaper, the *John Gripe*, continued to be published twice a week and it caused quite a stir among the English settlers as many began to question what Marsden was really concerned with: himself and his career as Justice of the Peace in Cavagnal, or the future of the French and English relations in all of Lower Canada.

On November 23rd, 1837, the British Army, under the command of Colonel Charles Gore, suffered a minor defeat at the hands of a well-fortified and well-armed Patriote force in the Village of St. Denis, south of Montréal. This defeat of the great British Army by a small group of farmers and shop keepers in rural Lower Canada shocked the whole English community in and around Montréal.

It also gave great meaning and a huge morale boost to the other Patriote strongholds around Montréal, namely at St. Benoit, Ste Eustache, St. Charles and in a small community west of Montréal called Cavagnal. F.X. Deschamps was elated and he asked William Whetstone to send out another copy of *John Gripe* as soon as possible.

One thing that Deschamps had not counted on was a surprise raid on the Mohawk Mission at Kanesatake later that week. Another set back was the defeat of a Patriote stronghold in St. Charles, south of Montréal in the Richelieu Valley.

Colonel Charles Wetherall and about three hundred and fifty troops battled a force of about one hundred Patriotes on November 25th. Many

Patriotes were killed and a few others were captured. The defeat of the Patriotes at St. Charles had made up for the British defeat two days earlier at St. Denis.

However, what concerned Deschamps in Cavagnal was what the Mohawk warriors would do now that their sacred Catholic Mission had been ransacked and burned by the Patriotes from St. Benoit. F.X. Deschamps had read what the legendary Mohawks of the Iroquois Nation could do if they were provoked. He had read about what had happened at Lachine and to the great Quebec hero, Dollard des Ormeaux back in the 1600s.

"The last thing that I want is to do battle with those savages from across the river," Deschamps told Whetstone and Hyacinthe Chaput on November 27th. "If Marsden cannot control them and if we are caught in a battle and we lose, which we could, God have mercy upon us from those bloody heathen Indians. I wish that our confrères over in St. Benoit had not burned their Mission. There was no need to do that."

Hyacinthe Chaput was the most radical of the three Patriotes who were discussing these matters, and he told Deschamps not to worry.

"We will defeat the wretched English and their filthy Indian friends. We have done that before and we will do that again."

Deschamps had to explain to Chaput that two very experienced former British Army veterans, Major John Marsden and Captain George Henderson, were now leading these "wretched English and filthy Indians." He continued to tell an unbelieving Chaput that other officers and non-commissioned officers of the Vaudreuil Loyal Volunteers were all veterans of either the Royal Irish Fusiliers, the Royal Navy, Hessian mercenaries, British Cavalry, or some other Regiment from the either the War of 1812 or the Napoleonic Wars.

"We are up against a well-trained and experienced group of men who seem to have whipped their raw recruits into a crack Militia force," he explained.

Chaput still did not seem too concerned. He knew that their mounted force of Patriotes would scare the English and Indians away as soon as they showed up.

"I am not so sure," Whetstone added. "I have heard from our spies that George Henderson has been training his men how to deal with a massed cavalry attack. Do you have any ground troops to back up your cavalry attack?" he asked Chaput.

"No, why should I?"

"Well," added Whetstone, "you need to learn a lot more about military tactics if you want to defeat this local militia. You cannot attack an infantry in square formation with cavalry. Not without infantry support. Look what happened to the great Marshal Ney at Waterloo a few years ago. He lost Napoleon's great cavalry while the Old Guard stood by awaiting their orders to advance. Had they, Napoleon would probably be still Emperor of France and maybe all of Europe and not out on some lonely island in the South Atlantic lying in a cold grave."

"Well, what do you suggest?" asked a visibly concerned Deschamps.

"We cannot back down now," said Whetstone.

"No, never," Chaput added in an agitated voice. "We will not give in. Fight I say, and rid the area of these two leaders, Marsden and Henderson. Maybe we can kill them before any confrontation can occur. They will be leaderless then. We cannot lose."

"You forget one thing," added Whetstone. "We already tried to kill George Henderson this past summer, along with three of his friends. We lost two men trying and another was wounded. He was a member of the famed 95th Rifles back in Spain and Portugal and that Regiment was known for their sharpshooters. He rarely misses and he is always alert, more so now than ever before since his home, family, and friends here in Cavagnal are at risk."

"What about attacking his family?" asked Chaput.

"You are more stupid than I thought," replied Whetstone. Chaput took a step back and Whetstone realized he had angered the Patriote leader. To Whetstone's astonishment, Deschamps spoke up and agreed with what he had just said.

"There are over fifty of the best Mohawk warriors from Kanesatake and Ganienkeh in the United States camped right now on his property. I would not try to attack his house or his family with such a force protecting them. Henderson is not stupid. I bet you that he knew that his family would be threatened and that is why he asked the Indians to camp there."

"So what do we do?" asked a now completely bewildered Hyacinthe Chaput.

"Well we could ask our dear Mr. Harwood over in Vaudreuil to have Marsden stripped of his title as the local Justice of the Peace," Whetstone replied. "That would really take some of the wind out of his sails. His importance in the community would diminish."

Deschamps added to Whetstone's comments that the Vaudreuil Seigneur, Robert Unwin Harwood, really outranked Marsden in the Vaudreuil Loyal Volunteers. "If we can get him to dismiss Marsden and maybe even Henderson and Lerniers, we may have a chance."

Chapter 30
What Price Is Victory?

They never got a chance to see their plan through. Though Chaput wrote a long letter to Seigneur Harwood, Harwood refused to do anything about the Patriotes' plan and remained in seclusion in his manor house in Vaudreuil.

The Vaudreuil Patriotes lost all hope for success when, on the 16th of December, 1837, Sir John Colborne led a large contingent of British Army regulars, two cannons, and one hundred and fifty militiamen from Montréal against a large Patriote force in Ste Eustache. The Patriotes were soundly defeated. Over one hundred Patriotes were killed, including their leader J.O. Chenier.

Troops from the barracks at Carillon attacked the Patriote stronghold in St. Benoit and burned the village to the ground. Hyacinthe Chaput had been present at Ste Eustache but he had been able to escape across the frozen river with scores of others.

Major John Marsden had called the members of the Vaudreuil Loyal Volunteer Militia to arms the day before and they were on duty all along the waterfront from the 15th to the evening of the 16th, awaiting retreating Patriotes from Ste Eustache. Marsden had been advised by fast courier that a battle would take place in Ste Eustache, and that he should have his men ready.

They were ready, though they did not expect to see any real action in the two days following the defeat of the Patriotes at Ste Eustache. However, unknown to them, F.X. Deschamps had organized a raiding party for the evening of the 16th. Seventy-nine mounted men and about thirty others in wagons were to attack Marsden's store and Schmidt's Tavern in Cavagnal.

Deschamps had also known that there was to be a battle down river in Ste Eustache and had let about twenty of his men go there in support of the Patriote cause. Hyacinthe Chaput was to lead the men, and Deschamps was to accompany him.

After the battle Deschamps had also fled across the thin ice of the Ottawa River. He wanted to be present for his specially planned raid on two of the most important bastions of English rule in Cavagnal.

While crossing the river just downstream from Pearson's point, two of his men were shot by Mohawk sharpshooters who had been strategically placed on the north shore of the river by Aron'hio:tas. One of the men, Auguste Major, had been with the raiding party from St. Benoit that had attacked the Mohawk Mission at Kanesatake. He had been recognized: the Indians had been looking for him.

Auguste had lived in and around Cavagnal for many years and was well known on both sides of the river. He had established himself as a great scout and woodsman. However, he made one fatal mistake by taking part in a raid on the Mission in a village where he was so well known.

The warrior who shot him in the back had also been present at the Mission, and immediately recognized him and shot him as he stepped out onto the ice late that afternoon. Of the twenty men from Vaudreuil who had participated in the battle at Ste Eustache, only nine made it back safely across the river that cold night in mid-December.

F.X. Deschamps, upon arriving on shore in Cavagnal, was immediately approached by five well-armed members of the Vaudreuil Loyal Volunteers and ten Mohawk warriors led by Chief Aron'hio:tas. Deschamps surrendered without a fight, as did the seven other men with him. They were arrested and placed under an armed guard.

Hyacinthe Chaput was the ninth man to make it back safely from Ste Eustache, and on December 17th he planned to take on George Henderson and John Marsden and avenge the loss at Ste Eustache. The rest of the Vaudreuil Patriotes in Cavagnal were still not aware of the results of the big battle down river from them and Hyacinthe Chaput was not going to tell them. He needed them to carry out his and Deschamps' plan to raid the Tavern and store the very next afternoon.

Though the Patriote cause was lost because of Colborne's victory at Ste Eustache, Chaput was planning one more battle that he hoped would benefit the Patriote cause throughout Lower Canada. He would be remembered as the man who led the Vaudreuil Patriotes to victory—or to death. Telling his men about the defeat at Ste Eustache would make them nervous and they would probably lose heart and give up the cause.

George Henderson was not aware that Chaput had made it safely across the river. He and the other members of the Vaudreuil Loyal Volunteers believed that the need for a militia was now over and that they would be soon going home. They were not aware that just two miles east of Schmidt's Tavern there was a mounted unit of eighty men and a column of fifty on the march west towards the now-celebrating group of militiamen. The Patriotes had left Vaudreuil on the morning of the 17th and, as they marched westward, more and more men had joined them.

George Henderson was about to be caught in a position he had not been in since Talavera. He had not been in command that day so long ago but he was now, as Marsden had left with twenty of the men to watch over his store and guard the western approaches to the community. There were still some Patriote sympathizers in Rigaud.

Both he and Marsden were concerned that those sympathizers just nine miles west of them would rally and join their fellow rebels in Vaudreuil. This would put the small English militia force in a very bad predicament, caught in the middle of two strong rebel forces. If the rebels could gather another force from St. Lazare and Les Cedres and attack from the south, the Vaudreuil Loyal Volunteers would be surrounded on three sides and have the river at their backs. They were divided into two separate forces, three miles apart, as it was.

Both John and George had discussed this grave matter but had hoped that their opponents had not seen the obvious problem. Luckily they had not, as their experience in military strategy was very limited and they did not have the battle expertise that Marsden, Henderson, and their fellow militia officers had.

George had sent out his pickets that morning and it was one of them that spotted the approaching rebels as they marched west on the King's Road. One of the first farms they came to was that of Christopher Roblin. They immediately killed his livestock except for his team of horses and then they set fire to the stable and house.

The Roblins had left for Schmidt's Tavern like most of the other English families east of it. Joseph Shouldice had hurried east after learning of Deschamps' capture and warned the local residents that there could be more Patriotes arriving from across the lake as the days went by.

Two Mohawk warriors who were patrolling the shoreline saw the smoke from the raging inferno at the Roblin farm and hurried back to the Tavern.

Shortly afterwards, one of the eastern pickets rode in with the news that there was a very large armed force of infantry and cavalry less than two miles east of them, heading that way at a rapid pace.

George Henderson immediately sent a rider west with a note advising Marsden of what was about to happen and suggesting that he return immediately. However, George recommended that at least half of the men that Marsden had with him should remain at the store to guard the western approaches.

"Now men," George called to the assembled militia. "We seem to be on the verge of a battle here in Cavagnal. If anyone would like to leave, now is the time."

Not one man moved and some of the women who were also present called out that they wanted guns.

"Sorry ladies. We just do not have enough guns and ammunition to arm everyone. There will be many wounded if this battle occurs and we will need your help with them. Dr. Grisenthwaite has just arrived down from St. Henry and he has quickly set up a makeshift operating room in the main dining room of the Tavern."

Mary Henderson was there, as was her daughter, Jane. So too were Mary Kilkenny Schmidt, Alice Shouldice, and Elizabeth Loland. The latter, being a well-known midwife in the area, had volunteered her services as Dr. Grisenthwaite's aide. She knew more about caring for the sick and injured than anyone else in the region, spare for the good Doctor himself.

Awen'rah:ton, Sori'howane, and their ten warriors stepped forward and quietly spoke to George as the rest of the militia and Mohawk warriors prepared their weapons. "We want to be your sharpshooters," they announced.

"That is exactly what I was hoping for," he told them.

"We remember your stories of when you were in Spain and how you and your men would be out in front and to the sides of your line regiments—out there harassing the enemy as they approached," Sori'howane said to his leader.

"Correct," George told them. "I want you to harass them as much as you can then fall back to our position."

"We will do just that," they told their long-time friend and now commander.

"Do you think that any of these Patriotes have ever been in a battle before?" asked Joseph Shouldice.

"Some may have been in Napoleon's army, and—if they were—they will probably still not have learned how to attack as we do. I am counting on that," replied George. "However, I believe most are just farmers like us."

"What about the cavalry?" Shouldice asked.

"I believe that they will not fight as a real cavalry unit because they do not know how," answered George. "I cannot see how they would have procured enough sabres or lances. They may fight as mounted infantry, carry guns, and—when they intend to fight—dismount and fight on foot.

"However, we do not know this and thus we must prepare for a cavalry attack. At least we have some stone walls and barricades to hide behind. We will not fight them out in the open. That could prove disastrous for us. I saw that at Waterloo. It was not a pretty sight seeing a line regiment caught out in the open by an attacking cavalry unit and not in square formation. They—the King's German Legion—were massacred to a man that awful day."

The Mohawk warriors from Ganienkeh had already left to skirmish with the approaching rebels, thus giving George and the others time to form their defense.

Hyacinthe Chaput was not aware that he would be attacking a well-prepared, though untested, militia. He believed that the English militia had dispersed since Deschamps had been captured. Nor had he thought to send out scouts in advance of his approach. He was expecting to surprise his enemy.

Chaput was blind with rage and revenge from the Patriote defeat in Ste Eustache. His only thought was to teach the English bastards of Cavagnal a lesson they would not soon forget.

Some of his men had tried to advise him that they should have more men out in advance of their column, but he ignored them. To further announce their arrival, his men set fire to Joseph Shouldice's farm as they passed by it. They had already set fire to the farm of Christopher Roblin's son as well. The thick black smoke darkened the sky east of Schmidt's Tavern, and many of the militia wanted to revenge the fires by putting the torch to Deschamps' store, but George and Joseph Shouldice held them back—difficult though it was for Joseph to that.

One of the advance scouts for the militia, Rotonni from Kanesatake, had hurried back by horseback after seeing the last two farms catch fire. Joseph Shouldice was livid and he wanted George to attack at that moment.

"We will wait awhile yet, Joseph," said George. "I know how it must hurt losing your fine house and barn for the second time in ten years. They will pay for it, either with their lives or in jail. You can trust my word on that, can you not?"

"I just hope you can promise that—or I will hunt them all down if I am not killed today. You can count on that, George."

"That is fine with me, Joseph. I will probably help you, too."

They both laughed and set about checking the men.

"Officer's call in five minutes," yelled George. Ebenezer Grampian, Sean O'Rourke, and Dugald Cameron were soon at George's side.

"I want you play your pipes as you have never played them before," George told Dugald, the big Scotsman from Côte St. Charles.

"You know I will," said Dugald. "I have brought along two other sets as well and my two nephews will be playing them. We also have two of the young Pearson boys from the Grand Côte on the drums. We will make them Frogs think that whole damn British army is down here waiting for them.

"By the way," asked Dugald, "what is your plan of battle today?"

George smiled and thought back to that day in June of 1815. He then announced, "Why, to beat the French, what else?"

They all laughed.

Ebenezer Grampian said, "methinks you stole that quote from old Nosey himself. Right?"

George only smiled and whispered, "He really got it from me that day."

There was more laughter all around, and George liked to hear it. It meant that his officers and men were relaxed and not scared.

The beat of a lone drum announced the arrival of the Patriote column. "What time is it?" George asked Joseph Shouldice.

"Twenty minutes to two," Joseph told his friend.

"Well, by two thirty this should be over, if all goes well," George responded. "I have trained these men as I would have my men of the 95th, and as long as they hold steady, we will win. If they run, God only knows what will happen."

George had not forgotten the Mohawk warriors from Kanesatake. Chief Aron'hio:tas and his warriors were placed all along the King's Road. Some were high up in the trees that lined the muddy path, while others waited just to the right of the main body of the militia, though slightly obscured by the thick brush.

George had lined up his militia in four rows. The front row was kneeling, bayonets fixed to their rifles. They would form a needle-sharp defense line if the Patriotes decided to attack on horseback. George had picked a narrow spot in the road near the Lerniers' house where a cavalry attack could not be used effectively.

The three other rows of the Vaudreuil Loyal Volunteers were lined up shoulder-to-shoulder and would volley fire by row on George's command.

"I figure about two volleys will stop the Patriotes, and between three and four will have them on the run," he thought. "It worked in Spain and Portugal—but those were seasoned troops, not untrained militia up against some rebels led by a fanatic. No telling what they will do," he thought.

Just as the Patriotes came into view, John Marsden rode up in his buggy. Ten of his men were right behind him loaded on two wagons. They were quickly placed in the line of militia after they loaded their weapons and some fixed bayonets. "I like your plan of operation," Marsden told George. "You seem to have your men ready and primed for a fight. Any idea of how many we are up against?"

"I estimate of at least one hundred and fifty—if not more. How is the west end?"

"Clear so far," replied Marsden. "I left ten men there as you suggested. Not enough to stop a large group, but enough to scare them."

"Hopefully no one from Rigaud will arrive. We do not need an attack from the rear. We could easily find ourselves out on the river by night fall if they do," George told Marsden.

The Mohawks were already taking their toll on the Patriotes as they began a steady fire from their hidden positions along the sides of the road. The mounted Patriotes showed no signs of dismounting, which worried George and Marsden. "If they charge us," Marsden asked, "will our men stand?"

"I think they will," said George. "It would be foolish to attack such a tightly packed force like ours on horseback on such a narrow road."

"You have picked your battle sight well, George."

"Thank-you, sir. I learned that one many years ago in southern France, near Toulouse."

"Look!" yelled Joseph Shouldice. "They're dismounting."

Chaput had quickly realized that his mounted unit could not be effective on the road. He had hoped to catch the English militia out in the open and run them down. However, seeing that he could not, he decided to put his eighty or more mounted men on the ground with the others.

The three sets of bagpipes and the beat of the drums of the Vaudreuil Loyal Volunteers soon drowned out the gunfire that was just two hundred yards down the road. The Mohawks had retired to the battle line of the militia. They had lost one man but, as Awen'rah:ton and Sori'howane now reported to George and Marsden, they had killed at least five of the attacking Patriotes.

"Good work, men," Marsden told his sharpshooters. "You have done well. Regroup and take up position with Aron'hio:tas over there."

The two Mohawks looked at George and then at Marsden.

"I think they want to be with me," said George. "Right, my brothers?"

"Yes, we do George," they replied. "Our Ganienkeh men can be with our brothers from Kanesatake but we are your brothers and we will be with you."

"That is fine with me," answered Marsden. "Now take up your positions."

Chief Aron'hio:tas' men were now firing as fast as they could let fly their arrows and what few guns they possessed. With the gunfire along the road, the sound of the battle marches from the bagpipes, the war whoops of the Indians, and the steady beat of the drums, the noise around the Vaudreuil Loyal Volunteer battle line was almost unbearable. The men had not yet been told to fire and as the Patriotes approached, and George sensed that some of the men were about to break and run.

"Steady men," he called. The Patriotes were about one hundred and fifty yards away when Marsden called his men to take aim. The Baker rifle was a deadly accurate arm in the hands of a well-trained man. George had trained his men well and he knew what the rifle could do at ranges up to three hundred yards.

"The Patriotes must be armed with some old muskets," George yelled over to Shouldice. "They have not yet fired on us."

"Waiting to get in range I guess," yelled John Cameron.

"Right," George shouted back. "So now is the time to let them know that we mean business."

"Volley fire by rank," George called to the men. The front row continued to hold their keeling positions. Since the cavalry unit had dismounted, the front row had removed their bayonets, loaded their rifles, and were about to be the first group of Cavagnal militiamen to fire their weapons in anger.

The four rows of militiamen fired as commanded, front row followed by the second, third, and fourth rows. At the same time, every one of the Mohawk warriors from Ganienkeh and Kanesatake fired. Arrows filled the sky as they rained down upon the now-terrified Patriotes.

The Indians had initially placed themselves to the right of the Vaudreuil militia. However, seeing an opportunity to sneak up closer to the approaching Patriote force, Chief Aron'hio:tas and his men cautiously ran along the thick hedge row that bordered the narrow road.

They were now in a position to completely outflank the Patriotes without them knowing it. There was a slight knoll to the left of the Patriote force and it was just behind this knoll that the big Chief had waited with his men. They would have the height advantage to shoot down upon the enemy.

Awen'rah:ton and Sori'howane were still at George's side when the firing commenced. Their three .50 calibre Pennsylvania long rifles gave a sharp crack as they each fired while the larger Baker rifles let go with a thundering blast. The volley fire of the militiamen was steady and in unison, each rank firing on the command of its officer.

Marsden was in his glory and showed it. He was wearing the now-faded red uniform that he had worn at Waterloo. Medals adorned his breast and he had on his big hat with a white plume. "I had this on at Waterloo," he yelled over to George.

"And I had this on, too," George responded, pointing to his well-worn green jacket. George had decided to wear his old uniform of the 95th Rifles for the battle. He had not worn it since coming home from France in 1815. Amazingly, it still fit him—though it was a little tight around the stomach. For today's battle he had taken off the army great coat to be able to fire his long gun with greater ease.

The fire from the Vaudreuil Loyal Volunteers and their Indian allies took an immediate toll on the ranks of the Patriotes. Hyacinthe Chaput had been in the lead, and since his men were not carrying rifles—but a wide variety of weapons that included pistols, shotguns, and some old muskets—they could not cause any real damage since their enemy was still way out of range.

The Patriotes who had arrived on horseback had left most of their mounts at Deschamps' store, where the five wagons that had brought most of the other rebels had also been stored. Some men had come by foot, and these poor souls were already tired from the long cold march from Vaudreuil.

Chaput called his men to continue to march forward even as the Ganienkeh Mohawks had begun to take shots at them. However, when the militia set off its volley fire with he and his men still one hundred and fifty yards away, there was nothing they could do but turn and run or to lie down and have the bullets pass over them.

The latter might have worked, but they chose the former and tried to turn and run. George had trained his men to fire two rounds a minute and the four ranks of militia were doing just that. In slightly over four minutes of continuous firing they had already broken the ranks of the Patriote force.

"Cease firing," yelled George. There were a few more shots from the Indians further down the road but they soon died out as well. The guns of the English and Indians fell silent.

One hundred and fifty yards down the road there was mass confusion. Scores of men lay dead or dying in the road, while others were running away back towards Vaudreuil or had their hands high in the air.

It was a stunning victory for the Vaudreuil Loyal Volunteer Militia. Not one of them had been killed and only two had minor wounds.

Some of the Patriotes had managed to get off a few shots before they were either killed or wounded. With the road so narrow and with the Patriote force approaching in a tight formation, all George and Marsden had to do was to have their men fire into the tightly packed ranks. This caused the force to come almost to a halt as the back ranks tripped and fell over the fallen front ranks.

George and Marsden had seen this done so often against Napoleon's troops that it was second nature to the two. When they saw how the Patriotes were approaching, they smiled at each other, knowing exactly what the other was thinking.

Chief Aron'hio:tas and his men were now behind the Patriote force, blocking off their escape, though some Patriotes had already grabbed a few of the horses that had been used by the Patriote leaders and galloped away east toward Vaudreuil. Many of the Patriotes were on their knees pleading for mercy as the Mohawk warriors swept down among them.

Aron'hio:tas had no intention of killing any more of the Patriotes, but laughed as his men took out their big scalping knives and waved them around. Their intent was to scare the Patriotes, but only the Mohawks knew this; the defeated Patriotes before them did not.

One Patriote, not wounded in the initial fight, took out a concealed pistol and took careful aim at the big Mohawk chief as he stood talking to some of his men. The Patriote never had a chance to get his shot off. His head was split in two by the razor sharp tomahawk of Rotonni. Blood and brains splattered all over the area and the man dropped, pistol still in his hand. He was the last man to die that day.

Though other men would succumb to their wounds, none would die a more violent death than the last Patriote had.

Hyacinthe Chaput was found under a pile of men. He had been one of the first to be killed. After his death, the other leaders of the Patriotes did not have the heart to continue the battle, but they could not stop the firing from the militia in time.

Chapter 31
Peace at Last

Only one of the Cavagnal defenders had been killed: Awen'rah:ton's seventeen-year-old son, Onasakenarat. The two militiamen who were wounded in the brief battle were quickly attended to by Dr. Grisenthwaite and Elizabeth Loland back at the Tavern.

On the Patriote side, however, things were a bloody mess. Though the members of the Vaudreuil Loyal Volunteers had fired for less than five minutes, their excellent training by Captain George Henderson and Major John Marsden had taken a terrible toll on the Patriote rebels.

Besides the five killed by the Ganienkeh warriors, forty six others died where they had fallen. Another twelve died of their wounds before they could be attended to by a then-very-busy Dr. Grisenthwaite and his staff.

Fourteen others had wounds that would eventually heal. Hyacinthe Chaput was identified as having been the leader of this Patriote force. F.X. Deschamps had been kept back at the Tavern and pleaded with his guard to try to stop the battle.

After a few minutes of deliberating with Dr. Grisenthwaite, Deschamps' guard escorted him at gunpoint down the road to the site of the battle. Unfortunately, they arrived a few minutes too late. The firing had already stopped and the battle over.

Deschamps slowly approached Marsden and George, his hands to his sides. Then he began to weep.

"I tried to get here in time to try and stop this carnage. I think Chaput would have listened to me," he told his long-time foes. "Look what has happened! We are all to blame. Hopefully this battle will end our conflicts and maybe we will live in peace from now on."

"I hope so," Marsden told the weeping man before him. "But before we do, you will be charged with having an armed force in the Seigneury of Vaudreuil."

"Hyacinthe Chaput was the main leader of this force," said Deschamps. "He lies over there."

He pointed to a blood-stained corpse with three bullet holes in its chest.

"He was a very radical man and, though we all planned this raid together, it was he who really wanted you all dead. I probably said the same thing once, but I would not have set fire to those farms down the road," he said, gesturing to the smoke rising in the distance.

"William Whetstone is the other leader of our local Patriote group. His brother Charles is also involved with us. I guess you already know that."

"I do," said Marsden. "My men at my store have orders to arrest them this evening, if they are still at home." Deschamps added that William should be at his house, as they planned to put out one last copy of the *John Gripe* the next afternoon.

Marsden called Sean O'Rourke over to his side. "Take your son Stephen and go to my store. Pick five of the men who are there and go and arrest William Whetstone and his brother Charles right away. Bring them here."

"Aye, sir, I will. Do you want them tied up?"

"No, Sean. That will not be necessary. Just explain what has happened here this afternoon. We do not want any more suffering than we already have."

"I will be back in about two hours," Sean told his commander. With that he headed west on horseback to arrest the co-leader of the Cavagnal Patriotes and his brother.

Marsden's plan to arrest the Whetstones did not materialize that day. The two men were not at home and had left for parts unknown, according to a man who was at William Whetstone's house when Sean O'Rourke arrived with his six men.

William and Charles Whetstone were arrested only four days later, on December 21st. Charles Schmidt and a party of the Volunteer Militia arrived at the Whetstone house and arrested the two Patriote supporters. William was subsequently taken to Montréal for trial.

"What shall we do with the bodies?" asked George. "We will load them onto our wagons and send them back to Vaudreuil for burial. Before that, we must have all the names of those who were present here, on both sides," answered Marsden.

John Henderson and John Cameron volunteered to take the names of the Vaudreuil Loyal Volunteer militia while Dugald Cameron, J.M. Lerniers, and Joseph Shouldice took down the names of all the Patriotes, dead and alive.

Most of the Patriotes were from Vaudreuil and points east. More than a dozen were from Ile Perrot. Only a small handful hailed from Cavagnal itself. Of the Cavagnal militia, all but five of the men were English-speaking.

"I wonder what the Governor will say about this carnage?" Marsden said to a tired and powder-stained George Henderson.

"I understand that we had no choice but to open fire. This was an armed force that already had burned three farms and was heading our way. We had to fire on them. It was them or us," replied George.

"I will write my report to Sir John Colborne and Governor Gosford. Will you write one as well, George?"

"I will John, as long as our reports match."

"They will have to," said Marsden. "Deschamps, the two Whetstone brothers, and some of the other leaders will either hang or serve time in jail. The others may pay a fine or will be released under strict observation. That will depend on the courts in Montréal."

George nodded his head and went over to check on the men who were now gathering up the arms of the Patriote force.

Before the remaining Patriotes were led west to Schmidt's Tavern under the watch of the militia, a man—dressed in a heavy woolen coat, a wool toque pulled down over his ears—slowly approached

John Marsden and George Henderson. The little man was with J.M. Lerniers.

Lerniers called to the two militia leaders to wait. "This Patriote has something to say to you."

Lerniers translated for the man since he did not speak English. "He says he is Onésime Legault from Ile Cadieux and has been a Patriote sympathizer for many years. However, he says that he has heard that there was a big battle at Ste Eustache and that the Patriotes were soundly defeated. Is that true?"

John Marsden replied for the Vaudreuil Loyal Volunteers. "Tell him it is true and that their leader, Jean O. Chenier, was killed along with over one hundred of their men, many more were captured and or wounded."

"Mr. Legault says that he was not aware of that battle until a few minutes ago, when one of our men told him." Lerniers continued to translate the man's story. "He says that none of the Patriotes here today were aware of that defeat except for Hyacinthe Chaput and F.X. Deschamps."

"That is why Deschamps was trying to get here, to stop the battle. He knew that these poor men did not know and that bloody bastard Chaput probably would not have told them so they would not lose heart and return to their homes and farms," responded George.

"Chaput must have really hated us," Marsden stated.

"He did," answered F.X. Deschamps, who had walked up beside the four men and listened to some of Onésime's comments. "Though I will always be a Patriote sympathizer and I know that I will either go to jail or hang, I admit that I once wanted you two dead," he continued, pointing at George and Marsden. "I was never the fanatic that Chaput was. He wished death to all the English and, when Chenier died yesterday in Ste Eustache, he envisioned himself as the next great leader of all the Patriotes in Lower Canada or as we call it Québec."

"It is too bad that these poor men from Vaudreuil, Ile Perrot, and wherever else, were led to their deaths by a man blind with rage and hatred. Your confession today may help your court case," announced John Marsden. "Though we have had many differences over the past few years, this testimony from your heart shows that you are really a decent man."

George stepped back and coughed. He thought he was hearing things. "I never imagined you would say that John," George told his commander and long-time friend. "However, I believe you are right, and from what Mr. Legault here has said and what F.X. is telling us right now, I think most of these men will receive light sentences and probably not be hanged."

Marsden added, "The leaders should pay. Chaput and Chenier have paid the ultimate price, with their lives. I guess you, F.X., and the Whetstones will serve time in jail but will not be hanged. I hope you will not—but that is up to the courts in Montréal and we will make a report on what you have said here today."

Marsden was sincere in his words and, like the rest of those present, realized that what had happened that day cast a very dark cloud over the history of their usually quiet little community of Cavagnal.

Marsden continued by saying, "I hope we never have such an armed rebellion again and take up arms against our neighbours as we have done these past few months."

With that, they all headed for Schmidt's Tavern for one final meeting. Most of the Patriotes were sent home after their names were taken down for reference purposes. Only F.X. Deschamps and three or four others would be kept under armed guard that night in George Henderson's well-used barn.

That evening, as darkness fell upon the area, a dull red glow could be seen in the north-western sky. Reports of a terrible rampage by Colborne's troops in the village of St. Benoit had filtered back across the lake by some of the Mohawks of Kanesatake.

The army garrison from Carillon had set upon the Patriote stronghold that same afternoon. After arresting any Patriote they could find, the troops raided the local tavern and hotel. Breaking into the liquor stores, the men got drunk; after raping many of the local women and young girls, they set fire to the whole village. Such provided the glow in the sky that the residents of Cavagnal could now see.

"God, it is Badajoz all over again," said a disgusted George

Henderson. "This will take years—if not decades—to mend now. Just when we hoped that we would once again be living in peaceful harmony with our neighbours the 'Great British Army' has once again ruined our chances."

Marsden was as disgusted as George, and he too remembered what he had seen that awful day in Spain, so many years before.

"The troops of the Carillon garrison were regulars and not militia, and that could prove to be one saving factor in all this mess," he said. "If only the poor Patriote sympathizers realize it."

"I hope so," said George, "but I somewhat doubt it. Only time will tell."

Aron'hio:tas announced that he and his warriors would be returning the next morning to Kanesatake. Marsden, George, and the other militia officers thanked the big Mohawk Chief and told him that if the Mohawks of Kanesatake ever needed help, the residents of Cavagnal would be there for them.

Awen'rah:ton had taken part in the battle, but it was a difficult time for him. He had been near his young son when he had been shot as they acted as skirmishers for the militia force. Awen'rah:ton and another Ganienkeh Mohawk had carried back the lad's limp and blood-stained body even though they had come under heavy return fire from the Patriote force.

After laying Onasakenarat's body beside a tree, behind the militia's lines, Awen'rah:ton had joined Sori'howane and George to continue the battle. He only really began to grieve when the firing had finally stopped and he had returned to his son's body.

"I am very sorry that this has happened," George told his Indian blood brother in a subdued voice, with tears in his eyes. "I feel responsible for his death."

"Do not feel that way, my brother," Awen'rah:ton replied. "He was a young warrior and he died a warrior's death: in battle. That is the way any Mohawk would want to die. Yes, I grieve for my son, but I am happy in the way he died, as a great warrior. He was defending a place he believed in, people he believed in, and people he loved. Though we do not come from here or Kanesatake we feel very close to this place because of you,

George Henderson, and your family. Do not apologize, Onasakenarat would not have wanted it that way."

"I understand," George replied. "Will you take your son home with you?"

"No, I wish to bury him here, where he died. New York is only our adopted land. However, I feel that Cavagnal could have been our real home after we were ousted from our old home near Kahnawake. He will be buried here in Cavagnal."

"That is fine, my brother," George responded. "We will find a decent place for him and say a few words over his grave."

"We will," answered Awen'rah:ton. "Then Sori'howane and I and the others will return to Ganienkeh for the winter. We will be back next year, if all goes well. Maybe we will hunt next fall, George Henderson. Hunt north of Kanesatake for a big bear or moose."

"Agreed," replied George.

With that, they headed back to George's home and a well-deserved night's sleep.

* * *

On December 18th, 1837, there was a proclamation from the Lower Canada Government stating that the Vaudreuil Loyal Volunteers would have the right to disarm all of the known Patriotes in the Vaudreuil Seigneury, given that the rebels were ready to surrender "en masse."

Major John Marsden and Sergeant J.M. Lerniers of the Vaudreuil Loyal Volunteers were selected to apply the new "Oath of Allegiance." The disarming of the Patriote supporters in Rigaud, Vaudreuil, and St. Lazare took most of the winter and into the following spring.

Marsden's role as leader of the Vaudreuil Loyal Volunteers changed from one of commander of a defense force to one of an armed force on the offensive prowl that took them all over the Seigneury.

Many throughout the region began to despise John Marsden, as it seemed he had a terrible hatred of the French citizenry of the region. Many people compared him to an English version of F.X. Deschamps, or even Hyacinthe Chaput.

Even George Henderson began to wonder about his friend and commander. Because things were being ruled under a martial-law style of government, George tendered his resignation as the Sheriff of Cavagnal on March 15th, 1838. Marsden accepted it without question and their friendship began to wane even more.

In May of that year, the newly appointed Governor, Lord Durham, granted an amnesty for most of the Patriotes who were still in Lower Canada. William Whetstone and F.X. Deschamps were released from jail in Montréal and they both returned to Cavagnal to resume their lives as private citizens. Charles Whetstone had only served a few weeks before his release.

Tensions were still high throughout the colony, and especially within the Vaudreuil Seigneury.

Robert Unwin Harwood, the Vaudreuil Seigneur, called for the dismissal of John Marsden that summer as the Justice of the Peace in Cavagnal, but Marsden remained in the position.

* * *

In November 1838, Curé Beauchamp of Ile Perrot reported at a meeting that the time was once again ripe for rebellion, and that they should continue until independence from England's rule was achieved.

Once again the Volunteers were called to duty. They drilled and patrolled the area until April of 1839 when they were finally disbanded for good. This time they were once again led by Major John Marsden and Captain George Henderson, but no shots were fired in anger.

"I guess we showed the cowardly bastards how we English really fight, eh George?" said Marsden as they rode back from Vaudreuil one afternoon in late March.

Accompanied by fifteen other militiamen, they had made a sweep along the shores and main roads in Vaudreuil. It was a routine patrol that Marsden had carried out most of the winter and he seemed agitated that they had not seen any action.

"Don't you think we saw enough bloodshed last year, John?" asked George.

"What do you mean by that comment, George?"

"It seems very clear to me—and most of the men in our company—that you are itching to have another battle with the Patriotes, if you can find one. I do not think you will. The main Patriote forces are south of here and Curé Beauchamp was only reflecting on his views—not the views of the rest of this region, I believe."

"If you do not watch yourself, George Henderson, I will relieve you of your command and have you arrested for insubordination and treason."

"Arrest me, John, and you will have a mutiny on your hands. These men here behind us and the rest back in Cavagnal are fed up with your extremely harsh treatment of the French Canadian residents of this area. Smarten up, John, resign your position with dignity. Think of some valid reason before you are ousted by Harwood—or Colborne himself."

"We used to be great friends," continued George. "However, during the past few months you have become power hungry and many of the local residents—who you truly believe to be your dear friends—actually despise you."

"Do you despise me, George?"

"No. I do not. However, I have a lot less respect for you now than I have ever had in the past fifteen years. Your treatment of the former Patriotes in this Seigneury and other members of the French Canadian society has been deplorable."

George continued his explanation to his leader as they rode westward along the King's Road towards Cavagnal.

"Not all French Canadians are Patriote sympathizers. You must realize that. We all live here in Lower Canada together. The French founded the colony and we English took it from them in war—we must now live together, in peace.

"Hopefully this recent rebellion will never occur again. As we both know, a rebellion has also occurred in Upper Canada, but it has not been as violent as this one and it is much different in its political background. That rebellion is not about relations between the French and English—but one of politics and reforms.

"Take it easy, John, or you will find yourself out of office as the Justice of the Peace and maybe find yourself with a bullet in your back. Because of our relationship and co-leadership of the Vaudreuil Volunteers, I have received death threats and many of my long time French-Canadian friends will have nothing to do with me. I regret that, but my I know that my initial duty was to my King—and now Queen—rather than to my friends.

"Do not only think about your own personal hatred of the French, John. Think about having to live here for the rest of your life under a constant threat of being shot, stabbed, or isolated from the whole community—French and English—because of your own personal hatred and gains.

"I am sorry for being so blunt, John, but it was about time someone close to you explained the facts. Down deep you are a good man. Do not let yourself be blindly led down a path of personal destruction. I rest my case. If you want to fire me, do so, but those men behind me will follow me—not you. You are alone. Make your decision."

John Marsden rode alongside George Henderson in silence for another few hundred yards before he reigned his horse to a stop, and turned to his second-in-command.

"George Henderson, I have threatened you with dismissal for your comments, but you have continued with your harsh words."
George thought that he was done for and was preparing for the worst, when Marsden resumed the conversation.

"Only a true friend and loyal supporter would have had the stomach to say what you have just said to me. I admire you, George, and I must admit that you are right."

The other men with them had pulled up alongside their leaders and were now listening to them chat.

"I have been very harsh on the local French. Even my dear wife Harriett has told me so. I ignored her and everyone else. I guess when you are power hungry, as you put it, one tends to wear blinders. I had only a narrow field of vision and did not see anything of what was happening around me. I am growing old and it is me who should now step down. I will, soon enough. Once we disband our militia.

"It will take years to mend what has gone on here in our little

Seigneury. Do you think that if I make a public statement and have a notice put up around the community that it will help?"

"I do not know," said George. "Most of the residents in our community, both French and English, cannot read or write. A written statement will go ignored.

"Go and see Seigneur Harwood and explain yourself; his word is well thought of in the Seigneury. When word gets out that you have apologized for your actions—and that you will disband the militia and return to civilian life—that may help."

"I will see what Harriett thinks of your plan, George, and let you know my decision tomorrow. Either way, the Vaudreuil Loyal Volunteers will be disbanded this coming Saturday, and all the men will be paid off. I am sure that the money they will receive will help them immensely."

"It will," replied George. "But do not even think that by disbanding the militia and paying off the men you will gain their respect. John, you are going to have to earn that respect. It will take months or years for them to forgive you—if they ever do."

* * *

On a warm Saturday in April of 1839 the Vaudreuil Loyal Volunteers turned out for the last time. Even the Seigneur of Vaudreuil, Lt. Colonel Robert Unwin Harwood, was present on the front lawn at Schmidt's Tavern.

The ceremony began with Major John Marsden calling the men to order and, under the command of Captain George Henderson, the one hundred and twenty men marched past the reviewing stand then turned and returned to stand at attention in front of their three commanders: Lt. Colonel Harwood, Major Marsden, and Captain Henderson.

Harwood was the first to speak.

"Though I have been separated from you men during the past troubles, I have been with you in spirit and thought. What you did was commendable. Even though many lives were lost at the Battle of Cavagnal two years ago, many more were probably saved by how you stood up against the rebels and fought for something you believed in: this great land of ours. You won. They lost, or we would not be here today beneath the great flag of our Sovereign Queen Victoria. Thank you, men."

There was polite applause from those in attendance. The next to speak was Major John Marsden.

"Stand at ease, men," he began.

In one fluid motion, all one hundred and twenty men took their heavy rifles from their shoulders and obeyed the order.

"We have gone through some very trying times over the past two and a half years," he began. "I want to commend all of you for your devotion and loyalty. Thankfully, none of us were killed or seriously wounded. Our foes lost many men and there are still many wounds to heal—though these wounds are not physical, but mental.

"I have been very harsh over the past few months and I wish to take this opportunity to apologize for my actions. I have already spoken to Sir John Colborne, our interim Governor, and have apologized to him as well. Only time will tell of what will happen here in Cavagnal in terms of the relations between the French and English.

"Let us hope that, from now on, we will all live in harmony and peace."

There was more polite applause from the audience and the men of the militia began to bang their gun butts on the ground. Alice Shouldice leaned over to Mary Henderson and asked, "What does that mean?"

"They are signaling their approval of what Marsden has just said since they cannot applaud him," said Mary.

"I am impressed," Alice replied. "Especially after what he has done around here."

Captain George Henderson was the last to speak before the men were paid off and released. "I have had the immense pleasure of commanding an excellent troop of men during the past two and a half years. You have been both loyal, dedicated, and—above all—professional.

"Major Marsden has given me the honour of reading this official dispatch that he received last week. 'On behalf of Her Majesty Queen Victoria, Sovereign of Great Britain and all her colonies, I wish to congratulate Major John Augustus Marsden and all of the officers and men of the Vaudreuil Loyal Volunteer Militia for the excellent professional work that they have done over the past two and a half years. If it were not for your training, leadership, and conduct under fire, Lord only knows what would have happened on that fateful and tragic day on December 17th, 1837. Go in Peace men, and return to your families. You will be always remembered as the men who saved the Vaudreuil Seigneury from the wrath of a small group of fanatics.' Signed, Sir John Colborne, Governor of British North America, April 6th, 1839."

All of the men cheered and once again stomped their gun butts on the ground. Everyone else gave the speech a rousing round of applause. They were a proud group of citizens who were gathered in the front yard of Charles Schmidt's Tavern that day in April of 1839.

Flags of Great Britain were everywhere. Major John Marsden called for three cheers for the Queen, and everyone joined in. Big Dugald Cameron began to play a rousing march on his well-used bagpipes.

Marsden called for calm and as his last duty as the official assistant commander of the Vaudreuil Loyal Volunteer Militia, called out, "Volunteers of Vaudreuil, dismissed. Come and collect your pay."

The men cheered once more and then they filed towards a small table that had been set up. Seigneur Robert U. Harwood and his clerk began paying the men.

Though they had been paid at regular intervals in 1837 and 1838, they had not been paid at all in 1839, a fact which had many grumbling. Each man was to receive over twelve pounds in wages, more than most would make in two years of hard work on their farms. George and the other officers were to be paid a slightly higher wage for having been officers in the troop.

As for the Mohawks who had served with them back in 1837, they had all been paid off when they had left for their respective homes, either in New York or Kanesatake. Each warrior had received one shilling four pence for each day in service and Chief Aron'hio:tas had received two shillings for his service each day while under arms in Cavagnal.

As an added bonus, the men were allowed to keep their rifles, all of their ammunition, and powder as well as their winter great coats and fur hats.

Each man would now have enough money to pay off many of his

debts, buy some livestock, and put some away for future use. Ironically, many of the former militiamen owed their once-enemy F.X. Deschamps money for supplies they had purchased at his store.

Peace had finally come to Cavagnal and the rest of the Seigneury of Vaudreuil. "Now maybe we can get on with our normal lives," George said to his wife, Mary.

"Yes, dear, we have been under arms too long. Too many have suffered, on both sides. We must start the plan we abandoned so many years ago to build a church in this community."

George smiled and hugged his wife. "Yes, my love. I whole heartily agree. I only hope that we succeed this time. Having infrequent visits from the clergy from Côteau du Lac or St. Andrews is not sufficient for this growing community."

Mary added, "God only knows when our own minister will be among us and preaching to us from the pulpit of our very own church."

Suddenly she mounted the small reviewing stand where, only a short time before, her husband and the two most powerful men in the community had stood. Never before had a woman addressed such a large crowd in Cavagnal.

"Ladies and gentlemen," she yelled. Few turned to listen, at first, but all looked when George fired his pistol into the air.

Mary began by saying, "Hopefully that will be the very last pistol shot in this community. Ladies and gentlemen, we are all gathered here together to pay tribute to the men who defended our homes so gallantly."

Joseph Shouldice gave a rough harrumph under his breath at Mary's last comment. His wife, Alice, poked him in the ribs and quietly said, "Listen to her."

"Peace is now here," continued Mary. "Years ago many of you planned to have a church built here in Cavagnal. Now is the time to have another committee formed so we can get on with our lives in a peaceful manner. All of us should be involved: men and women. Though this land is ruled by men, remember who our Sovereign, Queen Victoria. I am sure she would approve of having a woman on the board in charge of finding us a minister and building a church in which we may pray and praise the word of God."

All those present applauded and cheered, and some yelled, "Bravo, Mary Henderson."

George smiled and hugged his daughter Jane and the rest of their family. He had never seen his wife take such a prominent position in the community, and he was proud of her.

He thought back to that day on Dufton Pike so many years before and how it felt to pull up stakes in Westmorland and travel across the ocean to their new land and set up a new life.

Over the past fifteen years they had seen many hardships, death, and destruction—but they had seen many more wonderful things. Their family was healthy and growing steadily with strength and fortitude.

Yes, he thought. Now really was the time to forge ahead with plans for another new home and new life. This time it would be a new house of the Lord and a life of peace, harmony, goodwill, and religion in the community.

Mary stepped down from the stand and George and the rest of the Henderson family approached her with open arms. They hugged and cried as one big happy family. Around them everyone was clapping their hands and cheering.

The day had begun with the plan of disbanding a military force that had saved them from possible destruction. Now a woman in the community had taken the stand and had once more rallied the community together, not to raise arms against a common foe but to raise their arms towards the heavens and ask for the Lord's help in finding a minister for their soon-to-be-built church.

The new land called British North America, which the Hendersons had come to love and know as their own, had a new gift of life to be proud of: the birth of a new church in Cavagnal in the Province of Lower Canada.

Epilogue

Mary Henderson's desire for a church and a minister in Cavagnal did not see fruition until 1841, when the Anglican Bishop of Montréal created the new Parish of Vaudreuil for the Church of England. He appointed the Reverend James Pyke to the new Parish. In 1842, St. James Anglican Church was constructed about a half mile west of John Marsden's store.

Six years later the first Methodist Church was built up on Côte St. Charles; it was known as the Côte St. Charles Methodist Church, and the Reverend George Case was its first minister.

Most of the original settlers had come out from an extremely poor way of life in England, Scotland, and Ireland only to find even greater hardships in British North America. However, this new land and the new life they made for themselves were the foundations of the community that is now known as Hudson, Québec.

We can only thank God for those hardy folks of the early years here in Cavagnal. They forged a community out of the wilderness for us to appreciate today. It truly was a Frontier Adventure!

R. L. H.

Also available from PublishAmerica

A DEER IN WINTER
by Michelle Ordynans

A Deer in Winter is an inspiring story of survival. It's the semi-autobiographical tale of a young woman's odyssey as she escapes from an abusive home, endures homelessness in the cold of a New York winter, and survives sexual attacks and harassment. In the meantime, she continues her last term of high school while secretly homeless, in constant fear of being discovered and returned to her abusive household. Through it all, she sets her sights on meeting her ultimate goal—graduating high school and attending college in the fall so that she can eventually rise above her troubled background and build a better life for herself. All the rituals of daily life must be negotiated: how and where she sleeps each night, in the rain and snow; how she gets food; how she cleans herself and her clothes; and how she spends her evenings. Along the way she works, makes friends and boyfriends, and explores the fascinating sites of New York City.

Paperback, 206 pages
6" x 9"
ISBN 1-4241-6999-2

About the author:
Michelle Ordynans was born and has lived in New York most of her life, with her early childhood in Florida and a few years in Israel. She is married and has two grown children and several pets. She works with her husband and son as an insurance broker in New York City.

Available to all bookstores nationwide.
www.publishamerica.com

Also available from PublishAmerica

THE GAME OF LIFE
by David Shiben

Why are we here? What is the meaning of life?
Why is life so difficult? Why is the world in
chaos? Why does God allow such bad things to
happen to his people? Why don't we stop global
warming? Can we ever have peace on earth?

About the author:

David is just shy of the big
5-0. He was raised Lutheran/
Presbyterian. Early in life he
questioned   mainstream
religion, thinking many of the
good churchgoing people were hypocritical, praying for
one hour on Sundays and doing whatever the rest of
the week. They did not walk the walk or talk the talk.
He also found that the church could not answer many of the big questions
about life. David became disenfranchised with the church and wallowed
through a number of difficult years. In the mid 1990s, David began to
search for answers and started reading many self-help and spiritual books.
He started meditating and began his communion with the Supreme Being
and now answers these questions, explains living your life without fear,
and inspires provocative ideas and solutions to many of the world's
greatest problems—global warming, child abuse, war, prejudice,
government, the legal system, and the like.

Paperback, 244 pages
6" x 9"
ISBN 1-4241-9914-X

Available to all bookstores nationwide.
www.publishamerica.com

TUNNEL OF DARKNESS

by Rose Falcone De Angelo

Why are some people given the ability to see into the future or communicate with the dead? Is this a gift or a curse? The visions come uninvited and change an ordinary world into one of marvel, turmoil and sometimes fear. This is the story of Bernadette, whose psychic powers begin at the age of ten and carry her into the strangest places.

Paperback, 241 pages
6" x 9"
ISBN 1-60474-153-8

About the author:

Rose Falcone De Angelo was born in New York City's east side to Italian immigrant parents. Rose moved to Florida in 1986. She is the author of a book of poetry, *Reality and Imagination*. At ninety-one, she is the oldest published poet in the state of Florida and has intrigued all who have the privilege of knowing her. She is currently working on her memoirs.